Chicago waiter Mike C intrigue and romance as he becomes involved with Joe, an alien cop, who lands on Earth in pursuit of a dangerous mad scientist bent on taking over our corner of the universe. As Mike joins Joe on a wild adventure beyond anything he dreamed of in his life, Mike must balance his obligations to his nephew and his first lover-- with a little help from a drag queen in sequins and spandex and the well-dressed patrons of a leather bar.

Featuring a roll call of some of the best writers of gay erotica and mysteries today!

Derek Adams	Z. Allora	Maura Anderson
Simone Anderson	Victor J. Banis	Laura Baumbach
Helen Beattie	Ally Blue	J.P. Bowie
Barry Brennessel	Nowell Briscoe	Jade Buchanan
James Buchanan	TA Chase	Charlie Cochrane
Karenna Colcroft	Michael G. Cornelius	Jamie Craig
Ethan Day	Diana DeRicci	Vivien Dean
Taylor V. Donovan	S.J. Frost	Kimberly Gardner
Kaje Harper	Alex Ironrod	DC Juris
Jambrea Jo Jones	AC Katt	Thomas Kearnes
Sasha Keegan	Kiernan Kelly	K-lee Klein
Geoffrey Knight	Christopher Koehler	Matthew Lang
J.L. Langley	Vincent Lardo	Cameron Lawton
Anna Lee	Elizabeth Lister	Clare London
William Maltese	Z.A. Maxfield	Timothy McGivney
Kendall McKenna	AKM Miles	Robert Moore
Jet Mykles	N.J. Nielsen	Cherie Noel
Gregory L. Norris	Willa Okati	Erica Pike
Neil S. Plakcy	Rick R. Reed	AJ Rose
Rob Rosen	George Seaton	Riley Shane
Jardonn Smith	DH Starr	Richard Stevenson
Christopher Stone	Liz Strange	Marshall Thornton
Lex Valentine	Haley Walsh	Mia Watts
Lynley Wayne	Missy Welsh	Ryal Woods
Stevie Woods	Sara York	Lance Zarimba
Mark Zubro		

Check out titles, both available and forthcoming, at
www.mlrpress.com

ALIEN QUEST

Book One in the Alien Danger series

MARK ZUBRO

mlrpress

www.mlrpress.com

Copyright 2013 by Mark Zubro

Published by
MLR Press, LLC
3052 Gaines Waterport Rd.
Albion, NY 14411

Visit ManLoveRomance Press, LLC on the Internet:
www.mlrpress.com

Cover Art by Deana Jamroz
Editing by Neil Plakcy

Print format: ISBN# 978-1-60820-874-6
ebook format also available

Issued 2013

As always thanks to Barb D'Amato and Jeanne Dams.

"I'm trying to have a lifestyle here."

"He's straight."

"No man whose pants fit that tight in the ass could possibly be straight."

Mike Carlson examined the bartender-in-question's butt. "You're right about the pants, Hugo, but cheap, tawdry gossip says he's totally hetero."

Meganvilia, the drag queen at the hostess desk, said, "He's had a different woman pick him up each night this week. He may be cute, but straight or gay, he is a slut." Meganvilia wore a canary-yellow dress with a red feather boa draped around her three-hundred-pound-plus frame.

At the far end of the bar, the man in question was filling a large drink order. He wore a leather vest over his bare chest and broad shoulders. Tight leather pants clung to his slender hips. Mike was not about to tell Hugo, the most vicious gossip who worked at Oscar and Alfred's restaurant, that the night the bartender started working, Mike had asked the guy for a date and been unpleasantly rejected.

Mike poked Hugo's elbow again. "What I was trying to tell you, before you were so rude, is that, if you can tear your eyes away long enough from Mr. Unattainable, I think table twenty has stiffed you for their bill."

Hugo wrenched his eyes from his lustful musings and gazed at the very vacant table twenty.

"And," Mike added, "Table three wants you. They told me they asked for Cardassian wine quite a while ago."

"Merde, merde, merde," Hugo muttered, hurrying over to hunt for his missing customers. Hugo wore clothes that fit well about fifteen pounds ago. He had an over-stuffed sausage look, and his smile never quite lost its trace of vinegary sneer.

"Isn't Cardassian wine from *Star Trek*?" Meganvilia asked.

"Yes, but Hugo doesn't know that."

"Hugo told me he is still annoyed with you for not introducing him to the humpy number at table seven."

Mike surreptitiously inspected the gentleman and table Meganvilia mentioned. Mike had noticed that both men and women occasionally cast glances at the man. "I don't know him. I don't even know his name. If Hugo wants to meet him that badly, he can introduce himself to the guy."

"Hugo claims he's shy."

"Like a drag queen on a television talk show, he's shy."

"I wouldn't mind meeting the mystery man at table seven," Meganvilia said. "He looks just like a gymnast I dated for a few years back in the seventies. That build is divine."

"You could introduce yourself."

"I'm married to a truck driver who is extremely jealous. Maybe in another life."

Mike glanced at his watch. It was 10:00 P.M., and they would be closing the doors of Oscar and Alfred's in a few moments. The trendiest restaurant in Chicago didn't take reservations. At least half an hour before it opened, every day of the week in every kind of weather, a line formed waiting to get in. People often sat at the bar for over two hours before they got a table. Diners who arrived before ten would be seated eventually. After ten they were out of luck.

Hugo glanced up from the conversation he'd been having with four gentlemen in tuxedos at table three. He shot Mike a withering glance.

Hugo could be one annoying, dizzy queen, and Mike usually avoided confrontations with him.

It wasn't the job he wanted to have for the rest of his life, but Mike did enjoy being a waiter at Oscar and Alfred's. You didn't stop moving from the time they opened the doors, but the pay was better than most, the tips were great, and the food was fabulous. He saw that table eight's dinners were ready. He hurried to serve the pastas covered with artichokes, octopus, or asparagus that each of them had ordered. As he finished serving, he felt a light tap on his shoulder from the man at table seven.

For three nights running, the mystery man had been sitting alone at this prized position. From its place on a raised platform at the front window, you could gaze into the passing street or over all the customers in the restaurant. Mike didn't mind singles as so many of the wait-staff did, and this guy was an attractive man.

So far the stranger had been impervious to friendliness and pleasant chatter. He had simply come in each night and waited without complaining for the table he desired. As far as Mike could see, the man spent the entire time before and after being seated, either gazing placidly into the mirror behind the bar or staring calmly at the passersby out the window. He had evinced no particular interest in Mike or any of the patrons. Meganvilia reported that the customer insisted on that table in Mike's section each night.

The man had large shoulders and a narrow waist. He'd worn the same long-sleeve sweatshirt and tight, faded blue jeans every night against the early autumn chill. His black and white Nike running shoes showed only a few tiny scrapes and smudges. With his gold wire-rim glasses, blond hair clipped short, and a hint of five o'clock shadow, he looked like a university professor in his middle twenties. Mike admitted to himself that he wouldn't mind spending a great deal of time with this man naked in bed next to him.

Each evening at table seven, he'd ordered a completely different dinner including appetizer, soup, salad, entrée, dessert, and cappuccino. Obviously the guy wasn't worried about pouring in the calories.

Mike realized that some people came to a restaurant and asked for the same waiter for any number of reasons. Not too many did so because they knew their waiter would leave them alone, but that seemed to be the case with this guy.

The biggest oddity Mike had noticed so far was that the man always brought his own flatware to eat with. Mike hadn't been able to examine it up close. Casual glances had given the impression that the outer surface was some sort of bright, almost flowing, mother-of-pearl. Maybe the guy was a clean-and-germ freak. He tipped well, and he was no trouble, so Mike was prepared to overlook a great deal of odd behavior.

Mike made excellent tips because of his willingness to go out of his way for diners' eccentricities, and leaving someone alone was exceedingly simple.

The hunk at table seven motioned him closer. "If you're wearing white briefs, I'll buy them from you for twenty dollars."

Mike did a double take worthy of Groucho Marx. "I beg your pardon?"

Occasionally patrons hit on Mike. His mom often told him he had a handsome face. He ran along the lakefront three days a week and worked out often as well. He was in good shape, and he had a pleasant smile and an easy but very efficient manner with customers. He was always polite with those who came on to him, but he always said, "No." He didn't mix work with relationships.

The single at table seven let his soft brown eyes gaze wistfully into Mike's. "I'd really like to purchase them."

"What is this crap?" Mike asked.

The man smiled and said, "You turn me on."

"I don't know you," Mike said and hurried off.

Other than slapping his check down when the guy's face was turned the other way, Mike ignored him for the rest of the meal.

At one thirty, as Mike was counting his tips, Meganvilia spread the word that a six-foot, red-haired woman called on the bartender just after closing. The red-head and the bartender had sauntered out the door, gotten into her Porsche, and roared off into the early morning darkness. Hugo sullenly slapped the dollar bills he was counting onto the slightly damp top of the bar. He whined at Mike, "I could be convinced to forgive your earlier frivolity, if you would introduce me to the gorgeous guy at table seven."

"I don't know him," Mike said. He avoided adding details about the guy's unorthodox style of coming on.

"I saw him talking to you," Hugo insisted.

"He's just another customer."

"And the first trip to the moon was just another walk in the country."

Quickly Mike finished his nightly tally and slipped out the rear exit of the restaurant. He understood but had little patience with Hugo's soap-opera style of conducting relationships. He'd long since ceased to be amused by the soaring highs and depressed lows mixed with a continuous supply of sniveling gossip.

Behind the restaurant, the back alley was well lit, and the guys from the valet parking were always around. At the moment, one of them was gently pulling a red Lexus out of a parking space. A fine mist wafted along a cool late September breeze. The temperature was in the fifties but on its way down.

Mike pulled his down-lined jacket closer and hurried the half block to the street. As he neared the four-plus-one apartment house at the end of the alley, he heard a soft moan. He glanced around. No one else was in sight. He kept a small vial of pepper spray on the end of his key chain. He yanked it out of his pocket, flipped the safety cap off, and held the spray ready to fire.

Two

Seconds later he found the cause of the moan. Slumped between a dumpster and the side of a garage was the single from table seven.

The man groaned. For a few seconds Mike thought it might be an elaborate set-up for a mugging. He took several steps closer. Mike gasped at the grotesque twist of the body. Blood seeped along the pavement. He saw a gash ending in an ugly scrape along the guy's left cheek and an unsightly purple mark along his chin. Mike hurried forward and squatted down next to the injured man.

"You need a doctor," Mike said. "I'll call 911." He took out his cell phone.

"No." The negative was spoken softly but insistently.

"Come on, guy, we've got to get you to a hospital."

"No." The refusal was stronger this time.

"What's wrong? No insurance? They'll find a way to pay for you."

The man shook his head, tried to rise, but slumped back down onto the pavement. He used his hands to help pull his left knee close to his chest. He twisted his torso and let out a yelp. He breathed deeply several times then said, "That feels better."

"What happened?" Mike asked.

"A car with five teenagers in it drove past. They screamed 'faggot,' 'homo,' and 'queer' loudly and often. I ignored them. They must have thrown something out of their car as they drove past. I never saw it or them coming. Whatever it was, hit me in the head and stunned me. I fell. Before I knew it, they were on me. I was too dazed to fight." He touched his torso and his left hand. "They kept kicking me."

"Do you have anyone you want me to call? I could take you

to a hospital. You should go. You might have internal injuries."

"I don't think so."

Mike helped him up. For the first second or two when they touched, Mike felt a brief tingle.

The handsome stranger leaned against the dumpster. With one hand he pressed against his left side. "Does this happen a lot around here?" he asked.

"Gay people have to be careful in this neighborhood. Straight adolescents still feel the need to use us for target practice."

"Hell of a way to live."

"You're not from around here?" A suburbanite. Mike did not hold the same prejudice that many urban gays in Chicago had against their brethren from the boondocks who often drove miles just to be among their own kind.

"You could say that."

"This is a hate crime," Mike said. "Best way to fight back against gay bashing is to call the cops."

"Why is that?"

Mike gazed at the man carefully. "If we don't report the crimes, we remain invisible, and the cops won't deal with the problem."

The stranger held Mike's gaze without blinking. Mike felt uncomfortable, as if he were totally naked at high noon in the middle of Daley Plaza.

"Can I help you get where you're going?" Mike asked. "Do you have a car?

"No."

"No car, but not from around here?"

"Just got to town last Monday. So I guess I'm from here now. Will you take me home with you?"

"No." Mike thought about the remark the guy had made about his underwear.

The guy looked puzzled. "You don't want to take me home?"

"I don't know what dark corner of the planet you're from, but on the part I live on, we have a cup of coffee and chat on the first date. What is it with you?"

"I'm coming on too strong?"

"Like a berserk tank squadron."

"Sorry. A cup of coffee sounds good." He swayed a little and clutched his side.

"We'll get you someplace warmer, safer, and out of the drizzle. Then we can worry about hospitals, cops, food, and your social gaffes. What's your name?"

"Joe."

They walked to Coffee Supreme Cafe at the corner of Belmont and Broadway two blocks from the restaurant. Mike ordered decaf; the stranger, regular coffee. They took their beverages to a table near the side door that opened out onto Belmont. Even though it was after 2:00 A.M., half the seats were taken.

Mike noted the ugly bruise and no-longer-bleeding cut on the stranger. "You sure you're okay?"

"I hope so."

Mike enjoyed the thrum of Joe's pleasantly deep voice. Joe took several sips of coffee before heaving a large sigh.

"Why do you come on so strong?" Mike asked.

"It's what I heard the past few nights in a bar I've gone to. Those were lines I heard guys use on each other."

"Where was this?"

"Balls, Whips, and Chains on Milwaukee Avenue."

"You're a stranger, and you went there?"

"What's the problem?"

"That's the toughest gay leather bar in the city. Modeling your behavior after what you hear there is not recommended."

"I didn't know."

"Where are you from?"

Joe pulled in a deep breath. He looked around the coffee shop and leaned over close to Mike. "I need help. I need you not to be frightened."

Mike leaned back in his chair. Who had he gotten hooked up with? Was this guy some kind of nut case or worse, a criminal, a killer? "If you're in some kind of legal trouble, call a lawyer."

"There is no easy way to say this. I've wanted to wait, but I can't. I don't have that much time."

Mike had listened to those catch words far more often than he wanted to count in the past ten years. Usually it was the prelude to someone announcing he had AIDS. He'd seen too many of his friends die. Things were far better now with newer meds, but for an unfortunate few, they didn't work. He didn't have the emotion to spend on a stranger.

"There are hospices to go to, help agencies. I can put you into contact with people who will help you."

The stranger look confused. "Why would I need an agency?"

"You're not sick?"

"Except for some smashed parts courtesy of those teenagers earlier, I'm fine."

"Oh. I'm glad."

"Look there's no easy way to say this, and I am desperate. They don't put situations like this in any training manual." The stranger drew a deep breath. "I'm from another planet."

THREE

Mike examined him carefully. "You don't look alien. Although, maybe there's a little bit of Mr. Spock about your ears, not much though."

"I'm serious."

Mike chuckled.

The stranger looked nonplused. He caught Mike's eye. This time Mike didn't flinch as he returned the stranger's gaze. "Right," Mike said, "I run into a good looking guy who is mugged, and he turns out to be nuts. Good-bye."

"I can prove it."

"I'm sure you can."

"I can read the history of a person's life."

"You can read minds?"

"Just the memory parts."

"What a stupid power. It's useless."

"No it's not. Watch." Joe glanced around the coffee shop. "See that guy sitting in the corner by the window, the one with the beard?"

Mike nodded.

The stranger paused for half a minute. Mike began to get up.

"Wait," the stranger said. Mike hesitated, and a few moments later, Joe began, "He's a rapist on parole. He's spent the time since he was out trying to find a way to do it again, but he is petrified about getting caught."

Mike pointed discreetly toward a man and woman sitting three tables away. He put his hand over his eyes and whispered, "That man and woman had sex with an Albanian dwarf half an hour ago. The guy usually wears a purple bra on Saturday nights to entice Peruvian, lesbian poets to have three-ways with them."

"He does?"

"No, you ninny. I'm making it up, just like you did."

"I was telling the truth."

Mike briefly returned his gaze to the bearded man who appeared to be in his late fifties. "I don't know that guy and neither do you."

Joe smiled at him. "You came out to your parents when you were sixteen. Your dad and mom were surprisingly understanding."

"It's not as if my coming out was a big secret. And who the hell are you anyway to pry into my private life? What's going on here?"

"I'm trying to prove myself to you. I need help."

"I'll say. You can skip the history lessons. Of course, it would be interesting to have my own private alien and psychic. Hugo would go nuts. Whizzing off to another galaxy has its possibilities. Maybe I wouldn't have to listen to him brag anymore about how often he's been to Europe. Of course, then he'd probably claim he's been around the entire universe three or four times. Then again, maybe he has. That would explain a lot about Hugo."

"How about the first time you beat off? The story of which you have told no one."

"This is getting ridiculous. No one could know that."

"You were fourteen."

"I'm not sure I want to hear this."

"You fantasized about your best friend, Robby, who is straight."

"I still do. He was gorgeous then. He still is."

"You were in a storeroom at school."

"I was not."

"You were. It took less than a minute for you to reach orgasm. Then you took the semen on your hand, brought it to your mouth, stuck out your tongue, and..."

"Stop! No one knows that. Nobody. I've never told." Mike slumped back into his chair. "You couldn't have been watching. I locked the door."

"Correct. There were no windows. You'd just gotten out of gym class. Miss Ethridge, your eighth grade teacher, had sent you to get some cleaning supplies."

"You cannot possibly know that."

"But I do."

Tendrils of numbness snaked over and around Mike's skin. He shivered. He gazed carefully into the eyes of the alien. He saw soft brown, small flecks of gold, a calm glistening. "You couldn't... No one could... How...? No one can look into minds. I'm turning into a dithering idiot." He realized he had grabbed each elbow with his opposite hand, nearly pulling himself into a ball while sitting in the chair. He forced himself to put his hands flat on the table. He eyed the alien warily. "Should I be frightened?"

"Are you scared right now?"

"More than a little."

"I am not here to hurt you."

"What are you doing here? Why are you bothering me? You said you need help. How could I possibly help you, or is this one of those spaceship/kidnapping deals?"

"This isn't any of that Bermuda Triangle hokum. That's all over-active human imagination. The laws of physics don't get suspended at a whim. Things fall down. Gravity works."

"Is this one of those spiritual, save-the-Earth deals? We're not at war as much as we were in the fifties, so it can't be that. It's environmental, right? We're ruining the planet. If we don't shape up, your species will destroy the world."

"Give it a rest will you?"

Mike slowly leaned back in his chair and examined the man who had turned his world upside down. The guy might simply be a raving loony. Mike didn't know if he wanted to believe that or not. The alternative, that this really was an alien, was more disconcerting. The coffee shop was fairly crowded, and he didn't think the guy would try anything with so many people around. He'd felt sorry for him because he'd been mugged. He didn't look dangerous. Mike kept himself prepared to bolt if anything remotely dangerous began to happen. All that early-morning running along Lake Michigan would certainly pay off. He put his hand around the vial of pepper spray in his pocket.

"Where are you from? How did you get here? How long did it take? Tell me about your world. Why isn't the United States government after you? Wasn't your ship detected on radar?"

"You ask very intelligent questions."

"That wasn't an answer. Why haven't you been found?"

"I was hiding behind a comet and snuck in."

"You're kidding?"

"Yes. I read some cult on your planet believes it. I found it quite amusing. As if I needed to hide behind a comet. Besides, on your planet dodging secret government agents isn't that difficult."

"Get real. You can't land some spaceship undetected by radar. They've got to have a fix on where you landed."

"They don't on mine. It landed undetected. Sort of."

"Feel free to explain 'sort of' and where is the ship? Is some eight foot metallic robot guarding it?"

"Not this week. Would you believe a force field protects it?"

"Barely. Of course, I believe in the good fairy. Me."

"Not very funny."

"I've been working extra shifts recently. It's late, and I'm tired. So what am I supposed to do about you? I don't know any leaders to take you to."

"Most people would be happy to have a visitor from another planet as a house guest. They'd be gaga with excitement."

"I haven't been 'gaga' since I was two, and I don't remember inviting you to my home."

The alien stared into Mike's eyes.

"Stop that."

"Stop what?"

"Looking into my mind. I don't like it."

"I don't have to make eye contact to read your mind. Although I do have to be in someone's physical presence. If I don't want you to be aware of me doing it, you won't be. Does this mean you do think I'm an alien?"

"Belief is a bit of a problem right now, yes. I'm not sure what you could say that would convince me."

Joe said, "Well, for years on your planet, a good portion of the population believed an invisible all-powerful being created everybody. You want me to match that?"

Mike drew a deep breath. "You're probably escaped from a psychiatric ward, although you did know about that time at school." Mike shrugged. "You're more likely to be from the IRS, cloned by an all-powerful computer which is attempting to conquer the planet."

"How did you guess?"

"Magic. Remember, poof, I'm a fairy."

"Do you always run yourself down?"

"Are you gay?"

"Sort of."

"You're bi. I knew it. A raving loony and a bisexual. What a cop out, or wait a minute. Did Hugo put you up to this?"

"I'm not bisexual. You keep mentioning Hugo. Who is he?"

"You read my mind, and you don't know that?"

"I've read a couple of your memories. I actually know very little about you."

"I'm not sure Hugo is bright enough to think up something this nutty."

The alien stood up.

"Now what?" Mike asked.

"I really do need your help. I'll take you to my ship."

"Why?"

"You won't have any more doubts."

"Why didn't you just appear to the president?"

"What for?"

"He's the leader."

"Look, it wasn't random chance I found you. You've been to that bar, Balls, Whips, and Chains. You know your way around. More important was that when I looked in your memory, you seemed like a decent guy. At the restaurant you were kind and patient with all your customers, even with that table with three screaming little kids."

"How many minds did you look in before mine?"

"Only a few. It takes a great deal of energy. To actually look into a person's whole life takes quite a while. It's sort of like running a film backward. I can skip parts, and some parts I can't get in to. For the information about you, I checked a few emotional high points of your life. They stick out like sign posts."

"Are you controlling my mind?"

"I can't, but if I could you'd never know."

Mike figured that was all too true. He put on his jacket. The alien didn't have one. "You aren't cold without a jacket?"

"I haven't noticed the weather much. Do you have a car?" the alien asked.

"Yes, but it isn't here. I usually take public transportation to work. How far is this?"

"The ship is in the lake off downtown. Can we get a cab?"

"Not at this time of morning in this neighborhood."

"We'll have to take a bus."

"A bus? We're going to an intergalactic spaceship in a bus?"

"We could walk."

"I ran five miles already today, thank you."

"Then it's a bus."

"Why don't we just 'beam up' to your spaceship?"

"That option only comes on the luxury model spaceship."

"Bullshit."

"Okay, I was kidding about that. We're still years away from matter transfer technology."

"That sure makes me feel better."

They strolled over to Clark Street. The bus arrived. The alien did not have exact change. Mike managed for both of them with a nickel to spare.

Mike announced, "We'll have to get more change, take an intergalactic express, or walk back."

"I'm doing my best," was the alien's only retort.

FOUR

They had the entire bus to themselves. They sat in the wide back seat.

Mike said, "I can't believe we're taking a bus to a spaceship or that I'm believing any of this."

The alien swiveled his head on his slender neck, smiled at Mike, and rested a warm, muscular hand on his arm. "Would you relax?"

Mike jerked his arm away.

"This is not some kind of Vulcan mind meld," the alien said.

"If you haven't been here that long, how do you know about that?"

"I've managed to read the entire history of several people's minds. How do you think I catch all your references to Earth movies? You may not remember everything, but it is in there. All of the peoples' memories I read had seen *Star Trek*."

"Why don't you go see Agent Mulder? He's dying to have an alien in his life."

The alien grinned. "Are you kidding? The guy's a neurotic paranoid."

Mike smiled briefly then shook his head. He stared out the window for a few moments. The persistent mist had added an oily sheen to the early morning streets. At rush hour on a rainy day, it could take over an hour and a half to get from Belmont and Clark to downtown Chicago. Now it took minutes. They cruised through the Clark and Diversey intersection, past the long-closed Tower Records store at Belden and Clark, then on by the Chicago Historical Society, the Latin School and on to where Clark turned into a one-way street going south through the trendy night life section of the city.

Part of the reason Mike had gone along was sheer curiosity.

How had the guy known about him beating off at school? The main reason, however, was that at the age of twenty-seven he felt the need to do something spontaneous. It had always been important to him to have control over as much as he could in his life, but for the past six months he felt like he would rather just fling off all his clothes and take all the escalators at noon on a Saturday during the Christmas rush at Water Tower Place or quit his job and work on a fishing boat off Key West or go someplace like Bali and roam the beaches and mountains. Even more than that, maybe this would be an adventure. Besides the guy was really hot-looking, and Mike didn't get any feeling that the alien was dangerous. Mind altering, universe changing, skin tingling, mind whirling, brain racing maybe, definitely weird, but not lethal.

While they had been in the coffee shop, the mist had become wisps of clouds slowly becoming denser until they completely obscured the view of the skyscrapers on Michigan Avenue and the Loop.

As they crossed Division Street, Mike asked, "Why do you use that strange flatware?"

"My fingers aren't used to what you eat with." He patted his pocket. "It's simpler, and it's a little reminder of home. It has a special way of molding comfortably around my fingers. I didn't think it was obvious."

"It wasn't really. Tell me the truth about why you're here."

Joe sighed. "Why don't we wait until we get to the ship?"

"Why don't you tell me now?" Mike asked, "Or maybe I get on the first bus back north?"

"I could force you."

"If you wanted to force me, you could have done that without all this folderol. Don't you have some kind of Prime Directive to not interfere with native inhabitants and their lives?"

"Are you referring to that *Star Trek* deal again?"

"Yeah."

"I don't know how to get through to you, but *Star Trek* is not reality. The Prime Directive was a plot device used by clever writers."

"I did not take a stupid pill this morning."

"Sorry."

"How come you can speak English so well?"

"I can repeat everything that was in the minds of all the people's memories I've looked into. I know three Earth languages so far."

"Is Joe really your name?"

"You were expecting something unpronounceable?"

"Yes."

"I am Police Detective Joe from the Seventh Directorate of Violence Control, sub-category twenty-six, unmated, reared in concept house 152-86, implanted with series G through R anti-crime, series A to XX intelligence. Want me to go on?"

"'Joe' I can handle."

As they crossed Ontario Street, the alien rose and looked behind them. He seemed to peer intently for a moment.

"What is it?" Mike asked. He saw one car behind them. It was a dark, four-door sedan with four people in it.

"Nothing."

"Are we being followed?"

"I don't think so," the alien said. "I've been careful."

Just before Grand Avenue, the alien yanked at the buzzer rope. The bus jolted to a stop on the west side of Clark Street. Mike hesitated. The alien put his hands on Mike's wrist and tugged gently.

"Please, you must help me."

Mike liked the idea of an all-powerful alien asking for help. As long as he'd bought it this far, he let himself be pulled up from the seat. He followed the alien out the door. The car that Mike had seen out the rear window passed on the other side of the bus then ran the red light at the corner.

They walked east on Grand Avenue. The lights of a passing car illuminated the quiet, empty streets of the near North side at three in the morning. The street lights brightened the misted pavement with their orange glow. They continued on Grand past the North Pier building.

"What is your world like?" Mike asked as they walked under Lake Shore Drive.

"Not cold like this. I like these mists and gentle rains as you've had tonight. We don't permit variations in the weather. My planet has been climate-controlled for thousands of years."

A black Chevrolet pulled off the Drive and began turning toward them.

"Is that the same car that was behind the bus?" Mike asked.

"I'm not sure."

They ducked into the entrance to the parking garage to Lake Point Tower. Hidden in the shadows, they watched the car speed past. The occupants were muffled phantoms in the murky light of the interior.

The alien peered at it intently as it swept by. They waited until the car disappeared around the far side of the high rise apartment building and for the sound of the motor to die away.

They emerged carefully. Nothing else on the street moved.

"We need to hurry," Joe said. They were across the street from Navy Pier. The hulking form of Lake Point Tower loomed on their right.

The north side of Navy Pier was for vehicle access. Mike and Joe paced quickly to the pedestrian walkway that ran along the southern edge of the pier. The deepening fog hid them from all but the closest inspection.

"We have to climb the fence," Joe said.

"Figures. We won't set off an alarm?"

"My technology can beat your technology."

"I'm not sure that is completely comforting."

"How about slightly comforting?"

"Monolithic would be scarier but more secure."

The alien pulled a small device out of his pocket, ran his fingers over its face for a few seconds.

"It's safe now," Joe said.

"What was that thing?"

"Just a little friendly help."

Joe gripped the bars of the fence, quickly scaled it, and dropped to the other side.

"This is illegal," Mike said.

"You expected the adventure of a life time to be perfect?"

Mike glanced around, approached the fence, and squeezed his hands around the bars. "I haven't done something this illegal since Tommy Dickens and I snuck into the circus when I was ten."

"Ain't it great to be ten again?"

"That sounds like a cue for a Broadway show tune."

Choosing his tenuous belief in the reality of the alien over his apprehension, Mike glanced furtively around one last time, then quickly scaled the fence.

FIVE

Alarms did not sound. The sky did not fall.

The alien grinned at him and said, "I picked the right human."

They hurried along the walkway. Mike peered into the rapidly thickening fog. On their right moored next to the pier were a number of the large pleasure boats that cruised along the lake shore during the warmer months. Mike could barely see them. On their left they passed park benches, sculptures, and shuttered businesses.

Mike listened to the quietly lapping waters of Lake Michigan. He felt reckless and daring and a trifle like an outlaw. Although he didn't imagine strolling along the pedestrian walkway at Navy Pier after hours was a major felony.

On one of the benches a quarter of the way down, they saw a couple snuggled together, lips locked. The woman briefly opened her eyes and gazed at them. She held up a hand in brief greeting then returned to her nocturnal osculation.

Halfway down the promenade, about even with the gigantic new Ferris wheel, Mike looked back. Headlights rounded the far corner and stopped. Mike thought he saw vague shadows flit in and out of the beams of light. Someone fussed at the gate for several moments and then pushed it open. Seconds later a car bore down on them. A Chicago police car with Mars lights rotating followed the first.

"Run!" the alien yelled. He sprinted toward the far end of the pier.

The necking couple jumped up and dashed toward a parking lot ramp which Mike could never reach before the cops got to him.

Mike hesitated. The black sedan cruised to a stop ten yards from him. Four men with guns drawn leaped out. Behind them Mike saw two Chicago cops emerge from their car. The men from the black vehicle all wore dark business suits. Two of them and one of the Chicago cops took off after the alien.

Someone shouted, "Halt!" A shot rang out. Mike dove for the pavement and covered his head with his hands and forearms.

Mike couldn't see who yelled, "Don't fire, you son of a bitch." Footsteps rushed past his head. Seconds later hands grabbed him roughly, lifted him up, and flung him up against the side of the building.

"Spread 'em, you son of a bitch." The voice was husky and gravelly and distinctly unfriendly.

Mike squawked a protest but got himself slammed harder against the side of the wall. His legs were kicked wide apart. Hands groped quickly up one leg and down the other, then patted his sides up to his armpits. Out of the corner of his eye he could see several of the men talking to each other. He heard shots coming from the direction the alien had run then silence. His arms were pulled behind him and handcuffs were applied.

"What's going on?" Mike demanded

"Shut up, asshole," came the gruff, gravelly voice.

Mike got himself swung around by the handcuffs. He faced a man who stood about five-foot-seven. Mike looked back over his shoulder. A guy over six-foot-two held him from behind by the restraints. Both men wore open trench coats over their dark business suits. More cop cars had arrived. Uniformed police milled around gawking at the three of them.

"Who are you?" the man asked.

"Why am I under arrest?" Mike asked.

Very slowly and carefully the man asked, "What is your name?"

The calmness with which the words were spoken did not hide the menace Mike heard in his tone. He gave his name.

"What were you doing down here at this hour of the night?"

"Walking."

"Nobody takes walks down here at this hour. The gate was closed and locked. You knew you were where you weren't supposed to be."

Mike spoke as quietly and calmly as possible. "I was taking a walk."

"Who was the guy you were with?"

Mike shrugged. "Claimed he was an alien from another planet."

The Chicago cops guffawed. The men in the business suits stared at him impassively.

The gravelly voice asked, "Somebody says they're an alien, and you just decide to casually stroll around with him? You expect us to believe that? You must be nuts. There are no aliens."

"Then let me go."

Another unmarked Chevrolet and more Chicago police cruisers drove up. The new arrivals conferred briefly with their fellow officers.

Mike looked at the herd of cars. Besides the unmarked cars, there were at least six Chicago police vehicles by now, all with lights flashing and rotating. They didn't send this kind of power to enforce the park district closing laws, or at least they hadn't since the Democratic National Convention in 1968.

They turned their attention back to Mike. They took his wallet, hustled him across the walkway, and shoved him into the back of the second Chevrolet. Mike had to duck his head quickly to avoid banging it against the door frame. The door slammed before he could voice his next protest.

He was in the back seat of a car with a wire mesh screen between the front and rear seats. The door handles had been removed. He wasn't getting out until someone let him out.

Prior to this Mike had never come close to being arrested. He'd gotten his only traffic ticket for speeding on a California freeway when his parents had taken him on a trip out west when he was seventeen. He kept telling himself not to be frightened.

He also felt a little foolish. Why had he been so stupid to blurt out that the guy was an alien? In cold retrospect in the back seat of the cop car, he told himself he'd been silly to go along with the stranger. He knew he'd broken a minor law, but he'd been handled as roughly as a dangerous criminal. His fear began to increase exponentially the longer he sat in the back of the car.

If Joe really was an alien, and they had detected something on radar, then Mike's comment could certainly complicate his life. Mike didn't picture the police saying, "Oh, well, you're merely totally insane. That's okay then. You can go."

Mike watched one of the guys in a suit take his wallet over to the other unmarked car. The man riffled through the contents. He held one item up and examined it closely. Mike thought it was his driver's license, although it was hard to tell from this distance. Checking back on the card at intervals, the man tapped at a small computer terminal on the passenger side of his vehicle. Background check, Mike presumed. He watched police personnel arrive and leave. Some began filling out paperwork.

Mike tried leaning back, but his shackled wrists made it difficult. He shut his eyes and leaned his head against the side window. If he managed not to be thrown in jail, the worst of it was, he could never tell anyone else that he'd wandered off with a guy who claimed he was an alien. Hugo would lead the chorus of people suggesting he get serious help from teams of therapists. Telling the cops had been done in a moment of unthinking irrationality. He didn't know if he should say he was only kidding about the alien stuff, make angry protests, be demure, or demand his lawyer.

An agonizingly slow half an hour passed before two plain-clothes men approached the car. A Chicago cop in a starched white shirt and stiff uniform strolled over to join them. Mike could hear bits of their conversation.

"He's our prisoner," the short man said.

"I need something substantial to justify using all these people," the cop said.

Several moments of muttered conversation followed. Finally the short man growled loudly, "It's our case."

"Bullshit," the Chicago cop stated, and he turned and stomped away.

The two men in trench coats entered the car. The tall one started the engine and they began to move.

"Where are you taking me?" Mike asked.

"We need to ask you some questions."

"Am I under arrest?"

"Not yet."

"Who are you guys?"

"FBI."

"What's going on?"

"You should be able to tell us."

The men were impervious to any further questions Mike asked.

SIX

They drove to the Dirksen Federal Building, entered the underground parking garage, and pulled into a space marked "Reserved." They hustled him into an elevator, punched eighteen. The elevator rose and then opened onto a corridor with gray carpeting, white walls with no pictures on them, and pale yellow, wooden doors leading off in three directions. They took the left-hand way and led him into a room with no windows. The chairs were blue plush and well worn. A three year old copy of *Field and Stream* rested on a coffee table.

Two women entered the room moments later. They motioned for the men to leave.

The women wore gray skirts, gray blazers, and white blouses. Mike thought *clones and ciphers and cops, oh my*. One was slightly shorter than the other. The short one said, "I'm Special Agent Denise Henry from the FBI. We need to talk to you." She took off his handcuffs and handed him back his wallet.

Mike rubbed his wrists and shook his arms then checked his wallet. Everything looked intact. He exercised his right to remain silent.

"You told the other agents that the man you were with said he was an alien. What were you doing with him?"

Mike blushed and felt foolish. "He claimed he was an alien."

"He wasn't," Agent Henry said.

The other woman introduced herself as Special Agent Hynes. She said, "You're gay, aren't you?"

"What the hell?" Mike asked.

"Are you?" she snapped.

Mike was sufficiently frightened and angry to snap back, "Yes."

"You were lucky," the woman said. She explained that a

serial killer had been preying on gay men. Someone fitting his description had been seen lurking around Navy Pier in the early morning hours the last few days. They had staked it out but found nothing until this morning.

"But this guy knew stuff about my life."

"He stalks his victims. Tries to find out as much as he can about their background before he approaches them. To avoid detection, he moves around the country quite often. As far as we can tell, he only latches on to one victim in any city. We've been tracking him for several years now. We got a tip that he was in the area."

"How did you know which of us is which?"

"He was closer to the description than you. We've also spent some time checking you out since we picked you up. Right now, we think the other guy is who we want. Plus, he ran. You didn't. Not a sure sign of guilt, but a big hint."

Agent Hynes said, "You are very lucky to still be alive. How you people can just walk home with strangers is beyond me."

"Who are 'you people'?" Mike asked.

"Gay men," Hynes said.

"All kinds of people, gay and straight, go home with all kinds of people. You've never had a one-night stand?"

"I'm not the issue. The man who could have killed you is."

"Are you sure this was the guy?" Mike asked. "He seemed so -- well, he didn't seem like a killer."

"Are you used to dealing with serial killers, Mr. Carlson? Of course not."

"Trust us. We deal with them. They can be as ordinary as your next door neighbor. Remember they've got to live in proximity to someone. Those neighbors are usually the last ones to suspect."

"This is unreal," Mike said. "Can I go?"

"We need for you to tell us everything he said to you. We may be able to piece together clues from the slightest thing. You're the only one who's escaped from him. You could have very valuable information. Will you help us?"

Mike had the healthy distrust that almost all gay people have for official authority. From the Stonewall Inn to the latest raid on a gay bar in Chicago, he knew to be wary of cops.

The night had been so totally strange. He still felt more than a little silly, embarrassed, and frightened, but he was also starting to get pissed off. He was hesitant and distrustful enough of the police to begin with. Now he was also angry about the way he'd been treated. He decided to keep his answers as short as possible. He only gave the most basic information. He downplayed the alien connection. He left out any specifics Joe had used to convince him he was from another planet. It still mystified Mike that the alien knew about his first orgasm. He truly had never told anyone about the incident.

Mike didn't bring up the fact that they'd been trespassing and neither did the agents, maybe because it was a local ordinance and not a federal statute or maybe because the alien was who he said he was, and Mike was bait or a witness or maybe the alien was who they said he was, and Mike had had a narrow escape.

For the next hour he could feel their growing frustration, but now that the initial fright had worn off and the panic of being manhandled had subsided, his sense of reality and self-confidence returned. In fact the cops had been far more violence-prone and vicious and less forthcoming than the alien had. Not wishing to anger them, he asserted himself as calmly and gently as he could. Finally he said very quietly, "I've answered these same questions three or four times now. I wish I could help you more, but I think it is time I left."

Agents Hynes and Henry left the room for several minutes, then came back and said he was free to leave. There was no further hassle and minutes later he walked out. It was a little after six o'clock. On Dearborn Street facing the Calder stabile across the way, Mike looked up at the fog-enshrouded buildings and drew a deep breath. For the moment his feelings of fear and anger were triumphant. He vowed to call his lawyer as soon as he got home. Mike was also honest enough to admit to himself that a tiny part of him was also disappointed. What if Joe really was an alien? It would have been the adventure of a lifetime.

He was totally exhausted. He couldn't wait to crawl between the sheets of his safe and familiar bed. Pulling the covers over his head and sleeping for the next ten hours seemed like a reasonably sensible option. Eating vast amounts of chocolate didn't sound like a bad idea either.

To catch the 151 Sheridan bus north, he trudged over to Michigan Avenue. Before he'd left, he got change from the cops. They'd grumbled but given him the coins. Minutes later the bus lumbered slowly northward. The dense fog made it impossible to see more than a car length ahead. On the ride home, he nearly nodded off to sleep several times.

Instead of walking from Belmont and Lake Shore Drive, he decided to take a cab. He'd stop at his favorite all-night deli to pick up a pint of chocolate chip cookie dough ice cream. The very next vehicle coming up Sheridan Road pulled over at his hail. Mike hopped in.

"Belmont and Racine," he ordered.

The cab took off in a mad careen north for a short block then roared west on Melrose.

As soon as the centrifugal force eased enough, Mike leaned forward. "What the hell is going on?" he demanded.

The alien turned around from the front seat.

SEVEN

"Christ, not you again," Mike said.

They flew down the street to Broadway where the alien made a sharp right.

"Stop," Mike roared.

At Buckingham the alien made a sharp left. The cab never paused or even slowed long enough for Mike to try and jump out. The alien drove only a few feet on Buckingham to the alley, swung left into it, roared back to Aldine, made another left, pulled up to Broadway and made a sharp right and sped on. The light at Belmont and Broadway was red. Mike reached for the door handle. The alien slammed the brakes on. Mike pitched forward. The cab made a right turn on red, swung west on Belmont, and cruised rapidly forward.

"I don't suppose if I asked you nicely to stop the cab, you would?"

"No. Please listen to me. I'm sorry if I caused you trouble."

"They told me you're a serial killer."

"Why would I want to murder cereal boxes?"

"I am not amused."

"Your mother made you eat Shredded Wheat every day for breakfast? What's Shredded Wheat?"

"Something that's healthy for you."

"Oh. Why would that be bad to eat?"

Mike said, "Klatu Barada Nikto."

"What was that?"

"The only alien I remember from when I studied it in high school."

The alien look puzzled.

"It didn't work," Mike said. "Never mind." The light at Belmont and Halsted was green so the cab didn't stop. Mike was still prepared to jump at the first sign of slowing. "Where'd you get the cab?"

"I stole it. The driver left it running outside a convenience store."

"And that justifies taking it?"

"Transportation is the issue, not justification."

"Is that cop morality or alien logic?

"I had to find you and make sure you were safe."

At Belmont and Clark the light was red. Cars were backed up ten deep at the traffic lights. The alien wouldn't be able to plow forward recklessly. As the car slowed, Mike opened the door and leapt out before it came to a full stop. He stumbled for a few steps, then trotted off.

"Hey!" the alien yelled. He jammed the cab into park, jumped out, and hurried after him. Annoyed drivers glared at the alien as they inched around the vehicle blocking a lane and a half of traffic.

The alien caught up with Mike in front of the Lucky Horseshoe bar several doors down on Halsted Street.

He grabbed Mike's arm. "Hey! You can't run away."

Mike gazed down at the hand on his arm. "Yes, I can. One foot in front of the other, only faster than walking." He stared back at the cab. "You can't leave a cab sitting in an intersection."

"Why not? It isn't mine."

Mike shook off the hand. "Go to hell. Drop dead."

The alien said, "On the day after you graduated from high school, you stopped by your best friend Robby's house to pick him up to go to the movies. You were early."

Mike turned pale. "You couldn't know this."

"You had known him since kindergarten. His parents were divorced. He lived with his mom. You'd been in and out of each other's houses for years. Neither of you knocked. You walked in on him and his..."

"Stop! Nobody knows that."

"And you have never told, ever, especially the fact that you were aroused by the sight. It has been the most embarrassing moment of your life so far. After that you felt awkward being around him so your friendship slowly disintegrated. Everybody else just figured you drew apart because you were going away to different colleges."

"You talked to them."

"I don't know them. As far as you know, they never let on that they saw you. Do you think your friend or his mother could have been less embarrassed than you?"

Mike nodded. "What I saw was part of the reason I decided to get my BA in psychology, and then for a couple years I worked on getting my MSW. I wanted to understand what made people tick."

Mike stared at the passing traffic. He had never told anyone about what had happened that day. He had missed Robby's friendship. These days they saw each other about once a year. Things had never been the same after Mike stumbled on their incest. Part of his shame was as the alien had said. He wished he'd been able to watch.

He felt his knees go weak. He'd never fainted in his life, never even come close. He steadied himself against the building.

"Are you okay?" the alien asked.

"No," Mike answered. He gently shook his head at the alien's proffered hand. He took a few deep breaths. Then after several moments of staring at the alien, he said, "What do you want here with me? No lies, no evasions, just give me the truth."

"Okay, but can we move away from this public place? The government agents are brighter than I care to admit, and they are persistent."

Mike hesitated.

"I'm not a killer," the alien said.

Mike felt this was true. More than this simple feeling was the new revelation of something secret in his life being known. Powerful evidence that the guy certainly had some kind of unusual ability. Everything rational and sensible in Mike rebelled against the concept of aliens from another planet. Maybe drunks in the outback of Montana saw flying saucers, but not sensible people in the middle of the Lake View neighborhood of Chicago.

Of course, living near the lake front on Chicago's north side could be totally strange. The weirdness quotient in this neighborhood was high at any time. Halloween around here could be a religious fundamentalist's nightmare, but still. With a shudder he gave in to the probability that he was in the presence of a creature from another planet.

"We could go to my place," Mike said, "although maybe they're watching it."

"I would if I were them. I was going to pick you up in the Loop, but I needed to be sure you weren't followed. No one got on the bus at the stop with you or off when you did. As far as I could tell, the bus was not followed. Nobody tried to emulate my mad careen through the streets and that alley a few minutes ago. Still, they might watch your place just in case they thought I might try and hook up with you again."

"How would they know you weren't just some trick? They claimed you looked like a killer they were after."

"I doubt if they got a very good look. They were never that close. You gave them a description of me when they questioned you?"

"They seemed to have one already, but what they told me sounded pretty vague. I actually didn't tell them very much." Mike explained about his feelings toward cops.

"I understand," Joe said. "I'm probably safe unless others I've talked to have called, complained, or tried turning me in. They would have given them my description. I doubt if I have to worry, but for now I'd rather err on the side of caution."

"You've told other people you're an alien?"

"No, just you."

"I have to go home sometime."

"Can we talk about it first?"

"I'm hungry," Mike said. "Let's eat." He thought for a minute about what was open at six in the morning.

They walked up Belmont to Ann Sather's Restaurant, a landmark in the Chicago gay community. Darkness and fog enshrouded them. The few people who hurried past barely gave them a glance. The first tendrils of winter lurked in the cool damp. At the restaurant, they took a table next to the wall so they couldn't be seen from the front windows.

Eight

A waiter with a shining bald head took their order. Mike stuck to hot chocolate and the restaurant's famed cinnamon buns. The alien ordered toast and coffee.

"How'd you get away from the cops?" Mike asked.

"I ran."

"That's the whole explanation?"

"Yes."

"For an alien you leave a lot to be desired. Why don't you have technological powers that would awe them into submission?"

"I can help myself, but I can't use my technological power against humans. Nor am I allowed to use it to help them or give away its secrets. Although that last would be tough since I don't know how most of it works. I can fix a little bit of my ship, but not much."

"If it breaks down, you're stuck?"

"One hasn't broken down in over five thousand years. Perhaps if I simply mowed people down with psychic brain waves someone would probably notice. Submission from humans might happen pretty quickly, although it would draw attention to myself, and I would like to avoid that."

"Can you mow people down with psychic brain waves?"

"No."

"Do you have psychokinetic powers?"

"No."

"What earthly good are you? Oh, sorry, you're not from here. What would have happened if they had shot you last night?"

"I would have been seriously damaged."

"Killed?"

"I am not immortal." He touched the bruises on his cheek. "And I can be damaged."

"Are you a robot?"

"No."

"The FBI was obviously closer to finding your ship than you thought. Maybe you should have hidden behind a comet when you flew in."

"Thanks for the tip."

Mike said quietly, "What do you want from me? I'm in this now, just tell me."

The waiter delivered their food. Mike sipped at his hot chocolate while the alien talked.

"Another being from my world came to Earth over a year ago. There *is* a sort of 'prime directive' that says we are not allowed to visit less technologically advanced planets. It's the reason I have to be very careful about how I use my technology here. In an emergency I would have to use it to terminate myself before using it to harm the people here."

"You'd commit suicide rather than interfere?"

"I have no choice."

"Doesn't that scare you?"

"It's part of the training. It's the same on my planet. I cannot hurt anyone. All police are implanted with that principle. We don't violate it. We don't want to violate it."

"Why not just implant non-criminal behavior in everybody on the planet?"

"All implants are a choice for free inhabitants of my planet."

"The triumph of the individual or the group?"

"The current structure of our society is over ten thousand years old."

"Who am I to argue with success?"

"I'm a cop on my planet. I'm here after a criminal who

escaped. He broke the codes against implant experimentation, and I've been sent to find him and bring him back. I went to your restaurant because that is the last place I've been able to track him to. I know he had dinner there for two straight nights before he disappeared. At your table, the one I was at."

"How do you know these things?"

"It's in your head."

"How did you know this restaurant to go to?"

"Police work, asking questions."

"Have you found his ship?"

"No. I don't know if your police departments or special agents found it and him. In the normal course of events, his ship should be traceable by my ship's sensors. Also a tracking device is implanted in every criminal's body. I should always be able to locate him by that. A week ago, two days before I arrived, both his and the ship's stopped working. The ship can be hidden and shielded. His personal tracker should only stop if it is no longer implanted in him. He must have managed somehow to remove it. That is supposed to be impossible, but then so is escape. Removing the tracking device should have killed him. On my planet, it would kill him, but it didn't here. I talked to several people who saw him after the device ceased functioning. It is in your head that he was at your restaurant after the tracker stopped working. He may have found somebody who could remove it for him. The concept that someone here could perform such an operation is alarming. That is highly improbable but possible. He is bright enough to construct a device that could be used to do such an operation. It would take a great deal of knowledge, medical and anatomical, along with planning, organizing, gathering materials, just a ton of stuff. He is probably tampering significantly with lives of the people on this planet."

"But you can't find out where the ship is?"

"No. I should be able to, but so far I haven't. To hide a ship is not easy. This is not a stupid criminal. He's an astronomically brilliant, mad scientist. He would not hesitate to kill. I've got to find him and get him back to my planet."

"How? Does he have psychokinetic powers?"

"No."

"Can he read people's memories?"

"No. That's a power that's implanted in police where I come from, easy to find the guilty that way. Makes us judge, jury, and cop at the same time. The criminals can't lie. If they commit a crime, we know."

"That's invasion of privacy."

"That's efficient crime prevention."

"It's unconstitutional."

"Not where I come from."

"What's to keep the police from framing everyone?"

"The implants block such behavior. We're trained to enforce the law, not break it. We do have a review system which is like your appeals courts, one of whose major functions is to prevent that kind of abuse."

"Does everybody on your planet have implants?"

"The normal number is between five and ten, mostly for education and learning."

"Why aren't there implants to stop you from reading memories? Why doesn't it work both ways? Why aren't there implants to read or control minds or stop people from being criminals?"

"Thousands of years ago my planet was engulfed in Implant Wars. It was an era sort of like your nuclear age. Bigger, more powerful, more complex and dangerous implants were being created. A third of our population died in the last and most devastating of those wars. After that the regulation and peaceful use of the implants became enshrined in law. It took nearly a thousand years to wipe out criminals and rogue systems or planets that refused to comply."

Mike ordered another hot chocolate, and the alien, more

coffee. They consumed cinnamon buns and toast for several minutes in silence.

"How could this other alien mess things up here?" Mike asked.

"He could use advanced technology. To say that he could 'conquer' the world is overly dramatic, but as long as he is here, he is a danger to this whole planet."

"If he's such a danger, why did they only send one of you?"

The alien looked uncomfortable. "Your planet is not very important and poses no threat to us. Nobody cares much what happens here. You have no technology we need. What few resources you have that might be valuable to us would be prohibitively expensive to transfer all the way to my planet."

Joe blushed.

"Also, I shouldn't tell you this, but I'm not a very important cop, and I'm a screw up. My mission is roughly equivalent to taking a seasoned veteran detective in Chicago and busting him down to the level of a first year cop handing out parking tickets. The next step is firing me and undoing the implants. Sending me here was an alternative to throwing me out on my butt.

"On my planet they expect me to fail. If I bring him back alive, the advancement and the perks and the promotions would be phenomenal. He hurt a lot of people on my planet before he was caught. Most are content to see him gone. This is exile here for him."

"And for you?"

"I'd like to prove myself to my bosses and to myself."

"How do you know he hasn't just left?"

"I have a grid set up around Earth that would disable his ship if he tried to pass through it. He and his craft would reenter the Earth's atmosphere and burn up. That has not happened. My ship's radar would have picked that up."

"You're in contact with your ship? Maybe he left five minutes ago."

The alien reached in his pocket and pulled out a flat piece of metal about the size of a half dollar, only this was square. It was the object he had used to disarm the security system at Navy Pier.

"This is a communicator." He held it out to Mike.

It was slightly larger than the display part of an iPod, only the front, back, and even the slender sides were all screen. "I won't break it?"

"No. Probably nothing on Earth could even dent it slightly."

Mike held the cool bit of electronics in the palm of his hand. The surface was a display like a computer monitor. Half was dense with figures Mike couldn't decipher. He placed it gingerly back in Joe's hand.

The alien ran his finger along the display. "My ship's computer would talk to this, and I would know."

"An intergalactic beeper. Gee whiz, way cool."

"You're starting to get sarcastic."

"Sorry."

The alien tapped several times on the side of the communicator. A small but incredibly clear picture appeared on the screen. "This is him," the alien said.

Mike saw an older man with receding hair, a cleft chin, and very blue eyes. "I sort of remember him from the restaurant," he said. "He isn't an ugly bug-like creature." Mike paused then asked. "You aren't secretly an overgrown cockroach in disguise?"

"Sorry to disappoint you. There are no big or little bug-like aliens, which of course, would make it tough for them to conquer a demented atom, much less a planet. Nobody has cockroaches ruling their planets. No critters will come crawling out of my throat. Nobody is kidnapping earthlings to do sexual experiments with them. I am not in disguise. What you see is what you get."

"That's a comfort."

"His ship has not left the planet, nor is it in orbit. As I said, I have a grid around Earth that would damage him and his ship.

That has not happened. The residue would be detectable. No, the ship is hidden on this planet. My vehicle is larger and more sophisticated than the one he stole. Because his is smaller, if he shut down all the systems and shielded it, he could hide it successfully."

"What if a person from Earth found it?"

"They wouldn't be able to penetrate the force field to get to the outer rim, and even if by some miracle they did, they wouldn't be able to even dent the hull."

"They could report it to the media."

"Have you seen it on the news?"

"Obviously not. How big is his ship?"

"Maybe as large as a rounded-out city bus. If he got it underground somehow, it would be tough to find."

"You got yours under the lake."

"His ship doesn't have the capacity to do that. The basic workings of our ships are the same, but in sophistication, power, things it can do, his might be compared to a child's tricycle, mine to a space shuttle. The police have the best available equipment."

"Does he know you're here?"

"Not from his technology. He might assume they sent someone. If a person I've questioned reported it to him, he would need to become circumspect, maybe even suspend his operations."

"For how long?"

"Until the threat from me was neutralized."

"You mean until you were dead?"

"Yes."

"And anyone who helps you?"

"I doubt if he'd think you were important enough, but if you get in his way, he would not hesitate to harm you."

"Thanks for the tip."

"I'm trying to be honest."

"What if he's been captured by the same people who are after you?"

"When I circled back to see what the FBI agents were doing with you, I checked their recent memories. None of them indicated any recent powerful memories fueled by high emotion that show they had him."

"So, how am I supposed to help?" Mike asked.

"You're the last person I know who was in his physical presence. I just missed him. I need to find out as much as I can."

"Unlike you, he did not confide in me. Why not just pretend you were a real cop and ask me questions? Why the big revelation?"

"If you demanded police identification, I have none to show you. I don't have the capacity to duplicate any. Do you think they send the space shuttle up with a copy machine on board?"

"You mean you can cruise around the galaxy at speeds we can only dream of, and you can't do something simple like make a fake ID?"

"Being without official identification would cause suspicion. As a reasonably intelligent person, you would be wary. It would be more difficult to get to talk to you."

"And telling me you're an alien makes it easier?"

"We're here aren't we? The past couple days I did have some trouble without identification. Earthlings in America are very suspicious, but fortunately they also love to talk." He took a sip of coffee and then resumed, "Another reason I told you is that it takes too much psychic energy to keep that kind of secret every waking moment. Maybe it's what makes me a rotten cop. No training manual talks about the total aloneness of being the only one of my kind here. I needed to be honest and open with at least one person."

"Every gay person on the planet can relate to that."

"It's sort of the same with me. Besides questioning you, I need impressions, guesses, and I wasn't lying before, I do find you attractive."

"You're gay?"

"I am male, and I am attracted to you. You may label me whatever way is comfortable for you. I do not know why I find myself sexually attracted to you. Does everyone here always know why they're attracted to someone else? Plus, I need a guide to Earth ways. I don't know the terrain that well. I can read people's histories, but it is not the same as having someone I can speak with, share an honest thought with. I don't get all of the idioms here. I am limited by what I've read in people's minds, and I have no basis for evaluating what I've understood. Witness the gaffes I made in trying to make connections with you. I really did go to that bar. I read a man's mind. That's how he approached guys."

"How did you know I'm gay?"

"Read your memory."

"Why not just keep reading minds until you find him?"

"If I read all memories in just one person's mind, I am totally exhausted. You can't believe all the psychic garbage that's in there or how monumentally boring it is. I can try doing only high points, but mostly those are of major events: the birth of a child, the death of a parent, first sexual encounters, that kind of thing. Finding what would be helpful to me is difficult. Checking every memory in a person's mind for only the past two weeks would take time and there are millions and millions of people to try. I wouldn't know which ones to pick. It's easier to do it as if it were a regular police investigation."

"Why not do it like regular police investigation, but just read minds?"

"Don't you ever get tired of asking questions?"

"Not yet. I have lots more, and you haven't answered all the ones I've asked. It's tough you can't just use that memory power stuff."

"Earthlings are too different for it to be efficient. On my planet it only takes seconds to read the memories. Because of the physiological differences between us, it takes more energy to look into the minds here. One image I read in a person's mind captured it exactly. Reading earth minds is the mental equivalent of having to make a journey of a thousand miles while tracking through snow two feet deep. I get tired very quickly. No one on my planet knew what effect the difference in physiology would have. If this were my planet, I'd be done already. As I said earlier, I have to evaluate and make decisions based on what I see in people's memories. The ground rules are different."

"Or you could be telling me a pack of lies."

"I could. How would you know?"

"Why not reveal yourself to a cop and get help from a professional?"

"You ever just tried to casually walk up to a cop and ask about a case they're working on? Doesn't happen. Not on anybody's planet."

"You could use the same trick you worked on me. Convince them of who you are."

"Not a bad thought. Too big of a chance though that the one I picked would turn me in. I cannot read the future or what a person might do. I can make only an educated guess, based on the past I read."

"How did you know I wouldn't turn you in?"

"I didn't. I took a chance, based on the parts of your memory I did read, what I saw of you as you worked, and partly it was just a hunch."

"Hell of a chance."

"We're trained to take risks."

"How much of my memory have you read?"

"Only the parts I've told you about."

"Am I supposed to believe that?"

"I can't control what you believe. You should not underestimate your attractiveness and the positive impression you give as a waiter dealing with people. You have a wonderful sense of humor, and remember you're the last person to see my criminal."

"Does he have a name?"

"Vov."

"That's it? Not 'Vov Jones' or 'Vov Smith'? Just plain Vov?"

"I'm approximating the sounds in my language with yours."

Mike nodded. "Vov, the criminal. I've got it. Does sending federal agents mean the government now believes in UFOs?"

"They know something came from outer space that can change directions and speeds."

"They didn't try to shoot you down with jet fighters and rockets?"

"Mike, my ship is faster than the speed of light. It is certainly faster than anything anyone on this planet can shoot at me."

"After the fiasco this morning, how are you going to avoid the authorities?"

"They must have a much better fix than I thought on where my ship came down. Also, I have been asking a lot of questions of quite a number of people. I don't know if they have made a connection between my questions and the ship landing. Even if they don't have a photo, they still might have lots of people who can describe me."

"Maybe someone saw you at the pier and called the police."

"I doubt it."

"Half the people on this planet are running around with camera phones. They might even have you on tape. They told me you matched a description of a serial killer."

"They lied."

"Supposedly he's been hanging around Navy Pier."

"I have gone to the pier very late at night to get to my spacecraft."

"They've got some data based on what I told them this morning, although it wasn't much."

"I wish you hadn't told, but you were in a tight spot. I never dreamed they were that close. After this, I'll have to be even more careful. That's where you might be able to help."

"Not if they're watching me."

"I can't reveal I am an alien to dozens of people. Someone would tell. The authorities would find me, and at the very least, lock me up as having lost my mind. You, I have confidence in. From your memories, I know you don't tell secrets."

"Thanks for the compliment."

"At least they won't be able to find the ship."

"Why not?"

"It's not just in the water, it's fifty feet below the bottom of the lake."

"How were we going to get to it?"

"I'll take you."

"When?"

"Now, if you like."

They paid their bill and as they walked out of the restaurant, Mike asked, "How'd you get US cash?"

"All our spaceships, even the smallest, have working labs. Many minerals are universal or readily enough available throughout the galaxy."

"You can make gold from lead?"

"No, why would I bother? I had a few diamonds from home, and I took them to a diamond center, and I had some gold I took to one of those places that buy gold."

"They were the same as Earth diamonds and gold?"

"That's what the lab is for, to make sure they're the same."

Mike said, "The magic of science."

"What's that?"

"An old quote something about the key to the magic of science is that it works although I'm not sure I've got that exactly right."

"Does it matter? I've got cash."

"I guess not."

"My communicator can tie into bank accounts."

"You've been robbing people?"

"I siphon funds from those billionaires who have not paid taxes in the past ten years."

"They have taxes where you come from?"

"They have taxes where everybody comes from."

NINE

Part of Mike figured this would be the ultimate test: no ship, no alien. While fairly convinced, a small part of him was still torn between believing this was an alien and just some whacked out basket case. The information he'd been given in the past hour had certainly made it easier to believe Joe.

At the door of the restaurant, the alien carefully looked at the fog closing in on the pavement, passersby, and traffic.

"Foggy should help," Joe said. "If the fog is thick enough, it will be easier to remain undetected."

They strode down Belmont. The car headlights made little dent against the clinging mists. Mike remembered only once before being in fog this thick. As a kid he'd been camping with his family on Mt. Tamalpais just outside of San Francisco. He and his family had watched the fog drifting up the mountain and covering the surrounding countryside until it had reached them and covered the entire landscape in dense white. It was one of the most beautiful sights he'd seen in his life.

"Are we going downtown?" Mike asked.

"I moved the ship while the cops had you."

When they arrived at the lake front, they skirted the Belmont Harbor boat house. They heard footsteps and paused tensely. A lone jogger thudded by on the asphalt path near them. Even though the person was only ten feet away, he or she was little more than a darker shadow. They walked across the grass to the Belmont rocks. In high summer this area was crammed with gay people absorbing cancer-causing rays from the sun.

They heard and saw no one else. Mike caught the sound of water slapping against the rocks piled along the shore.

"Water's a little cold for swimming," Mike stated.

"We aren't going to swim. For one thing, I don't know how."

"You are possibly the most inadequate alien I have ever met or heard of or dreamt about."

"You dream about aliens?"

"Actually, no."

They walked along the very edge of the lake. The alien had his communicator out and was tapping gently on the surface of it.

"Walking on water has a certain appeal," Mike said. "I could impress religious fundamentalists, maybe start my own church. Donations are a good thing."

"There," the alien said.

"Where?"

"Here." Joe walked to the very edge of the water. The rocks at this point formed a shelf leaning out over the surface. Painted on the pavement and posted on the signs were warnings about no diving or swimming. The alien lay on his stomach with his head and shoulders over the tip of a large boulder. He reached down and seemed to peel off a very thin strip of clear plastic. He stood up and shook it out.

Mike thought it looked like a throw rug with the sheen and thickness of Mylar. It was about the size of a very large garbage can lid.

"What's that?"

"Over-water transportation."

Mike laughed.

"I show you something technologically advanced and you are amused?"

"I'm doing my best. How does it cling like that? It was invisible."

"More techno magic for your enjoyment. We're here to meet your needs."

"You mean you don't know."

"Not the foggiest."

"Is that alien humor?"

"Earth does not have a monopoly on dumb jokes."

Mike followed the alien down to a rock that was about even with the lapping lake water. The alien placed the Mylar-rug on the water where it floated. Mike thought it resembled nothing more than a piece of translucent, overgrown tinfoil.

The alien stepped lightly onto it. Instead of plummeting into the depths, the flotation device with Joe on it bobbed with the gentle waves. Joe held out his hand to Mike.

"You're not kidding, are you?" Mike asked.

"It'll hold the two of us safely."

"How does it work?"

"Interrelation of elements."

"What does that mean?"

"Technically, I'm not sure. Practically, it means we can safely take this to the ship."

"Where are the controls?"

Joe held out his communicator. Again he extended his other hand to Mike. A wicked thought of shoving the alien into the drink crossed Mike's mind. He shrugged off the silliness and faced the reality of otherworldly fear. His curiosity overcame his caution. Mike put out his hand and took the alien's. He felt a brief tingle as he had the first time he touched him. It felt almost like the electric spark when you scrape your feet on a rug as you cross a room with low humidity in winter. The difference was this left a pleasantly warm sensation.

Mike stepped on the wafer-thin lid. It was an odd sensation only in that he felt like he was standing on firm ground. A foot away he could see the rock he stepped from. The water around him swayed in the light swell. The flotation device barely seemed to move. It was as if it was adjusting itself to the weight above and the water below in a continuous stream, so that the surface they stood on remained firm and steady. More, Mike felt as if his feet were pulled to the surface, as if gravity itself had solidified, frozen around his feet. He felt no insecurity or feeling of falling.

Mike reached a hand into the fog. "Wow."

After several taps on the surface of the communication device, the flotation contraption began to move out into the lake.

"How can you tell which way to go?"

"Tracking device -- radar."

"Oh."

Mike felt weird and otherworldly as they eased through the fog. "How fast are we going?" he asked.

"A little over twenty-five miles an hour."

Whether it was because of the fog or the technological superiority of their mode of transportation, Mike hardly had a feeling of movement. The sensation of forward motion was smooth and pleasing. Mike could picture this as a pleasure craft on a peaceful lake.

"My last boyfriend had a racing boat," Mike said. "He desperately wanted me to be impressed with it. I drove it once. The damn thing could go fast. Unfortunately with him, I wanted to go slow."

"This isn't too fast for you?"

"I meant in our relationship."

"I knew that."

"This is fine."

Silence and fog enshrouded them. Mike thought it had begun to be a bit lighter. The sun must be burning off the fog. He wondered what would happen if it did before they got back.

"Not much farther," Joe said.

"Can the police radar find us?" Mike asked.

The alien held out his communicator. "On my ship I could detect human craft, but not with this. Even if their radar found us, in this fog they'd have to come within several feet of us to actually see us."

"What if the fog lifts? Then the whole population of the city will be able to see us."

"We're too far out, and we're not going to be out here all that long."

Mike felt them slowing and then come to a stop. They'd been on the water just over half an hour. They must have gone at least several miles out. The alien stared at the face of the communicator, then rapidly began to run his fingers over its top.

"Okay," Joe said.

In the mists the waves made soft sounds. For several minutes nothing happened except growing light. Mike thought he could see a few feet farther from the disc than before.

"How do you hide this thing under the bottom?"

"Gravitational displacement."

"What does that mean?"

"Stuff moves so other stuff can go where that stuff just was."

"Well, that's clear. I bet it's in all the physics text books."

The water in front of them began to churn and swirl. With a soft hissing noise a solid slab of metal began to appear as far as he could see in front of them. He could get no sense of scale from where he stood. No question whatever was rising from the lake was immense and that the alien was causing it to rise. After the initial soft hiss, the ship rose as silently as the fog moved.

From behind them and to the left, Mike thought he heard a noise, which quickly grew into the roar of a boat motor.

TEN

"Somebody's coming," Mike said.

Joe was already rapidly tapping the top of his communicator. The ship began to disappear.

"We better get out of here," Mike said.

The alien kept tapping. "I've got to bury the ship again." Seconds later Joe's fingers stopped moving. He gazed around. "It's safe. Let's go."

"Is it the cops?"

"I don't know. I can't take a chance. No pleasure boat is going to be out on the lake in this fog at this hour at this time of the year."

Mike said, "We must be pretty far out. I don't want to be run over by some tanker from Lake Superior."

"Hush," Joe said.

The other motor was much louder and seemed to be coming toward them. Whoever it was couldn't be moving too fast because of the fog. Joe began manipulating his communicator. Mike felt the disc turn. He whispered, "Are we going back to shore?"

"Yes," the alien whispered back.

The other boat's motor seemed to be almost on top of them. Still, Mike couldn't see anyone. Then the alien pointed. Mike saw the outline of the prow of a boat, with the logo of Chicago police department on its side. Then their craft was pulling them in the opposite direction. They began to move more quickly than they had before. In only a few moments, the sound of the other boat began to get farther away. Mike guessed it must have taken only about half as long to get back as it did to go out. He shivered with the knowledge that the ship was real, and Joe was, as he claimed, an alien.

At the shore, Joe peered intently around at the friendly fog.

He quickly replaced the disc under the rock where it blended with the gray surface. Mike could see no seam or fissure that marked its place.

As they walked toward the underpass where Belmont Avenue began, Mike thought he saw rotating Mars lights.

"Cops," Mike said.

They swiftly backed up.

"Which way?" Joe asked.

"I'm not sure. The police might have all the underpasses covered."

"I'd rather not run into them."

"Me either," Mike said. "Follow me." Mike led the way up the slope of Lake Shore Drive. The beam of a car's headlights rose, passed them, and faded. Mike listened intently. "Let's go." They dashed across the northbound lanes, clambered over the median strip, listened again, then hurried over the southbound lanes. Behind them they heard several cars whoosh by. They hurried across the strip of park to the Inner Drive then walked up Briar Street past Sheridan up to Broadway. It was well past dawn.

"I think we're safe," the alien said.

"I sure hope so," Mike said. "You really do have a ship."

"Yep."

No doubt about it, Mike realized. This was an alien, and he was in the middle of the greatest adventure any human could dream of. He shook his head. He'd been up all night. Mixed with his excitement was a desire to sleep for a week. Mike yawned. "You may not need to rest, but I've got to get some sleep. I'm supposed to work tonight."

They continued walking up Briar to Halsted, then cut across to Wellington and continued strolling west.

Joe said, "I want to go back to that bar where Vov was. I didn't get the answers I needed the other night. I know you've been there before. You would know things, people to talk to."

"If someone reported you to the cops, and you don't know who, how do you know which places they'll be watching? And why would the police connect that report to the ship that landed in the lake? They wouldn't know you were one and the same, unless they had pictures of you in both places or somehow they had matching descriptions."

"They probably aren't one hundred percent certain."

"They could be on the lookout for me after this, too," Mike said. "I could sleep at my place. They let me go so they aren't likely to arrest me. What if I'm bait? Where could you go to wait for me? How are we going to question people?"

"It would probably be better if we stuck together."

"If I go to work, they could pick up my trail there. It won't do much good for me to play hide and seek with the FBI. We'll have to think of something."

"I'd like to get undercover for at least a few hours," the alien said. "I don't want to chance going to my ship again until after dark."

"So what do we do?"

"If you're willing, we could try your place. As you say, I could just be some trick you picked up."

They walked up to Belmont and turned west to Southport and then north for a block and a half. Mike enjoyed the cool morning, with wisps of fog still hanging in the air, and now sunlight occasionally stealing through to illumine the multi-colored hues of the autumn-struck trees.

A half block from his house, Mike saw a uniformed police officer strolling toward them from the direction of Lincoln Avenue.

The policeman marched up to them. He was a narrow-waisted man Mike guessed to be in his late fifties. He wore a mustache. His blue uniform was creased and sparkling clean. Mike thought there was something odd about the way he was dressed. The cop spoke directly to the alien. "You need to come with me."

"What is this?" Mike asked. "What law has he broken?"

"That's no concern of yours." He put his hand on the alien's elbow. "Come along quietly to the precinct, and we'll get this all straightened out."

"Stop!" Mike grabbed the alien's arm and pulled in the other direction. "The guy's a fake."

The cop whipped his gun out, but before he could aim it at them, Joe's hand shot up and shoved the gun in the other direction. The cop stumbled toward Mike. To his own surprise, Mike shoved him hard. The cop backed up, stumbled on the curb, and fell into the street. His weapon skittered away. Joe leapt for it and kicked it across the street.

"Let's go," Mike yelled to the alien. They took off toward Belmont. Mike looked back and saw the cop dodging traffic toward where Joe had kicked the gun. Fifty feet down Lincoln Avenue, Mike pointed to an alley. They dashed down it.

Mike was in good shape, but he was puffing hard by the time they reached Diversey. The alien barely seemed to be out of breath.

"How'd you know he was fake?" the alien asked.

"Three things: First, his hat was wrong. Chicago cops all have that silly black and white checkerboard pattern along the hat brim. His didn't have that. Second, he said 'precinct' and not 'district.' People from out of town think we have precincts, or those who just watch police shows, think the same thing. Chicago has police districts. It's one sure way to tell the native from the tourist. One other thing confirmed it though."

"What was that?"

"He didn't use his radio to call for help. He just went for his gun. We were no direct threat to him, nor were we trying to escape. The real question is, if he wasn't a real cop, who was he? How did he find out where we were, and what did he want?"

"There's something else as well."

"What?"

"I was trying to read his mind, but he put up resistance. I was taught there was no way anyone on my planet or Earth could block me like that."

"If you're as incompetent as you say they think you are, maybe they didn't tell you everything."

"There are those on my planet who say the government lies to us."

"Ours does."

"Ours isn't supposed to."

Mike laughed. "Neither is ours. Is the guy you're chasing like a political criminal? Is it just the government is mad at him?"

"No. He's a genuinely evil, totally corrupt former scientist and doctor. His crimes against people were massive. Hundreds of thousands of innocent lives were lost."

"How long have you been hunting for this guy?"

"A little over two years."

"Seems like a long time."

"You ever try searching several billion square miles of space for one tiny speck?"

"There was one time..."

"I don't want to hear about it."

They spoke while they walked down alleys, keeping watch at every turn for anyone who looked suspicious.

"If this guy was from the other alien, and you're such a threat to him, why didn't this fake cop just kill you?"

"I'm not sure. If he could get my ship, the technology on it could be of great benefit to him. Without me alive, it would be impossible for him to find it."

"How would Vov know where we were and be able to get somebody there?"

"I don't know. He doesn't have magic abilities. He's got to be getting help from sympathetic humans."

"Yeah, why'd he even use a cop outfit, fake or real? What was the point?"

"If it looks like a cop making an arrest, people don't get suspicious."

"But wouldn't Vov know that you can read the human's memories?"

"If he thought he could shield that guy's mind from my probing, maybe he was over-confident. He's got to realize I would detect the shielding, or maybe his device was made to conceal even the fact that he was shielded. Even somebody as menacing and dangerous as this can make lots of dumb mistakes."

"How'd he know where to find us?"

"If he's in with the criminal element, who knows? We were on the street for only a little while, but maybe we were in that restaurant for too long. More likely he's got an 'in' with the FBI. He'd have had to follow you from there. I suppose he could have gotten your address. He can't have…"

The alien pulled out his communicator. He panned the device up and down Mike's body, front and back. The alien held the object close to Mike's butt.

"Take out your wallet," Joe said.

Mike did as he was directed.

The alien scanned the leather inside and out. "Here," he said, as he reached into an inner recess and pulled out a microchip-sized piece of plastic.

"What's that?"

"A tracking device from my planet. I was told Vov only had the ship and had no time to steal anything more."

"Maybe they lied again."

"Or worse, he has the capacity to manufacture these, or maybe he stole more things than they told me."

The alien held the chip on the tip of one finger, pressed the front of his magic dingus and held it over the tracker. After several seconds of reading the dingus's face he said, "This is from here. He made it on Earth with Earth materials. He's got to have one hell of a lab set up."

At the next cross street, the alien flicked the tracker onto a passing car.

"Why not destroy it?" Mike asked.

"I could only do that on my ship. I don't want to carry it around. Better than tossing it away is sending it where we are not. The license plate on that car was from Iowa. I'm not sure where that is geographically, but I know it isn't Illinois."

"Smart."

"We still need to get off the street," the alien said. "Vov has been able to track us all this time."

Mike said, "The FBI had my wallet."

"Then Vov has some connection with the FBI somewhere. That is not good. I need time to think and plan. Is there someplace we can go?"

Mike said, "I know the perfect place to hide."

ELEVEN

Carefully observing each person they passed, they hiked back to Lincoln Avenue. They caught a bus south to Halsted Street. Their destination was the Luxor Hotel at the corner of Webster and Halsted. Mike figured no one would ever look for them here.

Any list of the least desirable places to stay on Earth would include this establishment. Look up the word "sleaze" in the dictionary, and you'd find a picture of the Luxor Hotel. It had a reputation in Chicago's gay community as a place you could use for a minor encounter with a briefly significant other. Supposedly, there were sex orgies on the roof on hot summer nights. All year round on Monday afternoons they set out a lavish buffet for the transgender denizens of the hotel and their friends. On New Year's Eve they threw jockstrap parties which could set up a call boy's reputation for years. The darkest corner of the deepest basement was reputed to have a leather dungeon. Down there while people indulged in their favorite kinky delight, home movies of S/M activity were shown continuously.

Mike had been to the Luxor's New Year's Eve party last year. The waiters had all been mid-level pornographic movie stars. All of them had nubile, sylph-like bodies. All were barely a breath over the age of jail bait. Not a button or a bow much less a jockstrap covered their bronzed and over-buffed flesh as they served drinks, hors d'oeuvres, and dinner. Several ice sculptures and one liver pâté built in stunning replica of different brands of jockstraps adorned the sides of all the entrances and exits.

Late in the evening one of the waiters had followed Mike into the bathroom, but Mike had discouraged the young lovely. He didn't disapprove of a quick, but safe dalliance, and he certainly didn't mind pretty young men, he just preferred more masculine men with muscles, brains, compassion, wit, and a sense of fun whom he'd spent time with, getting to know and care for.

The lobby floor was tile-covered. Each of three walls had

one couch with ripped, dark-red vinyl cushions. A reception desk interrupted the depressingly ordinary fourth wall. An immense woman sat at the counter with an adding machine and what looked like a stack of bills. She introduced herself as Edna. Her eyebrows raised not the slightest when Mike and Joe showed up in the middle of the morning with no luggage and asked for a room. Whether it was a salacious assignation or a genuine check-in for overnight, her gaping yawn indicated her deep disinterest. Edna claimed a top floor suite was the only space available. Mike presumed it was the most expensive. Although this place couldn't charge what the Ritz did, it could overcharge as well as any over-priced Michigan Avenue hotel.

The elevator was being repaired so they had to walk up four flights. Faded maroon carpeting covered the halls and stairs. The risers creaked. In the room the carpeting was dingy brown. The furniture was nicked and scarred. The pink chenille bedspread was threadbare. On the walls the faded black and white pictures of over-muscled men were blotched with yellow stains. It was awful, but it had separate rooms and the towels looked mostly clean.

Mike preferred the separate bedrooms. While the alien had shown no tendencies to violence, Mike was glad he could at least lock a door between them. He doubted if he'd have to fight off an amorous alien, but he didn't want to take the chance either. As they'd ascended the stairs, Mike had thought about what the alien had said about being attracted to him.

Mike found Joe attractive, and he was curious about his anatomy. Were they similar? He wanted to touch the front of Joe's pants, to feel what was under the cloth, to touch his hair. What would it be like to make love to a hot-looking alien? Would it be different? Could he make Joe moan in pleasure? What could he do that would help that happen? The concept of sleeping with someone from another planet had a certain kinky appeal, but he knew he'd feel odd touching the creature's body. Mike had no intention of making any move on the guy. Nor would he show in any way that he was interested in reciprocating any initiative begun by the alien.

But he knew the longer he was with the alien, the more powerful the sexual attraction became.

Even more, after a disastrous fling with a married college hockey player, he'd decided that he would only sleep with a guy if he was in love. He felt some lust but was nowhere near ready to jump in the sack with Joe.

As they surveyed their urban oasis Mike said, "I'm exhausted, but I don't know how I could fall asleep. My mind is racing, but I've got to at least try to shut my eyes."

The alien said nothing after they decided on the sleeping arrangements. Mike left the sitting room, shut the connecting door, and locked it. Fully clothed, he flopped onto the bed. The pillow was as thin as a cheap paperback novel and just as hard. His body sank nearly to the floor on the overused mattress. As exhausted as he was, he wound up tossing and turning for a while. He finally fell asleep to thoughts of his own bed in his own apartment.

TWELVE

Mike woke staring at the water-stained ceiling. He listened for noise from the other room, but he heard none. The cracks in the ceiling were enough to tell him he wasn't in his own comfortable apartment. That much was reality. He thought maybe he was going nuts. Real people don't get involved in interstellar adventures. No one would ever believe Mike if he told them.

Mike rubbed his tongue along his teeth. He wished he had his tooth brush. His clothes felt rumpled and uncomfortable. He ran a hand through his mussed hair.

He thought, I'm frightened out of my mind. My whole life has completely altered. I'm not supposed to indulge in investigating criminal activities. I have no training for that and no inclination to do it.

Mike touched his stomach and chest. He touched his chin. Well I'm real, but maybe while I was asleep, Joe, from another planet, has been beamed to another galaxy.

He swung his feet out of the bed. After he took a shower, he put on his worn clothes, including his black boxer briefs. He wondered for a few seconds if the alien wore underwear, then shut out the image. He didn't want to know. Not yet.

He unlocked the connecting door and opened it. The alien sat on the couch staring out the window at the high-rise across the street. He turned and smiled at Mike.

Mike thought, if he smiles like that often enough, I will fall in love with him even if he turns out to be a gaseous vapor from Pluto in disguise.

"Good afternoon," the alien said. "It's nearly two. Did you sleep well?"

"I always feel peppy after a good four hours of tossing and turning."

"Problem?"

"Are you kidding? I've got the biggest news since the birth of Christ, and I can't tell anyone. It is possible I'm in some physical danger, and I'm scared. Other than that, everything is fine." Mike sighed, "Did you sleep or get some kind of rest?"

"I indulged in energy rejuvenation, yes."

"What the hell does that mean?"

"I'm twenty-eight of your Earth years. We age the same as you although we live about fifty years longer. Our mental abilities help us to remain youthful. We don't begin to look old until we are over one hundred."

"Why not find someone brighter than me, somebody who knows astrophysics and who would know what questions to ask you?"

"I'm not here to teach technology. Even if I had the knowledge, I have neither the permission nor the ability. I'm here to bring back a criminal."

"Maybe if you'd appeared to a high-tech scientist, they'd be able to ask you super-bright questions. I'm just a nobody, a gay guy with a rage to know cheap tawdry gossip."

"You sound a little tense."

"I don't often find an alien on the couch in my luxury suite. How about you? Are visitors from outer space just popping in on your planet all the time?"

"Yes."

"How nice for you. Do you need to shave? Do you go to the bathroom? Do you want a shower? Do you know what a shower is?"

"Yes to all of the above."

The alien stalked into the bathroom. A moment later Mike heard water running and then a screech followed by words in a language he presumed was native alien.

Mike hurried to the bathroom door and looked inside. Billows of steam rushed towards him. He could see the outline of the alien behind the shower curtain at the far end of the tub. Water cascaded in front of him.

"What?" Mike asked.

"How do you change the settings?"

Without looking at the alien, Mike reached in and twisted the dials until the water temperature was comfortable to his touch. "I'll put out towels," Mike said. Mike placed the unfluffy patches of cotton so the alien could reach them easily.

As the sounds of water cascading over a body issued from the shower, Mike shut the connecting door, walked to the phone and called his lawyer. David Smith had been a friend of his since they'd gone to St. Swithins Grammar School on the far north side of the city when they were kids. After graduating from law school, David had set up an office on Belmont just west of Broadway. On this Saturday afternoon, Mike called him at home.

THIRTEEN

"What did you do this time?" David asked.

"I haven't done anything ever."

"So why do you call me so often?"

"I covet your ugly tie collection." David wore everything from frighteningly pink ties covered with cabalistic signs to ones which pictured dead fish with eyes that glowed.

Mike said, "The FBI picked me up last night."

"Never had a client picked up by the FBI before. Maybe I'm moving up in the world."

"They claimed I was out walking with a serial killer."

"Better than bringing him to your apartment. Who was the guy?"

"He said he was an alien from another planet and wanted to take me to his spaceship."

"I've heard there's a lot of that going around these days. You should know better than to go off with strangers in this day and age, no matter what planet they claim to be from. Did he name his planet?"

"No. I would have used safe sex."

"There's that, but I was thinking of the Jeffrey Dahmers and that ilk." David loved dreaming up the most lurid scenarios that might happen if anyone he knew tried something even slightly out of the ordinary or made even the most minor change in their lifestyles. He wanted everything rigidly the same, yesterday, today, and tomorrow. Even more, for him, being negative was an art form. He referred to himself as omniphobic -- afraid of everything. Mike always wondered how David got himself out of his own front door in the morning to parade his fears among the denizens of the planet.

Mike felt odd not telling David that the person he was

referring to was about twenty feet away and taking a shower. He wasn't about to take people completely into his confidence.

David asked, "How'd they know you were with him?"

Mike told him what the cops had said about a guy hanging around Navy Pier, being a serial killer, and preying on gay people.

"I thought you were more selective," David said. "My official lawyer's advice is, do not go off with guys the FBI is after."

"Do I check the wanted posters at the post office first, or do I ask for criminal background checks?"

"Both."

"Doesn't sound romantic."

"I don't want you dead. Where did you meet him?"

"I helped him after he got mugged. I couldn't leave him there."

"You should have called the cops and an ambulance and had them take care of him."

"How do you check guys out?"

"I don't. As you well know, I'm in a sick, twisted relationship that has lasted three years. No, I don't want to talk about it. As is familiar to all who know and love me, we've driven three counselors to alcoholism."

David always talked about his lover this way, but whenever they appeared in public together, they were as nauseatingly loving as two guys who'd met a week ago and were still in lust with each other.

"What do I do if the FBI hassles me?"

"They have no logical or legal reason to."

"I already know that."

"If it happens again, be polite, tell them you've talked to me. Hand them my card and call me. Wait for me to get to wherever you are. I'll try to make a few calls to see what is going on. I have a friend on the Chicago police department. I don't promise anything."

Mike thanked him and hung up.

After the alien finished showering and redressing, they sat in the small alcove with the window overlooking Halsted Street. The alien's right knee brushed against him, then returned and pressed against Mike's left calf. Mike discreetly moved his leg.

The alien said, "I'm not going to hurt you. You could have slept longer."

"I was a little afraid of you molesting me while I was asleep, but I was too tired to stay awake."

The alien walked to the connecting door of the suite, closed it, and locked it from this side. He looked over his shoulder at Mike. He placed his palm on the door and shoved gently. The door swung open. "Security is not a strong point here at the Luxor."

Mike strolled casually across the room and tried the same experiment and got the same result.

"I find you attractive, but the rules are very strict," the alien explained. "We are not to have sexual relations on this type of operation. We also have severe taboos against interspecies intercourse."

"Why the rules against it? I wouldn't get pregnant and have an alien child, would I?"

"I don't know. I'm a cop, not a biologist."

"I have to go to work eventually," Mike said. "I've got to earn a living. You may be something new and different, but when your work is done, you'll leave. I still have to pay the rent."

"I certainly want to work saving the Earth around your schedule."

"Don't give me that crap," Mike retorted. "You said you didn't have any leads except going to Balls, Whips, and Chains. It is useless to go there until after midnight. I'm more worried about saving my own ass. How am I supposed to do that if an evil alien is sending his minions to harass me? Even if you left me immediately, wouldn't he try and kidnap me to force information out of me?"

"He doesn't have to kidnap you. If he can alter that fake cop to block my reading his memories, he most probably has the capacity to read your memory. He doesn't need you, just your memory."

"You said probably."

"Yeah. I can't guarantee you won't be kidnapped."

Mike looked around his grungy surroundings. "I'm not going to live in this dump for the rest of my life. I'm not going into some kind of witness protection program based on the word of an alien."

"I'm sorry," Joe said. "Things have moved much faster than I thought."

"Could the other alien be working with the police? Maybe you're the criminal."

"Then why would I need you?"

"You told me. You don't know the idioms or the nuances especially in the gay community."

"Have I asked you to do something criminal?"

Mike paused. "We hopped that fence."

"Something significantly criminal?"

"No."

"Nor will I. Even if you leave now, I am obligated by the laws of my planet to see that you are safe."

"But if you go off investigating, how are you going to do that? Wouldn't you need to be in my presence twenty-four hours a day?"

The alien walked to the center of the room and stared at the floor.

Mike let the silence lengthen.

The alien looked up at him. The dim light from the cloudy

day outside and the poor lamp light mingled in an eerie golden mixture which bathed the side of the alien's face. He had a nose that gave him a Greek-god profile, lips you'd want to kiss forever, long eyelashes, and bright eyes.

"Okay," the alien said. "I cannot guarantee your safety one hundred percent. I will promise to do what I can to save you, which is a great deal, but you can walk out right now. I will not pursue you, harass you, or punish you in any way, but you're right. Vov has knowledge of you. I had no idea he had such abilities. I'm sorry."

Mike gazed carefully at the alien for several moments. Mike couldn't see himself refusing. Yeah, it could be dangerous. So could crossing the street. "Do I still get to complain?" Mike asked.

"Of course."

Loud banging on the door interrupted their interspecies repartée.

"The cops?" Mike asked.

"I don't see how. You were on the phone with your lawyer while I was in the shower, but you didn't tell him where we were."

The pounding on the door became more insistent. A voice that seemed to come from far down the hall bellowed, "Stop that goddamn pounding?" This had no effect on the hammering their door was taking.

Mike turned to the alien. "No matter what happens, I want you to stop looking in my mind. You do it again, I walk, even if it means you fry my brains with a mental phaser."

"I didn't mean to offend."

"Tell me you will stay completely, totally, and entirely out of my mind."

"Okay."

Mike didn't have supreme confidence in the alien keeping his word, but at least the guy promised. Mike walked to the door and wrenched it open. Standing in the doorway was a bald man with a tattoo of a dragon that stretched from ear to ear over the top of his head. His hand was raised to continue drumming.

"Stop that noise," Mike said.

"Who are you?" the bald guy asked.

"Obviously not who you were looking for."

The alien came up and stood behind Mike.

The flames from the dragon's mouth swirled around the left ear of the man in the doorway. The tail formed a purple swirl around his right ear.

The stranger said, "You guys are hot. How about you become the ones I'm looking for?"

The alien put his arm around Mike's waist. "No thanks," the alien said. "We're spoken for."

"You sure?"

The alien gave Mike's bicep a gentle squeeze. "I'm sure."

The alien's touch was warm and pleasant. Mike shook off the comfortable, tingly feeling and shut the door.

Fourteen

"I want to stop at my ship, but I don't know how heavily guarded the lake front is," the alien said. "I may have to wait for night, and more fog wouldn't hurt."

"I can't imagine they have enough personnel to guard the entire shore line that closely."

"That patrol boat had to be blind luck."

"Maybe it wasn't," Mike said.

"I do have more confidence in their radar and detecting equipment. My little flotation device isn't really built for two. Without you, I can go faster. They're going to be hunting for my ship even more intensely."

"I want to try going home," Mike said. "Plus I want to visit a friend in the hospital. He has AIDS."

Joe said, "Good luck with him. I know it can hurt to see a friend who is ill."

"Thanks."

Joe said, "I need some time to observe the workings of the police along the lake front before I go out to my ship."

They agreed to meet back at the hotel just before Mike needed to leave for work. They parted outside the front door of the hotel. Mike watched Joe walk away. The alien had perfect buns. Mike shivered involuntarily.

Mike took a northwest-bound Lincoln Avenue bus from Halsted Street. He got off a block after his normal stop. He strode up Lakewood to Fletcher Street and turned east. He surveyed the houses and apartments with a wary eye. He walked half a block to the alley behind his house. The pavement was clean and the garbage picked up, attesting to the power of the local alderman to make her part of the city work.

He cautiously crept down the alley. He saw nothing untoward

or suspicious. Herds of nondescript people wearing dark sunglasses and sporting beige trench coats were neither skulking in dark doorways nor lurking in the front seats of black sedans. No one in or out of a Chicago police officer's uniform gazed malevolently upon the urban alley. Mrs. Benson's cat sat on the corner of the backyard fence and glared at Mike, the same as it often did when he came in from or went out through the alley. The lack of bright lights in the rear always made Mike uncomfortable using this entrance at night. Now for the first time while it was daylight, he found himself tense and wary. The back door was hidden by large bushes and a bend in the back wall. Once beyond it and finding the space clear, he was thankful for the cover.

Mike moved about his third floor apartment quietly and carefully. He didn't know how long he'd be gone. He grabbed his gym bag and tossed in several pairs of clean underwear, along with socks, shirts, pants, and a black leather jacket. As an afterthought he threw in some running clothes. If he could help it, he wasn't going to be a prisoner of his adventure. From the bathroom he took his toothbrush, deodorant, and shaving equipment.

On the way out, he tried to ease quietly past Mrs. Benson's apartment door. The landlady's three rooms were crammed with pictures of her children, grandchildren, and great-grandchildren. She applied so much rouge to her face that it looked as if she mashed her face into vats of make-up every morning. Her door swung open just before he arrived at the bottom of the stairs.

"Something funny is going on," she said. "Somebody knocked on your door around six this morning and then almost once an hour since then, but you weren't home, and they went away. It was different people every time, but all of them looked furtive. They all double-parked down the block so I couldn't get the license numbers on their cars."

"What did they look like?"

"Once it was two women in gray outfits. The other times it was younger men in tan trench coats. You aren't in trouble are you?"

"No, I don't think so."

"Then about ten minutes before I heard your footsteps upstairs, a Chicago cop rang your bell. You're sure you aren't in trouble?"

"Fairly sure."

"Well, if you have a problem, you come to me. Mildred Benson is someone you can count on. You sure you're all right?"

"I'm fine," he answered.

"I worry when you don't come home. Have you found a new beau?"

"No, Mrs. Benson. It was just a very late night."

"Be careful," she warned as he eased his way to the door. "Always use a condom, Michael."

He gave her a cheerful wave and left. Mike appreciated her concern, although he could get mildly annoyed at her intrusiveness at times. Several of the tenants referred to her as "Mom" Benson.

He walked down to Belmont then west for three blocks until he got to the Harvey Milk Hospice. He signed in at the reception area and waited for his friend Darryl to respond to being paged. After five minutes of pacing the floor, he asked the clerk to try again. Still no answer.

She smiled apologetically and said, "He might be napping, or he could be so deep in conversation, he didn't hear. He's a handful." She shrugged. "I'll take you up."

She led Mike through the foyer, up three flights of stairs, down an antiseptic hallway, and around a corner. The walk through these corridors always reminded Mike of his college dorm. He heard a loud, strident voice carrying down the corridor.

The receptionist said, "I'm sorry. We try to keep it very quiet."

"I've been through this before," Mike said.

When they were near enough, Mike could hear Darryl's voice decreeing and decrying as he was wont to do. He was saying, "That is so not true. Fred Tomaine is the worst thing that ever happened to this community."

"Sssh! Don't say things like that." This was a voice Mike was not familiar with.

"Don't shush me. No one has ever liked me telling the truth. The pantywaist faggots who call themselves activists in this town have got to understand what they've done wrong, and what they need to do to set it right. I don't have time for all this polite crap."

Mike smiled to himself. Darryl hadn't changed much since he'd been radicalized when he'd gone off to college. They had met while Mike and Darryl attended St. Margaret's High School in the near northwestern suburb of Centerboro. Over ten years ago they had fallen in love in that mad, usually inept way only teenagers can. Darryl was the first guy Mike had ever loved or had sex with. Passion and lust had ruled their days for over a year of sneaking behind their parents' and friends' backs. No one had ever caught them. Their ardor had cooled during the last semester of their senior year, and then Darryl had gone to Boston for college, while Mike had stayed in Chicago. At school they'd both met someone new.

After five years, Darryl had come back to town committed to causes, a self-described super-radical, who found groups such as ACT-UP too tame, superficial, unorganized, scattered, and ill-led. Mike agreed with the causes but not the tactics. Darryl was ready to put up a picket-line up at a moment's notice, prepared to man the barricades for truth and justice, eager to tell his version of the truth loudly and continuously. Most of what he said was strident and accusatory. Numerous times people he'd worked with in radical gay groups had asked him to tone down his rhetoric. Three people had filed slander lawsuits against him. He'd vowed to live to see his accusers rot in lavender. Mike doubted if Darryl would be alive long enough to see either victory or defeat.

The two men in the corridor turned at their approach. Darryl was in jeans that were tight on his body about twenty pounds ago. Today he had shaved. He wore a yellow silk shirt that only for a moment distracted Mike's gaze from the sallow complexion and the dark circles under his former lover's eyes.

The other man was over six feet tall and must have been in his fifties. He waved briefly to Mike and scuttled off down the corridor.

"Coward," Darryl called after him.

The receptionist warned Darryl about making too much noise and then left. Mike hugged his friend.

Darryl nodded his head in the direction of the recently disappeared antagonist. "He's stupid and a coward. He used to be one of the most important gay bar owners in this city. Now he's dying like the rest of us. I hope he's sorry for his timidity."

"What did he do to hit his temerity limit on Darryl's politically-incorrect-temerity-index?"

"He thought silence equaled safety."

"Do I know him? Do I want to know him?"

"No."

They entered Darryl's room. The only decoration was a battered and torn poster of Che Guevara that Darryl had found at a flea market in Newton, Iowa, three years ago. It was one of the few personal things he had saved when he'd been forced to get rid of most of his belongings before moving into the hospice. Mike sat on a green vinyl-covered chair, Darryl on the bed, the only two places to sit.

"I brought you today's book."

Darryl still read voraciously, but he had ordered Mike to stop bringing him stacks of books. He'd asked for one a day at the most. Today's installment was *Hard Candy*, the twelfth in the Cat Marsala series by Barb D'Amato.

"I've got today's rumor. Have you seen CNN?" Darryl asked.

"I've been a little busy."

"You've got to keep up with the news."

"I try keeping in touch with my own life. That's enough for me."

"Philistine. If you listened, you would know there are big

rumors swirling around about a cure for AIDS."

Mike groaned.

One of Darryl's mechanisms for dealing with his condition was to read every single item in every magazine, newspaper, or Internet report about the latest medical developments. Besides prescribed medicines and orthodox regimens of treatment, Darryl also indulged in every schlock cure that made the rounds. He made weekly forays to three university libraries to keep up both with the learned medical journals and the popular literature. He'd been to five different countries chasing down rumored cures.

"Don't groan at me," Darryl said. "It was at this big conference."

"Was that a vaccine or a cure?" Mike asked.

Darryl had tried a regimen of the drug combinations which had proved to be effective with over seventy percent of patients. Darryl had been among the unfortunate thirty percent that they did not help.

"It's supposed to be practically a mob scene at the Mokena Universal Health Care Clinic. People were demanding to be let in. I've been on the phone most of the afternoon. The AIDS underground says this thing might have real promise."

"How many times has the secret underground network announced the same thing?"

"You always try to take away my hope."

"I remember the horrible depressions you go through after each one of these turns out to be a failure. You want to believe so badly. So do I, but be careful with your hopes."

"If I want to get my hopes up, I will get my hopes up."

Mike took his friend's hand and held it. Darryl started to yank it away then stopped.

After several moments of silence Darryl said, "You're the only one who comes to visit me, and all I do is get snotty with you. Sometimes I wish I wasn't so rude or so frightened."

Mike caressed Darryl's hand. "You want today's massage?"

Darryl nodded. He took off his shirt and lay down on his stomach on the bed. Mike ignored the lesions on his friend's back, as he'd gotten used to doing. He took the lotion from the side of the bed and spent fifteen minutes stroking and kneading Darryl's torso. By mutual agreement this was done in silence with only classical music playing on an iPod with Darryl using headphones which Mike had bought him as a moving-in gift. Today's selection was a Mozart horn concerto.

Mike found giving the massage soothing. He usually didn't mind Darryl's total self-absorption. When Mike showed signs of upset from his own life, Darryl usually missed them. Today, Mike found this comforting. He wasn't ready to talk about the alien. He didn't know if he ever could.

As a teenager, he'd fallen in love with Darryl's bubbling enthusiasm and daring, as well as his willowy build. He'd begun to lose interest in him after he finally realized that they talked mostly about Darryl's life, Darryl's problems, and Darryl's world, but he still felt some of the old affection when he saw him.

When Mike finished, Darryl turned over. He said, "Thanks for still coming to visit."

"I hope the treatment you heard about really is something. Have you heard of this place before?"

"Mokena Universal is on the 'healing circuit,' although I've never been there before. Up until now they haven't done much with AIDS-related opportunistic infections. They have as schlocky or brilliant a reputation as any of them, depends on whether you improved or got worse, which is how opinions usually run."

"Do you want me to go with you to check it out?"

"I've got an appointment with my regular doctor tomorrow. I'll ask Greta Ghoul what she's heard."

Darryl always gave the medical personnel who dealt with him gallows-humor nicknames. Greta was a gray skinned woman with a European accent. Her gentleness had managed to penetrate

Darryl's defenses.

"I've been feeling a little better lately," Darryl announced. "I may try to sneak out again tonight. This dump is nice, but it is short on excitement."

"Be careful," Mike counseled. "You've already been thrown out of one of these. You don't want to lose this place."

"I'm not dead yet," Darryl responded, "and a guy who was here last week told me I could have his last leather outfit. You going out tonight?"

Mike hesitated. "I'm probably going to Balls, Whips, and Chains."

"That's still my favorite bar of all time. Maybe I'll meet you there."

"Great," was what Mike said. *How will I explain the alien*, was what he thought. He'd rather not have Darryl joining him and the alien. Then he chuckled at the concept of boyfriend as weird alien. He'd wound up with one or two of those.

"What?" Darryl asked.

"Just pleased that you might get out."

A few minutes later, Mike left.

FIFTEEN

Back at the Luxor, the alien had not returned. Mike waited half an hour. He didn't know if he should be concerned or elated. If this were cheap crime fiction, he thought, the story might be called "The Case of the Disappearing Alien." Mike's doubts resurfaced. What if he went to work, and the fake cop brought reinforcements and tried to kidnap him off the street? He waited as long as he dared, then, confused and worried, took a cab to work.

Mike had strong ambiguous feelings about the failure of the alien to show up. Beyond that, Mike knew he was attracted to the alien physically. He'd felt mild lust when he waited on him the first time, but human or no, Mike's experience with dating told him to go slow in any relationship. He admitted to himself that he was curious and interested. He didn't want the alien to be gone.

In the park across the street from the restaurant, Mike saw Joe. After a wary look around, the alien dashed across the street. "I just missed you at the hotel," Joe said. "I wish you'd have waited."

"Where the hell were you?" Mike demanded.

"You were worried?"

"More mystified and confused. You were supposed to be at the hotel. Where were you, and why were you late?"

"You ever try to visit an intergalactic spaceship in Lake Michigan with herds of cops keeping watch?"

"Only once. So what happened?"

"Always with the questions."

"You're the alien. You expect me not to be curious? If I'm going to be able to tell my grandchildren about this, I want to have my facts straight."

"I spent huge amounts of time avoiding the hordes of police in and around the lake. I did not get to my ship. I thought maybe toward sunset the fog would redevelop. It wasn't nearly thick enough. I'm reasonably sure the ship will be safe where I left it. I just wish I'd had more time this morning."

"Too many cops? That's it? That's the whole explanation?"

"I have to be discreet and careful. I know you'd prefer something magical or technologically other-worldly."

"I have met an inadequate alien."

"You're disappointed, but you're tough. You can handle it."

Mike sighed. "I've got to get to work."

"I'll be watching to make sure nobody harms you. Let's meet in the alley when you're done. It's less public back there."

Mike agreed.

Inside the restaurant Mike wanted to have a quiet shift. Seconds after he walked in, Hugo sidled up to him, stuck a finger in Mike's chest, and said, "Rumor is you met some mysterious stranger last night. Word is, he is totally hot, hot, hot. My spies saw you at Coffee Supreme Cafe over on Belmont."

"There's nothing to it, Hugo. He was an alien from another planet who'd been mugged. I helped him out."

"It's not nice to make fun. Deep dish needs must be filled."

"Hugo, get a life."

Hugo drew himself up. "You need to remember that you are not above the rest of us. You are human. Gossip will out. You're not all that much taller, thinner, and more muscular than Justin Verlander. You can't afford to be snippy with Miss Hugo." Verlander was a hot, young pitcher on the Detroit Tigers.

Mike said, "Go scratch your own eyes out."

Hugo stomped off.

Meganvilia sashayed over to him. Tonight he wore a pink caftan over yellow chiffon.

"Love the outfit, dear," Mike said. "Traffic won't be able to miss you."

"I want every boy on the north side to stare."

"They will," Mike assured him.

Meganvilia poked a big knuckled thumb in Hugo's direction. "Is the evil empress on the prowl?"

"Yes."

"Be wary. Once the bitch gets an idea in her head, she is merciless."

"What can she do? Get me fired?"

"Anything is possible."

"She's a dizzy queen who needs a life. That gossip crap went out when I was in junior high school. I can't believe anybody listens to that stuff or even puts up with it."

"She has lots of friends who think she is witty and clever." Meganvilia put a hand gently on his forearm.

Mike said, "He's the kind that gives our sexual orientation a bad name."

Meganvilia patted his arm then said, "You're more testy than I've ever seen you."

"Sorry. Tough day." Mike had known Meganvilia since the third grade. He liked and trusted him. They had never been lovers but had been confidants for years. Nevertheless, he doubted if he could find a way to give him today's real news.

Mike was spared telling either truth or lie as he spotted his lawyer. David was waving to him from the front of the line of customers waiting to enter. Mike unlocked the door and managed to keep the herd of starving diners out in the cool night air as he let his friend in. Today David wore a tie with a picture of a black and white spotted cow with the saying "Save the Cows" on it. The rest of his ensemble was wedding and funeral gray. He was five feet six with a mass of freckles and gold-rim glasses, sort of Huck Finn stuck in a library. They spoke at a table in the rear, out of sight of the crowd.

"I talked to the FBI," David said. "According to what they said to me, and we all know the government never lies to us, you are not a suspect in an investigation. Supposedly, no one is following you."

"I tried going to my place earlier. On the way there I didn't notice anything suspicious."

"Would you know what to look for?"

"I talked to Mrs. Benson, the landlady. She's the nosiest old woman on the planet. She said I had visitors. From her description, some of them sounded like the FBI agents who questioned me."

"They told me you wouldn't be bothered." David sighed. "What did you tell her they wanted?"

"I didn't. She didn't ask. She respects our privacy. She seldom pries, but she lets us know she's watching out for us and herself, of course. She's curious about everything."

"She's a god-send. My landlord lives in Cuba or Pago Pago or someplace where we can't get at him. There are three lawyers in the building besides me, and we're all suing him for something or other."

"Did you talk to the Chicago police?" Mike asked.

"I have an excellent source in the department, a gay man at the command level. He says the whole serial killer story they gave you is bogus. He hasn't been able to get much more than that. He said he'd keep checking for me."

Meganvilia unlocked the door and customers started filing in. David decided to dine. Mike put him at table seven. Moments after the first rush had settled to a steady influx, Mike saw agents Henry and Hynes from the FBI push their way into the restaurant. Mike glanced out the window to the crowded street. He saw no sign of the alien.

Mike motioned for David, who hurried over.

Agent Henry strode up to Mike and said, "We have to talk."

Mike pointed at David, "This is my lawyer. He'll be accompanying me."

"Are you going to sing?" Agent Henry asked.

"I didn't know the FBI had a sense of humor," David said. "I thought we'd get all the witty lines."

"Deal with it," Agent Henry said.

"I've got customers to feed," Mike said.

"This won't take long."

Mike hesitated. "I guess Meganvilia can handle a couple of hot meals for a few minutes."

Mike hurried over to the drag queen and explained what he needed.

Meganvilia said, "You're lucky the owner's not coming in until later. I'll cover for you." Meganvilia patted Mike's butt with a hairy hand. "Run along and talk, dear. I may even be able to deflect Hugo."

Mike, his lawyer, and the agents used the deserted manager's office for their conference.

"Where'd you go after you left our office this morning?" Henry asked.

"Is my client a suspect?"

"We're just curious. We stopped by your place to ask you a few more questions, but you weren't in, all day. Where'd you go? Weren't you tired?"

"He doesn't have to answer that."

"I was off in an intergalactic spaceship, whizzing around the universe, but I needed to get back to work tonight."

"I'm not laughing," Agent Henry said.

"I'm trying my best," Mike said.

"What did you want?" David asked.

Agent Henry glared at him.

David said, "You claimed you had a few more questions.

What are they?"

"If he's going to give us crap, why should we ask them?"

"If you're just trying to dick him around, give up. Either accuse him of something or leave him alone."

"He may have had contact with a serial killer, or maybe he's the killer we're after."

Mike's nervousness increased several notches.

David said, "That is so much bull. There is no serial killer."

"Maybe we can find something on you, Mr. Smith?"

The lawyer responded, "I'm twenty-seven, gay. I shoplifted a cap gun from a Kmart when I was five. My mother made me give it back to the manager. I have three unpaid parking tickets from when I attended the University of Illinois Chicago campus."

Mike tapped his order pad on his left hand. "I have to get back to work."

"I'd like you to leave my client alone."

"We'll be in touch," Agent Henry said.

They left.

"I don't know," David said. "Something weird is going on. You should probably stop making comments about that intergalactic crap. It just annoys them."

"Why didn't they ask more questions?"

"Maybe because I was here. Maybe they're trying to push you until you make a mistake and confess."

"Maybe they could torture it out of me."

"They obviously think you're connected to something."

"I don't need this nonsense."

"If they try to hassle you, just call me. You've got my card in your wallet?"

"Yes, David."

"Don't lose it."

"Yes, mother."

After several more admonitions, David returned to his meal.

Mike served four drink orders in quick succession and soothed the rattled nerves at several tables. While he was waiting for a fifth drink order, Hugo approached again.

"Who were those women?" Hugo asked.

"That was my Uncle Ajax and his lover in high drag."

"You don't have an Uncle Ajax."

"I don't?"

Mike picked up his tray of drinks and hurried off. Every chance he got throughout his shift Mike glanced out the window. As night deepened mists of vapor began to reappear. So far the fog did not look very thick.

Mike was never happier to see a work day end. Before he left, he stopped in to see the owner. Mike needed to take his vacation time before the end of the year. He asked for and received three of his allotted days. Combined with his normal two days off, he would have five days in a row to not have to worry about work.

Mike walked out the rear of the restaurant and glanced carefully around the alley. The redeveloping fog remained thin and wispy. The guys parking the cars were admiring a pink Porsche. As Mike strode forward, he eyed every possible hiding place more carefully than he would if he knew an anti-gay militia was planning an ambush. He kept his vial of pepper spray with the cap off in his right hand. He didn't know if this would work against an intergalactic attack, but he'd do whatever he could to defend himself, as ineffective as that might be. Joe's assurances that he'd be protected were one thing; seeing the otherworldly technology work, quite another. Mike was sure he didn't want to be part of any attack, successful or not.

As he stepped to the end of the alley, the alien emerged from between the dumpsters and gave him a devastatingly sexy grin.

SIXTEEN

"Where to now?" Joe asked.

"Before we can go to Balls, Whips, and Chains we need to change clothes."

"Why? I got in wearing this." The alien still wore the tight jeans and sweatshirt he'd had on in the restaurant the night before.

"Did people answer your questions?"

"Not much."

"Because you didn't fit in. Trust me. I have a black leather jacket that will get me into any part of the bar, but I don't have extras. We'll have to buy you some appropriate clothes. We don't need much, but we'll have to have something. I can't afford to subsidize an alien. Do you still have cash?"

"Plenty."

On the northwest corner of Halsted and Clark Streets stood a building that had been a variety of restaurants, bars, and other businesses over the years. All had failed. No one knew why. The corner was a great location with excellent foot traffic possibilities. Its latest incarnation was as Sally's Leather Boutique. The establishment opened at three in the afternoon and didn't close until three in the morning.

Sally was an enormous leather queen who presided over his shop from a front counter. When Mike and Joe walked in, the three-hundred-pound proprietor smiled at them from behind the cash register. A male assistant approached them. Mike thought the kid might be one or two breaths over the age of eighteen. Mike was certain the guy had been hired because he was young and his slender body fit perfectly in a leather harness and tight black-leather pants.

"May I help you, Gentlemen?"

"We're stopping at Balls, Whips, and Chains. My friend needs the bare minimum in order to fit in and to be allowed into the basement."

Every gay man in the city had heard of the basement of Balls, Whips, and Chains. That section of the bar was open from midnight to five in the morning seven days a week. The dress code for getting into the bar wasn't that severe, but for getting into the basement pit, the rules were very strict. Enforcement was done by a guy sitting on a motorcycle placed athwart the head of darkened stairs. His nickname was Beefsteak. He was fat, bald, and mean. No plea worked with him. If you qualified, he nodded his head and moved the front wheel of his Harley. If not, you languished in the upper reaches, which would normally be outré enough for the most depraved tastes. At Balls, Whips, and Chains it was rumored that male or female you could find someone to fill any same-sex fantasy you ever had. Mike had been there four or five times and still had not explored even half of the vast establishment.

The thing Mike most liked about Sally's was the incredible leather smell. Masculinity oozed from off the racks of clothes.

The young clerk responded to Mike's comment. "I understand, sir. I can fit sir with the basics. Will you both be purchasing?"

"Him, yes. Me, maybe."

"I'm buying for each of us," said the alien.

"Good, I could use a few things," Mike said.

The clerk measured their waists, inseams, and shoulders. Mike thought the young man's hand lingered at their crotches an inordinate amount of time.

"Both you, Sirs, have twenty-nine inch waists and forty-four inch shoulders."

They spent half an hour rummaging through enough rugged clothing to fill any butch queen's wet dream. By the time they were finished, Mike had decided on a chain metal harness and then leather items: a modified jock-strap/cod-piece, chaps, and a vest. The alien purchased an indoor/outdoor flannel shirt, heavy leather boots, metal studded bicep and wrist bands, a belt made of spent bullets welded together, a leather cap, and a two-inch wide dog collar with more metal studs.

As to this last Mike said, "If you want that, we should get the leash that goes with it."

"I don't get it."

"It's a slave-master thing."

"Isn't slavery illegal in this country?"

"But not in people's imaginations."

"Oh."

"I hook this to your collar and lead you around with it."

The clerk said, "Sir is right. If Sir wears this, Sir would be allowed in any leather dungeon in the city, public or private."

"Anything to fit in," the alien said.

In the changing room in the back of the boutique, Mike took off his shirt to try on the harness.

Three other men stood around in various states of undress. One was a great bear of a man in tight, leather short pants. Except for the immediate vicinity of his forehead and eyes, hair stood out on every square inch of the exposed parts of his body. A second denizen was a short, emaciated man in full leather who kept wrapping and unwrapping a whip around various parts of his cow-hide outfit.

The third stood in his white briefs in a corner in front of a three-way mirror. He was trying out leather straps of every kind. Mike tried not to stare, but as the guy's body moved to and fro, Mike saw deep red scars, and numerous welts across his pecs and his entire back. He had a long, narrow face with black eyes, eyebrows that pointed up in the middle, and a bushy, black mustache that drooped around his mouth.

Mike nudged the alien and whispered. "That guy was in the restaurant earlier."

Joe looked toward where Mike had inclined his head. The

alien whispered back, "The one with all the red marks?"

Mike nodded.

"I haven't seen him before," Joe said. "I doubt if he followed us."

Mike said, "He didn't seem strange in the restaurant." He saw a tattoo of a teddy bear just above the waistband of the man's shorts.

The alien was silent a moment then whispered, "No recent strong emotions, no blocking. I doubt if he's from the criminal I'm here to catch."

"Would he necessarily know the person he was working for was an alien?"

"No, but at least I didn't get anything like I did with that fake cop."

The changing room itself had a reputation as a place not immune to the occasional intimacy among the clientele who couldn't wait to indulge their lusts in more private quarters. For now none of the men present got naked, no one made an untoward proposition, nobody suggested a brief torture. Nothing odd happened while Mike and the alien donned their attire.

Mike did notice the alien eyeing him carefully. "You look good in that harness," the alien noted.

"You're both very hot," the bear of a man commented.

"Thank you." Mike blushed. Glancing at himself in the mirror, for one of the rare times in his life, Mike thought he looked sexy. Usually he thought of himself as okay looking, although he did sometimes get compliments. The alien looked good enough to star in porno movies. Moments later, back in their regular clothes, the alien paid for their purchases and they left.

Halfway down the block, Mike peered over his shoulder. The man with the red scars and teddy-bear tattoo was nowhere in sight.

"We need to get rid of our old clothes," Mike said. "We can't go into the bar carrying packages. We'd look stupid. Do we dare try going to my house?"

"I think you can safely. I'm not sure about me. Right now the police would be suspicious of anyone you were with. I'm not worried about anyone Vov might send. No earthling can harm us now that I'm being more careful."

"Couldn't somebody just shoot one of us with a high powered rifle or maybe teenagers heave bricks from afar?"

"Not anymore."

"Why not?"

"I expected an elaborate technological attack. I didn't expect to get clunked on the head. I recalibrated my communicator as best I could. I don't have the background or knowledge of the physics involved to explain it to you."

"I bet you say that to all the guys. If no earthling can hurt you, why'd the other alien send that lone cop?"

"I don't know that he was alone, or maybe he thought you would be alone. That blocking power thing has me worried. If the human was conscious of it, that has implications for how far Vov's plans have gotten. On the other hand, maybe all the cop was supposed to do was delay us long enough for Vov to get there. Remember Vov does not have monolithic power. Neither do I. Also, if Vov is making friends with earthlings, presumably he'd have to do it carefully. If it was criminal activity he wanted them to do, would he want or be able to trust them completely? I doubt it. He'd more likely pose as a criminal than an alien. It's easier."

"That I can believe."

"Maybe we should just go to the Luxor."

The debate about going to the apartment became moot as they stood on the corner of Sheffield and Belmont. A black sedan pulled up to the curb, and the doors swung open. Agents Henry and Hynes emerged with their guns drawn. Joe draped an arm across Mike's shoulders. Mike moved closer to the alien and put his arm around his waist.

"This the person you were with last night?" Agent Henry asked.

"Are you going to accost every guy I talk with or take a walk with?"

"Is this the person you were with last night?" Henry reiterated.

Mike felt the alien tremble slightly. He didn't know if it was from fear, or if the alien was preparing some blast of technology or mind control to destroy the insistent FBI agents. Mike clutched Joe more closely. He noticed the alien had a scent unfamiliar to him, but altogether pleasant -- new mown hay on a summer's morning mixed with warm earth and perhaps a hint of roses in spring.

Mike said, "You need to talk to my lawyer."

Henry said, "Your lawyer isn't here, and I'm talking to you."

"They train you in being arrogant bullies?"

"Answer the question," she snapped.

Mike said, "This is a perfectly wonderful man who I met several weeks ago. We've been dating. He is not the person I was with last night."

"Where'd you meet?"

"Here's my lawyer's card. Good-bye Agent Henry, Agent Hynes. Have a nice day."

Mike's heart raced as he gently steered the alien around the two FBI agents. He kept his arm around Joe's waist and strode purposefully forward. He expected at any moment to be waylaid, but they made it unmolested to the next corner.

In front of Bittersweet Bakery, the alien said, "I thought you said your lawyer talked to them and everything was okay."

"They lied."

"The police can do that?"

"Cops on your planet don't lie?"

"We don't have to. We know who's the criminal."

"I forgot. You read memories."

"You didn't turn me in."

"I know. I'm in this now." If he had any doubt about the alien, he'd passed up his chance to get rid of him. Opportunities for simply running in a mad panic had presented themselves, but that wasn't Mike's style.

Mike hailed a passing cab, and they journeyed in silence back down Belmont to Halsted and then south toward the Luxor. At the eternally busy corner of Halsted, Fullerton, and Lincoln, Joe abruptly got out of the cab.

"What?" Mike asked. "You won't ride in a cab you haven't stolen?"

"We need to be certain we aren't being followed."

They tossed some money to the cab driver then walked up Lincoln past the Biograph Theater. A block north they waited in the bus zone for public transportation. They bustled aboard with their packages, easily making change this time. They took the bus to Ashland where they switched to a cab again and took it west for a mile. They walked south on Western Avenue for several blocks then turned back east. After several more switches, they were satisfied they were not being followed. They wound up approaching Halsted down Armitage Avenue.

In the living room of the Luxor suite they dumped their purchases on the couch. Mike began to undo his belt. He found the alien boldly staring at the front of his pants.

"What?" Mike asked.

"I've never seen a human naked."

"They were nearly naked in the changing room of the boutique."

"A leisurely inspection with a willing person is very different."

"You haven't seen it in people's minds?"

"You can watch naked people on videos. Is it the same as in person?"

"No."

"Do you mind if I watch you?"

Mike was interested in seeing the alien naked, but under Joe's intense scrutiny, his curiosity shrank faster than John Wayne Bobbit's dick. "Is this junior high? I'll show you mine if you show me yours? I'm not a kid. Maybe we should change in separate rooms."

"You're not curious about me?"

"Yeah, but there's lots I'm curious about that I don't know about."

"Like what?"

Mike thought for a second. "The size of the prick of every quarterback in the National Football League."

"Why are you interested in that?"

"Why not?"

"I could find out for you. It could take a while."

"Every desire for a cheap thrill doesn't need to be filled. If we fall in love and decide to get married, we'll have plenty of time to get naked and do exploring. Let's just get on with it."

He opened his gym bag and pulled out clean socks and underwear. He looked at the alien, who was unbuttoning his shirt. "Do you wear underwear?"

"I'd like to see you in yours, or could I wear a pair of yours that you haven't washed yet?"

Mike sighed. "This is more kinky than I bargained for. For an alien you have a lot of earthly fetishes. Are you sure you aren't human?"

"Guaranteed, one hundred percent alien. I'm bright enough to recognize that which turns me on. You want me to go into the other room?"

"You can if you want to."

Mike tossed him clean underwear and socks then turned his

back. He slipped out of his clothes, pulled on new briefs, flung on a pair of old jeans, and put on the leather accouterments they had just purchased. If the alien wanted to stare at his naked butt or brief-clad rear, he was welcome to. He was not about to be part of some intergalactic, early teenage lust.

SEVENTEEN

Moments later, looking as studly as several dead cows could make them, they left the Luxor, took a bus up Lincoln Avenue to Southport, exited and walked north for four blocks. They passed Mike's second favorite bakery in the city, Brownie Magic, crossed Addison and walked past the Music Box Theater. The midnight showing of *Henry, Portrait of a Serial Killer* was just letting out. Several of the men and a few women stared at them. One openly gaped.

"People are staring," the alien said.

"A famous mystery writer once said that if you wanted to hide something the best place was right out in the open."

"I feel ridiculous," Joe said. "You're not the one being led by a leash attached to his collar."

"I may be holding the other end of the leash, but I'm just as chained as you are. Some of our gentler citizens may never have dreamed they'd see people dressed like us, but in the bar you'll fit right in."

As they walked, the area turned into one of warehouses and small factories. As they turned left on Byron, Mike looked back. He said, "Isn't that the guy with the scars and welts who was in the changing room at Sally's Leather Boutique?"

The alien looked behind them. "I don't see anyone."

Mike stopped and gazed back. The street was empty. He said, "I want us to be careful. If nothing else it's awful late at night to be wandering around the streets of Chicago."

The wisps of clouds from the recurring fog seemed to cluster around the pale orange streetlights. Mike was glad for his leather jacket. The night was becoming distinctly cool.

They halted halfway down the block between Hermitage and Ravenswood Parkway. The businesses, the factories, and the mansion on the block all abutted onto each other, often blurring the distinction of where one started and the other left off.

Built far back from the street was an old mansion, the only house on the block. The place was an immense affair. From the angle they were approaching it, Mike could see there had been at least three distinct additions. It resembled an unhappy marriage between a Victorian gingerbread monstrosity and a Medieval castle. It was gargantuan and garish and kept a small sculpting company in business with concrete patchwork, repairs on old gargoyles, crumbling moldering plinths, and garish plaster statues purchased at rummage sales throughout the mid-west.

Two giant oak trees stood on each side of a path that bisected the front yard. A grand, wide staircase led up to a door that looked like those that enclosed the darkest cells of the most dangerous prisoners in the most horrific dungeons. The alien reached for the black cast-iron door handle. The door didn't budge. It was locked.

"They can't be closed," the alien said.

"How'd you get in before?"

"I walked in while other people were entering."

Mike leaned in front of the alien and pulled a metallic chain on the side of the door. "You gotta know the territory," he said.

The door creaked open in the best tradition of such doors in horror movies. Mike gazed into the impenetrable darkness that greeted them.

"Atmosphere," Mike said. "It's what I like about the place."

They stepped into a vestibule barely larger than a walk-in-closet. The walls were covered with black burlap. The only break in the darkness was to their left down a passage with a dim red light at the end. They walked several steps down this until a space opened up on their right. This was the coat check room run by a person in full dominatrix drag whom Mike presumed was a woman until the person offering to take their coats did so in a basso-profundo rasp. They declined.

Five steps further on, the passage turned to the left. They

were greeted by a man with no shirt. Suspenders made from a bicycle chain held his leather pants up over his protruding gut. Mike noted that he could have used a bra to contain his flabby pecs. He glanced at the face and then peered hard. The handlebar mustache and close cut gray hair were vaguely familiar.

"Professor Armbrewster?" Mike asked.

"Mike Carlson! If I'd known you were into this scene when you were a student, you wouldn't have had to study as hard." His eyes made a lustful tour over Mike's torso, stopping to peek into his opened jacket to the harness underneath.

"I enjoyed your class," Mike said. He paused under the scrutiny. "I didn't know you worked the door here."

"Only now and then. This week I've been working for a friend who's on vacation. Plus tonight our club is having its monthly meeting."

Mike wondered what club it was. He paid his cover charge and paused as the alien dug into his own pockets to pay his way.

"Hold it, fella," the bouncer said. He held up his hand in front of Joe. "I told you to stay out."

Mike turned back. The bouncer was glaring at the alien.

"He's with me," Mike said.

"I don't care if he's with the queen of England."

"What's the problem?"

"He's been in here harassing customers. Somehow he got down into the Pit without the proper clothing. He started questioning people in the middle of one of the hottest water sports scenes we've ever had."

"I'm sorry," the alien said.

"Sorry doesn't cut it. I said don't come back."

Mike eased past the alien and leaned his body against all of the professor's fat flank. He rubbed his crotch deliberately and slowly up and down the mounds of leather-covered flesh. The professor's arm snaked around Mike's waist and pulled him even closer. Mike put his lips close enough to Armbrewter's ear to cause goose pimples to flash over the older man's skin.

Mike whispered, "He's new to the scene. He's with me now, and he won't cause any trouble." Mike let one hand caress one of the professor's pierced nipples. Armbrewster opened his legs wider to make room for an obviously expanding bulge down the left leg of his pants. "What do you say?" Mike asked.

"Well, okay, if you vouch for him."

"Yes." He grabbed the alien and pulled him into the bar. Six feet past the entryway, Mike pulled Joe close and whispered, "Is there anything else you haven't told me?"

"Several million things. You want me to start now?"

"Later."

The ground floor room they entered might once have been the old parlor, front hall, and dining room of the original mansion. It had been converted into one large bar room. The only seats clustered around a circular drink dispensing area in the rear.

The main feature of this part of the ground level at Balls, Whips, and Chains was the dense, smoky murk.

The music in this room was throbbing disco with the bass turned to full blast so at times you felt like you were in the middle of a thumping heartbeat.

As Mike's eyes got used to the dimness, he saw that the floor was crowded with men gawking at the twenty-seven televisions which ringed the ceiling. Each was recessed a foot into the walls of wooden paneling painted solid black. All of the screens showed a grainy, black and white film of two fat, old, bald men smoking cigars and listlessly slapping at each other. No sound came from the movie. The walls and floor were painted as dark and uninvitingly as the walls. The ceiling alternated mirrors with black-light posters of men whose muscles were rounded and pumped up with the greatest bulges saved for the exaggeration around the crotch area.

The alien pointed at a video screen. "Is that sexy?"

"It is if you're one of the three people in the universe into that scene. Anybody on your planet do that?"

"Not for video. Don't they have pretty guys or at least decent-looking guys in these things?"

"You're a porn film critic? Everybody knows all the guys are ugly in S/M porn."

"I didn't," the alien said. He glanced around the room. "I hope you know some of these people, although how you could see them in this darkness is a mystery to me."

Besides the television screens, the only other lights came from three sources: the numbers on the cash register, the glowing eyes in a cow's skull which hung on a far wall, and a set of blinking red lights wrapped around the tip of what was reputed to be the longest and thickest dildo in the world.

"I haven't recognized anybody yet," Mike said. "Let's move closer to the bar and cruise down here first."

Mike discreetly checked out a few of the better-looking guys. He had mixed feelings about running into any of his friends. They'd be curious about Joe, but most would be too discreet to ask direct questions. Getting their help in finding Vov might be awkward. They would have tons of questions which Mike was not prepared to answer.

The alien shamelessly let his eyes make contact with those of all the other men. He smiled broadly at the ones who stared back at him.

When he noticed this, Mike said, "Stop that."

"Stop what?" the alien asked.

"Staring is too obvious. It could mean you're interested. It's not part of the code."

"What code? There isn't any code."

"Yes, there is."

"Tell me about it," the alien said.

"Maybe later. Unless you know what you're doing, staring

at people is out. Don't be obvious. I thought this was a secret mission."

They stood against the wall under the gigantic sex toy with the glowing and blinking end and watched the crowd.

"You knew that guy at the door," Joe said.

"Yes."

"He was awfully nice to you."

"He has reason to be."

"Why?"

"You didn't see it in my memory?"

"Look, if I know things from your memory, I'll just tell you. I don't want to turn our conversations into a debate or a guessing game. I would like talking to you to be pleasant. It is as much a treat for me to be open and honest and talk to a human as it is for you to talk to me. I'm curious about lots of things, and I promised not to look in your memory."

Mike felt chagrined. "Sorry, but I'm as new at this as you are. The professor had a reputation among the guys at school. He was much better looking five years ago when I took a class from him. He mostly liked to have sex with blond males. I'd never done it with a prof. I waited until I was sure I'd never have him in class again, and I seduced him. It was a turn on doing it with a teacher."

"It's not supposed to be?"

"Depends who you're talking to. Why can't you read people's thoughts?"

"The implant device isn't programmed for that."

Mike nodded. He leaned his shoulders against the wall and placed one foot against the wall behind him. "I mean how soon after someone thinks a thought does it become a memory? Isn't it instantaneous? Why can't you simply wait those few seconds to read their thoughts and emotions?"

"They're different parts of the mind. I don't know the

technical explanation. I follow neural paths related to memory."

Mike wasn't sure he bought that explanation, but he had no basis for further argument against it either. Mike peered intently across the room. "I know that guy, Skipper Henderson." He nodded his head in the direction of a lanky man in his mid-twenties. "Come on."

They caught up with Skipper as he ordered a beer at the bar. Mike introduced them. Skipper stood over six-feet-three with soft red hair parted in the middle and hanging to the tip of his ear lobes and then cut off abruptly.

"How's the writing going?" Mike asked.

"Rejection one hundred fifty-three came in the mail today."

Skipper wrote torrid gay-romance novels, over-written gay-historical novels, over-wrought gay-fantasy epics, and cheap tawdry pornographic short stories. He'd sold over a hundred of the porno pieces and one legitimate short story to a magazine that folded after publishing two issues. He had taken the story to a printer, gotten each page blown up, and framed. Then he hung them on the walls of his one-room apartment.

"Which one got rejected this time?"

"*The Queen Roared at Midnight.* The one with the drag queen who saves the kingdom for the young gay prince, but the drag queen can't stay in the kingdom and live happily ever after. He has to roam the world in sadness, singing popular Broadway show tunes."

"Leaves you an opening to write a sequel."

His rejections didn't normally discourage Skipper much anymore. His side job as porter in an expensive whorehouse did. He always said his job gave him tons of grist for the mill of his fiction. He claimed most people wouldn't believe half the stuff that went on.

"What are you up to tonight?" Skipper asked. "I thought you'd sworn off this place."

"Why'd you swear off coming here?" the alien asked.

"I broke up with my last boyfriend here."

"He was a creep," Skipper said. "I told you that. You were better off when he dumped you."

"That's what everybody keeps telling me." Mike pulled Skipper and the alien into a corner. "We're here looking for somebody."

The alien pulled out his communicator. A few quick taps and Vov's face appeared.

"Cool," Skipper said. "That's the smallest sized iPod I've ever seen. The picture is perfectly clear. How do you get one of those? I've never seen anything like that for sale."

Skipper was heavily into electronics. He'd computerized the client list at the whorehouse. When finished, only he and the owner knew the special code necessary for access. If they were raided, no client list would ever be found. He had set the system up so that if someone without the code tried to retrieve any information, the entire hard drive along with the program would automatically erase itself.

"Something I sort of worked on myself," the alien said.

"Wow. You figure out how to market that, you could be rich."

"Have you ever seen the guy in the picture?" Mike asked.

Skipper peered intently. "I don't think so. He hang around here?"

"Yeah."

"How come you're looking for him?"

"Joe's a private investigator, and I'm helping him."

Skipper raised an eyebrow which in the dim light made his face seem remotely sinister. He had a long face on top of his lanky form. His tight jeans emphasized his narrow hips. He wore a black leather jacket without any shirt underneath.

"You brought a detective in here?" Skipper asked. "Does the management know? Do the owners? This could be a big problem, Mike. Are you sure you know what you're doing?"

"He's okay," Mike assured him. "He's not with the official

police. I said private investigator."

Skipper shook his head. "I don't know, Mike."

The bartender brought over a glass of beer and placed it in front of Skipper.

"What's this?" Skipper asked.

The bartender was wearing only leather boxer shorts and white athletic socks that peeked over the top of his construction boots. He leaned over and spoke to Skipper. "The guy at the end of the bar sent it down." He nodded towards a man who looked to be in his late forties. He had long shaggy hair down to his very broad shoulders.

Skipper smiled fleetingly. "See you guys later." He sauntered toward his benefactor.

"Let's try downstairs," Mike said.

The guardian of the depths, Beefsteak, gestured dramatically with a limp wrist to make some point to the bear of a man he was speaking to. He turned to Mike and Joe. He touched the center of Mike's leather harness. "You have the most perfect pecs I have ever seen. You work out?"

"No, just lucky, I guess."

The front wheel of the motorcycle moved and down the stairs they marched.

Eighteen

Dark red light illumined their pathway. Hanging from iron spikes on the wall on the left were seven wheels from a motorcycle, a 1964 Ferrari, a ten speed bike, the helm of a seventeenth century galleon, a Conestoga wagon, a child's tricycle, and allegedly the real left front tire from the vehicle James Dean was riding in when he crashed and died. On the right was a ten-foot-long mural of predatory animals done in charcoal on a gray background. Vicious animals leaped and lunged at frightened prey in scene after scene of violent death.

At the bottom of the stairs they entered another murky room. The walls alternated between lines of pebbled rock or mottled gray bricks. Mike led the way with some confidence to the right, down a short hall, and into a slightly more well-lit room. As he turned the corner to enter, the alien grabbed Mike's arm. He pointed back the way they'd come and whispered, "Isn't that the guy with the red scars who was in the leather store?"

"Where?" Mike turned quickly. He saw only empty hallway.

"He's gone. He was there a second ago."

They retraced their steps all the way back upstairs. Beefsteak gave them an odd look when they asked if he'd seen a man with deep red scars and numerous welts on his body.

"Is there a problem?" Beefsteak asked.

"I promised to meet him here," Mike said.

"Haven't seen anybody like that," Beefsteak said.

They returned downstairs to the room with better lighting. Here men gazed at a large screen television on which the management permitted only the showing of sporting events. College wrestling was very popular. The more butch and studly the event, the more likely it was to appear on the screen. Currently there was a late extra-inning, west coast baseball game showing. The announcers sounded bored.

At the bar they stood next to several men discussing buying Canadian municipal bonds. Mostly, however, the denizens of this room clutched cans of beer in silence, only occasionally drawing sips from them. Two or three posed with one foot up against the wall, bare chested, jeans tighter than spandex, emphasizing what they were selling. Most guys simply lounged more than casually in their denim and leather, staring straight ahead. A few, depending on their level of expertise or desperation, interest or lack thereof, were trying to catch or avoid someone's eye.

The alien nodded toward two men in conversation at the far end of the bar. "Isn't one of them the bartender from Oscar and Alfred's?"

Mike discreetly checked out the two studs clad in tight leather from head to toe. "It is. What's he doing here?"

"Why shouldn't he be here?"

"He's supposed to be straight."

"Straight people don't come here?"

"Only if they're lost or they're selling something."

As they approached the men, Mike noted the bartender stood closer than a lover would to the man he was talking to. Mike tapped him on the shoulder. The man gazed at him indifferently and growled, "What?"

The alien showed him the communicator picture and asked if he'd seen the man.

The bartender said, "No." He turned his back on them.

Mike and Joe walked away.

"I don't like him," the alien said.

"Got that right," Mike commented.

Darryl walked into the room. Mike spotted him. He said, "That's the friend I visited in the hospice earlier. He'll probably know more people here than I do, and he's most likely to have answers to your questions."

Joe said, "You didn't tell him about me?"

"I'm not sure I'll ever be able to tell anybody about you. This whole thing still feels unreal to me. He'll probably think you're a new boyfriend."

"You could use that private investigator line."

"You're lucky I thought of that. I had no idea you were going to drag that communicator thing out. Skipper's an electronics expert. He might have gotten suspicious."

"I've got to use it," Joe said. "I'll be very discreet."

"Just remember, you're a detective."

Darryl wore a new pair of very tight black jeans that made him look like an emaciated teenager. His black leather jacket engulfed his frail torso.

When he saw them, Darryl smiled brightly.

"You snuck out," Mike said.

"Definitely. Who's the man at the end of your leash?"

Mike introduced them.

Darryl immediately pulled the alien close and stuck his thigh in Joe's crotch. "Tell me all about yourself," Darryl demanded.

"I'm a detective."

"Detective as in mystery-Bogart-Bacall-adventure or as in cop-fascist-pig-brutality?"

Mike said, "That's detective as in don't-be-obnoxious."

"I love it when your voice gets threatening and menacing and even deeper."

"Be nice, Darryl."

"I'm always nice."

Darryl ground his hip against the front of Joe's pants. "I'm getting to know him. I need to see if I approve of him for you."

"Thank god we've started quoting Broadway show tunes," Mike said.

Darryl grabbed Joe's left butt cheek.

"Nice and firm," Darryl announced.

"You never grabbed my butt in public," Mike said.

Joe gave Darryl a bemused look and asked, "Do you want to feel how firm the front is?"

"Mike's not usually the jealous type, but I'll behave anyway, until I can get you alone. Where did you graduate from college?"

Mike said, "Darryl's a degree queen. He also loves twenty questions."

"I don't mind," Joe said. "I have several degrees in law, criminology, psychology, social work, and population maintenance from numerous state universities."

Mike had to admire the alien. He'd answered with as much of the truth as sounded plausible without answering specifically.

Darryl threw his arm around the alien's shoulders and said, "Why don't you hustle over and get us a couple drinks? I need to chat with Mike for a minute." He handed the alien a twenty dollar bill. Joe glanced at Mike who undid his leash. The alien sauntered off.

"What the hell is going on?" Darryl demanded.

"Great flaming angels are descending from heaven to offer me riches and joys beyond all my dreams."

"Don't try and be a comic with your Uncle Darryl. It's not nice to fool with Darryl. He gets revenge. Since when are you hanging around with detectives?"

"He's a private detective not a cop detective."

"Besides the fact that he's a hot man, why are we interested in him?"

"We who? I'm not pregnant. Are you?"

"Are you in love?"

"We're looking for someone."

"The two of you?"

"Joe and I."

"When did you meet him?"

"Last night."

"Some guy you met a day ago and you're playing detective with him, and he's got a dog collar and you've got the other end of his leash?" Darryl glanced at the alien who was trying to get the bartender's attention. "He is a hunk. I'm not so worried about your taste in men as I am about your common sense."

"I loved you."

"Some people are lucky."

"Darryl, what did I say about the last guy you dated?"

"Nothing."

"Precisely. You always love intrigue and conspiracy theories. Here's your big chance. Shut up and help."

Joe returned with three very cold bottles of beer. Mike reattached his leash.

"Who are we looking for?" Darryl asked.

Joe looked at Darryl then Mike who shrugged and said, "He wants to help."

"I want to know what the hell is going on."

Joe pulled out his communication device. He pressed his fingers on the face rapidly then cupped it in his hand and held it out for Darryl to see.

"What is that?" Darryl asked.

Mike said, "A secret new electronic device that Apple would kill for."

The alien held it up so Darryl could see the picture. "This is who we're looking for or anybody who has seen him. I know he's been in this bar."

Darryl gazed at the picture a moment. "Nope. Never saw him. Is he some kind of desperado?"

"Yes," Mike said.

"I need to know all if I'm going to help."

Darryl hitched up his belt and grabbed his crotch vigorously as he caught the eye of a man with a pierced navel across the way. When the man didn't deign to glance in his direction, Darryl returned his attention to the alien.

Joe said, "We need to question people who've seen him. We don't know who to ask."

"And I'm not sure who to approach," Mike added.

"I don't know anyone down here," Darryl said. "Let's try the dance bars upstairs."

NINETEEN

They did not return the way they'd come. First, they entered a series of rooms Mike had never known existed. All were very dark. Mike heard only occasional slurps and moans, but he couldn't see the inhabitants who perpetrated the noises.

Darryl seemed to know his way through the warren of downstairs rooms crowded with men. From somewhere near what Mike thought must be the rear of the old mansion, they ascended several flights of stairs to a landing lit by a bare bulb painted purple. Two doors led off the landing. Darryl picked the one on the left. Mike thought they might not be in the mansion proper anymore but in one of the warehouses that abutted it.

"How do you know which one to pick?" the alien asked.

"I have magical and mystical powers," Darryl replied.

Mike said, "Somebody showed him, but he gets off on playing the overly dramatic know-it-all."

"Type cast once again," Darryl said.

The first room they entered upstairs was lined with black leather cushions nailed on all four walls from floor to ceiling.

"Looks just like my Aunt Sylvia's bedroom," Darryl said.

"Only if Aunt Sylvia was a biker-dyke," Mike commented.

"You've met Aunt Sylvia?" Darryl asked.

"Not yet tonight," Mike said.

A bar about twenty feet square was in the middle of the floor. At each corner was a platform on which a nearly naked woman danced. The dancer closest to the door they entered was thin and sylph-like. Progressing then to the right around the bar, larger and larger women danced on each corner. The fourth looked like she might crash through the wooden supports at any moment. Glancing at her, Mike thought of the dancing hippos in the movie *Fantasia*. Several of the leather-clad women were stuffing dollar bills into the crotches of the dancers. As many were in line for the heftiest woman as for the thinnest.

Numerous red, yellow, and orange spotlights caught the women in lurid poses, but at least this illumination made the room brighter than the ones below. Mike, Joe, and Darryl were the only three men in this room.

Mike felt uncomfortable in what was obviously a woman's enclave. He didn't know if men were even allowed in this section of the bar. While Mike gazed at the heaviest woman, Darryl strode casually forward. He took out a dollar bill and stood in line to give the dancing behemoth the money. Mike noted some of the fifty women in the room. None seemed to pay him any notice.

When Darryl returned from his foray, Mike whispered, "I didn't know you had heterosexual tendencies."

"Mary will join us in a minute. We better get out of here. Women are beginning to snarl under their breaths."

"I don't hear anything," the alien said.

"Trust me, they're snarling."

Darryl led them through a mirrored maze to what Mike guessed might have been a sun porch before someone dumped all the plants and painted every window flat black. The roof consisted of sky lights through which patrons could gaze at the star-lit heavens. The view over their heads to the faintly visible stars was only obscured by a skull and crossbones painted on the center pane of glass. Men and women clustered around a bar which stood near an exit sign.

"How many bars does this place have?" Mike asked.

Darryl said, "If you didn't only come here for leather lust, you would know it has enough watering holes to overwhelm South Dakota."

"What will Mary know?" the alien asked.

"She's a place to start. I wouldn't dream of asking questions without knowing someone."

"Do I have to keep this leash on?" the alien asked.

"Yes," Mike and Darryl said simultaneously.

Mary arrived minutes later. Her black leather bathrobe concealed much of her bulk as she swayed into the room, spotted them, and trundled over. Several people greeted her raucously as she traversed the distance to them. When she arrived, she hugged Darryl, asked how he was, and greeted Mike and the alien cheerfully.

"I only got ten minutes. Marsha, bitch-goddess and wimp, got beaten up by Melinda again. So we're all doing extra sets. What do you need?" All this seemed to rush out in one breath from her voluminous lungs.

"It's urgent," Darryl said.

"Everything's always been urgent with you, Darryl. I get worried only when you turn it up to desperate." She patted the alien's hand. "Darryl's whole life has been on fast forward."

Darryl explained the purpose of their visit then said, "Show her the picture."

The alien held out his communicator.

"Wow. What kind of phone is that? It's perfect." She squinted at the face. "I've never seen him, but I know who your best bet is: Howard. He knows everybody. I saw him earlier. He was all bummed out about something. Wouldn't tell me what."

"Is he dancing or tending bar?" Darryl asked.

"Dancing. You know who he is?"

"The blond who sometimes wears the purple fishnet jockstrap?"

"That or very tight and very sexy military uniforms. He's flexible. Tell him you know me and that I sent you. If you find out what's bothering him, let me know."

They took one of the back ways downstairs. Darryl claimed it would be shorter. Mike had thought he was reasonably familiar with all the twists and turns, swirls and eddies of the upstairs portion of the immense Victorian mausoleum, but he got lost on the way downstairs, once opening a door into a broom closet. Another time he peered through a doorway where he saw two guys in Medieval executioner's hoods shaving all the hair off a third guy's lathered body.

Their progress was further slowed by Darryl insisting they pause to gaze at any particularly kinky scene. The alien's innate curiosity didn't help any, and Mike wasn't averse to staring briefly. A simple trip down three flights of stairs turned into a thirty minutes of unslaked lust. Mike noted that no matter where they were, the throb of deep bass music penetrated, sometimes mute as a rumble of far off thunder, most often loud as a heart-throbbing annoyance.

When they arrived at the men's dancing bar, set up the same as the women's, Darryl scanned the crowd then said, "I don't see him." They made a circuit of the room with the same result.

"I know where they change," Darryl said. "Follow me."

Moments later they entered the dancers' dressing lounge. The small room was strewn with clothes and hot men. Narrow lockers lined one of the walls. Twelve or so guys were in various states of undress, those soon to go on in more clothes, those recently off in less or nothing. Mike found the sight agreeable, and more than his interest stirred. While gazing at one guy, he bumped into Joe and wondered if the alien was similarly affected. Joe unhooked the leash from his collar and, after Mike let go of his end, stuffed it in his back pocket.

Of the men nearest to them, they saw one guy snorting coke, another reading an organic chemistry text, two smoking cigarettes, two more playing Cribbage, and a couple of young lovelies were in a corner passionately making out.

The guy next to the door, a young man in bright polka dot boxer shorts said, "Out! This is off limits. The john is across the hall."

Mike said, "We need to see Howard."

"He'll be out in a few minutes. You'll see all of him then. Get out before I call security."

"Come on, guy," Mike said.

Darryl said, "I see him." He pointed toward a young man near the back, lounging in a straight-back chair with his legs draped on a desk. He wore a brown, Illinois state trooper's uniform.

Howard noted their interest in him, unfolded himself from his reclining position, and came forward. "Wha's up?" he asked.

Darryl said, "Mary suggested we talk to you. She'll be down in a few minutes to explain. We need some information."

Howard looked at the three of them and shrugged. He took them to a room behind the locker room. It contained an old, oak teacher's desk and several folding chairs.

Howard turned a chair backwards, flung a leg over the bottom, sat down, and rested his hands on the back. Mike wondered if this was studied or natural. Howard began without preliminary. "I don't get off until four. My basic fee is two hundred an hour. I charge extra for couples and anything kinky. I don't usually do three, so that would be more. It's gotta be safe sex. I'll do rough stuff to people, but I don't get whipped or hit."

"We don't want to buy you," Mike said.

Howard was a handsome man, and his uniform made him look very studly. Mike wouldn't mind a few dates with the guy or, to be honest, even casually groping him here and now as he sat spraddled in the chair. Of course, he could wait a few minutes and dump money into his underwear or fishnet g-string and grab a quick feel or two. Something about groping him while he was in that uniform appealed to Mike.

The alien broke into his lustful thoughts. "We'd like to ask you a few questions."

"Are you some dumb-ass trying to get a date with that old 'I'm-a-writer' crap to get us to talk? That line's been used a lot around here lately."

"We could be cops."

"I can smell cops a mile away." He pointed at Mike and Joe.

"You two are too hot-looking to be cops." He pointed at Darryl. "He's got AIDS. You aren't cops."

"You're right," the alien said, "but we do need to ask you some questions."

Mike and Darryl nodded.

"Well, if Mary knows you guys and sent you down here." He shrugged. "What?"

The alien held out the communicator. "I need you to look at this picture and tell me if you've ever seen this man."

Howard took one look, gasped, rose, tottered backward, and was saved from falling only because he ran into the desk.

"What's wrong?" Mike asked.

Howard gulped, shook himself, and began edging toward the door. "No, way, man. I don't know anything. Keep away from me." He fled the room.

TWENTY

The three of them gaped at each other for a couple seconds then followed. Howard was not in the dressing room. When they reached the hall, it was empty.

"Let's try to the left," Joe said.

Mike and Darryl hurried after him. When they got to a turn, they saw velvet darkness. They groped their way forward. They encountered a few doors that were locked when they tried them. At the end of the hallway, they found two guys kissing. Neither was Howard. Each was hefty with a beard. They wore flannel shirts and bib overalls. They claimed they hadn't seen anybody. The one in the red-checked shirt told them to get lost and turned to entwine his tongue with his buddy's.

The trio backtracked to the dressing room door and headed in the opposite direction down the hall. The first two doors they came to were locked. The third opened onto stairs that led down into blackness.

"Is this another entrance into the pit or to some other basement?" Mike asked.

"I wish there was a light," Darryl said.

The only illumination came from the rectangle of the door behind them.

"Someone is down here," the alien said.

"How do you know?" Darryl asked.

"Can't you hear him?"

Mike cocked his head and strained to listen. He heard nothing.

The alien led the way down. Mike reached for a railing, but empty space greeted his grasping hands in both directions. He found neither hand-rail nor wall to clutch. Black, empty space led off into a total void in all directions. They crept carefully downstairs. Mike counted eight steps before they reached the bottom. Peering into the darkness the three of them clustered together.

"Where is this person?" Darryl asked.

"There." The alien pointed.

A pink blur swayed in the darkness. Seconds later Howard's body slumped at their feet. He gasped desperately for breath. The alien knelt next to him. Blood oozed from Howard's ears, nose, and both eyes.

"Can you do something?" Mike asked.

Suddenly Howard's body arched up. He gasped, screamed, fell back, his body twitching.

"What's wrong with him?" Darryl asked.

"I don't know," the alien said, "but there's nothing we can do to help. We need to get out of here."

As suddenly as the body began jerking, it stopped. They watched the chest rise and fall rapidly.

"We've got to report this," Mike said. "We can't leave him here. We've got to get him some help."

"I don't want to be involved with cops at this point," Joe said. "You've had enough hassle, and it'll only get worse if I'm involved in this."

"What involvement with the police?" Darryl asked.

"We can't just leave an injured person here," Mike said. He groped for the wall and fumbled for a light switch. He found one about six feet from the stairs. He flipped it up. The illumination from the overhead light was better than an ailing firefly but not by much. Mike could see deep recesses and dark shadows of passages that crept into further darkness.

The alien dashed up the stairs and closed the door. Mike heard Joe step tentatively back down. A shiver went up Mike's spine.

"Why'd you close the door?" Darryl asked.

"If we don't want cops, I want us to still have options not to have somebody see the door open and decide to investigate. So far it is only the three of us who have seen this."

"Could he have fallen down the stairs?" Mike asked.

"Maybe, or it could be drugs," Darryl suggested. "Enough coke to fry his brain, literally?"

"Hard to tell," the alien said.

"What was he so frightened of?" Mike asked.

"It was after he looked at your picture," Darryl said. "He must have recognized the person. Must have had a bad experience with him, had to be something wrong."

"Maybe he was already drugged up," the alien said.

"Maybe somebody tried to kill him," Mike suggested.

"Murder," Darryl said.

"He isn't dead," Mike pointed out.

"It's still spooky," Darryl said, "And anyway we can investigate, the Hardy Persons."

"You'd make a hell of a Nancy Drew," Mike said.

"I've always wanted to try drag," Darryl said.

"This is serious," Mike said.

"Everything is serious," Darryl said, "unless you're dying, and then it's either a joke or a tragedy. I didn't know Howard. I don't feel tragic. I don't feel like laughing either. What are we going to do?"

"Look, he seems to be breathing okay now," Mike said, "but none of us are doctors. There could be something seriously wrong. Those spasm things looked really wrong. We've got to do something."

"Is he in immediate danger?" Darryl asked.

"I don't know," Joe said.

"We could take him with us," Darryl said.

The alien eyed him carefully.

Darryl said, "We walk out with him between us. If we're seen, people will think we're taking a boozed up or drugged out buddy home."

"Possible," Joe said.

Mike said, "We're going up the stairs and past over a hundred people and nobody's going to ask any questions? You're both raving loonies. We need professional help."

"We could take him to a hospital ourselves," the alien said. "When he comes to, we can question him again."

Mike eyed the darkness beyond the light. "Can we get him out from down here without going back up?"

Darryl said, "Him bleeding like this is going to make it tougher."

"The bleeding has stopped," Joe said.

"We still need to clean him up," Mike said. "You could maybe carry a drunk friend lots of places, but somebody bleeding or bloody would certainly cause a commotion." Mike hurried upstairs and convinced a too-busy bartender to lend him a towel and a glass of water. Mike answered the dubious look with, "We're trying a new torture." The bartender simply nodded at this and turned to his next customer.

Back downstairs Mike cleaned all the blood off Howard. Carrying the comatose dancer up the stairs turned out to be the toughest part of the whole operation. The limp body nearly slipped out of Mike's hands as he tried to keep the head from lolling back and holding onto his shoulders at the same time.

Mike and the alien propped Howard between them and then proceeded down the hall away from the stairs leading to the main floor. They got a few odd looks from one or two guys they passed. Several nodded sympathetically. One asked if he could help. Two guys congratulated them on not letting a friend drive drunk. Through a warren of vacant rooms behind the torture rack they found another set of stairs leading up.

"Where does this lead?" Mike asked.

"We're going to be in the back garden," Darryl said.

They lurched up a final flight of stairs. Darryl swung open a door, and they were outside in the cool night air.

Despite the early autumn temperature, men lurked in corners of the vast garden. Even with the leaves fallen from sheltering hardwoods, the evergreens, the high walls, and the lack of light kept this a secluded place for a rendezvous, a place to meet a stranger for a few minutes of pleasure, or perhaps find a lover.

"Which way?" Mike asked.

Darryl nodded. "There's a gate on the side of the house nearest the street."

They found the exit where Darryl said it would be. As they stumbled out onto the street, Joe and Mike almost dropped Howard. They steadied the still unconscious man carefully between them and then started down the street.

In the middle of their fumbling, Mike's arm came into contact with Joe's. He felt the becoming-familiar pleasant tingle. He also found himself becoming aroused. He hadn't been turned on in such an inappropriate forum since the tent in his jeans when being called to the chalk board in seventh grade. If Darryl noticed, he would feel the need to mention it. Mike had no idea what Joe's reaction would be. What Mike did know is that it felt good.

Joe said, "We can't walk far like this."

"We've got to get him to a hospital," Mike said. He looked around for Darryl. He spotted him propping himself up against a tree.

"What's wrong?" Mike asked.

"I hate hospitals unless I'm dragged by my balls by several burly male nurses. I'm also tired. I think I better take a cab back to the hospice."

He stepped away from the tree, staggered momentarily, and began to tumble to the ground. Mike caught him before he landed. "I think maybe you should stick with us," Mike said. "We can get a taxi over on Ashland Avenue. It's only a couple blocks away. Can you make it that far?"

Darryl, leaning heavily on Mike, only managed a nod.

The little band lurched down Berteau over to Ashland. Mike helped Darryl into the front seat of the first empty cab. Then Mike and the alien eased Howard into the back seat and got in.

"We should drop you off first, Darryl," Mike said.

"It's okay. He's in worse shape than I am. At least I'm conscious."

They directed the driver to take them to St. Bridget's, one of the few hospitals that still took the indigent. In the emergency room, someone only passed out and not in immediate danger took less priority than squalling babies and bleeding accident victims. The three of them waited with Howard. They occasionally noted furtive glances from the less oddly clad denizens who sat nearby. Mike did his best to ignore them. At one point, while they briefly were the only ones in the room, the alien checked Howard's pockets. He found three condoms and twenty dollars in singles -- nothing else. It was half an hour before Howard was taken for examination.

Darryl sat between Mike and the alien. Mike was worried about how pale Darryl was, but his friend insisted he wanted to stay and that he was okay. After Mike returned from one foray to the bathroom, he found Darryl slumped in his chair with his head on the alien's shoulder. Darryl was fast asleep with the alien's arm around him.

"Is he okay?" Mike asked.

"I think he's just tired," Joe said.

An hour after Howard had disappeared into the depths of the ER, Darryl awakened. In answer to Mike's questions, "I'm feeling much better, thanks, just tired. What's happening with the kid?"

After being rebuffed by numerous hospital personnel, the three of them became insistent about getting answers concerning the condition of their acquaintance.

A suspicious doctor asked, "Are you family?"

Darryl immediately said, "Yes." Mike knew Darryl had dealt with recalcitrant hospital personnel. There were numerous jurisdictions where gay lovers of many years had been denied access to their partners because of the missing technicality of family.

The doctor shrugged and said, "You know what kind of drugs he was on?"

"Was it drugs?" Mike asked.

"I don't know. I can't find anything organically wrong, but there's a lot of drugs that people take that we wouldn't be able to find in an examination down here. He could come around, or he could be in a coma the rest of his life. I doubt if we'll know anything tonight. He certainly doesn't look like he's going to die. I suggest you go home and come back later today. We'll have had a chance to observe him and run some more tests."

They dropped an exhausted Darryl off at the hospice. He insisted that Mike call him as soon as possible with any information on Howard or the man they were looking for.

As they took the bus back to the Luxor, Mike said, "Could you read Howard's memories?"

"No. Whatever happened to him blocked my probing. Plus it is nearly impossible for me to get into a sleeping or unconscious human mind. I get mostly gibberish. Reading a memory is like trying to follow a million neural paths. For a person who's asleep, many of the neural paths shut down or are blocked. I can't get past them. I'm not sure anyone on my planet could."

TWENTY-ONE

The Luxor lobby was quiet. The "Out of Order" sign had been removed from in front of the elevator. Mike stepped into the car tentatively. Someone had painted the lush woodwork a flat gray. The elevator's upward movement was slow and laborious, made with grinding noises that sounded as if, down in some ghastly basement, there were minuscule beings grasping tiny chains as they raised the car link by rusted link. He vowed to take the stairs from now on, no matter how inconvenient.

It was nearly five in the morning. With little conversation, they went to their separate rooms and slept.

Mike rose just after nine, feeling peculiarly unrefreshed. He found the alien awake as before.

"I'm going for a run along the lake," Mike said. "I want to do something normal for a little while. Do you want to come along?"

"Sure."

Mike tossed him an extra pair of gym shorts. "You don't have a jockstrap do you?"

"What are they?"

"You should wear underwear as you run."

"Would it bother you if I didn't?"

"Aren't you uncomfortable flopping around, or is your anatomy that different?"

"You show me yours; I'll show you mine."

"Forget it. You can use what you wore last night."

Mike enjoyed the run down the paths of Lincoln Park north from Fullerton. The weather was pleasantly cool, clouds alternating with sunshine. The alien looked sexy in the borrowed running clothes. Each of them got numerous stares from both men and women. More than ever Mike felt he'd like to explore the bulge in the front of Joe's running shorts.

Back at the Luxor, Mike showered and changed into the jeans and sweatshirt that he'd worn the day before. In the other room he tossed the alien a pair of underwear and waited while he used the shower.

They grabbed sandwiches at a cafe just west of the corner of Fullerton and Lincoln Avenues.

"What's on the agenda today?" Mike asked.

"We get Howard to talk, or at least I read his memory. He's the main lead I've got left."

They returned to St. Bridget's Hospital. Howard was gone. Hospital personnel could discover no record of his being there. Mike and the alien discussed, cajoled, and argued for half an hour with various staff members, but they got the same story from all of them. No one named Howard had been treated or admitted. The shift that had been working when they had brought Howard in had gone home earlier that morning. They could return later to question them if they wished.

On the street outside, Mike said, "We can try talking to the large woman dancer from the bar. She might know where he lives, or maybe Darryl knows Howard's last name or at least how to contact Mary."

Mike used his cell phone to call Darryl. His friend's first words were, "Marry him."

"Who?"

"Joe, the guy in the bar, marry him. If I was going to live a while, I'd have proposed marriage to him last night."

"I think I'm going to get to know him a little better before I take any major steps."

"What's to know? He's pretty. He's funny. He's got an interesting job. Last night was excitement and adventure. What more do you want? How many people do you know who are detectives?"

"At the moment one is enough."

"Have you been to bed with him yet? Why didn't you tell me about him yesterday?"

"Darryl, as you know, you can be a little self-absorbed."

Darryl sighed. "I know. Don't marry him, and you'll be sorry. What happened at the hospital? I was too out of it last night."

"How do you feel?"

"Do I sound sarcastic, demanding, and obnoxious?"

"Yes."

"Then I'm normal. What happened?"

Mike explained.

Darryl responded, "All records of him completely wiped out? Incredible! It must be a hell of a powerful operation to do that kind of shit. What are you involved in?"

"I'm just helping this guy. Maybe the emergency room was just too busy, and Howard slipped through the cracks in the system. For all we know, he could be in some hallway in the hospital sleeping his brains out."

"I don't know Howard's last name. I'll call Mary and ask her. I'll get back to you as soon as possible, but she's out a lot. This could take a while."

Mike thanked him. Under prodding, Darryl admitted that he had slept through the night without waking up for the first time in nearly a year. He felt completely refreshed. He'd had something exciting to be involved in again. They'd yelled at him for sneaking out, but for the moment they were not going to make him leave.

"I think the head of the place likes my politics," Darryl said. "So far, I'm okay."

"Have you been to your doctor yet today?"

"I have an appointment later. I'm going to ask about that cure at the Mokena Universal Health Care Clinic."

"I'll go with you if you decide to go," Mike offered.

In the gray September sunshine on the street, Mike explained to Joe what Darryl promised to do. Mike finished, "It's my grandmother's birthday. My parents are having a party. She's going to be eighty. I love her very much, and I don't want to miss the celebration. My family would never forgive me if I didn't show up. I would never forgive me if I didn't go. I also want to see how she likes my present."

"We've got to work on finding Vov."

"How? You have no leads. The bar last night was a bust. I'm the last one to see him. Well, I don't have a clue beyond that. At the moment Howard is a dead end, if not an actual dead body. Until Darryl finds Mary or the hospital shift comes back on duty, there's nothing to be done. Sorry, maybe you'll have to find another human to harass."

"I don't know where to start," the alien said. "You were my last hope."

The guy looked totally woebegone. Mike felt sorry for him.

"Come with me then. If the police are following us, they will be more convinced than ever that you're a guy I've met, and we're dating. Do you think your criminal alien has enough minions here on this planet to track down my entire family and figure out we're going to a party?"

"No."

"I had a real life before you showed up. Bills to pay, places to go. You said you wanted to learn more about Earth first hand, not just from people's memories. Here's your chance. You've never been to an earthling birthday party."

"Only in a couple people's minds. I'd like to learn more about people, but not from their memories. I know it's unscientific, and people on my planet would laugh, but I just want to watch and observe."

"This will be the real thing. You'll get to meet my nephew, Jack. You can examine the mind of a criminally insane fourteen year old."

For several moments the alien gazed at the hospital, the

passing traffic on Lincoln Avenue, and the businesses opposite. "I have no idea where to go or what to do next." The alien glanced up and looked directly at the late September sun. He drew a deep breath and said, "Okay, the party it is."

More carefully than two carjackers, they snuck down the alley behind Mike's three-flat. In the garage Mike unlocked the doors of a 1956 Chevy four-door coupe.

Joe said, "This doesn't look like the other cars I've seen."

"It's Darryl's. He had to get rid of it to be poor enough to get into the hospice. He was too fond of the car to sell it. I think the real reason I have it is because he didn't want his sister Myrtle to get hold of this beauty before or after he dies. He hates her. Darryl says she's had her eye on it for years. Darryl lives to get even."

Mike pulled out into the alley, drove over to the Kennedy, and took the expressway out toward O'Hare Airport. Traffic was light at noon on a Saturday.

As he passed the Rosemont Horizon, Mike yawned. Four or five hours of sleep a night was not enough, but for the adventure of a lifetime, he was willing to make sacrifices. He could sleep when the alien was gone.

Mike turned onto Highway 53 north to Algonquin Road and took it two miles west. He drove into the upper middle-class subdivision of Belle Starre where his parents lived.

TWENTY-TWO

"Is your nephew Jack really a criminal?" Joe asked.

"I think he is."

"What's he done?"

"What hasn't he done? He got his first suspension from school in first grade. He spent an entire recess trying to take chunks out of as many kids on the playground as he could. He's had a career of biting and bullying, theft and arson, tantrums and suicide attempts. One of his nuttier incidents was in fifth grade. He was in the principal's office being disciplined. The principal turned around to check some information on the computer. By the time she turned back, Jack was naked and smoking one of the principal's cigarettes. I used to baby sit him when he was small. He behaved pretty okay for me, but I think he was afraid of me."

"Why was he frightened of you?"

"I wouldn't put up with his crap. His mother, my older sister, should have stopped putting up with it when he was two. Even worse, her ex-husband has joint custody. His parenting skills are non-existent. He's an accountant by day and an outlaw biker on nights and weekends. He's taken the kid with him on some of his journeys. He rides him on the back of his motorcycle. On occasion my sister has tried hard to change herself and help her kid. I think it's hopeless. She has trouble following through, whether on suggestions from the social workers or even commands from a judge. I don't know who's the bigger problem, the mother or the dad."

"The kid is only fourteen?"

"And he's a homophobic creep. He doesn't have the nerve to say things to me outright, but he does that teenaged under-the-breath trick. So far, I've chosen to pretend not to hear. You'll meet him along with everybody else. My grandmother is the most wonderful woman. You'll like her. My mom and dad will wonder if you're my true love. My brother will want to talk sports. He's got season tickets to the Bulls, Bears, Cubs, Sox, and Blackhawks."

"Those are all sports teams in Chicago, right?"

"Yeah."

"Got it. How does he find the time to go to all those games?"

"He's got his own business selling lawn furniture wholesale. He probably makes more money than all the rest of us combined."

"Why is the party at one in the afternoon on a Saturday?"

"My grandmother has a boyfriend who wants to take her out to dinner tonight. Rumor is that he's going to propose marriage."

Nearly twenty cars lined both sides of the tree-shaded street. Mike pulled the Chevy into the last few feet of the driveway and let it stick across the side walk and a foot into the street. Before the car came to a full stop, two children around five years old dashed out of the house. They let the screen door slam behind them. Mike got out of the car and held out his arms to them. The boy and girl leapt into his arms. He returned their hugs and kisses.

"What'd you bring us, Uncle Mike?" they demanded.

"A new friend," Mike said.

They gazed at Joe. Mike introduced them.

"Is he going to be another uncle for us?"

"Maybe."

Mike let the kids down. The boy walked up to Joe. "Are you going to be nice to Uncle Mike?"

The alien squatted down so his eyes were level with the boy's. "I'm going to take him on the biggest adventure of his life."

"Cool. Can I come with?"

"I wish you could," Joe said.

A man who looked like Mike, only with a stockier figure, bushier hair, and a mustache, came out of the house. "Yo, Mike."

Mike hugged his older brother and introduced Joe.

"You follow sports much?" Larry asked the alien. Mike left them to their conversation.

Almost fifty people showed up for the party. Around two Mike found himself alone with Joe in the kitchen.

"I like them," Joe said.

"They like you," Mike told him. "My mom said you had beautiful manners. That's her highest compliment."

Mike's aunt, Tiffany, swept into the room. "Mikey!" she shrieked and rushed to embrace him. Aunt Tiffany wasn't as gargantuanly proportioned as her personality seemed to indicate. Although her figure could most kindly have been called "pleasingly plump," it was the aura of her perfume, her loud clothes -- today a bright fuchsia pants suit -- and her bubbling personality that made her seem to fill up a room.

Aunt Tiffany monopolized Mike for the next fifteen minutes. People wandered in and out of the kitchen, and some kid or another always seemed to be underfoot. Mike's brother invited Joe to see his sports memorabilia collection someday.

As Aunt Tiffany was hugging Mike good-bye, the door to the kitchen swung open. A handsome boy in his early teens strutted in. Aunt Tiffany glanced at him and sniffed. Her whole personality deflated into a puzzled frown. "Hello, Jack," she muttered and scuttled out the door.

Except for a face full of freckles and lack of height, his nephew resembled Mike a great deal. The boy glanced at his uncle.

"I see you brought another one of your faggot friends." The boy imbued this statement with enough teenage snarl for a whole street gang.

Mike leaned down slightly. His hand stopped just short of gripping the boy's upper arm. Physically harming a child was not Mike's style, much as he might want to throttle the boy. Mike used a fingertip to tap the kid's shoulder.

Jack began squirming and growling as if he'd been assaulted. "This is physical abuse," the boy whined. "I'll call my mom."

Mike spoke softly, "You may try any manipulation with anyone in this family you want, but I will beat the living shit out of you if you are ever rude to me or any of my friends."

The boy ran off. Moments later his sister strode in. "What did you say to my son?"

"Nothing you shouldn't have said years ago."

"How dare you?" she began.

Mike held up his hand. "We've had this argument before. I'm not having it again."

Mike left the room. He wished he knew how to make a screwed up teenager less screwed up. He doubted if promising violence was a smart approach.

He took Joe to his old room. His parents used it as a guest room, but it was still decorated with his pictures, posters, and mementos. The alien glanced at his shelf of books. Mostly they were old textbooks mixed with a few paperbacks which were mostly fantasy epics. Joe picked up a one volume edition of Tolkien's *Lord of the Rings*.

"That's my favorite book of all time," Mike said.

Joe hefted the paperback. "Books are a foreign concept to me," he said. "Our implants give us the knowledge we want."

"Works for me," Mike said.

Joe replaced the book and examined the shelf above them. He touched a baseball which had one dark smudge on it.

"It's from a game. I caught a home run at Wrigley Field when I was fourteen."

"We don't have games like that on my planet."

Mike was about to ask what kind of sports they had on his planet when there was a knock on the door. His grandmother and aunt, Dahlia, rushed into the room.

"Eighty roses." His grandmother gave him a tearful kiss.

"Mike, they're beautiful."

Mike said, "When I got here, and they hadn't been delivered, I was worried. I was afraid I was going to have to call the florist."

Mike's mother and sister-in-law walked in. They gushed about the plethora of multi-hued roses filling the living room. Mike had ordered them delivered with vases to save time and energy. They all proceeded to the living room. With the whooping and hollering about his gift and the opening of presents, nearly half an hour passed before Mike realized the alien was not present. He freed himself from the celebrating mob and hunted for him.

He found him in the basement. Joe was sitting side-by-side with his nephew, Jack. Their upper arms and legs at the knee were touching. Mike knew his nephew hated to be touched. In front of them was a large screen television set. In their hands each had a set of individual controls for an electronic game. The alien was causing a character to perform complicated maneuvers and violent actions on the screen.

"I've never gotten to this level," Jack said in awe.

"Want me to show you again?" Joe asked.

"Yeah." This said with eagerness, no affectation, and without a trace of teenage snarl.

The screen switched, and Jack began to punch buttons while the alien explained maneuvers. After five minutes the game finally got the best of the boy in spite of the alien's help.

"That was great," Jack said. "How'd you learn this? Can you stay and show me more?"

Joe looked up at Mike. Jack looked between the two of them and seemed about to lapse into teenage sullenness.

"I can't stay as long as I want this time. I can come back. We need to go."

"You can't tell anyone," Jack said.

The alien held the boy's gaze. "I would never break my trust to you. What you've told me is between you and me."

Jack grinned. "I like him, Uncle Mike."

Mike couldn't remember the last time he'd seen his nephew smile.

"I'm glad," Mike said. "I'm sorry I threatened you earlier. I'm shouldn't have said that."

Jack looked startled and muttered, "S'okay."

Mike said, "The party's starting to break up. We should go."

Jack stayed close to the alien as they said their good-byes and nice-to-meet-you's. Jack followed them out to the car. As the alien moved to get in the Chevy, Jack touched Joe's elbow and said, "I hope you come back soon."

The alien ruffled the boy's hair. Mike forced himself not to gape. He'd never seen Jack give or accept affection. Mike wasn't aware of anyone in the family who'd seen it happen either.

Mike heard his sister's voice calling Jack. The boy hunched his shoulders, jammed his hands into his pockets, stared at the ground, and inched toward his mother's voice.

"What did you do to him?" Mike said as they drove away.

"We talked, plus I read a few of his memories. He's very close to his counselor at the high school. They play one-on-one basketball together. I'm not sure I understood that."

Mike explained.

"Your nephew enjoys that a lot, but he hasn't taken him into his complete confidence. Jack is afraid of men."

"Why?"

"His dad has been beating him up and having sex with him since he was six."

Mike slammed on the brakes. Only their seat belts kept them from being flung around the car.

"Why are we stopped?" Joe asked.

"I'm turning around. This is going to be made public, and it is going to come to a halt immediately."

"Father and son will both deny it."

"I don't care. You can say it is so."

"How? That I read his memory? Who would believe me or you? They'd probably lock us up. At the moment he trusts me. He told me he isn't supposed to see his dad again until the Thanksgiving holiday."

Mike said, "Between now and then, we must think of some way of keeping them apart. My lawyer will think of something."

"That might work, but wouldn't it be better if Jack was able to tell on his own?"

"Possibly, but that creep is never going to touch him again, memory or no memory."

"You can't just physically attack the man on a random basis. Have you ever beaten someone up? Attacking people requires training of some kind."

"I think I have a right to overreact here. This is horrific."

"Maybe I shouldn't have read the boy's memories. I wanted to help. Despite your statements, I sensed that you cared very deeply for him."

"And will you be around to be part of his life after you have caught the criminal from your world?"

"Probably not, but you will be. You know, Jack likes you. If he could confide in anybody in the family, it would be you. He doesn't understand about your being gay, but he still likes you." A car behind them beeped. Mike pulled over to the side of the road.

"Is Jack gay?"

"No, he's a very screwed-up, heterosexual fourteen-year-old."

"I heard you say you'd never reveal whatever he told you."

"He didn't talk about being molested. What he disclosed to me, I will keep secret. What I just told you is in his memory. He has almost enough trust in his counselor to disclose this to him."

"I thought reading memories exhausted you."

"I read a few emotional highlights. Obviously, for a teenager there aren't as many as for an adult, but all of his centered around his father and what he's done to him."

"I should tell at least one other member of the family. My mother would be the best. She could handle it better than any of them. She wouldn't panic. She's the one in the family who is in charge of reality checks."

"Maybe she can be first," Joe suggested, "but we should wait until we have confirmable proof in human terms."

"I guess you're right. How'd you get him to trust you?"

"I can't use the technological wonders of my planet on people here, but mastering the technological parts of your planet is reasonably easy, especially something as simple as that game. When I came into the room, he ignored me as I watched him play. He loses himself completely in front of it. All other memories are blocked out. He's conscious of only the game. It is very soothing to him. Being able to advance multiple levels is even more soothing. Each time he lost, he immediately started again. He was very good at the game already. I started by making several simple suggestions. He was resentful until he realized what I said worked. I showed that reaching the top level and beating the machine completely was a real possibility."

"He likes you because you haven't crossed him yet."

"Do I want to?"

"Probably not. If what you're doing works, and we can stop his dad, great. I hate the damn electronic games, but if it would help him, I'll learn them. Whatever works." Mike pulled away from his parking place. "I wonder if my sister knows what his dad has been doing."

"I didn't read into his memories deeply enough to know. I do have a question. How can a child get that far in the education system with that many problems?"

"What do you mean?"

"His situation wouldn't be allowed to happen on my planet."

"How do they handle messed-up kids on your planet?"

"Each year, in every school they take the worst problem children in each grade and separate them out."

"What happens to them?"

"They take them to special schools. They try various implants, chemical injections -- what you would call drugs, and various therapies. They have a great deal of success."

"And if it doesn't work?"

"It seldom doesn't."

"Your job exists, so it can't be a perfect system."

"Slightly less than three percent of the people in your country are in some way connected to the criminal justice system -- in jail, on parole, or on probation. Less than one half of one percent of the people in all of our star systems are. Our population is over one hundred billion, so that still is half a billion law breakers, but if our procedures worked like yours, the criminal justice system and all its attendant workings would bankrupt us. You're driving over the speed limit."

Mike looked at the speedometer as he drove toward the Northwest Tollway. He was going fifty-five in a thirty-five-mph zone. He slowed down.

"I'm still really angry about what's happening to Jack."

"You'll be able to do a great deal to fix it. First, we've got to be able to get Jack to talk about it. It wouldn't do any good to try and force it out of him."

"You're right. He'd probably get even more defensive. How is the poor kid even handling it? What was in his memory?"

"I didn't have time to read extensively, but you know how he's handling it. What does everybody in the family think of him -- that he's a criminal in the making. Now you know why. You can't help today. I've given you some information, so you can try and help in the future."

"I still feel like I should go over to his father's house and do something violent."

"Maybe it will come to that. For now, let's concentrate on helping Jack and consulting a lawyer before you do anything rash."

"Yeah." As they paid the toll just before the Kennedy Expressway, Mike said, "I called Darryl. He set up a meeting for us with Mary. He gave me the address."

Twenty-three

Mike exited the expressway at Addison and drove east to Cliff Street, filled with rows of bungalows and two flats built in the thirties.

It was nearly four o'clock when they rang the bell. Mary was in her bathrobe with her hair up in curlers. Sans costume, glitter, and atmosphere, she looked porcine and unkempt. She led them into a living room with faded carpets, torn and tattered drapes, and threadbare furniture and offered to brew them fresh coffee. They demurred.

She plopped onto a sofa and propped her feet on a plastic table. "What's Howard done?" she asked.

The alien said, "He hasn't done anything. We're worried about him. He had an accident at the bar last night. We took him to St. Bridget's Hospital."

"Is he okay?"

"We don't know. He was gone before we got there today. We stayed with him as late as we could this morning, but we couldn't find anything out."

"There was a stink at the bar last night. The owner was pissed. He doesn't like it when the dancers take off in the middle of a shift. A few of them find a john for the night and leave to earn a lot of quick bucks. Howard could get fired. He's pretty and popular, but there's always another pretty one willing to be just as popular. I told you last night that he's been bummed out about something, but he wouldn't tell me what. You don't think he's in real trouble, do you?"

"We want to make sure he's all right."

"I don't usually give out the other dancers' addresses, but Darryl vouched for the both of you." She wrote on a piece of paper and handed it to them.

It was nearly five. The sun had only managed to burn through the fog in the last hour. The sunshine seemed to be occurring more by tolerance from than by triumph over the clouds.

Howard's apartment was two blocks west of the corner of Milwaukee and Belmont Avenues. The outside of the building was grime-encrusted maroon brick. Bits and pieces of the crumbling exterior crunched under their feet as they approached the front door. No one answered when Mike pushed the little white button under Howard's name.

A child of about ten rode her bike up to the door as they were inspecting the mailboxes for an indication of a manager or landlord. Mike and Joe used the time-worn expedient of following the child inside after she unlocked the door. Since there was no elevator, they were forced to walk up five flights of stairs. The corridors smelled musty. The walls needed painting. A few of the ceiling fixtures lighting the hall worked.

Howard's apartment was the last one on the left. No one answered their knock.

"I don't like this," the alien said.

"The apartment house, the corridor, the door, or the lack of an answer?"

"All of the above."

"You know he could simply have refused treatment at the hospital and walked out. Right now he could be merrily romping about the city or committing the atrocious crime of having coffee with a friend."

"You really believe any of that?" Joe asked.

"I think I'd prefer to believe all of that."

"Let's try the neighbors."

They stepped four feet to the nearest door across the hall. The alien knocked. No one answered.

Mike leaned close to the door. "I think I hear music."

The alien knocked louder.

"Maybe they left the stereo or television on," Mike said. "We keep this up we're going to draw attention to ourselves."

"We've got to talk to these people." The alien bashed his hand against the door which was flung open while he was in the middle of his second bash.

Dressed only in skimpy red gym shorts, a male in his early teens peered out at them. The boy's acne was evident from lower torso to hairline on his head. Mike caught a glimpse of a girl about the same age peering around a door further inside the apartment. She was almost as scantily clad as the boy. She saw Mike catch sight of her and ducked back out of the room.

The boy said, "Can I help you?" He clutched his knobby shoulders. Mike saw the indentations at the side of the boy's nose that said he normally wore glasses. Mike thought he might have been all of thirteen.

Joe said, "We were wondering if you know anything about your neighbor across the way."

"No. I never talk to him. My mom might. She isn't home."

"When is the last time you saw him?" Mike asked.

"Gosh, I don't know. I gotta go." He closed the door.

"Gives a new meaning to day care," Mike said.

"How so?"

"Babies making babies. I hope to hell they're using condoms."

No one answered at the next three doors, but at the apartment closest to the stairs, a woman who looked to be in her early sixties answered. She wore a navy blue business suit. In one hand she clutched a can of pepper spray.

"What are you doing up here?"

"We're looking for Howard Martinelle from down the hall in 5L."

"You cops? You got some kind of identification?"

"We're friends of his," Joe said. "He hasn't been to work in a few days, and nobody knows where he is. He was supposed to meet us for lunch today."

Mike looked at the alien with admiration and then uneasiness. The lies sounded absolutely real and plausible.

"He's missing?" the woman asked.

"Nobody's seen him," Joe said. "Everybody's worried. We knocked, but no one answered. We're trying to find out if any of the neighbors might help us."

"Why don't you check with the management?"

"We will," Joe said, "but sometimes neighbors meet and talk."

"Howard rarely talked to anybody. He had a stream of men up here. I know he's gay, and I know I'm supposed to be liberal and all, but I don't like the place being used as a whorehouse."

"You're sure he was a prostitute?" Mike asked.

"What kind of friends are you that you don't know what he did?"

"How do you know he was a prostitute if he didn't talk to his neighbors?"

"Stands to reason. You don't bring that many strange, older men to your apartment, never the same one twice. What are we supposed to think?"

Mike shrugged.

She continued, "I heard he was going to be thrown out. There was a ruckus down there several nights ago. Woke us all up. I nearly called the police, but who wants to answer their questions all night long? I don't like to meddle."

"What was the ruckus?" Joe asked.

"Loud shouting, banging doors, furniture or something being thrown around, probably glass, because I could hear it shatter."

"When was this?"

She thought. "Three nights ago."

"Who could let us into his apartment?"

"You really think something could be wrong?"

"We hope not."

"You can try apartment 1C on the first floor. That's where we drop our rent checks every month."

Mike and the alien marched all the way downstairs. The door to apartment 1C was opened by a man in his late fifties. He wore a short-sleeve, white shirt open over his hirsute chest. His belly bulged over blue Dockers pants held up by pink suspenders.

After they explained their concern about Howard, the man said, "I don't want to be involved with the police. I get hassled enough by tenants demanding this and that. I got city inspectors crawling all over this place half the day and night."

"At least let us check in his apartment," Mike said. "We aren't the police. We're just worried about our friend."

"Well, the owner does want him out. Maybe this'll be the final excuse."

As they trudged back up to the fifth floor, between puffs of heavy breathing, the manager gave them more information. "I haven't seen him since the big fight three nights ago. I know he's a hustler. I heard he does a lot of S/M work. Maybe a client got out of control. Howard screams at me when it's time to pay the rent. I'm just the guy they're supposed to give it to. Why yell at me? He's always late with his rent. He assumes because he has a cute butt he doesn't have to pay on time."

The hairy guy unlocked the door. The first room they entered was a mass of shattered glass, strewn dishes, and disheveled clothes.

"My god!" the manager exclaimed.

TWENTY-FOUR

Mike and Joe strode in ahead of him. The kitchen was on the left. It was as large a mess as the living room. The sink had stacks of unwashed dishes and glasses piled to six inches above the top. Dirty dishwater rose to about half way up the filth-encrusted mound. Cockroaches feasted on food remnants. The refrigerator had only mustard, ketchup, sour milk, and a loaf of bread with the first hints of mold on it.

In the bedroom all the drawers in the dresser were upended, their contents strewn about the room. The mattress lay askew on the box spring, which itself had deep rents showing the internal metal. The only evidence Mike saw of S/M were issues of *Drummer* magazine torn and scattered around the floor.

The manager stood at the door to the room shaking his head. "I guess I'm going to have to call the police."

"Yes," the alien said. "It would be best."

They found a phone without a receiver. A cursory look failed to turn it up. "I'll have to go downstairs and call. I'll be dealing with the goddamn cops for hours. I'll stay downstairs to let them in. Better not touch anything." He paused at the door. "Or maybe if you stole all this shit it would make it easier for everybody." Muttering curses he left them.

"I thought you didn't want the police around," Mike said.

"We needed him to leave so we could look the place over and get the hell out."

"Could the other alien have done this?"

"I don't know why he would."

"What are we looking for?"

"Connections, anything non-terran, something suspicious or out of the ordinary."

"How would we know what's ordinary in this chaos?"

A guy who looked to be about sixteen appeared in the doorway.

"Who are you guys?" he asked.

"Friends of Howard's," Joe said.

"I've never seen you before."

"We haven't seen you either," the alien said.

The stranger had black hair and taut muscles on a slender frame. He wore blue jeans and a sheepskin-lined denim jacket. The shirt-tails of a purple-and-white flannel shirt hung to his knees. Mike didn't think the kid was shaving more than one day a week yet.

"My name's Kyle Flannery. I was supposed to have a date with Howard. Who are you guys?"

"I'm a detective," the alien said.

"Cops, huh. I was afraid it would come to this."

The alien let the presumption that they were official police go uncorrected.

Mike introduced himself without any title and asked, "How'd you get in?"

"I pressed the buzzer downstairs. No one answered. One of the other tenants came by. I walked in with him."

"The buzzer didn't ring up here."

"It doesn't work a lot."

"You know Howard well?"

The kid began edging toward the door. Almost casually the alien got behind him. The kid looked from one to the other of them.

"I haven't done anything wrong," he said. He looked about ready to cry.

Mike said, "Kyle, we don't want to bring harm to you. We're just looking for Howard. We're not going to hurt you."

"What happened here?"

"That's what we're trying to figure out. What can you tell us?"

"I'm not sure."

"When did you talk to him last?"

"I've called a dozen times and stopped here every night for a week. Finally, last night I went to the bar where he worked."

"They let you in?"

"Howard showed me a secret place you can get in through the buildings connected to the bar. I only saw him for a minute. He got real mad and told me to leave. When I didn't, he threatened to have me thrown out. I thought he loved me. Yesterday I finally got him to promise to meet me tonight. Has something bad happened to him?"

"Do you have any idea who trashed this place?" Joe asked.

"He's not very neat, but he never leaves it this messy."

Kyle walked into the kitchen, then stuck his head in the bedroom and walked back. "This is incredible, totally crazy."

"How so?" Mike asked.

"He's been acting so weird lately. I've been worried about him."

"Is there anything missing?" Joe asked.

"Hard to tell," Kyle said.

"His toothbrush and razor are still here," Joe said. "If he was going somewhere, it wasn't a planned trip."

Mike figured they had only a few more minutes to get this guy out before the police arrived. A whole host of crimes -- murders, burglaries in progress, active domestic disturbances, among others -- would take precedence over this one, but eventually the official police would show up.

Mike said, "There's a coffee shop at the corner. Why don't you tell us all about it down there?"

"Don't you have to make reports?"

Mike felt odd slipping into a semi-cop mode as he said, "We

do nothing but make reports. Maybe they'll have donuts for us to eat in the coffee shop. We can be comfortable while we talk. There's no body here. We're not sure there's even been a crime. We just need to talk."

They shut the door on their way out and walked downstairs. As Mike stood outside with Kyle, the alien stopped at the manager's apartment. He returned in moments, and they left.

Mike and the alien sat on one side of a booth with dark maroon, plastic covers on the seats. Kyle sat on the other side. The restaurant claimed to have the freshest pancakes in town. Mike wondered if this was a valid or important claim. How unfresh could a pancake get, unless they were yesterday's leftovers reheated? The grease on the walls looked like it might have come over with the Mayflower.

Mike and Joe ordered coffee. The kid ordered a soda.

Kyle said, "I'm not sure I should be talking to cops."

"We're not going to arrest you for being underage. Nor are we going to arrest Howard for having sex with you."

"You could tell my parents."

The alien said, "If we want to bust you, all we have to do is get your identification and take you to the station. What we want is information. You be honest with us, and we don't tell your parents."

The kid sipped his drink. "Everybody says the Chicago police are homophobic creeps."

Joe took Mike's hand, entwined his fingers with his, and placed the combined fist upon the table. "We understand more than most."

Kyle said, "Gay cops? I heard there were some. Are you really gay?"

"We want to help you," Joe said. "We're being honest with you. Why don't you be honest with us?"

"I wish I knew more adults who were gay. Howard's nice and all, but he doesn't really explain things. Sometimes I thought he was just using me for sex."

Mike suspected "sometimes" was an understatement. As would most gay men, he understood the kid's fears and loneliness.

A cop car pulled up outside the restaurant. Two young-looking cops, a male and a female, got out and swaggered toward the apartment house.

"You said you were afraid it would come to this," Joe said. "What did you mean by that?"

"I'm worried about Howard. The only reason I know him is because he went to high school with my sister. I guess I needed him more than he needed me. I really like him, but lately I've gotten the idea he didn't want me hanging around."

"He do anything specific to give you that impression?"

"I don't know." Kyle thought a minute. "I guess he was sort of cold and distant. I've never been in a relationship before. I don't know what that is supposed to be like. I didn't know if I should say anything to him or just go away. I didn't know anybody I could talk to about it."

"How old are you?"

"Eighteen."

"Tell me the truth," Mike said, "or no matter how gay we are, your parents get called."

Kyle hesitated then said, "Sixteen, next month. That doesn't mean I'm too young to be in love and have sex. My parents don't care what I do."

"You're sure about that?"

Kyle shrugged.

Joe asked, "Besides pushing you away, did he do anything else unusual lately?"

"I left messages on his answering machine. He used to always call me back. He must not have gotten them."

"I didn't see an answering machine," Mike said.

"Maybe whoever wrecked his place took it."

"Why?" Joe asked.

No one had an answer to that.

Kyle said, "He was always honest with me, or at least I thought he was."

The kid looked miserable. Howard had probably simply begun to lose interest in an underage, nervous, gay teenager.

"He would have told me, wouldn't he, if he wasn't interested in me? I told him I loved him last weekend."

"Sometimes people get frightened as you get closer to them," Mike said.

Mike felt sorry for Kyle. He wished he knew how to help. He wondered if the alien was reading the boy's memories. He hoped he wasn't. The poor kid deserved his privacy and didn't need somebody intruding on his pain. On the other hand, if the alien was doing some psychic delving, perhaps they could get some important information quickly.

"Why are you worried about Howard?" Joe asked.

"The last couple times I've been over he's gotten these weird calls. He winds up arguing over the phone with whoever calls. I could hear the other person's voice from five feet away. They really screamed and shouted at each other. Then Howard would have to go out for an hour or two. One weekend when I was staying over, he was gone all night."

"What were they fighting about?"

"It sounded more like Howard didn't want to do something."

"Did he ever say who it was or where he went?"

"He didn't explain anything. He told me if I still wanted to come around, I'd have to get used to the way adults acted, that I wasn't to behave like a sniveling little brat."

Mike doubted if Howard was much more than three or four years older than Kyle.

"You put up with that?" Joe asked.

"He yelled at me a lot, but my parents yell at each other all the time. I guess that's the way adults deal with each other."

"It doesn't have to be," Mike said.

Kyle shrugged. "I hope not."

"Can you remember anything else?" Joe asked. "Even the smallest thing that might give a hint about where he is?"

Kyle thought a minute. "Two things, I guess. One time when he left I decided to follow him, but I didn't get far. He got into a limousine in front of the apartment house and took off. The other was, I started coming to his apartment when he wasn't there. I wasn't supposed to do that. I'd come when I had a bad day. Kids at school trying to rough me up or calling me names sometimes gets to be too much. My parents told me I'm smarter than all the rest, and I should be able to figure ways to make kids like me. As if a high IQ is an open door to having friends. Parents can be so naive. Anyway, I don't think he told many people about me. He never introduced me to any of his friends. Once he came in when he didn't expect me. He had somebody with him. I only saw the guy for a second. They argued out in the hall. They were pretty furious with each other, but I couldn't make out what they were saying. The fight didn't last long, but afterward Howard screamed at me. I left pretty quick. We made up later, but we were never the same after that."

"Would you recognize the man he was with?" Joe asked. He reached for his communicator and showed the picture to Kyle.

"It was too quick. I couldn't say either 'yes' or 'no.'"

"Would you recognize the limousine?"

"It was just an ordinary black limo. I didn't even think about getting the license plate number."

"One of the neighbors told us that there was a big fight a couple days ago."

"I don't know about that. I just know about those times I told you."

"We can try and get the phone records," Mike said. "We can

have some idea of who Howard called out to and who called in."

"What am I going to do?" Kyle asked.

"What do you mean?" Mike asked.

"Howard was the only gay guy I really knew. I can't get into most of the bars. I want to meet other people like me."

Mike knew exactly what the kid was talking about. The most significant feeling he remembered about his youth as a gay teen was the sense of being the only one, of being totally alone in the world.

Mike reached over and took the kid's hand. "You will meet other people like yourself. High school will probably be tough. I wish I could make the pain go away for you, but I can't. When you go to college, being gay will be easier. For now there are youth groups that you can go to that are designed especially for gay teenagers. I can show you in the gay newspapers before we leave. The most important thing for you to remember is that you can lead a happy life and have friends and good times and be fulfilled. Being gay does not have to hold you back."

Kyle became misty eyed, "Thanks," he gulped. "Lots of the time Howard didn't seem to have much use for me, except for... in the bedroom."

"I know this sounds like your mother," Mike said, "but you do use condoms?"

"Usually."

"From now on, always. Promise me."

"Okay."

"And if you didn't use condoms, you need to be tested for STDs including HIV."

"I couldn't."

"Please think about it. There are ways of being tested anonymously."

Kyle promised he would give it some thought.

They picked up a gay newspaper on the way out the door.

Mike pointed out the names of places where Kyle could go to meet other gay teens and where he could be tested.

As they were standing at the curb, Mike held out his hand, but Kyle gave him a fierce hug.

"Can we meet to talk again?" Kyle asked.

"You've got to take charge of your life," Mike said. "You need to meet people your own age."

Kyle looked crestfallen. "How do you know what I need?" he asked.

Mike was nonplused. He simply did not want a relationship with an underage kid -- platonic or otherwise. Obviously Kyle, in the way teenagers could, had formed a strong attachment to him very quickly.

"If you're ever in danger or in trouble or if you think of something you've left out about Howard, give me a call." Mike wrote his number on the front page of the paper. Mike put his hand on Kyle's shoulder. Briefly, he massaged the thin shoulder through the jacket. Mike said, "We both care about you and want the best for you. If you need to talk or call, great. Remember, you are not alone. You'll be fine."

Kyle gave him a wan smile, a brief wave, turned, and strode away.

Mike and Joe watched Kyle for several moments. "Poor kid," Mike said.

"Why?"

"I know exactly what he's going through."

"That happens to all gay people on this planet, loneliness, getting picked on?"

"Things have gotten somewhat better in the past decade, but it still can hurt very, very much to be young and gay."

"Wasn't he using Howard as much as Howard was using him?" Joe asked.

"I guess you could say that. Did you read his memories?"

"No. If we can get through to people by talking, I'd rather do it that way. This way is easier."

"Got it."

"I need to get access to phone records."

"Skipper Henderson might be able to help. We can call him from the Luxor, and then I need to go with Darryl to the Mokena Universal Health Clinic. I promised him. Whether it's a cure or an elixir or whatever, it is probably bogus, but he wants to go."

Joe stopped in the manager's apartment again. Then they returned to the car and drove toward the Lakeview neighborhood.

Mike asked, "How is it that you're so good at lying?"

"We take acting lessons as part of our training."

"Sort of a real, live cop show."

"The ones on your television are all amateurs. Do you believe my lies?"

"Which are those?"

"Good answer. I only lie when I have to, and I always tell as much of the truth as I can."

"You're very convincing. Which lies have you told me?"

"I've told you the truth."

Mike wished he could believe that.

"What'd you say to the manager when we left?" Mike asked.

"The first or second time?"

"Both."

"I just said we were going for coffee. If they needed us, we'd be back. The second time, I asked what the police had said."

"You weren't afraid the cops might still be around to question us?"

"The cop car was gone when we got outside. I figured I was safe. If it had still been there, I'd have walked away."

"What if they'd come into the restaurant?"

"You think every cop in the city has a description of us?"

"They could."

"We haven't done anything. Why would they be looking for us? Anyway the manager said they seemed to be a couple of bored rookies. There wasn't any blood or any corpse or any screaming people, just a mess. The cops told him to forget it. Howard hasn't been missing that long. If we want to make a missing person report, we can wait twenty-four hours and then come to the station."

"Not much help."

"No." The alien seemed to hesitate a moment then said. "I'd like to go with you and Darryl to the clinic."

"Okay, and from Darryl's room, I can call Skipper. Remember him from last night?"

"The one who writes novels?"

"Yeah. He's an electronic genius. He can get into things that nobody else can. Although, if what you said about mastering our technology is true, maybe you can do it. Why can't I just give you a computer and let you get the information?"

"An electronic game is simple. You just have to be faster than the rather simple logic of whoever set it up. I could break into the telephone network faster than somebody computer illiterate on your planet, but someone who is familiar with systems would be better. It might take me twenty-four to forty-eight hours, depending on how well guarded they have their lines. We'd have to find a computer that has the proper access. I'd have to learn the language of the computer, the codes, the processes. While trying, I might inadvertently tip someone off to my search. It would keep me occupied too long. It will simply be more efficient if we can use someone you know."

Twenty-five

It was seven in the evening by the time they got to the Harvey Milk Hospice. The weather was pleasantly cool with a slight breeze from the south.

They found Darryl lying on top of his bed. He was fully dressed. His eyes were closed, his skin was pasty white, and his breathing was shallow.

"Darryl," Mike whispered.

Darryl opened his eyes about halfway. He grinned. "I'm having a no good, very bad day."

Mike sat on the bed next to Darryl. He took his hand. The alien sat in the chair.

"You shouldn't have gone out last night," Mike said.

"Don't play mother to me. You don't need ..." Darryl's voice trailed off.

Darryl not finishing a tirade worried Mike more than the weakened physical condition. Darryl lived to orate.

"It's okay, Darryl. I'm here." Mike caressed his friend's cheek, brushed the hair back on his head. "Do you need to go to the emergency room?"

"No, I still want to go to that clinic."

"Darryl, I don't think that's such a good idea."

"You suggest I wait until I'm dead? I can't get much worse. I can make it."

"How?" Mike asked.

"When I talked to Greta the Ghoul earlier today, she couldn't tell me 'yes' or 'no' about this treatment, but I don't have a choice."

Mike nodded reluctant agreement.

Darryl glanced at Joe. "I told Mike he should marry you."

Joe said, "If I decide to marry him, first I'll ask you for his hand in marriage."

Darryl patted Mike's forearm. "If you can't have me, you'll need somebody studly." He prodded one of Joe's biceps. "This one will do nicely." Darryl grinned and began levering himself up and off the bed.

Mike shook his head. "You picked a hell of a time to play matchmaker."

Darryl managed to swing his feet off the bed. With Mike's help, he struggled into an upright sitting position. That accomplished, he held still and breathed deeply for several minutes.

"Darryl, really," Mike began. "It's early Saturday evening. They won't be open."

"The AIDS section is open twenty-four hours a day. Whether as a service to customers or a slick way to make more cash, I don't care. I've got to give it a try. They say there are lines all the time. You've just got to get in line and wait. If there's a chance I won't die..."

"If it's another dead end..." Mike began.

"We don't say 'dead end' to a person with AIDS. Help me up." Darryl held out his hand.

Joe said, "I think we can help him enough to get him there and back."

"An ally," Darryl said. "You make a lovely piece of cavalry all by yourself. You can lend your lovely muscles to the cause. Did you guys talk to Howard?"

"Not yet."

Mike decided to drop his objections. As Darryl said, "What was the point of waiting until he was dead?"

Before they started out with Darryl, Mike called Skipper Henderson.

"How was last night?" Mike asked.

"Mr. Drink Buyer was just another guy who wanted to take

me home, beat me up, and piss on me."

"A romantic."

"Did you find who you were looking for?"

"No."

"The man you were with was really hot. Is he a boyfriend or trick?"

"Neither, yet. We need a favor about the guy we were looking for." Mike explained about being hassled by the police and that they needed to be discreet about locating the phone records for Howard Martinelle. "Can you do it?"

"For you, honey? You and I had the best sex I've ever had. You were the very sweetest man. Besides, when you read my manuscripts you tell the best lies about how great they are. Of course I'll do it. Might take until Monday afternoon because it's the weekend. It will take time no matter when I do it."

Mike thanked him.

Darryl began to stand up. Mike put his arm around him to help him up. Darryl stumbled. Mike and the alien caught him. "Let's get going," Darryl half snapped, half pleaded.

Leaning heavily on Mike and Joe, Darryl made it down to the big old Chevy. They laid Darryl carefully in the back seat and propped him up with several pillows that Joe retrieved from Darryl's room. He also brought a blanket to wrap him in.

"This is style," Darryl said.

"This is nuts," Mike muttered as he maneuvered the car out of the parking lot and drove down Belmont toward Lake Shore Drive.

"I heard that," Darryl said.

"Congratulations," Mike said. He told him about their day, leaving out the parts about what was in his nephew's head and anything he thought might give Darryl a hint about who the alien really was.

"I met your grandmother once," Darryl said. "I remember

her, very Italian, very smart. She knew we were a couple before we knew we were a couple. I liked her. She made the best spaghetti sauce I have ever had."

They took Lake Shore Drive to the Stevenson Expressway to the Dan Ryan Expressway until it ended. They drove down Interstate 57 to Interstate 80 and exited at Harlem Avenue.

On the way the alien said, "I thought they had these new drugs that were helping people with AIDS, almost curing it."

"That's the good news," Darryl said. "The bad news is they don't work with everybody. I'm one of the unfortunate minority. I'm sure we'll meet others in my position at the clinic tonight. If belief were the whole battle, everyone would live, but desperate people can only hope."

They took 191st Street west two miles to the gleaming edifice that was Mokena Universal Health Care Clinic. A customer could get any kind of health food, drink, or supplement. The counselors, never referred to as "doctors," spoke a wellness, New Age doctrine that was soothing to many and drew thousands of clients every week.

A billionaire computer programmer had died and given his entire fortune for the development of a research clinic, with the caveat that the entire facility be dedicated to discovering methods of natural healing. They had purchased a hospital that had gone bankrupt several years before.

A ten-story central core housed administration and research. Six wings spread out from the center, three to the west and three branching out to the east. Each of these was dedicated to trying experiments on particular diseases. According to Darryl, the section used for AIDS had only been staffed in the past few months.

In front of this complex and facing south was a one-story building which was an emergency facility. No ambulances showed up at their door. The owners of the clinic were careful not to advertise themselves as doctors or as offering medical services. If they did, they could be in trouble with any number of regulatory boards, as well as be sued for every mote of dust in the place by disgruntled patients. Nor did they ever dare call their products, "drugs." Other governmental nasties would descend on them for daring to do so. They gave their clients treatments or elixirs or compounds or whatever their Yankee-peddler instinct could come up with as names for what many people considered snake oil.

The exterior of all the buildings was glass and polished bronze, so that the building seemed to shimmer even in the darkness. In blazing sunlight it could be seen for miles.

The flat parking lot stretched for acres and acres around the complex. At that hour on a Saturday, the cars clustered around the entrances. There might have been several hundred vehicles, but they were dwarfed in the immense sea of asphalt.

In the parking lot, small electric shuttles ran twenty-four hours a day picking up and bringing back clients, relatives, and friends. They deposited Darryl in one of these and took seats just behind him. The driver was an acne-scarred teenager who was chewing a wad of gum. She drove slowly and carefully, making sure each speed bump was crossed with nerve-soothing slowness.

"If she goes any slower, I'm going to slap her," Darryl muttered.

If the teenager heard, she gave no notice.

At the entrance there were two mini-vans with the names and logos of two local television stations. Inside and far to the left were television lights where someone was being interviewed.

This part of the old hospital had been completely renovated. According to the original dedication still on the wall in the lobby, the complex had been built in the late 1940s. The interior of the clinic was blond wood and plush carpets with the walls covered with well-spaced muted paintings featuring pastoral scenes.

The clinic desk was to the right. Even at that hour, the waiting room was filled with sitting and standing people. Six nurses and their attendant staff dealt with the patients. The clerk who was assigned to them smiled in the middle of what must have been mass chaos for days. She was very efficient and very pleasant but very honest. She told them Darryl would have to wait for a preliminary check-up, which was what all these people were waiting for. Then they would have to join the long list of people who were waiting for appointments for the experimental treatment. Such an appointment might not happen until next week.

Darryl's voice was shrill and loud as he began, "This sounds like a load of crap."

Mike was no longer embarrassed by Darryl's tirades, but he still wasn't happy about them. Darryl often got more action than others who simply accepted what the medical establishment told them. This tirade lasted a good five minutes.

Most of the people in the room studiously ignored them. The clerk simply kept a bland smile on her face throughout. When Darryl seemed to be finished she said, "Sir, we can talk as long as you wish, but it is not going to alter anything. You're simply going to exhaust yourself needlessly."

"I'm not exhausting myself, I'm dying," Darryl said. "I don't have time to wait on some list."

"I'm sorry, sir, but everyone in this room is dying. Over half of them are worse off than you are."

Mike thought, for once emotional blackmail is not going to work for Darryl. He didn't know if he was glad about that or not, and then felt guilty for thinking it. The clerk told them it would be at least an hour before Darryl could see a counselor.

"We only have so many counselors," she said. "Although if you'd have been here during the week, it would have taken just as long."

"Does this cure really work?" Mike asked.

"You'll have to wait and speak with the counselor."

They found two vacant seats at the far end of the vast waiting room. Darryl immediately slumped into a chair. He said, "I'm exhausted."

Joe sat with Darryl while Mike went in search of food. He decided to take the way that led past the television cameras. He saw that at the moment it was just several reporters in front of a fountain area that had the clinic logo and a bronze American flag hanging on the wall behind it. On one side of the metallic banner stood three bronze figures: a man and a woman comforting a child of five or six.

When Mike came back with orange juice and cashews for all three of them, Darryl was listening intently to several people argue about political realism, Michel Foucault, and gay marriage.

Mike half listened to their conversation for a few minutes. He had one of his books for Darryl from his car. He tended to buy the books for his friend in batches of seven to ten. He kept them in a box in the trunk of the Chevy. He'd picked out a Jonathan Kellerman mystery as they got out of the car. He'd assumed they'd be waiting for a while, so he wanted something.

Darryl perked up as the conversation intensified. His passionate interjections became more frequent. The alien seemed to be totally caught up in listening to Darryl and the group he was orating with. Mike had heard any number of Darryl's harangues several hundred times. He pulled out the Kellerman book. He found Milo, a cop and the main character's close friend, one of the best depictions of gay people in literature.

He'd finished two chapters before Darryl was called. The crowd had not diminished. In response to Darryl's questions, the nurse had said it would take at least an hour for the preliminary consultation.

Mike and Joe strolled down the corridors, which except for the AIDS wing, were mostly quiet. They discovered that several were still totally uninhabited. From the foyer of the central core, they could see empty hallways leading to all the wings, both the used and unused. The air was still. The emergency exit lights created dim shadows. Fixtures in the center core were covered with cloths. Some were even in the original plastic packaging.

"This is kind of odd," Mike said.

"What?"

"I thought they had all this money, but this looks like they stopped before they finished renovating and haven't been back inside since. He ran his hand over the top of a computer monitor. He showed the alien the thick coating of dust that resulted.

"Maybe they just didn't have as much money as they claimed," Joe said.

"Or they're just a schlock organization with an expensive front."

"Hey!" shouted a loud angry voice.

Twenty-six

Mike and Joe turned to see two burly men hurrying towards them from the far end of one of the deserted wings. The men, who looked like rejects from an ugly linebacker competition, approached Mike and Joe warily. They wore security guard uniforms. Mike noted that they kept their hands near their guns.

"What the hell are you two doing here?" one of them shouted from two paces away.

"Taking a walk," Mike said calmly.

"Walk somewhere else!" the guard bellowed. "This area is off limits. Out! Now!"

Mystified and annoyed, Mike and Joe found an exit and walked outside. The sodium arc lights in the parking lot left a soft orange glow over everything.

"That was odd," Mike said. "Did you read their minds?"

"They thought they were doing their duty, nothing unusual."

Mike said, "There was no need to be that pissed off. Do all cops anywhere in the universe have that same, I'm-pissed-with-the-public approach, or were these just two angry ex-jocks who are never going to be anything but what they are?"

"Some cops let the badge go to their heads."

"On your world, too?"

"All over the universe, I'm afraid."

They strode to the edge of the parking lot farthest from the buildings. The perimeter of the grounds was surrounded on all sides by a parkway about twenty feet wide. Mike could still see the furrows of lines in the sod. The trees were little more than sticks with a few browned and withered leaves attached. They strolled along the grass. The clinic was to their right. A corn field was to their left. Mike could see the un-harvested stalks bend against the rising wind.

"They said it was going to warm up," Mike said. "Wind feels pleasant."

"I like the wind on your planet," Joe said.

"You don't have breezes?"

"Nor gales, nor hurricanes, nor tornadoes, not much of anything in the way of weather. Everything is climate-controlled and strictly regulated. Makes farming a dream, but for a romantic, it's kind of hell."

"Golly shucks, Camelot."

"What is that?"

"A fantasy paradise. Are you a romantic?"

"If I understand what you mean by that, I guess I am. Maybe that's what makes me a not-so-good cop. I tend to listen to people before I read their memories. A good cop isn't supposed to do that."

"But don't people lie?"

"Of course. Criminals in every solar system seem to be about the same. None of them ever did anything."

They reached the opposite side of the clinic from the emergency entrance. Across several fields, they could see cars and trucks rushing by on Interstate 80. They paused to observe for a few minutes and breathed the night air.

Mike swept his hand at the heavens. "Where is your home?"

The alien gazed at the southern sky for several minutes before answering. He pointed. "It's behind that cluster of stars. If we were outside Earth's atmosphere, you could see them more clearly."

"What's its name?"

"In your language it sounds like Hrrrm."

"What is it like on your planet?"

"What do you mean?"

"Are people happy? Do they have houses, pay rent? Does the

government control everything?"

"Population has been steady for thousands of millennia. Some want there to be fewer people. Some want there to be an increase but with more colonization for the excess."

"Is Earth in danger?"

"Of being colonized? No, we are an incredibly civilized people, more or less. Our explorers take pride in going to uninhabitable worlds and making them viable. In your solar system, it'd be like earthlings going to Mars and having it be a working colony in fifty years and self-sustaining in maybe a hundred. Even for us that doesn't happen very often. It costs an incredible amount of money, but people still do it for the adventure and freedom from regulation."

"Why didn't you do it?"

"I like my adventure mixed with regulations, so I became a cop."

"What is your life like?" Mike asked.

"What do you mean?"

"I guess, like, do you live in a house?"

"I live in a glorified dormitory when I'm on duty. As cops we are socialized to deal with masses of our fellow beings and with loneliness. My home is a modest house on the edge of a city with a population of one billion. There are mountains a few miles away where I go climbing and look at the sun and the stars."

"Sounds kind of pleasant."

"It can be."

"Do you have anyone special?"

"No."

"What happens when you catch Vov?"

"I take him back."

"He just gives up?"

"Probably not. I'll have to disable him, somehow." They

began a second circuit of the exterior.

"Is this going to do Darryl any good?" Joe asked.

"No," Mike said, "Or at least, I doubt it. I can't imagine any of these health fads making the slightest difference. They are a way to snatch tons of money from frightened people. It isn't illegal. Some might call it immoral. For the desperate, it gives a few moments of hope. My friend is going to die. No matter how many times I think of it, face it, try to ignore it, his coming death still hurts."

"I'm sorry."

When they arrived at the point in the parkway facing the rear of the hospital, they stopped. The shadows were darkest here. "What's that light?" Mike asked idly.

In a field about a half mile away, a headlight beam seemed to be dipping and jiggling over the uneven surface. In general the light seemed to be moving toward them.

"I don't know," Joe said.

They watched in silence for several moments.

"Must be some kind of all-terrain vehicle," Mike said. "Kids run around on trails in fields all over the Midwest. I used to on my aunt's farm when I was a kid. Some farmers don't like it, though. Teenagers either scare the animals or tear up fences or hurt themselves and try to sue. I thought they were illegal out here."

Twenty-seven

The headlight beam slowly approached the parking lot. They could hear the vehicle now, with its motorcycle-like roar. When it came within range of the arc lights, Mike saw that it was indeed an ATV. It pulled into the parking lot at some distance from them. Joe put his hand on Mike's arm. "There's something odd about that thing."

"What?" Mike peered at it closely. In the sodium arc lights, the driver appeared to be a man in his early thirties. "He's a little old to be cavorting around on one of those things, but I don't see why not. No reason to discriminate because of age. Why don't you just check his memories?"

"He's too far away. It's not like I can reach miles away to look into a person's mind. I need to be within normal speaking distance." Joe pulled out his communicator and began rapidly tapping the face. Moments later he turned pale.

"It can't be."

Mike tensed. "Is it Vov?"

"No, but almost as bad."

The vehicle now headed straight for them. The headlight beam grew rapidly brighter, catching them both in its glow.

Mike asked, "Are you, me, or both of us about to disappear in a puff of intergalactic smoke? I want to tell you, I am not in the mood for beaming around the galaxy."

"It's...aw nuts." As the vehicle headed toward them, Joe said, "The closest thing on your planet to what he is would be a bounty hunter or pirate. My communicator picked up his implants. He brings Vov back, he gets money."

"Wouldn't you?"

"No, I'm a cop. It's my job. I get medals and a new chance at a career."

"Why aren't there lots of bounty hunters looking for this guy?"

"We don't get a lot of escaped convicts. Earth is also out of the way. It isn't cheap to get here. Any bounty hunter faces the possible danger from a deranged criminal. Make no mistake, the guy we're after is a brilliant, evil, deadly alien. Not a big chance of success for a large outlay of private money."

"Weren't you expensive to send?"

"I'm a government employee, a not totally unnecessary and certainly justifiable expense. My guess is the guy approaching is probably the only one. There isn't a big call for pirates and bounty hunters. In the past few millennia, their numbers have dwindled. Not much for them to do. Nuts. No matter what, say absolutely nothing about the fact that you know me as an alien."

"Why not?"

"Because you would endanger both my existence and yours."

The stranger slowed more than necessary for every speed bump. He piloted the vehicle in fits and starts, which Mike judged couldn't all be due to the terrain. The driver seemed amusingly inept or very new at piloting such a vehicle.

The rider waved at them cheerfully and pulled to a stop with the front wheel of the ATV three inches from Joe's left foot. Joe didn't flinch. The driver tried revving the engine, but it coughed spasmodically and died.

The ATV driver dismounted, took off his helmet, and smiled at them. He was over six feet, slender with broad shoulders, black hair, a firm jaw, and dark brown eyes. He spoke to Joe. "Fancy meeting you here."

"I have to talk to him, Mike. I'll be back in a few minutes."

Joe beckoned to the newcomer, who gave Mike an ironic bow and then walked off with Joe. The two of them talked near the edge of the glow from the sodium lights. Mike heard none of the conversation. They looked as different as any two earthlings. Neither gesticulated angrily, and Mike thought he'd hear them if they raised their voices to each other.

Minutes later both aliens approached Mike. He felt unease at their advance upon him. The newcomer wore a self-satisfied smirk. Joe hung his head.

"Evening," said the other alien.

"Hello," Mike said. "I'm Mike Carlson."

"I'm Zye." The new alien extended his hand. Mike felt the same tingling he had when he touched Joe. Zye turned away, hopped on his ATV, and started it with a roar. Then vehicle and driver meandered slowly away. Mike and Joe resumed their stroll on the grassy parkway.

"What's all this about?" Mike asked.

"It's a reality check for me. He reminded me that nobody on my planet expects me to bring the criminal back, that nobody cares if I bring him back. He suggested I give up and leave."

"How'd he know you were here?"

"He wouldn't say how he found me. Police reports aren't open to the public on my planet, but bounty hunters are enormously resourceful. This guy is a master. Over the years he's made some spectacular catches. He got enough bounty from his hunting to be able to buy his own planet. This is sort of a lark for him -- a challenge."

"Who did he think I was?"

"I'm not sure. He knows you're not from my planet. The technology he has with him would show him that. He probably assumes you're an earthling I've duped into doing what I say."

"How do I know I'm not?"

"Because you are free to leave any time you want. I will not compel you to stay. I would not compel your silence."

"Lot of good my saying I met an alien would do."

"Zye and Vov might be using humans for contacts as well. Howard and that fake cop are examples. They would need as much help with the idioms as I, if not more. I can read people's histories. They can't."

"Why'd he come to this clinic on this night?"

"I didn't put enough blockers on my communicator's signal. I was over-confident or being my usual inept self."

"Why'd he show you he was here?"

"To gloat, to irritate me. Bounty hunters look on cops more as nuisances than as enemies. Bounty hunters aren't legal on my planet, but our laws don't have effect on other planets, so they can operate anywhere off world with impunity. Maybe he does simply want to bring the bad guy back for a reward."

"Why wouldn't you both work together? Since you won't get a reward anyway, why not help each other out? Either way you get Vov back."

"It doesn't work that way. Bounty hunters work independently. He would kill me to get the prisoner."

"Isn't that illegal?"

"In my star system, yes. On your planet, yes, but this is a dicey situation. Your laws can't touch us. My enforcement powers in my star system are limited by our laws. I'm not supposed to act outside the law no matter where I am."

"Why didn't he just kill you now?"

"He thinks because I'm here, I might have a clue."

"What kind of clue could be here?"

"He wouldn't tell me. I didn't tell him what I know, nor do I want to give him a hint of how little I've been able to find out. Bounty hunters aren't successful because they act rashly. He'll bide his time."

"Can you kill him?"

"I have no reason to."

"How long has he been here?"

"He wouldn't say."

"Is he a threat to me?"

"Yes."

"A vigorous 'no' would have been much more pleasant."

"If he knew that you knew the truth about me, he would have killed you on the spot."

"Why?"

"You're not important to him in the slightest. Alive, you might cause a problem. It's good enough for him to want you dead. Plus, technically, I've interfered with an indigenous civilization. I've broken the law, and I'm afraid you're the remnant of my misbehavior, equally part of the problem and so expendable."

"Two days ago interstellar beings were not trying to murder me. I'm trying to figure out how I'm better off now."

"What can I say?"

"How about that this has all been a bad dream and you're going to give me a free subscription to the *Blond-Viking-of-the-Month-Club*."

"What's a Viking?"

"A fantasy that isn't going to come true any time in the next millennium. And for sure they would kill me?"

"They certainly wouldn't mind violating the laws of my star system."

"Gives a whole lot of depth to the notion of *thanks for sharing*."

"We aren't supposed to interfere with the local species. It's one of the reasons I'm a bad cop. I like people too much. I want to listen and hear their stories. It seems almost cold and cruel how I know when the people on my planet are guilty. I can be aware of their entire lives in seconds. Justice is quick and merciless."

"But I thought you said it was perfect."

"But those who set up the system are not perfect. Shouldn't we check on Darryl?"

"I want straight answers here. How is this guy going to affect what we're doing?"

"I don't know. I have better implants than he does. My ship is far more technologically advanced than his, but he's like any bounty hunter. I'm sure he's got tricks up his sleeve. If he gets this guy, my chances of getting a career back home are nothing. I might as well set the instruments on my ship for the other side of eternity as bother to go back to my planet."

"It can't be all that bad."

"Sure it can. It could even be worse."

Mike said, "It could be raining."

"What's that?"

"A gag line from a great movie."

Joe asked, "You ever been to the other side of eternity?"

"Not recently."

"I doubt if it's amusing."

"One can hope."

Inside the clinic they looked around for Darryl. The crowd waiting to be interviewed was no smaller than when they entered. As they walked up to the nurses' station, they heard what sounded like a loud squawk and a significant crash.

Moments later the swinging doors that led to the examination rooms burst open. A female security guard with the height and heft of a pro wrestler had hold of Darryl by his left ear. Darryl was attempting to swat her, but every time he got a fist around, the guard gave him a good shake, and Darryl dangled like a rag doll.

"I'll bite you," Darryl warned. "I have AIDS. You'll die."

"Use that threat on someone who cares."

"I'm a sick man," Darryl said. "How dare you treat me like this?"

"You wait your turn. You do not hassle the staff. You want a chance for the treatment, you better behave."

She deposited Darryl in front of the nurses' station. Darryl looked at Mike. For the first time ever, Mike thought Darryl looked chagrined. His friend leaned heavily against the counter. Mike moved to prop him up.

The nurse looked at Darryl severely.

"Your preliminary examination is done." She slid several forms over to him. "As soon as all your paperwork is in, we will consider giving you an appointment for putting you on the list for a meeting with a counselor, possible treatment, and the method of payment."

Darryl started to say something, but finally he just hung his head. "All right," he mumbled.

Mike and Joe had to almost carry Darryl out to the shuttle train. He leaned heavily on them both. His friend was silent and in pain. Mike thought of trying to get him admitted to a hospital right then.

As they neared the shuttle, Mike glanced back at the entrance for a moment. "Look!" he said.

Darryl muttered, "What?"

The alien looked back over his shoulder where Mike indicated.

"Is that the guy who approached us on the street wearing the fake cop uniform?" Mike asked.

"I think so," Joe said. "Can you handle Darryl yourself?"

"Yeah."

Mike put one hand around Darryl's waist and one of Darryl's arms around his shoulder.

As the alien hurried off, Mike saw the fake cop disappear into the building. Mike and Darryl struggled into the shuttle. His friend was so light, he knew if necessary he could simply carry him.

When they got to the car, Darryl said, "Hold me." Mike hugged his friend, then got him settled in the back seat. Mike started to close the door, but Darryl held onto his hand. "Wait a few minutes." Mike looked over the parking lot but didn't see Joe or the fake cop. Mike sat on the seat and rested Darryl's head in his lap. Darryl briefly opened his eyes.

"He's in love with you," Darryl said.

"Who's in love with me?"

"Joe."

"Don't be absurd," Mike said. "He's..." His voice trailed off.

Darryl shut his eyes. "Don't argue with me," Darryl muttered. "I know love when I see it."

Mike wasn't sure whether he flat out didn't believe Darryl, or if he was afraid to believe him. Being insightful about people was not Darryl's strong point.

Darryl sighed deeply and shortly thereafter fell asleep. Less than five minutes later Joe hurried back.

"How is he?" Joe asked.

"Exhausted. Asleep. Did you find out anything?"

"No. I followed him as far as that central rotunda with all the dust and unopened equipment. I couldn't use violence, and they wouldn't answer my questions. Something is odd about this place."

"Is there a connection between the fake cop and Vov?"

Joe shrugged, "There's got to be. He's working with humans or using them at least. I doubt if he's revealed who he is or his powers. He would have no need."

Mike sat in back with Darryl. They wrapped the sick man in his blanket and set the pillows around him. Joe drove while Mike cradled Darryl's head and upper torso. He wakened briefly as they accelerated onto Interstate 80.

Mike said, "You don't look so good, Darryl. Should we bring you to a hospital?"

"No, I'm just tired."

"What happened?" Mike asked him.

Darryl yawned and snuggled into Mike's arms. "I was an obnoxious twit."

"That's not unusual. What did they say?"

"The treatment costs thousands of dollars. I don't have the money."

"I thought these health food places were in business to sell their wares," Mike said. "I've never heard of them charging that much. Isn't it usually drink this bottle of vile fluid and call me from Nirvana?"

"I don't know," Darryl said. "I need to find a way to pay. When I come back next, they want me to bring financial records."

"That sounds suspicious to me," Mike said.

"Me too," Darryl said. He yawned again. Moments later he

muttered, "Thanks," and fell back to sleep.

Joe's driving was much steadier than when he'd been dashing about the streets in the cab. "You drive pretty well," Mike commented.

"Spaceship, car, video game, it's all a matter of hand-eye coordination."

Mike thought, "Or you've been here longer than you claim." But he said nothing about this thought. He said, "Zye wasn't so good driving that ATV."

"It has something called stick shift. I wouldn't know what to do either."

At the hospice Mike carried the sleeping Darryl inside and up to his room. His former lover weighed barely more than he had when he was twelve years old. Darryl woke briefly as they took his shoes off and tucked him into bed. He muttered thanks and fell back to sleep. They mentioned their concern for Darryl's condition to the receptionist. She promised to have someone check on him.

Joe said, "Should we give St. Bridget's a try again?"

"It's one of the few leads we've got, and the shift that was working when they brought Howard in should be on duty."

At the hospital they got very little consideration. A terrible accident on Lake Shore Drive had all the emergency room personnel tied up. The few brief answers they got were all akin to, "We don't give out patient information," or "Go away we're busy."

Back at the Luxor, Mike called his answering machine. He punched in the two-digit code to get his messages. He had three. One was from Skipper Henderson telling him to call no matter what time he got in. Mike wondered if he'd gotten the phone information already. The second contained several moments of silence, punctuated at the end by a sudden click. The third was from Mrs. Benson asking him to call her immediately. Unlike Skipper, she did not leave a time limit, but Mike couldn't imagine waking her up as late as it was.

He dialed Skipper's number.

"I didn't wake you?" Mike asked.

"No. I'm working on my new short story, *The Stupidest School Principal in History*."

"Doesn't sound like a very catchy title."

"Everybody's a critic."

"Sorry. You left a message on my answering machine."

"Yeah. I thought you'd want to know. It seemed pretty important. I saw that guy you were looking for. He was in Balls, Whips, and Chains."

"When?"

"Tonight. I called just after I got home. I must have seen him around ten. I came home early to get to work on the new story and decided to call."

"Thanks."

"I'm still working on those phone numbers. I should have something early in the morning."

"Great. I'll call you."

Mike hung up and told the alien the news.

"We should go over there," Joe said.

"Okay."

Mike and Joe changed and headed for the bar.

Twenty-nine

On the other side of the street and down the block from Balls, Whips, and Chains, Mike and Joe paused.

"Why are we stopping?" Mike asked.

"I'm wondering why he would go here unless he's using it as a place to recruit humans. Although I'm not sure why he'd pick there."

"Haven't you asked yourself that question several times before?"

"Well, yeah."

"And the point now is?"

"If he knows I've been here, why did he come back?"

"Does he know you've been here?"

"I presume so."

"Well there's a comfort."

"I wish I knew what was in his mind."

"When we meet him, we'll have to ask him."

"If there's time."

"What does that mean?" Mike asked.

"He's not going to happy when I find him."

"Is he going to try and kill us?"

"Probably."

"We're looking for somebody who is going to kill us. Does this seem like a rational thing to be doing?"

"It's my job."

"Well, that makes me feel better. Will you be able to stop him?"

"I've come a lot of light years to do just that."

"I could be in danger."

"Yes."

Mike stood in thought, looked at Joe, glanced at the night sky. He asked himself the question asked early in the *Transformers* movie. Fifty years from now would he wish he'd stayed and shared the adventure or would he always regret not being part of it? His answer was the same as in the movie.

He nodded his head. "I'm in."

"Let's walk past the place and around to the back," Joe said. "We've got some feel for the layout. Let's see if we can't find a less public way in."

"I wish we knew where that kid, Kyle's, secret entrance was," Mike said.

"We didn't think to ask. Maybe if we see him again."

"We could try the way we left with Darryl."

"Even that had too many people. I'd like to find the way in that is the least public."

Mike followed the alien. They watched a group of three men walk up to the front door and enter. At the cross street north they turned left and walked to the entrance to the alley.

"Let's walk this way," Joe said.

Mike did his best Groucho Marx imitation. Joe stared at him.

"What was that?" the alien asked.

"An old joke I happen to like more than I should."

"Oh, maybe you can explain it to me later."

Joe entered the alley. Rotting garbage was scattered among dented dumpsters. A car with smashed windows and all the tires off rested on its left side. The lights at the ends of the alley were lit, but none in the middle were working.

"Are you sure this is safe?" Mike asked. "I seldom choose back alleys in dingy sections of Chicago to take my evening constitutional."

"No, I'm not sure it's safe. I will protect you, which is better than several tank battalions on your side."

Mike hoped it was true.

The alley behind the bar complex was as dark as any nightmare Mike could conjure up. He wanted to believe the alien's assurances that this was safe. Occasionally he did hear a rustle. Got to be rats, not humans. He stuck close to Joe's left shoulder.

Half way down the alley Joe said, "That bar complex is more vast than I imagined. Look."

Mike followed the pointing finger. "See, it was already joined with the six buildings next to it, but it also connects with the factory past that. All those buildings are really a single unit."

"Maybe they're just next to each other. There don't have to be passageways."

"But there could be. I'd like to do some exploring in all of those if I can. There's got to be a way back in there. If Vov has set up a laboratory, he would need a lot of space for making and creating."

Mike looked at the chain link fence topped with razor wire. "We aren't going to climb that?"

"Not if we don't have to."

The alley did not go through to the further cross street but made a sharp right turn. An immense three-story factory connected on their left with the row of buildings that started with Balls, Whips, and Chains. This factory stretched to their right nearly half a block to the El tracks. Between them was the fence. From the alley to the building was a twenty-car parking lot.

"Can't we just go in the front door, like we did last night?" Mike asked

"Vov could have spies working for him. I'd rather sneak in. Zye could have discovered this place as well. As a last resort, we'll go in the front door."

First, they followed the fence to the El tracks. The alley ran to a small underpass large enough for only one car at a time to drive through. The embankment for the El tracks was flat gray cement at least twelve feet high. The chain-link obstruction was connected to the bricks of the underpass to a height of eight feet above their heads. They quickly ducked through the underpass but found only more factories and empty parking lots.

They followed the fence back down the alley the way they had come. Around the factory it had been high, stout, and nearly new. At intervals further down behind the other buildings, it was bulged out, worn out, or in slight tatters.

"Could an alien ship be in there?" Mike asked.

"The factory building is big enough, but my sensors should have detected something if it was in that building." He pulled out his communicator and gave it a final check. He shook his head, "Nope, nothing."

They found a break in the fence about two hundred feet down from the bar. They were forced to crawl on their bellies to get through the break. Mike held the chain as wide apart as possible for Joe, and then Joe did the same for Mike. As he squirmed under the fence, Mike felt something skitter across his ankles. His involuntary jump caused the bottom of the fence to poke him sharply in several spots. He gave what he thought was a small startled gasp.

Joe turned back on him and snapped, "Hush."

Mike subsided. He wasn't particularly squeamish about rats. He also didn't want to have one as a best friend. After he was back on his feet, Mike checked himself for possible punctures. He was sure the fence was rusty and feared his skin had been broken. He felt nothing like oozing blood.

They were in back of a small, boarded-up building two doors down from the mansion with the bar entrance.

"No telling how far the bar goes or where the other businesses begin or end," Joe said.

They started back toward the broad and deep factory building. No one challenged them. No dog snarled and lunged. All was quiet and serene, a peaceful oasis in the urban maelstrom. In the distance Mike heard sirens. The urban glow seeped into the darkness at indistinct intervals, leaving patches of lesser gloom amid the deep black.

After negotiating several more chain-link barriers, which Joe had to help him over even though he was in good shape, they arrived at the final obstruction before the factory. The final fence was nearly new. Even in the dim light, it seemed to gleam. None of the windows in the factory were broken out. As far as Mike could see, the thousands of small square panes were totally intact. The ground around the factory had been swept clean. No broken beer bottles, crushed soda cans, used condoms, or other debris marred the surface.

One thing was comfortingly familiar. The bricks on the factory walls were dingy. Even in the dimness, Mike could make out the dirty black and gray smudges that covered most of the surface.

Mike mentioned all this to Joe in a low, quiet voice. The alien paused. "You're right," Joe said. "I don't know what it being this clean means. I really want to see inside."

None of the buildings whose backyards they had passed through gave any hint of access to their insides. The dumpster near the alley in the last business before the factory proved to be what they wanted. "We can move this over," Joe said. "We can climb on it and jump over the fence."

"A six foot drop."

"About that."

"This is breaking and entering."

"Only entering. We haven't broken anything yet. You want to wait here for me?"

"And pigs have wings." Mike stifled any of his other objections. This was the biggest adventure of his life, and he wasn't going to chicken out now.

As they moved the dumpster, the wheels squealed and squeaked. When they ceased moving it, they waited to see if their activity brought any inquires. All remained quiet. After a few moments, Joe scrambled up as Mike held the dumpster in place.

"Who's going to hold this for me?" Mike asked.

"It's pretty stable. Let go."

The dumpster was in a corner of the backyard. The only tree in the alley hung deep shadows over it.

Mike let go. Joe flexed his legs on top several times. "It's fine," Joe said. He took several steps, and then with a graceful jump that would have done an Olympic athlete proud, he leapt over the fence. He landed on his feet, stood, and turned back to Mike.

Mike scaled the side of the dumpster. He stifled thoughts of arrest, prying eyes, dangers, and warnings and scoldings he could imagine from his mother and father. He took several steps and jumped. Joe grabbed his arm, or Mike would have fallen backwards. When he landed, he felt the jar in his ankles and back. Quickly, Joe had his hand in Mike's armpit and was helping him to stand upright.

They rushed across the pavement, Mike's favoring of his ankle costing them precious seconds. Flitting from shadow to shadow around the warehouse was simple, because most of it was in impenetrable darkness.

Every door was securely padlocked. They followed the perimeter around until they arrived at the El tracks. The factory came within a foot or so of the embankment. A feeble light above the tracks cast a checkered glow down on them through the crenellated fence at the top of the embankment. At ten-foot intervals, metal struts which supported the tracks above stuck out from the walls.

"What's that on the second floor?" Joe asked as he surveyed the rear of the building.

"A door that leads nowhere?"

The opening was hard to make out, but it looked as if about fifteen feet above the pavement was a portal which might have, at one time, led to a fire escape. It was within two feet of one of the support pilings for the El tracks at the top of the embankment.

"I'm going to climb this and see what I can see," Joe said. He immediately began to ascend. Across from the door, Joe stopped. He held onto the metal with both legs and one arm and reached out to the former door. Joe quickly climbed back down. "That's no good, but I think I saw something two struts down."

They were completely behind the factory building. The El tracks approached the factory in a curve at this point. Twenty feet down the alien climbed again. As his head reached the level of the train tracks, Mike heard the distant rumble of an El train.

"Get down," Mike urged.

The alien held on. The noise of the train built into an ear-shattering, nerve-snapping rumble. Mike winced and hunched his shoulders. After the train hurtled past, he looked up to see the alien carefully examining a small outcropping.

It took only a few seconds for the alien to quickly scramble back down.

"Damn, that thing is loud," Joe said.

"What did you find?"

"That overhang used to be a wider opening. The boards are loose. We can get in that way."

"Won't we have to put our feet close to the tracks to get in?"

"Yes."

Joe climbed back up. At the top he stood for a few seconds as he hung between building and tracks. His arms outstretched above him rested on the bricks. His feet came within inches of touching the tracks. With a lunge his torso began disappearing into the factory.

Mike felt the cool metal and bits of flaking rust as he climbed. The small bolts and rivets as well as the crossties gave his feet and hands places to hang on. Through the opening he could discern the outline of Joe's body.

Mike looked up and down the curve of the tracks. He could

see only about fifty feet in either direction. Joe held his hands out towards him. Mike rested one hand on the aged factory bricks, fixed his feet carefully on the girder, and began twisting his body. He got both hands on the bricks and began pushing against the top of the embankment with both feet.

He heard the first faint rumbles of a train. His feet began to slip. He lunged forward. If the alien had not been there to catch him, he would probably have fallen to the ground or, worse, backward onto the tracks.

He felt the strong hands on his arms. The light on the front of the train became steadily brighter. The clatter became a roar then a thunder. He scrabbled his feet against the wall and, just as the train passed their location, found himself squirming his torso through the window. By the time the northbound train passed, Mike was on his feet. He looked back to see a face staring out at them from the back of the train. Moments later the face was gone. The never entirely silent night-noise returned.

Luckily the muscles Mike had worked on for years and Joe's assistance had gotten him into the building safely. He also found himself enjoying each time his body touched Joe's. His heightened sensuality might be inappropriate at such moments of danger and dismay, but his body was responding to the tingling warmth of contact with Joe. He liked it. Even more than that, the adventure itself with a hot man was turning him on. Maybe this was part of the lure of an action-adventure hero. Mike thought, "Jason Bourne, here I come." He shook his head. No time now for fantasies to come true.

Thirty

Mike examined his new environment. The urban glow seeped through the nearly opaque windows. As his eyes adjusted to the incomplete darkness, Mike realized they were on a metal walkway that stretched both left and right. The walkway continued to the far walls on either side and then stretched into the distance as far as he could see. The floor below them was starkly empty. At the first corner Mike and Joe came to, they found a set of steps leading to the ground floor.

Mike felt frightened and excited at the same time. He'd on occasion dreamt of violating the law. Certainly he'd never contemplated doing it so deliberately. Navy Pier the other night had been odd. This was illegal with a capital felony. Here he was with a near stranger from another planet outside the bounds of anything he'd experienced before. He wondered at his daring and his willingness to abandon caution. If the alien was controlling his mind to weaken his sense of obedience to the rules, he certainly couldn't feel it. What Mike did feel were his clammy hands and the sweat streaming down from his armpits. Certainly the alien hadn't removed all fear and good sense.

On the ground floor they stopped and reconnoitered.

"Just as clean is it was outside," Joe said. He had his communicator out and was tapping rapidly on the console. "The ship has never been here, nor can I find any definitive traces of either Vov or Zye."

"This is cleaner than the streets of a powerful alderman's ward," Mike commented, "or maybe the owner is anal retentive."

Their footsteps were neither softened by an accumulation of dust nor made harsher by a layer of grit. Without direct light it was difficult to tell, but as far as Mike could observe there was no garbage and debris. No potholes or ridges of cement marred the floor. The feeble light was enough so that they didn't have to grope their way forward. They followed the wall on their left. Their feet made little noise as they eased forward down the length of the building. They found a door in the wall at the far end from where they'd entered. They judged this portal to be closest to the intersecting building which would, with any luck, lead eventually back to the bar.

Mike smelled new wood and varnish. The handle gleamed dully in the dark.

"It's got to be new," Mike said.

"I agree."

Joe put his hand on the handle and turned. The door was not locked. Carefully they peered into this new opening. More silence and a deeper blackness than the factory greeted them.

Mike strained to listen. "I don't hear anything," he whispered.

"Neither do I."

They entered the new building. It must have at one time contained offices. It was as vacant as the factory. However, the light from the street was less evident. The windows had been covered with carefully applied sheets of cardboard. Still, occasional motes of city light escaped into the darkness. Mike saw swirls of dust and tracks of small animals on the floor. An un-dusty path made by occasionally observable footsteps led back toward Balls, Whips, and Chains.

"Are you scared?" Mike whispered as they entered the new room.

"Please don't talk."

For several minutes they paced carefully from room to room until they came to another newly built door. At one point, Mike thought he heard distant shouts. He couldn't tell if they came from the street outside, behind, in front, or even above or below.

Joe paused, and they both listened, but the noise was not repeated. Each building presented its own warren of rooms to ease through. They always chose the way that seemed to head back to the bar. Each new door opened as if it had recently been oiled. This made Mike as wary as anything else. Obviously someone was used to traversing this path. He hoped whoever it was did so in the day time. He could think of no excuse to give to a cop or an owner or a casual stranger about their presence here.

They traversed two more buildings. Mike guessed they were still two or three buildings away from the bar when they heard the noises again. This time they clearly heard shouts and outcries from several different voices through the portal to the building ahead of them.

"What is it?" Mike whispered.

They were in a front hall. Mike and Joe craned their heads to gaze into a front room. Indistinctly through a window covered only with a bed sheet, Mike thought he could make out the pulse of flashing red and blue light. "Cops?" Mike asked.

"I think so. Something odd is going on. Hush."

They listened. Mike thought he heard footsteps rush by on the other side of the door. Silence followed. Joe eased open the connecting door. They were gazing into a deserted bar. No liquor bottles lined the shelves, and the chairs were on top of the tables. Red emergency exit lights lit three doorways, but not the one they peered through. The shouting was more distinct and almost continuous. They entered the room. Joe shut the door. Mike heard a distinct click. Mike felt the handle. Unlike the others, it had locked behind them. He nudged Joe and pointed this out. The alien nodded he understood.

"This must be the way Kyle got in," Mike whispered.

Joe nodded.

As they eased themselves toward one of the exits, a door on the far side of the room suddenly burst open. A man in his early twenties rushed into the room. He was dressed in a thong and a baseball cap.

He saw them. "Cops!" he shouted. "They're raiding the place. Everybody's being arrested. Run!" He began to bolt toward the other side of the room.

The alien grabbed the newcomer by the arm.

"Are you cops?" the young man asked.

"No," Joe said.

"Then let me go. I've got to get out of here. No one knows I'm gay. No one knows I'm a dancer. I'll get fired from my teaching job. Let me go."

"Is there an exit this way?"

"I don't care. The cops are back that way. I'm going to find a way out if I have to crawl through the sewers. Let me go." With a wrench he freed himself from the alien's grasp and ran. They heard doors slamming.

"He could just be going in circles," Mike said.

"I hope not. Why would the police raid this bar?"

"You want the long or short explanation of police and raiding gay bars?"

"How about short for now and then you can do longer at our leisure?"

"Raiding gay bars is a nasty tradition that goes back many years. Political and moral imperatives of the ignorant and bigoted sometimes overcome good sense."

"Sounds like the history of the world."

"Yours or mine?" Mike asked.

"Both."

"We don't want to get caught in the bar raid. If the other alien is here, what would he do?"

"If Vov and Zye are looking for each other, it would be paramount in their minds. They'd be less worried about trying to get the hell out."

"Why would Vov be looking for the bounty hunter?"

"Zye would probably be a bigger threat to him than me. I can bring him back dead or alive. The bounty hunter would just go with dead. Vov would perceive Zye as a threat and want to neutralize him."

The next rooms they found themselves in were storage rooms with mountains of beer cases piled nearly to the ceiling. The last one had a set of steps down and no other exit. They trudged warily down. The door at the bottom of the steps opened into vast darkness. Mike thought he could make out a bare bulb dimly shining some fifty feet away.

Joe said, "I think this is a far end of the basement area where we found Howard."

"Are you sure?"

"No."

They eased toward the light. The bulb glowed at the intersection of three hallways.

"Which way?" Mike asked.

"Who's there?" called a voice that trembled. Five men dressed in leather appeared from around a corner.

"We aren't cops," Mike said.

"We're lost down here," a man with a goatee said. "We've got to get out. Everybody upstairs is being arrested."

"Are there any more people down here?" Joe asked.

"We left a group about thirty feet back that way at the bottom of some stairs. This place is immense." Moments later they heard a number of voices and the shuffling of feet. Their small group retreated down a corridor and into a tiny room. Seconds later a much larger group of men appeared and the two groups of men crowded together.

"How many cops are there?" Joe asked.

"The place is swarming. Cops in uniforms, plain clothes. It's worse than anything I've ever read about happening in Chicago."

"Anybody know a way out?"

Joe nodded. "Mike, will you take them to the empty bar room? Break the door down if you have to. You can lead them out from there. I'll find you."

"Shouldn't you come back with us?"

"I've got to check this out."

"Who's down here?" shouted a stern voice. Moments later they heard the same voice say, "Get me some light and some more men."

The alien shoved his hand into his pocket and then held it out to Mike. "Here, take this."

"What?" Mike began. It looked like the alien's communicator.

"No time now," Joe said. "Hurry." He slipped the communicator into the front pocket of Mike's jeans.

Reluctantly, Mike led the group of about twenty men back the way he'd come. Up the stairs and through the storage rooms, they hurried. The door to the factory was still very locked.

"What good is this?" one man asked.

Mike explained. "It's a way out, through the empty buildings down the street from the bar."

"Not if it's locked," one said.

Two well muscled men picked up a barstool and rushed toward the door. The barstool splintered and large cracks appeared in the door. Quickly several men seized another ersatz battering ram.

"Follow the dustless path," Mike told the man in the goatee. "Find an opening in a building at a great distance from this one and get out."

At the fourth assault the door splintered into pieces. The men rushed through. The man in the goatee said, "Aren't you coming with us?"

"I'm going back for my friend," Mike told him.

"Good luck." The man in the goatee followed the retreating figures.

Mike retraced his steps through the rooms to the stairway. At least he had a sure way out if he found the cops too close. He heard neither voices nor the sound of moving bodies. He crept down. Through the portal at the bottom, he could still see the bare light bulb. Then he saw flashlights. He heard a high-pitched voice say, "I don't care how dark it is down here. We've got orders. A foot-by-foot search, we've got to find all of them."

"What for?"

"Just do it."

Then Mike heard footsteps at the top of the stairs behind him.

Trapped.

Thirty-one

Mike didn't dare wait to see if the men approaching were friend or foe. He eased into the darkness away from the flashlights. He moved right with one hand on the wall for a guide, more careful than a heart surgeon attempting his first transplant. He didn't want to trip and fall and make the slightest noise.

The wall was not continuous and even. Rooms opened off from it. He kept his hand touching the walls as he maneuvered through the maze. Quickly, he lost his sense of direction.

He'd been in the maze at least fifteen minutes when the voices became more distant and the flashlights beams became less frequent. His hand touched wood, which turned out to be the bottom of a set of steps. These hugged the wall and so could not have been the ones where they found Howard.

Suddenly a flashlight beam appeared twenty feet to his right and began probing toward him. He leapt for the stairs.

"Halt!" ordered a voice.

Mike scrambled forward. When he was half way up, the beam caught him.

"Halt!"

Mike raced up the stairs and flew through the door above. He was in a dark corridor. He turned right. Dim red light shone, and he suspected he was in part of the bar proper. He also thought he caught a whiff of smoke. He swung open the first door he came to and leapt inside. He was at the bottom of a stairwell. He wasn't sure he wanted to be above ground level with cops below him and possibly above him. He didn't want to stay in the same place either, when the door could burst open any moment and reveal him. As he rushed up this new flight of stairs, he regretted not following the other men out of the complex. He heard nothing behind him. The next door he eased open, revealed the bar that the women had been dancing in. It was completely deserted. It was also oppressively warm.

"Fire," he heard someone shout.

For the first time, Mike heard wailing sirens near at hand. Several more wisps of smoke entered the room. A man wearing only a bikini bathing suit rushed into the room. He had been one of the dancers on the bar the other day.

"The place is on fire!" the newcomer shouted. "I think the cops torched the place."

"Which part of the bar is on fire?"

"A lot of the ground floor."

"Let's try the roof," Mike said. He remembered vague advice about always climbing to the top. He thought maybe this was if you were stuck in a high-rise fire. He didn't care now. Down was not an option.

"Which way?" Mike asked.

"I don't know," the dancer said.

"Let's try this way." Mike led the man as best he could back the way they had gone when they were here with Darryl. They managed to get to the floor with the bar with the sky-lights.

Mike saw licks of flame back the way they'd come.

"Jesus, we're going to die!"

"Not yet, we're not," Mike answered. "Come on." There were two exit signs. The first one led down into heat and flickering light. The second led upward. They climbed the steps. Mike wondered if Joe were still in the building. He was worried for himself but found his concern for the alien much larger than he expected. He had no time to sort out his feelings. He felt the communicator in his pocket. Not knowing what magical, mystical, or technological power it contained, he had little desire to touch it. Nevertheless, it comforted him.

At the next landing, they met two men wearing tight blue jeans and flannel shirts with the sleeves cut off. Their faces were smudged with soot.

They were headed the way Mike had just come from. "Not that way," Mike said.

"We just came up from the other way."

"Is there another choice?"

The nearly naked dancer whimpered. "I'm going to die."

"Be still," Mike commanded. "Is there a way to the roof?"

"We used to have parties up there," one of the men said.

"Where's the entrance?" Mike asked.

"This way."

Ten feet down the corridor, he swung open a door. Steps led up to a locked door. Mike and the two blue-jeaned men braced themselves to batter at it with their feet. After the first few times, they coordinated their efforts. Quickly, the door began to be loosened. "One more," Mike said.

Suddenly, the knob fell off, and the door burst open. They were greeted by a chaos of lights and sound pulsing in the night sky. About thirty feet away bits of flames and puffs of smoke escaped through gaps in the roof. In the opposite direction a group of six people were lowering themselves one by one down the spiral staircase that led to the back garden. The staircase now served as their only escape from the fire.

Sirens screeched from every direction. Voices screamed and shouted. The roof was flat in spots and in others was pitched at different angles.

Mike had to lean forward to keep his balance, sometimes stooping over and using his hands to guide himself to the edge. He joined the group at the staircase, and looked over the side. Flames were spilling out of the windows in the path the fire escape took down. The next man in line, the dancer in the bikini, hesitated at the top. Several people urged him forward.

"I'll burn if I go this way."

Others shouted for him to get out of the way.

Mike looked back. Through a doorway he saw the alien

emerge. Joe had his arm around a blue uniformed cop, leading him to safety. Mike shouted at him and hurried forward.

Mike saw Joe let go of the cop who immediately sagged to the ground. Joe turned to go back into the building.

"Stop!" Mike yelled.

Joe gave him a quick grin then disappeared back inside. Smoke poured out of the opening. Joe reappeared in moments propping up another cop. He laid the second one down next to the first.

"Are you okay?" Mike asked.

"Fine. Are you?"

"Not yet. Can your technology save us?"

"Actually it's the smoke that would probably do us in, and I can't stop that. The technology helped me find you." He touched the communicator in Mike's pocket. "This is a spare. I wanted to be able to find you."

Mike looked at the cops. Each was young, maybe a day or two out of the academy. Both were severely burned around the legs. Their uniform pants were gone below the knee, and their wounds blistered up and down their calves. "Why'd you save them?"

"They were hurt. I cannot let a human die if I can help it."

"Even if you and I die?"

"We aren't going to die. I hope."

Together they moved the cops toward the edge of the roof. Four people were gathered at the top of the fire escape. The dancer was nowhere to be found. He must have gone down the staircase. Mike looked over the edge. About halfway down, flames from three windows completely engulfed the metal. Mike placed his hand on the railing. He removed it immediately from the scorching heat.

Mike realized there was no possible way to get down short of rescue or jumping. In the street he saw numerous engine and truck companies. Two ladders were already extending toward the roof. Water from numerous hoses cascaded toward the building.

Mike wondered if they'd make it before the fire reached them. Only so many people could fit on a ladder at a time, and they were four stories from the ground.

"Can you just stop the fire?" Mike whispered.

"No. We're going to be fine. Look."

A ladder reached the roof five feet from where they were. Two firemen began scrambling up toward them. Mike watched the tops of their hats get quickly larger as they neared the top of the ladder. Thirty seconds later the first rescuer reached the top and leapt onto the roof. "Anybody hurt?" he asked.

"Here," Joe said. He pointed to the cops.

The fireman pulled out a hand radio. "I've got two injured up here. Get another ladder in this vicinity."

The second fireman reached the roof. He briefly consulted with his partner. He turned to the small assemblage. "You're going to be fine. We're going to carry down the injured people. You're going to follow us one by one. The other ladder will be here in a few seconds, and we'll be able to go even faster."

The second fireman took one of the unconscious cops and disappeared down the ladder. The other helped each person begin his descent. The other ladder arrived. Two more firemen appeared. One immediately took hold of the other cop and started back down. Mike and Joe were the last two civilians left on the roof.

Mike put a hand on the tar. "It's starting to get warm."

"We're safe," Joe said.

When it was their turn to climb down, the fireman explained, "Put one hand here, the other here, swing your legs over, and ease yourself down. Anybody afraid of heights?"

They shook their heads, no.

"Good. Let's go, I'll be right behind you."

The alien leaned over and kissed Mike on the lips. Mike felt an unexpected erotic jolt. The danger dampened his desire, but he was willing to pursue the feeling as soon as he could.

Mike reached for the ladder as he had been instructed.

The climb was more harrowing than he expected. The distance from the ground surprised him. About halfway down he looked back up to where Joe was descending. Then Mike glanced back between his feet at the waiting rescuers.

"Don't stop!" someone shouted.

Mike felt his sense of equilibrium become shaky. He gripped the ladder tightly. He glanced up at the night sky.

Joe called to him, "You okay?"

Mike nodded. He resumed his descent. Occasionally, he caught glimpses of the crowd across the street being kept back behind barricades. He saw squadrols -- the Chicago version of the old paddy wagon -- and squad cars and fire trucks filling the entire block.

At the bottom of the stairs he saw several police officers. Could this be some of those from the raid? Was he risking arrest when he got to the bottom?

A loud, creaking groan split the night and thirty feet away part of the wall collapsed. Flames burst into the night, and the police officers below rushed toward this new disaster.

When Mike was ten feet from the street, he saw that one of the squadrols was on its side and in flames. He wondered how it had gotten caught in the fire. He scrambled quickly down the rest of the way. Joe followed moments later.

THIRTY-TWO

Firemen led them down the street. Halfway down the block they found both of the cops Joe had rescued. They were on stretchers. One was being loaded onto an ambulance while the other waited. Each had an oxygen mask over his face. The one still waiting was conscious. He spotted them and waved them over.

The young cop took off his oxygen mask. He gasped, "You saved my life. Thanks."

A paramedic replaced the breathing apparatus. "Time for that later."

Seconds later a man in a leather vest hurried up to them. "Come on you two. They're still trying to arrest people if they can catch them."

"We just got down."

"Don't argue. That's how they're proving who was inside. If they weren't busy trying to control the crowd, you'd probably have been arrested already." After he and Joe took a few steps to get away, the guy in leather moved to the next group.

The cop was rushed into the ambulance. As it started to pull away, Mike got a good look at the crowd for the first time. These weren't spectators at a fire. Hundreds of angry people were throwing rocks and bricks at any cop they saw. Behind the crowd, Mike observed a squad car being rocked by ten or so men. Suddenly one of its windows was smashed and moments later it burst into flame. The crowd cheered. Mike saw pieces of pavement whistle toward an approaching squad car. Nothing was thrown at the firemen. The crowd's wrath was directed toward the cops.

Between houses and down alleys, Mike saw other groups of men and women. There must have been over a thousand people in the immediate vicinity, and more were arriving every minute.

Mike spotted Hugo and Meganvilia among the mob. Hugo wore his work outfit: too-tight black jeans and T-shirt. Meganvilia was in a dark blue evening gown covered by a purple cape. Mike pointed them out to the alien. Others in the crowd looked like they'd been out at clubs, some as if they'd just been dragged out of bed. Mike and Joe hurried toward Hugo and Meganvilia.

"What the hell is going on?" Mike asked.

"Were you inside?" Meganvilia inquired.

"Yes."

Meganvilia pulled him close and crushed him in a very masculine embrace. She unclutched slightly and looked him in the eye. "Are you all right?" she asked.

"I think so."

The drag queen stepped back a pace and eyed them both carefully. "You're a little dirty, but you're breathing. Do you know what happened?"

"I'm not sure," Mike said. "It was a bar raid, and then the place caught fire. I don't know how it started. Were you guys inside?"

"I wasn't," Hugo said, "but word is flashing through the community. The cops raided the bar. No reason, no excuse, no warrant. There must have been hundreds of people inside. I heard the first ones they tried to drag away were some lesbian socialists. They started to fight back. Things got out of hand fast, and now everybody in the community is rushing here."

"I got here only a few minutes ago," Meganvilia said. "I walked all the way around the crowd from here up to Montrose. The action on this side is nothing." He pointed at the still smoldering squadrol. "At least we got one. The big crowd is just south of Cullom Avenue. I saw at least a couple thousand angry queers doing battle."

"How'd the fire start?" Joe asked.

"I heard it was the cops," Hugo said.

Meganvilia spoke up, "Some people said it was an accident.

The place was a fire trap. From the first alarm guys were madly scrambling to get away."

Above the noise of sirens, Mike heard a chant from down the street. Soon everyone in the crowd was shouting, "Stonewall! Stonewall!"

Hugo poked Mike and sidled up to Joe. "Introduce me."

Mike performed quick introductions. Joe eased himself away from Hugo and put his arm around Mike.

"Was anybody trapped in the fire?" Mike asked them.

Meganvilia said, "I saw you coming down from the roof. You might have been the last ones out."

"We won't know about anyone trapped until they put out the fire," Hugo said. "If anyone died, it's because the cops killed them." The crowd surged around them. A knot of uniformed officers huddled together about half way down the block. There were three abandoned cop cars between them and where Mike watched. Toward the bar, Mike could see firemen moving hoses, spraying water, pointing. He could not hear their shouts.

The chant of "Stonewall" faded away for a few moments then started up again.

Mike and Joe said "Goodbye" to Hugo and Meganvilia and maneuvered their way through the crowd. Before they left the mob, Mike saw a man nearby pick up a piece of pavement loose on the ground. Across the street was a cop car. The man heaved the missile toward the vehicle. It hit and shattered the windshield. Several cops from the group down the block started in their direction, but the crowd was too big for so few cops. The police retreated. A Molotov cocktail flew through the air, rolled under the car, and, seconds later, burst into flames. An instant after that the car itself caught fire.

"What'd he do that for?" Joe asked.

"History."

"You'll need to explain that sometime. Let's get out of here."

They threaded their way between buildings and quickly

distanced themselves from the chaos and noise. Several streets away they saw a group of mounted policemen arriving. Mike and Joe ducked down an alley out of the light. Fifteen minutes later they were sitting close together on a bus bench on Lincoln Avenue waiting to return to the Luxor.

"Did you see Vov?" Mike asked.

"No, but he was there at some time this evening. My communicator found remnants of what you would call his DNA in several rooms."

"The empty warehouse was odd," Mike said.

"Yeah, it would be a perfect place for him to set up a laboratory, if he was daring enough to do so in town. I was expecting a more remote location."

"His stuff isn't there yet," Mike pointed out. "Maybe it was something for the future."

"Or it had absolutely nothing to do with him." The alien sighed.

"Did he set the fire?" Mike asked.

"I don't know," Joe said. "He may have."

"Why?"

"There is something odd about that place."

"I didn't mean why there; I meant why would he bother to set the fire at all. What is Vov trying to accomplish?"

"What do you mean?"

"When we first talked he was an escaped criminal."

"He is."

"Yeah, but he's doing a lot more stuff than just being a crazy criminal. Why burn stuff down?"

"I'm not sure. Maybe he wanted someone in there to die."

"He'd risk all those other people dying just to kill one person?"

"Vov would probably sacrifice the population of your entire planet if it served his purposes."

"He's a demonic, mad shit."

"Pretty much, or he wanted to destroy evidence of his existence, cover his tracks so I couldn't track him." Joe shrugged. "Sorry I don't have better answers."

"This is scary," Mike said. "Does he want to enslave the planet?"

"I doubt it."

"But why Earth?"

"Beg pardon?"

"What's he doing here? Does he need Earth materials?"

"He's a genius. Who knows what he could create mixing Earth and Hrrrm materials?"

"What did we ever do to him?"

"Are you asking or whining?"

Mike persisted. "What's he want here he can't have elsewhere?"

Joe sighed. "There are several reasons he might have chosen Earth." A few cars meandered by as their occupants spent their lives oblivious to an inter-galactic intrigue on the bus bench on the corner.

"What?" Mike asked.

"Well, you're out of the way. You're backward in all the important ways. No one in my home system would care much about this solar system. Plus, if he needed minions, he might think it would be easy to gain allies here or at least people easy to bend to his will. Your species has a history of being amenable to killing each other, quite cheerfully and brutally for that matter."

"And your people aren't?"

"You want to hear this, or you want to pick on all the species in the galaxy?"

"Let me get back to you on that." Mike watched the shadows of dawn creep across the pavement and storefronts. He turned to Joe. "Ultimately, what's he out for?"

"Himself. In all likelihood, he's trying to build himself a powerful enough ship with enough weapons to have an impact in other parts of the galaxy."

"One ship could do that much damage?"

"He could set himself up as a bounty-hunter or pirate on a distant world. He could do recruiting in my part of the galaxy, as I suspect he is doing here on Earth. He can't do all this stuff alone. He's got to have humans around to do the barge toting and bale lifting."

"Aren't your people afraid of his doing such recruiting?"

"No. Could he build a ship capable of breaking through the power grid on a single planet? Probably. He wouldn't be able to take over a whole star system, but he'd be able to recruit enough likeminded people from my world to take over and successfully defend a small planet in a remote corner of the universe."

"Like Earth."

"You guys would be beneath him, but he'd be happy to use you, so yeah, Earth and its population would do."

They sat in silence for several minutes. "You saved those cops," Mike said.

"I told you; I couldn't let them die. I wish I could say it was something noble, but that's my training."

"What if I hadn't found my way out?"

"The communicator would have led me to you. I would not have let you die and not just because of my training."

"You kissed me."

"I know."

"I liked it."

"I'm glad."

"When the fire started," Mike said, "I was afraid you wouldn't get out."

"Why did you come back?"

"I was worried about you."

"Thanks."

"I know you can take care of yourself without my help, but still, I've seen you damaged. Could your technology have put out the fire?"

"With the power on my ship, probably. Without it by the time I mastered the technology of rearranging the miniscule bits inside the atoms, most of the city could have burned. It would probably be easier to move a planet out of orbit."

"Can you move a planet out of orbit?"

"On a really good day, I can maybe move a small moon."

On the bus they sat together. Mike felt comfortable with their legs and shoulders touching in the narrow seat. The warmth and tingle gave him gentle comfort. Several people stared at them in the early morning dimness. He and the alien both smelled of smoke. Mike caught a glimpse of himself and the alien in the mirror above the driver. Their hair was askew, their clothes wildly rumpled, their faces streaked with sweat, soot, and dirt.

"What was all that about Stonewall?" Joe asked.

Mike explained about the significant moment in gay history. "There's a great movie about it called *Stonewall*. We can rent it."

Mike shut his eyes and leaned back against the bus seat. The uncomfortable metal and plastic felt almost soothing in its ordinariness. He reached over and clasped Joe's hand. Their fingers entwined. Without opening his eyes he asked, "How late is it?"

"It's got to be near six in the morning."

"I need some sleep." Mike felt his eyes drooping. In the lobby of the Luxor fifteen or twenty people were chattering animatedly. When Mike and Joe were spotted, the group rushed toward them. The questions were rapid fire, "Were you there? What happened? What did you see?"

Mike and Joe gave brief answers. It turned out a few in the crowd had been in the initial rush to see what was going on.

Mostly they were trading in rumors. Several claimed "the whole north side was burning down."

Except for the area immediately around the bar, Mike had found the streets mostly quiet and deserted. He assured them that the north side was intact.

On the walk up the stairs, they still held hands. Part of him would prefer to sleep for a week. He'd never been this physically and emotionally exhausted, but Mike thought a great deal about the alien's kiss and he very much wanted it to happen again.

Sleeping with Joe would be an excellent cap to the day, but he was hesitant about suggesting it. He remembered the alien's taboo about having sex with an earthling. He did not want to be rejected, either. When their hands unclasped, he felt a loss. The alien simply walked to his alcove and sat down. Even if he wasn't human, Joe looked as exhausted as Mike felt.

Mike felt the communicator in his pocket, took it out, and turned back. "What is this thing really?" he asked.

"A marvelous magical device." Joe smiled. "It doesn't do laundry, maid service, or windows. After that, it's pretty versatile." Joe took one out of his pocket. "Mine is a prototype which supposedly has more power than any other model manufactured. I haven't been able to prove that yet. Yours is an obsolete model. Not good for much anymore."

Mike held his out to Joe. "You'll need it back."

"I've got mine. Why don't you keep it?" Joe said. "It might come in handy."

"You sure? I won't accidentally vaporize the planet?"

Joe smiled. "No, but hang on to it -- that way I'll never be able to lose you."

Mike nodded and smiled and went to bed.

THIRTY-THREE

Mike awoke after less than four hours of sleep. He showered and once again found the alien perched in the alcove overlooking the brick building next door.

Joe had a bottle of orange juice and two glasses in front of him. He poured one for Mike and handed it to him.

"Is there news?" Mike asked.

"The television isn't working."

Mike called his answering machine. Numerous friends had phoned to exchange news about what had happened. There was a second reminder from Mrs. Benson asking him to call first thing in the morning. He also had several urgent messages from his mother. Mike called her first.

"Jack is missing and your sister is frantic. She went to get him up for school, and he was gone. His bed hadn't been slept in."

"I'm not sure how I can help," Mike said.

"Did he say anything to you Saturday?"

"No."

"Rosemary called Lennon Kazakel, her creepy ex. She told him Jack was gone. She said he went crazy. He threatened her. I'm worried about what he might do."

"Why did she even call the creep?"

"She thought Jack might have gone there."

"Right. We can't let him find Jack," Mike said. "What are the police doing?"

"Not much, I'm sure. He's just another runaway to them."

Mike spoke as reassuringly as he could. He hung up and then dialed his landlady.

"Are you all right?" Mrs. Benson asked immediately.

"Yes."

"I thought I recognized you on television. I couldn't be sure. It was a distant shot of people climbing down a ladder from the roof of that bar."

"It was me, Mrs. Benson."

"You sure you're all right?"

"I'm fine, thanks. What have you seen on the news?"

Mrs. Benson was a news junky -- everything from MSNBC to CNN to the local all-news station were her constant companions.

"The mayor was on all the news shows. Representatives from the gay community made statements. It sounded like people are pretty angry about this bar raid. At the moment they don't believe anyone was killed in the fire. A couple of cops were rescued by a patron in the bar. Several people were hurt in the riot that followed. The fire is out, and they're sifting through the rubble for anyone who was trapped. Almost that whole side of the block went up in flames. What were you doing up on that roof? Do your parents know you were there?"

"I'll tell you the whole story, Mrs. Benson, but not right now. You've been leaving messages on my machine."

"Yes. You have a visitor."

Mrs. Benson was not likely to play nursemaid to any of Mike's ex-lovers.

She continued, "Your nephew Jack is here."

"What?"

The phone was silent for several moments. Then Mike heard his nephew's voice. "Uncle Mike? I need some help. Can I stay with you?"

"Sure," Mike said. He halted. The kid didn't need to hear any kind of hesitation. "Put Mrs. Benson back on the line. We'll come get you." He put his hand over the receiver and explained to Joe.

"We can't go to your place to get him," Joe said.

"I know."

Mrs. Benson came back on the line.

"Can we meet you and Jack someplace? It's complicated, but I don't want to come home if I can avoid it."

"If it's to help you, it isn't a problem," she said.

They agreed to meet at the corner of Halsted and Belmont. Mike called his parents and gave them the news.

"Thank God," his mother said. "I'll call your sister and tell her he's all right. She'll have to call the police and tell them. When will you bring him home?"

"I'm not sure what's going on or why he ran away," Mike said. "I'll let you know after I've met with him."

After he hung up, he called Skipper. His friend had the list of numbers he was looking for.

"It's a long list," Skipper said. "I didn't know what you were looking for specifically, so I got everything. I think they might have been on to me after a while. I covered my tracks well, but someone might know that this number's records were tampered with. Sorry about that."

"It's okay. When can we come pick them up?"

"Any time this morning at work. You heard about the riot outside of Balls, Whips, and Chains?"

"Yeah, we were there."

"Wow! You'll have to tell me about it. It's a miracle everybody got out alive."

"Yeah."

Mike hung up and looked at the alien. "Did you have anything to do with no one dying in that fire?"

"I did what I physically could. I am not Superman."

"You may not have power yourself, but your little magic dingus sure does."

"Didn't we have this conversation already?"

"Does Vov or Zye have one of those?"

"This is more advanced than anything either of them could possibly have. Like I said, this is an experimental model. I was trained on it before I left. If he got hold of one of these and learned how to use it, I would be in deep trouble, as would your planet."

They walked north on Halsted Street past trendy art galleries and over-priced clothing boutiques. The morning air was pleasant, still warm for late September. A layer of wispy, gray, high clouds covered the sky. Mike bought a *Sun-Times* at a news stand. The fire and riot had happened too late to make the morning editions of the paper.

People and traffic passed on the streets as if it were a normal day. There didn't seem to be any more or fewer police on the streets. No one eyed them suspiciously.

Mrs. Benson and Jack were waiting for them on the corner. Mrs. Benson wore her summer house dress, pure white with bright yellow daisies dancing throughout the fabric. Jack had his usual scowl on this face. He carried a black backpack, the zipper dangling half off, deep rents and tears on the back. His jeans drooped on his hips, revealing red boxer shorts only slightly covered by his too short black T-shirt.

"Nice boy," Mrs. Benson commented.

Mike refrained from raising his eyebrow.

"Hi, Uncle Mike, Joe." Joe's return greeting was grave but friendly.

"Have you eaten?" Mike asked.

"I made him a little breakfast," Mrs. Benson said.

"It was great," Jack said. "She made everything from scratch. My mom and dad only ever open packages."

"I have errands to run," Mrs. Benson said. "We'll talk later."

"Thanks for helping." Mrs. Benson strode purposefully down the street.

Mike noticed that Jack stood near the alien. The boy looked from one to the other of them.

"We haven't eaten," Mike said. "Why don't you come with us?"

"Sure."

Jack fell in step between them. They walked to Ann Sather's restaurant. It wasn't crowded at this hour on a Monday. They sat in front at a table for four.

"Can I have coffee, Uncle Mike?" Jack asked.

Mike had no idea what the correct parental thing was to say about coffee. He didn't much care if the kid drank it.

"Sure," Mike said.

After they ordered, Jack looked everywhere but at them.

"You ran away," Joe said.

Jack's eyes came to rest on Joe's. "Yeah."

"Do you want to tell us why?"

Jack seemed to close in on himself. He became very still. Mike stifled an impulse to ask about the boy's dad.

They waited quietly. Joe's eyes never wavered from looking at Jack.

Finally, Jack said, "I couldn't take my mom anymore."

"What happened?" Joe asked.

"She just doesn't get it." Silence again. "I won't go back to her. You can't make me."

"Nobody is going to make you do anything for the moment," Mike said. "We're just trying to understand and help as best we can."

The familiar teenage whine crept into his voice. "Usually nobody wants to hear my side of things."

The two men waited.

Jack took a sip of his coffee, made a face. Mike moved sugar and cream nearer to him. "My dad lets me get coffee when we're traveling together."

Mike nodded. More silence. Their food arrived. More silence.

Mike and Joe concentrated on eating. Jack said, "Gay people molest little kids."

"Who told you that?" Mike asked.

"Everybody knows it."

Mike explained, "If you look at statistics and studies, you'd see that most molestations are done by straight men who are familiar with the victim, usually a relative. I can go on-line or to the library with you and show you the studies if you want."

"That's okay." He hesitated, looked from one to the other of them, looked down, muttered, "You never tried nothin'." He waited another few moments. Mike didn't interrupt his reverie. When the boy finally looked up, he said, "I guess I believe you."

"What happened last night?" Joe asked.

Jack gave a world weary sigh. "My mom and I were fighting about me going out with my friends. We always wind up fighting about it. Then she started hassling me about cleaning my room. I wanted to play computer games. Since you showed me that one, I've been working on it for hours. I've beaten it a couple times. I've been calling all my friends. It is so cool. She wanted me to stop playing and do work. She threatened to send me to my dad's. I told her I was never going there again. Then she hassled me about that, asking me questions for over an hour."

Jack pointed at the alien. "I guess she got really mad when I said you were the only one who was nice to me. She hit me then. I probably deserved it, but she hasn't hit me in years, since I was little. It surprised me. I had such a good time with you. I wanted those feelings again. I ran out of the house. I know I shouldn't have."

"How'd you get to the city?"

"I went to a friend's house, but he wasn't home. I know where you live, Uncle Mike. I go to the city more than my mom knows. I take public transportation all the time, and I have friends who are old enough to drive. We go to concerts sometimes."

He gave them a guilty look. "Are you going to tell her all this stuff?"

"We won't tell her what you don't want us to," Joe said. Mike nodded.

Silence descended again. Throughout most of the conversation Jack looked at the alien. Mike wondered if he should leave, but he got no sign from either of them. If leaving would help Jack to talk, Mike was willing to go.

The waitress filled their coffee cups and took away Mike and Joe's empty plates.

"Why won't you go to your dad's?" Joe asked.

Jack got misty eyed. Finally he said, "I'm scared," and stopped.

"Of what?" Joe asked.

"My dad."

"Why?" Joe asked.

Jack stopped looking at the alien and stared out at the street. His body was completely still. He barely did more than blink for five minutes. Abruptly he started to cry. Joe put his hand on top of Jack's and leaned closer to him. Mike had never thought to see his snarling and sneering nephew in this state. What happened next was even more startling.

Suddenly Jack was out of his chair and flinging his arms around Joe and burying his head in Joe's shirt front. Jack began sobbing and talking at the same time. The words were difficult to make out, but as Jack cried, Mike heard him say over and over again, "He hurts me." Joe's arms encircled the boy protectively and held him tightly. At no time did Joe look up to see if anyone was watching. He concentrated his full attention on the boy.

The waitress came over and asked softly, "Is he all right? Can I do anything?"

"He's going to be fine, now, I hope," Mike said.

When the crying subsided, Mike placed several napkins in Joe's hands. He passed them to Jack who used them to wipe his nose.

"I don't want him to ever hurt me again," Jack whispered.

Joe used one hand to caress the back of the boy's head. "We'll never let him hurt you," Joe promised.

Jack pulled in a deep breath. He shook himself slightly, but he did not leave the protection of the arms around him. He looked up at Joe. "Are you going to make me go back?"

"No," Joe said.

Mike said nothing, but he wasn't sure Joe should make such a strong promise. He knew Rosemary would be pissed. She might be an incompetent mother, but she became very protective of her rights if she felt they were threatened. He didn't see how they would be able to care for Jack as they ran around on the alien's quest.

Finally, Joe eased Jack back into his seat. Joe moved his chair so he could keep an arm around Jack's shoulder. The boy was breathing easier with only intermittent snuffles interrupting his words.

"What's going to happen to me?" Jack asked.

"If we're going to stop your dad from hurting you, we need to know more," Joe said, "but we're not going to make you tell us anything you don't want to. You've told us enough that we can begin a few things. The more you tell us, the easier it will be."

Jack nodded. He hung his head. The alien patted his shoulder and squeezed it. Mike heard Jack mutter, "He touches me." He paused. "He touches me...down there." Jack nodded toward his crotch. His whole story spilled out changing from angry mumbles at the beginning to steely fury by the end.

When he paused and seemed to have finished, Mike said, "I'm so, so sorry. We will never, never let it happen again."

Jack met his eyes. The boy nodded. "Okay."

Mike said, "Jack, part of stopping this is making calls to officials. Your dad will go to jail."

"I hope he dies."

This was enough for Mike. He pulled out his cell phone. He called his lawyer and told him the situation and what Jack had said.

David said, "I'll have the son of a bitch arrested as soon as possible. You going to handle the family stuff?"

"Yes." He gave David as much information as he had about Jack's father's movements, place of work, and residence.

"Won't be hard to find," David said. "Good luck with your family."

Mike stepped away from the table and called his mother. He gave a brief outline of what Jack had told them and of what he had put in motion in terms of arresting the father.

His mother rallied around instantly. "I'll call Rosemary. She was angry when I told her where he was, and she wanted you to bring him back. This should put a crimp in her style." His mother didn't waste words excoriating her former son-in-law. "Anything I can do?"

"We'll probably keep him for at least today. He's pretty vulnerable."

Mike had no idea where they would take him. Certainly they couldn't bring him to the Luxor. Two adults in that place were one thing. A minor who was in crisis was impossible.

His mom said, "Your father and I will back up any decision you make. The police will move today?"

"Yes."

"Don't worry about your sister. She might not always be connecting with reality, but this is the limit. This is the worst that could be happening. Good luck with Jack. Thank God, you were able to help him."

"It was Joe more than me," Mike said.

"He sounds pretty special."

"He is."

Back at the table Jack was giving Joe a brief smile. Mike patted

Jack's shoulder. "Saying all that stuff was really brave."

"Thanks, Uncle Mike."

Mike paused and placed his hand on Joe's shoulder as he walked behind him. Joe reached and patted the hand. Jack watched the movement.

"Are you guys like a couple?" Jack asked.

"We're good friends," Joe said.

Jack nodded.

"I made some calls," Mike said. "Your dad is going to be arrested. You're going to have to talk to the police."

Jack nodded. "That's what Joe said. I guess I'm ready."

"Do you want me to call your counselor at school?" Mike asked.

"Maybe. I don't know yet."

"We'll take it slow," Mike said. "The police will be enough for now. My lawyer will call my cell phone."

Joe said, "We have some errands to run. Would you like to come with us?"

"Yeah, cool."

Mike gave Joe a surprised look, but he did not object. It was the alien's investigation. If it was okay with him to have an earthling nephew along, he wasn't going to disagree.

Jack excused himself to go to the washroom.

"You were magnificent," Mike said.

"Thanks. He's got a rough road ahead of him."

"I don't want to leave him on his own. We're really taking him with us? I'd be willing to stay with him, and you could talk to people. He's emotionally vulnerable right now. I hate to risk anything going wrong."

"I need you with me. I don't want to leave him either. I hate to not be with him, but we've got to follow up whatever we can as quickly as we can."

Mike said, "If necessary maybe we could ask Mrs. Benson if she'd watch him."

"We'll think of something. We've got to meet Skipper pretty soon."

Mike groaned. "I said we'd meet him at his place of employment."

"Is that a problem?"

"It's a whorehouse."

Joe laughed. "The kid's having more adventures than he bargained for."

"I'm responsible for him. What if my family finds out I took him there?"

"Are you going to tell them?"

"No, but Jack's a smart kid, he could figure it out."

"Are you objecting morally, ethically, or logistically?"

"I guess it wouldn't be awful. I've been inside. It looks more like the interior of a Boston bank than anything else. On average the Luxor is far more risqué."

"You've been inside?"

"To meet Skipper."

Joe grinned at him.

"So, I was curious. I've never needed to pay for sex. Never wanted to, either. Besides, at this hour of the day we're not likely to run into anything more salacious than a naked statue."

Jack returned. He'd washed his face. They paid their bill and left.

THIRTY-FOUR

They took a cab to the whorehouse on LaSalle Street just north of Chicago Avenue. From the outside it looked like a normal townhouse. Mike didn't want to go through long explanations with Jack. He knew they weren't taking much of a chance of corrupting his morals by bringing him in.

They knocked on the front door. Skipper answered. Upon seeing Jack he frowned at Mike. Mike said quickly, "My nephew showed up unexpectedly. He's with us for the moment."

Skipper led them up a set of hardwood stairs into a magnificent foyer. A cut glass chandelier in the main hall hung from a stained glass skylight four stories above. The woodwork was deep maroon mahogany. The Spartan furniture consisted of a large antique desk and two tables in a dark wood. Each table had a simple vase with three red steel roses in it.

Each wall had one painting. All four were pastoral scenes in muted water colors. A phone made of antique brass sat on one corner of the otherwise uncluttered desk. A door closed above them, followed by the sounds of footsteps coming down the stairs. An attractive man in his mid-twenties appeared. He was dressed impeccably in a dark blue Armani suit, perfectly matching tie, a sparkling white shirt, and black dress shoes.

He smiled at all of them. Skipper took a business card out of the desk and handed it to the newcomer. "That's the address," Skipper said.

The man said, "Thank you," in a deep, mellifluous voice, smiled at them again, and left. Mike guessed he was an escort just receiving the address of a client he was about to visit.

Skipper took a sheaf of papers out of his desk. "This is what I have for you. I wish you could tell me what was going on."

"We don't have time now," Mike said. "We need to go someplace to examine these. I promise I'll tell you as much as I can as soon as I can."

Mike felt relieved when they were standing back outside. The sky was clear and the air was warm. Mike realized they had no place to go to examine the phone list. He looked at the alien. Mike guessed he was having the same thought.

"It's a nice day," Mike said. "Why don't we walk over to Bug House Square and enjoy the warmth?"

Bug House Square, officially known as Washington Square Park, was famous in the distant past as a place where speakers went to give political harangues for any cause. In the more recent past, it had been notorious as a place to pick up hustlers. Nowadays it was mostly a reasonably pleasant patch of green just south of the Newberry Library.

They sat on a bench. Skipper had provided them three pages, single spaced, dense with phone numbers.

"These numbers mean nothing to me," Mike said.

"Why do you guys need all those phone numbers?" Jack asked.

Joe said, "I'm a detective, and I'm looking for somebody."

"Why didn't you just go to the police station?"

"I'm a private detective."

"Like on television?"

"Yep."

Jack then asked, "What kind of place was that?"

Mike realized he was grateful he was not a parent. "A friend's house."

"Oh. It was beautiful."

"Which of these calls are local?" Joe asked.

Mike examined them. He still had to think to remember where each of the new suburban area codes was. In the past several years Chicago and the suburbs had been divided into five separate area codes. He still had trouble remembering which of his friends' numbers went with which prefix. He studied the list. None of the numbers leapt out at him as significant.

"I wonder if we can get back in Howard's apartment," Joe said.

Mike knew the situation was becoming impossible with Jack. The kid also looked like he was getting bored. He decided to try Mrs. Benson. If he could have gone home, he'd have taken care of Jack himself. Despite what the alien needed, he knew Jack was his first priority.

He called his landlady. She was in.

Mrs. Benson said, "You've got another problem. There is this large biker person camped outside the apartment house. He accosted me when I arrived. He asked if I'd seen your nephew. I didn't like the looks of him so I told him, 'No.' He says he's the boy's father."

"He is." Mike said. "He's dangerous." Mike gave her a brief outline of the problem.

Mrs. Benson was, as always, practical. "Want me to call the police?"

"I'll call my lawyer first. He'll know what to do." Mike called David.

His lawyer said, "Keep the kid away from there. I'll handle it."

"Can you take the kid for a few hours? I've got to be several places."

"He's your nephew."

"I've got a lot of conflict here. I wouldn't ask if it wasn't important."

"I've got court at one this afternoon. I can't, sorry. Why not try Meganvilia? She brags about her ability to handle any kind of man or beast."

"But a teenager?"

"Neither man nor beast. You've been friends with Meganvilia for ages, but what is known to only a few is that Meganvilia volunteers to help troubled gay teens at several north-side shelters."

"Meganvilia?"

"She's quite good at it. Please, don't tell her I told you. I would trust her implicitly, and she owes you a million favors. Call her. She'll be happy to help out."

"A drag queen for my nephew?"

"How many choices do you have?"

Mike called the drag queen. After several comments about the rioting the night before, Mike said, "I need help with my nephew."

"Is this nephew as in 'hunk from out of town who wants to have a good time,' or nephew as in 'closet case -- hide the naked men,' or what?"

"This is nephew as in 'abused child who needs a safe place to stay.'"

"And you can't take care of him because?"

"He's a troubled kid, but I think he's had a breakthrough." Mike filled Meganvilia in on the case. He concluded, "The father is camped outside my apartment house."

Meganvilia spoke clearly and distinctly. "I understand about child abuse. Of course I'll take him, not just as a favor to you. Don't worry, no one will get to him."

"He's a handful."

"So am I. I've never met a fourteen-year-old I couldn't deal with."

"He's straight."

"I'm not prejudiced."

"He's pretty depressed."

"Honey, I have a Ph.D. in depression. I'm very, very good at it."

Mike returned and told them about the presence of Jack's

father.

"I won't go near him," Jack said.

"We won't make you," Mike said.

Joe said, "Jack, we're going to make sure nothing bad happens to you. You trust us?"

Jack nodded.

Joe continued, "But we also need to get some detective work done."

"I have a friend you can stay with." Mike sat down next to Jack. "This guy is a flamboyant gay man. If that's not okay with you, Jack, we'll find someplace else."

Jack nodded gravely. "I'm sorry for all those mean things I said about gay people. One of my friends told me he was gay. I don't mind. I said those things to make you mad."

They drove to Meganvilia's. The drag queen was in a floral print muumuu. He shook Jack's hand silently. Mike made sure Meganvilia had his cell phone number and told him to call if there was any kind of emergency. Meganvilia did not question why Mike was staying at the Luxor. The drag queen looked at Joe, Mike, and Jack, nodded his head and said, "Everything's going to be fine."

As they drove away Mike said, "I'd trust Meganvilia with my last dime."

THIRTY-FIVE

At Howard's the manager said, "The owner wants his stuff out. You guys want to take it with you?"

"Not yet," Mike said. "It's been less than twenty-four hours, and he's getting evicted? That's kind of fast and kind of cruel."

"The owner's been looking for a reason to get rid of him since forever. The owner is a shit, and he doesn't like gay people. He can't discriminate openly, but he can act like a shit as quickly as he can when he's got an excuse."

"We need to do an inventory," Joe said.

The manager accepted this and let them in. They cleared off the kitchen table, spread out the phone logs, and then hunted for any kind of address book. After fifteen minutes Mike found a torn and tattered book amid a pile of papers in the bathtub. It looked like it had gotten wet and then dried. They could make out most of the numbers. A few pages at the beginning were missing.

They examined the book and the numbers.

"Why are we doing this?" Mike asked.

"We're looking for something that doesn't have an easy explanation. We're trying to match up names. We may have to call some or all of these. Vov, or Zye for that matter, could be using any one of these names. We'll start with numbers that are on Skipper's list and in the address book. After that, if necessary, we can call all the rest of them."

Using his cell phone, Mike began punching in phone numbers. From those who answered, he simply asked if they knew where Howard was. Most expressed surprise that he was missing. Two hung up as soon as Howard's name was mentioned.

Joe asked Mike about those.

"Might have been clients. They wouldn't want to be called."

After over an hour and a half, Joe took over the phoning chores. No one who answered knew anything. No one hung up on him. He also redialed those that had been busy or not in when Mike called.

After another hour and a half, Mike said, "This is useless. It is getting us nowhere, and over a third of them have been disconnected, or we get no answer. Calling everybody in your address book and explaining something to them takes forever."

"Boring police work is the same on any planet."

Mike ran his eye over the phone log. "Here's the day of the big fight. We got in touch with everybody except this disconnected number in the 815 area code."

"Where is that?"

"South and west of here."

"He didn't call it after that day, but he called it three times that day."

It took several minutes for Mike to check the numbers in the address book carefully. "There's no matching name or number here."

"How can we find out who this was?"

"I'll call Skipper."

Skipper's first words were, "How could you bring that kid here?"

"I'm sorry. I had no choice. I'm really sorry."

"It's good only Charley saw you. He's a friend and will keep his mouth shut. I almost died when you waltzed in here with a teenager."

"I'm really sorry," Mike repeated. "It really was an emergency, Skipper. Things have been crazed lately."

"The sky did not fall because you brought him here, but do me a huge favor would you? Don't bring him again, ever. I like my job."

"I promise. It really was an emergency."

"I can believe that," Skipper said. "I talked to Hugo just a few minutes ago. He said you were almost trapped in the fire last night, and then you were in the middle of the riot. What happened?"

Mike gave him a brief synopsis. He concluded, "I'd have told you more when we stopped, but I didn't want to linger with the kid in tow."

"I understand. I wouldn't mind being rescued by a fireman." Skipper added, "Although I'd want the circumstances to be a little less fraught with peril."

"You and me both," Mike replied.

"I bet they won't be hassling gay people in this city after this," Skipper said.

"I hope not," Mike said. "Skipper, I need another favor about these phone numbers." He explained about the disconnected number.

"I'm annoyed about your nephew, but you're a hero from last night. It shouldn't be a problem, but I'll have to be very careful. It's getting a little late to find anything today, but I'll give it a try. For sure I'll have it for you tomorrow."

"Great, thanks." He hung up.

He told Joe what he'd gotten.

There was a knock at the door. Joe and Mike looked at each other.

"Who?" Mike began.

Joe shook his head. He had his communicator out and was tapping it rapidly. He put his lips next to Mike's ear. "It's Zye. I don't want him to see you with me again. I don't want him to get suspicious. Hide in the bedroom. I'll deal with him." He shoved the phone log and address book into Mike's hands. Joe said, "Whatever happens, do not come out of the bedroom."

Mike darted into Howard's bedroom and closed the door. He heard Joe cross the room and unlock the door. He did not hear footsteps back so he figured they were talking in the doorway.

Mike assumed what followed was a conversation. He recognized no words. He heard a sort of melodic humming punctuated by occasional deep bass notes. There was a brief silence then a sound like a gunshot. Mike remembered the alien's dictum about not leaving the room. He heard nothing for several minutes. Then rapid footsteps approached the bedroom door. Mike shrank into a corner.

Joe walked into the bedroom.

Mike breathed a sigh of relief. "What happened?"

"We argued a few minutes. He wanted to know what I was doing here, that kind of thing. I told him to get lost."

"What was that gunshot?"

"Wasn't a gunshot. He tried to use his level of technology against me. My communicator can beat whatever he had with him. The confined space caused a repercussion, sort of like a sonic boom."

"Did any of the neighbors notice?"

"No one appeared."

"What happened to him?"

"He retreated. He'll be back. I have to assume he's got more technology to throw at me. He certainly wasn't prepared for the power I had."

"Is he okay?"

"He'll need to use the medical supplies on his ship sometime in the next forty-eight hours, but he'll be fine."

Mike wasn't sure he was glad about that or not. "Are we in danger?"

"Not immediately. We should leave anyway. We're pretty much done."

"What did you two talk about?"

"He was in the bar last night."

"What is so important about that place?"

"We'll have to ask Vov when we meet him. Zye either didn't know or wouldn't say."

Before they left, Mike made several calls. Mrs. Benson was in a chipper mood. "You should have seen it, Mike. Three squad cars showed up to get this guy. He resisted." She chortled into the receiver. "This was one time I loved the Chicago police. First, they bent him over his bike. Somehow he got away. He tried to run, but one of them tackled him. Then he hit two of the cops. It was glorious. By the time they were through with him, I think his left arm was broken, blood was pouring from his nose, his lip, and from above his left ear. The part I liked best was when they banged him face first into the pavement -- numerous glorious times."

"That's police brutality."

"That's the least that should happen to a child molester."

Mike called Meganvilia. After Mike said, "Hello," all Meganvilia said was, "Talk to him." Mike worried that they'd had a fight.

Jack said, "Uncle Mike, she's weird."

"I know."

"It's a guy, right?"

"Yep."

"I'm showing her how to work her computer."

Meganvilia got back on the line. "They teach children entirely too much in school these days."

"Everything all right?"

"Fine. My lover's going to be home soon. We'll probably go out to dinner."

"We can join you."

"Excellent. I want to get to know your new Mr. Right."

"I'm more concerned about Jack."

"He's a good kid. Everything's going to be fine."

Mike called his mother. He told her about the arrest.

"Rosemary is frantic," his mother said. "She's under sedation at the moment. I told her she's going to have to calm down and listen. We've had a parade of social workers in here at the house today."

"How'd her ex know to come to my place?"

"I told Rosemary Jack was with you. She wanted to go to your apartment and wait. I told her to meet me here, and I'd go with her. She talked to her ex before she came. She blabbed." His mother clicked her tongue. "He beat her. Whether it was before or after she told or both, I don't know."

"Is she all right?"

"Severely bruised and some minor cuts. Psychologically she's a mess. Is Jack there for me to talk to?"

"He's with my friend. I'll have him call as soon as possible."

"Okay. The doctor said Rosemary might sleep until tomorrow."

Mike promised to call the next day.

They left Howard's apartment and walked downstairs. Joe walked out the door first. As Mike's foot hit the stoop there was a tremendous explosion.

Thirty-six

Mike barely felt the concussion. Several of the windows in the building behind him shattered.

Mike gaped at the blue aura that surrounded Joe. He then realized that he himself was encapsulated by a blue cocoon of pulsing light. A second explosion sounded. The alien was calmly working his communicator. The second explosion seemed to stop in mid-noise.

Mike saw pedestrians flat on their faces and cars stopped in the middle of the street. A red orb the size of a bowling ball pulsed toward them from the top of a building across the street.

"Hold still," Joe commanded. His fingers continued to race as he talked. "That was a mistake. He revealed his position."

The orb approached Mike's body. He didn't move. When the red orb touched the blue aura, there was a brief pfft, and the red ball disappeared completely. He felt a slight distortion in what he saw and then a wave of dizziness. Moments later an ear-splitting cry rent the air. Then silence fell. Joe turned to Mike.

"We better get out of here. People are going to want to ask questions that we don't want to answer."

The blue aura faded. Mike held onto the building.

"You okay?" Joe asked.

"I was nauseous for a few seconds. I guess I'm okay. Are you all right?"

"I'm fine."

"What about all these people?" Mike asked.

People who'd been caught in the explosion began to pick themselves up. Others were pouring into the street asking what had happened and pointing at the two of them and back up at the roof top across the street. Several ran up to them and asked if they were all right.

"We're fine," Mike told them. "Was anybody else injured?"

No one was.

"We need to go," Joe said. He placed an arm on Mike's elbow. Mike heard the sound of sirens.

He found he could walk on his own. After they turned the corner and put several blocks between them and this new phenomenon, Mike asked, "What was that?"

"The bounty hunter decided to attack."

"It was him and not Vov?"

"I'm sure of it."

"Today's next question," Mike said, "is fairly obvious. Why was there a blue aura around me? Around you, I could understand."

"It was the communicator I gave you. You could not have been harmed. My prototype reacts automatically to a stimulus such as Zye used. It's what you would call an electronic-weapons response. You were in such close proximity. Mine automatically linked up with your communicator."

"But it couldn't protect you from the brick those teenagers threw?"

"Or keep me from getting kicked. Once I was dazed I would have had trouble fighting back. It's a sophisticated weapon designed for repulsing the kinds of attacks that would happen on my planet. It is not calibrated for an earthling heaving a brick from behind. At the time my communicator was on its normal setting, which automatically deflects any attack from a device known on my planet. If I'd have seen the brick coming, I probably could have vaporized it. I didn't. I wasn't on guard enough. I'm learning."

"Nobody has an anti-teenager device," Mike said, "but whoever invents one is going to be very, very wealthy."

On the bus to Meganvilia's Mike asked, "What did you do to Zye? I thought you couldn't kill him."

"I can't. I didn't. He is, however, more than ever, painfully aware of how much power I have."

"Can you tell me what you did?"

"Sure. I made a noise occur that even the dogs on Earth cannot hear. It is designed to pierce any protective device he's got. Took me a few seconds to activate it. He'll be very, very sick for an hour or so. With any luck it will make him think before attacking us again."

Dinner with Meganvilia and her lover, Ray, was extremely pleasant. Ray was a bear of a man, cuddly and hirsute. Mike remembered he was a cross-country truck driver. He told numerous amusing stories as they dined at Carson's for Ribs on Peterson Avenue.

While Jack was in the washroom, Meganvilia asked, "Why, pray tell, are you staying at the Luxor?"

"I can't explain everything right now. For the moment it's more convenient than my apartment."

Meganvilia looked from Joe to Mike and gave him a knowing smile. "Whatever works for you. If you see the owner Edna, tell her I said hello."

"Huge, ugly old woman?"

Meganvilia nodded.

"How do you know her?"

"I know everybody," Meganvilia asserted.

"Can Jack stay the night?" Mike asked.

Meganvilia and Ray nodded. "I like the kid," Ray said.

Meganvilia added, "And I can finally get on-line with that damn computer."

When Jack returned, Mike and Joe took him aside and said, "Your dad's been arrested, and your mom's in bad shape." Mike gave Jack the details.

"What's going to happen to me?" Jack asked.

"I'm not sure yet," Mike said. "Social workers, your counselor from school, the police, and I don't know who all you will have to meet. I promise to keep you safe and not let harm come to you. Do you believe me?"

"Yes."

"Good. Joe and I have to do more investigating, so if it would be all right, would you be willing to stay with Meganvilia and Ray for the night?"

"You're giving me a choice?"

"Yes."

"Most people only tell me what to do."

"I'll still want to do that sometimes," Mike said.

"I'll stay with Meganvilia." His face brightened. "This means I don't have to go to school tomorrow."

Mike nodded. As they were leaving, Jack hugged both Mike and Joe.

On the bus to the Luxor, Mike said, "What's next? I could use some sleep."

"I guess there's nothing at the moment. We'll have to see if Skipper gives us an address to match that phone number in the morning."

"It's not that late," Mike said, "but I wouldn't mind going to bed early."

THIRTY-SEVEN

The lobby of the Luxor was filled with men in white outfits.

"Is this a hospital convention?" Joe asked.

"It's a white party. It's a big AIDS benefit. Lots of cities have white parties. I don't know where they originated."

"We look out of place."

"You betcha."

A large television was on in one corner. It was tuned to the local all-news station. Mike and Joe stopped by to look. The screen was filled with scenes of the rioting the day before. The recap showed the rescue from the roof. Mike didn't think he was all that visible. Joe was clearly seen for about five seconds.

Mike murmured in Joe's ear. "Anyone might recognize you from that."

"All too possible." They listened to the coverage. They saw the mayor appear and appeal for calm. Joshua Pierson, an openly gay, Illinois state representative, shook hands with the mayor and made the same appeal. In the lobby of the Luxor, there were murmurs of approval at the state representative's appearance. One of the men in the crowd said, "See, they've got to listen to us now." Several local aldermen and representatives from other gay groups spoke.

Mike found himself leaning against Joe. He liked the feeling. "I'm tired." He put his arm around the alien. Mike felt warm and safe and aroused. Joe did not move to break the contact. The studly young anchor on television read a brief report about a mysterious explosion on the north side. Several eyewitnesses were interviewed. They gave contradictory accounts of what happened. Only one mentioned an odd blue aura.

"If we're not careful, we'll become as obvious as an elephant in the living room," Mike said.

"I agree," Joe said.

Mike and Joe watched the television until the national news came on. As they took the stairs to their room, Mike kept his arm around Joe's waist. Joe reciprocated. When several people passed them going down the stairs, they broke the contact. After the strangers passed, the alien and Mike put their arms around each other again.

At the door to their room, Joe looked at Mike carefully. "I thought you wanted us to keep our distance."

"You saved those cops. You risked yourself for them and for me. You were wonderful with Darryl. I've never seen anybody deal with him so well in such a volatile situation."

"I like Darryl. I wish I could be that brave in the face of imminent death."

"And the way you helped Jack is great. With any luck this will turn his life around."

"I hope so."

Inside the door of their suite, Mike said, "I'm afraid I might be falling in love with you. A bit of it is the allure of making it with an alien. I'm not some saint here. Some of it is lust. Some of it is warmth and gratefulness."

Joe moved close to him. They stood a foot apart. Mike rested his hands on Joe's waist.

Mike continued, "I may not be able to ever tell anyone I've been to bed with an alien, or at least get anybody to believe me, but that's one part of it."

As Mike paused, Joe simply kept gazing into his eyes. The hand on his arm felt warm and comfortable.

"I also think you are very sexy. I know we haven't known each other that long, but I've seen you be kind and gentle and brave, and you're funny. The only reason I'm hesitating from saying I'm in love is because I'm afraid you're going to leave. When your criminal is caught, you'll be gone, and I'll be left. I'm not good at pining and sighing hopelessly for a lost love. I also know that you've got strict taboos about having sex with me. I'm not great with rejection, but I've got to admit that I would like to have sex with you, and I wish you could stay."

Mike took his hands off Joe's waist. Joe turned and walked to the window, to their view of the brick wall next door. He stared out. Time stretched to a minute, then two.

Mike said, "I guess I'll go to bed."

"You underestimate yourself," Joe responded. He walked back to Mike and stood a foot from him. Joe placed his hands on Mike's shoulders.

Joe said, "I mentioned already that I'm curious about you as an earthling and as Mike Carlson. I've wanted to have sex with you since I first saw you. I have found that reaction in myself more than passing curious. For all the advanced technology and supposed wisdom on my planet, I feel passionate physical desire for you. Perhaps if we were truly wise, we would realize analyzing such desire is useless. I don't understand love as you talk about it. I do know that I enjoy being with you. You, yourself have a marvelous wit. You are a sexy man. I don't blame you for being reluctant, because it is against all the rules for me to stay here after my job is done. I'll have to go back with him. I could promise you I'd come back, but that is hardly realistic, no more realistic than what I'm going to say next."

Joe put his arms around Mike and drew him close. Mike returned the embrace. Their faces were inches apart as he continued to speak. "I will try and find every and any way to Vov, which I must do. I will not lie to you even at this moment. Staying here is unimaginably impossible." He sighed deeply. "Against all implants and orders, if I understand your concept correctly, I have fallen in love with you."

Silently they gazed at each other. Mike listened to the alien breathe. Mike so very much wanted this moment to be special and perfect. They moved into a fierce embrace. He felt Joe's arms around him and the familiar tingle increase as arms and legs entwined, as torsos became mashed tightly together. Mike felt their cheeks and ears touch. He nuzzled Joe's neck and ears, caressed the back of his head. He felt Joe's muscles through his sweatshirt and was very aware of the tingling touch of the alien's hands around his torso. Their lips were centimeters apart.

"And," Joe murmured, "against all orders and directives, I want to have sex with you."

Mike ran his hands through Joe's hair then exerted slight pressure, pulling their mouths together. He felt the touch of Joe's lips. Their lips met and tongues meshed. The exquisite co-mingling of their tongues and torsos threw him into ecstasy. Mike felt Joe's strong arms, their torsos straining together, legs bending to touch at as many points as possible. The now familiar tingle enveloped him.

THIRTY-EIGHT

Mike awoke in the hotel darkness. He heard distant, vague shouting. He turned over and reached for Joe. City light streaming in through the window showed the alien sitting up at the head of the bed. The soft light bathed his naked upper torso. Mike was pleased when they'd finally gotten naked that Joe had no noticeably alien physical differences from him. Mike rested his hand on Joe's thigh. The alien gave him a brief smile and tapped several times on the face of his communicator. He peered closely at the results.

"Nothing," he mumbled. "Just the denizens of the Luxor having fun."

The alien placed the communicator on the table next to the bed. He schooched down, turned to face Mike, and pulled him close. Mike sighed contentedly and returned the embrace. He basked in the joy and delight of the best love-making he'd ever experienced. He shifted so that his lips were a quarter inch from the alien's ear. He whispered, "Is that the kind of sex they have on your planet?"

"I've never been involved in three hours that were remotely this wonderful," Joe replied.

Mike's cell phone rang. He saw it was his mother and answered. "How is Jack?" was her first question.

"Doing okay. How is Rosemary?"

"You sister and reality are doing as best they can. You know how oblivious she can be. I've been in touch with the school. The guidance counselor Jack trusts turns out to be the social worker in charge of Jack's case."

"We should all meet," Mike said. "I'll set it up." They talked for a few more minutes discussing logistics.

Then Mike called Meganvilia who began without preliminary, "The kid's okay. Who said he was a problem?"

Mike went over the situation.

"We'll probably wind up meeting at Jack's school."

"We'll bring him in whenever you set it up."

After another round of phone calls, Mike had the meeting with Jack and all interested parties set up for early that afternoon. Jack's counselor at school, Mr. Rostov, was instrumental in making things happen on an emergency basis.

As soon as Mike hung up, his phone rang again. His caller ID said it was Kyle Flannery, the guy from Howard's apartment.

Mike said, "Kyle, what can I do for you?"

"You told me to call any time."

"I'm glad you called."

"I found Howard, or at least I found someone who says he saw him. He's at that Mokena Universal Health Clinic."

"Who told you this?"

"I went back to Howard's place this morning. I found a guy there. He said he was Howard's lover."

"Can you describe him?"

"Not much older than me, brush-cut hair, lots of zits." Neither of the other aliens. "Maybe you should check this place out. It's that big clinic that all the rumors are going around about an AIDS cure. They said he was a patient there. He claimed Howard called him. This guy told me that when he phones, they insist Howard is not there. He doesn't believe them, but they turned him away at the door. He doesn't know what to think or do. He said he's worried about Howard."

"Do you remember his name?" Mike asked.

"Brandon O'Bannion." Mike didn't remember that name from the phone list or rolodex, but it was a long list. They'd have to check.

"We'll take a trip down."

"You guys aren't cops though, are you." It was a statement

not a question.

"Why do you say that?"

"I tried calling the police to get hold of you. There's nobody on the force named Mike Carlson."

Mike didn't want to get into this now. "I'd like to meet to talk," he said.

"You don't need to. I almost didn't call you. You older gay guys always lie." Mike guessed to a sixteen-year-old, he must look ancient. Kyle continued, "But you said it was so important. At least you didn't try to use me for sex and lie to me to try and get that. Why didn't you tell me the truth?"

"I let you believe what you thought and didn't correct you."

"You lied," Kyle insisted.

"Yes, I lied. I really would like to meet with you and try to explain." Mike wasn't sure what he could tell the kid that would be believed. "Will you believe me if I promise not to lie?"

"I don't know."

They agreed to meet. Mike hung up and informed the alien. They checked the phone log. Brandon O'Bannion had been one of the no answers. They called again. Mike let the phone ring fifteen times before he hung up.

"We better get out to that clinic," Joe said. He pushed back the sheets.

"Wait," Mike said. He sat up, caught the alien's eye, and held his hand. "Before we go careening out of here, I want to say that I enjoyed what we did very much. I'd like to do it together with you for a very long time."

The alien leaned over to Mike and kissed him. "Me too," he murmured.

Thirty-nine

Mike and Joe arrived at Jack's school ahead of the others, and when Meganvilia and Ray arrived with the boy, they sat down with Jack and explained what was going on.

Jack listened to them with eyes that didn't waver from Mike's or Joe's when they spoke. His first question was, "Am I going to have to go with my dad?"

Mike said, "No."

"Is my mom going to go nuts?"

Mike said, "We're going to get her through this, and we're going to get you through this."

Joe said, "You know we won't let anything bad happen to you?"

Jack nodded. He lowered his head. They barely heard him say, "Can I live with you guys?"

Mike said, "Let's get through all this. If that's what you want, it's okay with us."

Joe said, "Of course."

Meganvilia was in what she called, "business man's drag." She wore a dark gray, pin-striped business suit with white shirt, gray and black striped tie, black socks, and black Florsheim shoes. Ray, the truck driver, also appeared in a conservative suit. All this attesting, Mike thought, to the seriousness with which they were taking the situation, and the commitment they had to Mike and his nephew. Mike had never seen Meganvilia conform to the expectations of non-drag society. Meganvilia prided himself on dressing the most outré of anyone in the room. After them, Mike's mom and dad entered with Rosemary in tow.

Finally, the school personnel walked in. Jack's counselor, Mr. Rostov, the one he played basketball with, wore a blue sport coat, white shirt, and a blue striped tie. Mike told them that David would be serving as Jack's legal representation and would arrive as soon as he could, most likely with up-to-the-minute information on Jack's father.

Once everyone was seated and water, juice, or coffee was provided to those interested, Mike's sister, Rosemary, said, "I don't want any of these people here. This is between me and my son."

Mr. Rostov, who ran the meeting, began, "This isn't a court hearing."

Rosemary said, "I don't understand what's happening."

Mr. Rostov said, "We're going to do a lot of sorting out. This will take a while, but we're going to do what is best for Jack."

Rosemary banged the table. "I know what's best for my son."

Mr. Rostov spoke in a low, soothing voice. "And as the mother, you're very important in all this, but Jack is old enough now to speak for himself so I'd like to hear what he has to say."

"I'm his mother," Rosemary said. "What I say goes. Doesn't it?"

The alien who'd seated himself next to Rosemary, put a hand on her arm and said, "We know you want what is best for your child."

Mike thought, if he touches her, is he controlling her mind? Then he remembered that Joe didn't need to be touching people to read their memories.

Rosemary gave Joe a weak smile and sat back in her chair.

Mr. Rostov said, "Jack?"

He looked at all the adults, licked his lips, grabbed the water in front of him and took a sip. He put his hands flat on the table. "I won't go to my dad's any more, ever."

An hour of emotion passed. The two key moments were Rosemary sobbing into her mother's arms and the alien putting his arm around Jack who remained tearless.

In the middle of the meeting, the school secretary appeared with David, Mike's lawyer. David set his briefcase down as another round of introductions took place. David's tie was a muted shade of pink, the most conservative one Mike had ever seen him wear. First David asked Jack, "You okay?"

Jack shrugged.

David smiled, "I have some good news." Jack brightened. The others leaned toward him. "I have been very busy. Turns out your father has several outstanding warrants in Florida. Plus the police here are charging him with attacking a police officer while he was being arrested. So it's going to be harder for him to get bail."

"Harder?" Mike's mom asked. "Not impossible? After what he's done?"

David explained, "There hasn't been a trial and a verdict. That'll take time. I think I can keep him in jail for a while, but I can't guarantee it."

Jack said, "I won't go near him."

Mike said, "We won't let that happen."

Rosemary said, "I can protect him."

Mike's dad said, "You haven't so far." They were among the few words he'd spoken, but everyone became very silent for long moments as their import finally seemed to penetrate Rosemary's understanding. She held onto her mother's arm with one hand and clutched a sodden tissue in the other.

They spent an hour going over where they thought Jack might be safe. Finally, Meganvilia said, "That evil man knows where Mike lives. He knows that Jack has been living with his mom at his grandparents' house, but he doesn't know where Ray and I live. He doesn't know we exist."

Jack broke in. "I'd be safe there. He couldn't possibly find me."

The school people had numerous objections and concerns. Ultimately, the family met in the hall. Mike said, "This is the one place Jack will be for sure safe. It is the best solution."

Jack agreed.

Mike's mom and dad supported Mike and Jack. Rosemary gave in. They rejoined the school personnel and explained the family decision.

"It'll be a transition time," Mr. Rostov said. "We'll work out a more permanent solution eventually. We must consider Jack's safety first. The worst is never going to happen. Now we can work on the best."

Smiles and sniffles followed a round of hugs from his mom and Rosemary. Jack hugged Joe and smiled at Mike.

In the parking lot, Joe and Mike stayed behind for a few moments after the others left. He said to Meganvilia and Ray, "Thank you so much, so very much."

Meganvilia said, "Glad to help."

Ray said, "Call any time."

Meganvilia pulled Mike aside and whispered, "Michael, what the hell is going on with you and Joe?"

"I wish I knew."

But Joe had come up beside them and heard. He said, "Mike is helping me in an investigation."

Meganvilia raised an eyebrow. "Investigating what's between his legs or…?"

Mike smiled. "All of the above."

Once back in the car, Mike called his answering machine. There was a message from Skipper. He had the address of the disconnected number which was somewhere in the 815 area code. It was in Will County near Kankakee. They headed south first for a stop at the clinic in Mokena, then on farther south.

After entering Lake Shore Drive, Mike said, "Were you controlling our minds in there? When you touched Jack, were you manipulating him?"

"Only with warmth and understanding."

Mike let it go. If the alien was all powerful, there wasn't much he could do about it but get his heart broken.

FORTY

Mike and Joe left the car in the commuter parking lot near LaGrange Road and 191st Street and hiked over to the clinic. The weather forecaster on the all-news station on the car radio had said there was a stationary front draped over northeastern Illinois. South of the front, the air would feel like summer -- north, like a cold, clammy fall. Strong storms were predicted within the next twenty-four to forty-eight hours.

They inched their way carefully around the perimeter to the far side, away from the twenty-four hour AIDS clinic and saw no cars parked in this part of the lot. Mike said, "This whole side of the complex looks deserted." From their vantage only emergency exit lights shone in the hallways and rooms. One of the shuttle buses sat abandoned fifty feet from them.

Joe tapped at the front of his communicator. "There's no one from my planet in there at the moment."

"Any humans?"

"I can't tell from this." He tapped again. "I can't get an exact fix, but I get evidence of abnormal electrical activity in the central tower somewhere above the fifth floor."

Mike gazed upward. "I don't see any lights up there."

"There's definitely activity above the fifth floor."

"You're sure?"

"As sure as I can be."

Mike said, "But there could be nasty, unfriendly human guards."

"There could be."

"We could just waltz past the entrance to the AIDS clinic."

"I want to take as few chances of being seen as possible. Vov or Zye or both could have spies around here anywhere."

"You are not a comforting alien."

The alien smiled at him. "I'm going in. You may stay out here or come with me, as you see fit."

"I see fit to not let my ass sit out here in the middle of the prairie. Can't you be more certain about who's in there?"

"This thing is no good for picking up humans. It can't be a lot of people or more lights would be on."

"Or it could be a lot of people sitting there in the dark waiting for us."

"Maybe. You coming up?"

Joe moved abruptly from their hiding place out into the open. After an instant's hesitation, Mike followed. Joe smiled. "I'm glad you're coming with."

Mike said, "I must be nuts."

Without running, which might have drawn the stares and suspicions of unseen eyes, they hurried across the parking lot.

They arrived unchallenged at the door at the far end of the clinic from the AIDS-care entrance. Down the hall they could see a few exit lights gleaming faintly at distant intervals. The door was locked.

Joe took out his communicator. "Maybe I can give the alarm an electronic breakdown. It'll take a minute. I want to do this without setting it off."

Joe's fingers worked for several minutes. Even though they stood in deep shadow, Mike wished he would hurry.

"Problem?" Mike asked after the time began to stretch uncomfortably.

"Technology can be a bitch. It's easier to blow something to smithereens than it is to carefully calibrate this to softly and gently take a piece of electronics apart atom by atom, and it takes a hell of a lot longer." He was silent for several more moments. "There." The alien reached for the door. It didn't open. Joe said, "Nuts."

Mike put his hand on Joe's arm. "Wait a second. What if he was lying?"

The alien stopped with his hand on the door. "Who?"

"Kyle, the kid with the tip. Maybe the bounty hunter or the evil alien got to him. We don't know who really gave him this information. That lover story could be a hoax."

They looked at each other. "A fine time for that insight," Joe said.

"We could be walking into a trap," Mike pointed out.

"I knew that."

"You could have mentioned it to me."

"I've had suspicions about this place. With it being this late, here's our chance to explore. So much the better if we find Howard. We'd better be ready to defend ourselves if we're attacked."

"Will the communicator you gave me protect me as it did before?"

"As long as we're near each other, it will give you some protection."

"That's one of the things I like about you, definitive answers."

"They both need me to get to my ship. As long as they want that, they won't want me in the hands of the police."

Joe began hunting on the ground at the entrance.

"What?" Mike asked.

"We need a rock to break the glass in the door."

"Have I mentioned that for an all-powerful, interstellar alien, you leave a lot to be desired?"

"An annoying number of times."

"Sorry."

Mike helped him look. The grass, clipped short as a putting green, yielded nothing. They dashed back to the dumpsters, which turned out to be empty. Ultimately, Mike offered to run back to the car and get the jack-handle.

Mike trotted carefully over the uneven ground. The night was cool and clammy. He broke a slight sweat under his T-shirt and jeans. He thought some about the illegality of what they planned to do, but mostly he thought about the sex they'd had. Mike had never enjoyed himself so much. Building a relationship on sex was no panacea, but having great love making didn't hurt either. Mike found the jack, and taking every precaution, quickly returned. He handed it to Joe.

The alien took off his shirt and placed it on the ground next to the door. Mike followed suit. Joe swiftly raised the jack and bashed the glass. The safety glass turned into a million shards that tinkled to the ground. The noise was muffled by the clothing outside and the rug within. It still sounded frighteningly loud to Mike. He said, "Half the planet could have heard that."

"No doubt. They will probably arrive any moment."

They waited several moments to see if anyone responded to the noise. All remained quiet. They brushed off their shirts and put them back on. Unable to think of any other objections and unwilling to be left behind, Mike followed Joe as he slipped inside the door of the clinic.

Forty-one

They darted from shadow to shadow until they came to the central core of the clinic. They huddled behind the unused reception desk. The dust-encrusted, plastic covering rustled at their slightest movement.

"Where are the security guards?" Mike whispered.

"I don't know." The alien sounded exasperated.

They listened to the silence. "Let's try the stairs," Joe suggested.

They crept to the door next to the sign that said, "Stairs." Joe peered through the safety glass then slowly depressed the handle. The door swung open quietly. At each landing the faint red exit signs gave off enough light so they were not groping around in total darkness. Essentially each floor described a circle around the central core of elevator shaft, stairs, washrooms, and nurse's station. The rooms were on the perimeter of the circle. All were completely empty of people or furniture.

Outside each door on every floor, they listened cautiously, and Joe checked his communicator. He still could not get a fix on the electrical output. At each landing they also opened the doors a centimeter or so to have some visual contact first.

When they reached the eighth floor, the door was locked. Joe ran his fingers over the front of his communicator. "The odd electrical emanations are coming from above us."

"Is this a force field?"

"No. Something from my planet is running in conjunction with electricity from your planet. Mixing power from my planet and Earth technology can distort my readings. I won't know what it is specifically until I examine whatever is causing the odd readings. When we get through this door, I bet we don't have to worry about human guards anymore. Whatever is beyond here must be something Vov or Zye didn't want random humans to have access to."

"Unless those random humans have been taken into his confidence and are waiting on the other side of this door with large baseball bats."

Joe gave Mike what Mike would call an impish grin. "Does everybody on your planet worry like you do?"

"You've read more minds than I have, you tell me."

The impish grin disappeared. Joe placed his hand lightly on the door then ran his fingers around the entire edge of the opening. "This is completely sealed."

"I forgot to bring my magic door unsealer," Mike said. He followed the alien's gaze as it traveled along the wall. Several panels with handles ran along the walls of the landing. The first yielded easily and revealed a fire extinguisher and water hose. The second contained a set of electrical controls. The third wouldn't budge. This one looked like an opening to a heating or air-conditioning duct. Finally Joe asked, "Could I have the tire jack?"

"Battering the door down might be a bit noisy."

Joe muttered. "I'll use your head for that."

"I heard that," Mike said.

"I'm going to gently pry this panel open. If there is the slightest noise, I will stop."

The slight squeak the metal made as it opened seemed to echo in Mike's ears. Maybe a demented mouse might have heard it five feet away.

Joe stuck his head in the opening, looked left, right, up, and down. He retracted his head. "I don't know how far this goes. I'm going to try it and see if it leads to a way up. I'll check it out and then come back for you."

"You're irritated."

"Yes."

"*The Adventure of the Irritated Alien* has a catchy sound to it."

Joe gazed at him.

Mike mumbled. "Sorry."

Joe said, "Dumb jokes when people are nervous is also a universal character trait."

"I wish that was more reassuring."

"I'll be back."

Joe climbed into the duct. Mike heard soft scrabbling sounds of cloth against metal for several minutes. Then silence. He put his head into the opening and looked in the direction Joe had disappeared. He thought he saw a faint shadow move. The duct was barely large enough to permit a man to slither through. Mike was not eager to try to imitate a snake.

The minutes stretched with maddening slowness. Mike leaned against the cold cinder-block wall. He noted the last paint job was beginning to flake in several corners. He strained to hear the slightest sound. His hands were clammy. Worries returned about being caught in here. He had no excuse anyone would believe. He trusted Joe would return. He just wished it would be soon.

The time stretched long enough for Mike to begin contemplating following after the alien. Once again he gazed into the duct. He saw nothing, but he thought he heard a slight scrape. Quickly, he pulled his head back. He listened at the sealed door, but there was no sound there. He could see only one flight of stairs up or down. He didn't think the noise had come from either of those.

Then he heard it. A definite noise that rapidly turned into the sound of soft cloth swishing gently against metal. Mike looked into the duct and saw feet approaching. He had no idea if they were the bottom of Joe's shoes. He stepped down the flight of stairs until only his head from eyes up was visible.

Moments later two black and white running shoes appeared in the opening, then white socks, and the legs of a pair of blue jeans. Joe fully appeared moments later.

Mike hurried back up the stairs.

"You okay?" he asked.

"Yeah. That thing is a little more cramped than I like."

"What did you find?"

"The duct work follows the curve of the inner tower. About six feet past where you can see, there's an opening to the elevator shaft. It's a short stretch from the duct opening to the elevator door. I managed to prop that open. That's what took so long. I didn't see or hear anybody, but we should hurry to get back."

"We're going through there?"

"I'm not going to be able to unseal this door. I suspect Vov gets up here by a special key in the elevator. This is the only way."

Mike nodded. "Let's do it quick. The longer we wait, the more I'll think about how nuts this is."

Joe smiled. He turned and scrambled back into the duct work. Mike glanced around the landing, stuck his head in the opening, then moved quickly forward.

Mike had never thought of himself as claustrophobic, but this began to make him feel uneasy. He used hands, shoulders, hips, knees, and feet to push his body along. At the same time, he remembered to go as silently as possible. This slowed his progress enough that his fear of being enclosed in this small space surrounded by the whole building began to grow more than uncomfortable. He noted the duct turning. As it did, the faint light from the landing began to disappear. He took comfort in being able to see the bottom of Joe's shoes. He didn't want them to disappear in the darkness.

He was into his second vow of never chasing after aliens when Joe's shoes disappeared in the ever-dimming light. Mike shut his eyes and continued to inch forward. Slow seconds thumped by like a bass drum beating a funeral dirge. He willed himself to move forward. His hand touched empty air. Before he could withdraw it, he felt a hand on his. Mike opened his eyes. Faint light had returned.

"We're at the elevator shaft," Joe whispered.

Mike looked down. Dim lights lit the bottom of the shaft eight floors below. He looked where Joe was. The alien squatted on the ledge of the slightly open elevator doors. The air duct had opened slightly at the end so he could move more freely.

Joe pointed and murmured. "You can get hand and foot holds here and here. I'm close enough to give you a boost and a hand. We're not going to die hurtling down this shaft."

Mike acted before his fears could paralyze him. First he moved his body a third of the way out, turned sideways, and gripped two handholds. As he pulled himself further out, he turned his torso so his chest faced the wall. Halfway out he shifted his grip to the side of the opening for the elevator doors. He felt Joe's hand under his left armpit. His feet touched the edge of the duct. He paused.

Joe said, "Shove off as far as you can and push upward. There's an outcropping above your head on your right. Put your hand in that as soon as you can. You can swing from that."

Mike nodded. He looked down, then quickly back up. "Let's do it," he said.

He felt the alien's helping hand. He placed his shoes on the edge. He began to shove upward. One of his feet slipped. It began to swing out. He grabbed for the outcropping with his right hand. His fingers touched metal. In seconds he was squatting next to Joe on the elevator ledge.

"Let's not do that again real soon," Mike said.

"We're here to meet your needs," Joe said. "Whatever you want, I want."

"A pool and matching pool-boy to go with it."

"Not on this planet."

Carefully, they turned to face the doors which were open about six inches. They listened for several minutes. Then Joe checked his communicator. "Still no sign of a living alien up here," he stated. Joe eased the access doors open wide enough for them to slip through. This corridor was as quiet as the entire rest of the complex had been. It smelled more antiseptic than disused.

Mike saw dust gathered at the edges of the tile near the walls, but the center of the hall was dust free. Any cabinet they came to was unlocked and empty, not a bandage or bottle of medicine anywhere. The nurse's station in the center of the hall was uninhabited.

At each corner, at each doorway, at any junction -- they paused to listen, their eyes straining to penetrate the darkness. Half way around the circle, the alien held out his hand for them to halt.

Joe looked at the display on his communicator. "Something is in the next room. It is not an alien. It's like a remnant." Joe shook his head.

The door was three quarters open. When Mike got his head around the woodwork, he saw a human foot. They inched their way into the room. Several machines had dim digital displays. Mike couldn't make sense of the readouts. He vaguely recognized several of them from visits to the hospital with Darryl and from television doctor shows. The light from these showed a young male.

Joe had his communicator out and was running it over the machines.

Mike examined the body. For all Mike could tell, the man could be anything from simply asleep to being in a deep coma. Close up he could see Kaposi Sarcoma lesions on the face and upper arms.

Joe touched the face. He spoke very quietly and very gravely. "Vov has been experimenting on humans."

"For what?"

"I can't tell. I don't know enough medicine. These machines have infinitesimal bits of materials from my planet in them. Like computer chips, only much more minute. Still it was enough to set off my communicator. That's the unusual electric discharge that I picked up."

"Maybe he was trying to cure them."

Joe ran his communicator up and down the body. He studied the read out a few moments. "I don't believe that." He swept the communicator up and down the body again followed by a longer inspection of the communicator. "This man is near death, but it isn't from his human diseases. Vov has been experimenting on him. That's what is killing him."

"Like the Holocaust," Mike said.

"I remember that from one memory I read. Yes, this would be like that."

"That is terrible."

"As awful on my planet as it is on yours. I'm sure Vov doesn't care about the inter-galactic laws he's broken, but if I ever bring him back to my planet, he would be executed. There hasn't been an execution on my planet in fifteen centuries, but this is beyond all decency."

They crept from room to room. They found three more rooms with people in them. All were deeply unconscious and hooked up to ventilators. Mike could see they all had KS lesions.

They found the doors to the stairs going up unsealed. They advanced to the ninth floor. Here all the rooms had humans in them. Each one was in the same condition as the ones on the eighth floor.

"Are these people going to die?" Mike asked. "Can't we get some human help in here for them?"

"I don't know."

The tenth floor reverted to the almost deserted status of the eighth. Halfway around their circuit, Mike heard a soft moan. It was the first noise they had heard in the past half hour that indicated a possibly conscious human nearby. Joe pointed to the room across the hall. The alien looked carefully before and behind them and then checked his communicator. He nodded. They inched across the floor. As they had with all the others, they stopped with one of them on each side of the open door.

There was another moan. Mike thought he heard the word "please."

Joe craned his neck around the opening. He slid his foot forward an inch. Mike could see the end of a bed. The door to the washroom was open. As Joe moved slowly forward, Mike followed. There was no television in the stand attached to the ceiling. There were no chairs to sit in. Joe listened at the door to the bathroom, then proceeded on.

FORTY-TWO

They found Howard on the bed. Howard was covered up to the neck with a sheet. His eyes were closed. Next to the bed was a table covered with syringes, scalpels, bottles containing different colored liquids, and items Mike wasn't sure of the purpose of.

Stretched out on the floor in the corner was the body of a male human in his early twenties. He wore faded blue jeans and a muscle T-shirt.

As they approached the bed, Howard let out another moan. They stood on opposite sides of the bed. Joe put his hand on Howard's shoulder. At the touch Howard groaned loudly and tried to twist about on the bed. The sheet slipped halfway down his torso. Mike let out a soft gasp. Lines of scabs eight or nine inches long and half an inch wide ran diagonally from his left shoulder to his right side. It looked as if strips of his skin had been ripped out.

"My God," Mike said.

"He's nearly conscious, but I can't read his memories," Joe said. Gently he placed his hand on Howard's head and turned it slightly. Howard began mumbling and squirming. Joe's shoulders slumped.

"What's wrong?" Mike asked.

"Look."

Mike hurried to the other side of the bed. Behind Howard's left ear was a hole slightly smaller than an eraser head but open and deep into the skull. The sides of the wound looked as if they had been seared to preserve it in that state.

"What is it?" Mike asked.

"Someone tried to put an implant into his head. What little I can read in his memory says basically that his body has been through a traumatic shock. I've heard of this too. When implants first became common on my planet, there were still occasional failures. Victims' brains would be paralyzed for a while. With one or two it became permanent, and they died. For thousands of years there have been no problems. Obviously Vov botched this one badly. I don't get the distortion from a sleeping or unconscious human here. I get synapses almost completely destroyed. Neuron paths shattered as if they'd been blown to bits."

"He experimented on him."

"Yes."

"Can you help him?"

"If I was at my ship, I could possibly prolong his life a few hours. I think he's going to die soon."

"You mean this was done recently?"

"I have no way of telling. The sheets aren't bloody. He doesn't smell and isn't dirty, and we've seen no cleaning supplies of any kind. So my guess is he hasn't been here that long."

Joe examined machines hooked up to Howard while Mike checked the man on the floor. His body was still warm, but he wasn't breathing. Mike moved him slightly. When he saw the right side of the man's head, he gave an involuntary gasp. That half of the man's skull was complete mush. Mike found the man's wallet. He found the identification. "Brandon O'Bannion found his friend," he stated simply.

Suddenly Howard gasped. His eyes opened wide, and his head swiveled violently from side to side. They hurried to the bed.

"Howard," Mike called softly. He placed his hand on Howard's arm.

"Mom? Dad?" Howard's voice was weak.

Mike sat on the bed and held the hand tightly.

"Help me!" Howard croaked.

"We'll do what we can," Mike said. "We should call 911."

"Yes, call," Joe said.

Mike tried his cell phone but there was no reception. He looked at Joe and showed him the dead phone. Joe said, "Probably interference from the bits of my planet up here."

There was no phone in the room. Mike said, "I think there was a phone at the nurses' station."

Joe put his hand on his arm. "Go quietly and be careful."

The hall was totally silent as Mike slipped carefully the twenty feet to the nurse's station. He found an unplugged phone. He fitted the clip at the end of the wire into the wall socket and prayed for a dial tone. Seconds later the comforting drone came alive. He phoned quickly and gave their location.

The 911 operator said, "Don't they have emergency personnel there?"

"No. We're the only ones here." He told about the bodies and no personnel.

"Is this some kind of joke?"

"There isn't time to explain. We have injured people here." He refused to give his name. The 911 operator started to get annoyed at him, but Mike hung up on her.

Mike cautiously returned to the room. He saw Joe sitting on the side of the bed holding Howard's hand. Joe spoke softly and quietly, "Yes, I know, Son, I love you as well."

"Dad," Howard spoke between gasps, "I'm sorry. I'm really sorry. I should have apologized long ago."

"It's all right, Son, I understand."

Howard shut his eyes, and his body seemed to shrink. Mike saw his chest continue to rise and fall.

Joe looked at Mike. "He's slipping in and out of consciousness."

"He thought you were his dad."

"The most prominent memories I could find were ones from when he was a child. There are a few other patches in there. I got a confused picture of a row of corpses."

"What does that mean?"

"I don't know, nothing good. It was a comfort to him, so I let him think I was his father. It will make his last moments more bearable."

"Help is on the way," Mike said. "I told them about the other patients."

"I doubt if help will arrive in time for Howard. I suspect Vov has planned for such an eventuality. I'm afraid people will get hurt."

"Can we do anything?"

"We'll do as much as we can," Joe said. "I managed to discover one other important thing. Howard has been to Vov's ship."

"You're sure?"

"Yes. The memory is seared in deeply and is accompanied by great fear."

"Can you find the ship now?"

"I hope so."

The door burst open.

FORTY-THREE

The bounty hunter and two other men marched into the room.

"You aren't the paramedics," Mike said.

"Not hardly," Zye said.

One of the men with him asked, "Should we kill them?"

Zye held up his hand to forestall their action. He gazed at Mike for a few seconds and then smiled. He turned to Joe. "Naughty, naughty, you broke all the rules. I saw that magic aura in the street. They will not be happy when I get home and tell them that you gave him a communicator."

"I can live with it," Joe said. "I thought you'd be out of commission longer."

"You're not the only one who's got medical technology."

Joe pointed at the men behind the bounty hunter, "Who are the humans?"

"Friends."

"Isn't that illegal?"

The bounty hunter laughed. "I don't play by anybody's rules except my own." He indicated Howard. "I was trying to find out what this one knew."

"How'd you know he was here?"

"Sources."

"Was it Kyle?" Mike asked. "You didn't hurt him, did you?"

"Shut him up, would you?" Zye said to Joe. "He gets very boring very quickly."

"Why do you care about Howard?" Joe asked.

"Same reason you do. I think he knows where Vov's ship is. I need that information. I need to keep him alive."

"He isn't going to live long," Joe said.

"What did you do to him?" Zye asked.

"We just arrived. Was it you or Vov that tried to do an implant?"

Zye moved around to examine the wound in Howard's head. "I don't have the training to do that. His mind must be nearly gone. Did you read his memories? You know where Vov's ship is?"

"His mind is destroyed," Joe said. "What few memories remain are of his childhood."

"So you say."

"Did you see the bodies on the floor below this?" Joe asked.

"Yes, it's Vov's experiments on patients," Zye said. "To make money, he's been trying to invent cures. From what I can find out, he seems to have something that works with AIDS patients. I suspect he's also been trying to give them implants. He's enslaving humans, curing them if it suits his purposes, making money off them for sure. I haven't been able to find where he invents his cures, but he's been using these people to try things out on, to experiment, to make money, to see what effect the changes he's made in implants have." He nodded at Howard. "Not working too well, but he needs money to finance an operation on a scale that he wishes to have. Humans are suckers for any kind of crap."

Mike swallowed his fury at this willful violation of human life. There was no time for anger now.

"Why he would want an empire here, I can only imagine. I was forced to burn that bar complex down, but he escaped. I think it was part of a future factory."

They heard sirens in the distance. Out the window Mike saw an ambulance turn into the compound. Zye saw his look and glanced downward at the emergency vehicles. Zye said, "I'm sick of this." He turned to the human minions with him. "Start with the guy on the bed. Shoot him."

Neither Joe nor Mike could react quickly enough. The

firearms thundered. Mike saw blood pool and spurt from at least four separate spots on Howard's body. Blue auras erupted around Mike and Joe.

For a few seconds Zye worked what looked like a communicator. One of his minions fired a gun at them. Nothing penetrated the auras. Mike realized Joe must have set their protection for Earth-based attacks.

Zye said something in his native language. Then the bounty hunter and his minions turned and ran.

"We'd better do the same," Joe said.

With a last look back at the lifeless body, Mike followed Joe out of the room. The bounty hunter and the others had already disappeared.

"Quickly," Joe said. "The paramedics won't know where to look. Vov's people could get in here, and all the bodies could be moved by the time an official was convinced to have the place searched."

Mike heard the elevator start. They took the stairs. At the eighth floor, the sealed door had been completely removed from its hinges.

Joe said, "I guess Zye isn't as worried as I am about being found."

As they proceeded down, Mike thought he heard footsteps in front of them, but they met no one. At the ground floor door, Joe peered out carefully. They heard shouts from a distance.

"I don't see anybody," Joe said. "Let's go."

The noise they heard was coming from the back of the complex. Zye and his men must have tried to sneak out the rear entrance. Mike and Joe dashed through the corridor and out toward the front. They passed through the disused emergency entrance quickly and dashed for the deeper darkness of the fields around the perimeter. They saw a fire engine hurrying down 191st Street.

"Who were those two guys with Zye?" Mike asked when they

were safely in the car in the commuter parking lot.

"The few seconds I examined them showed me very cold personalities, as if they were immune to a lot of normal human feelings. What's a terrorist group?"

"Raving loonies who would stop at nothing to get their own way."

"That's what these guys are from. Violence begets more violence. Zye may or may not be able to keep control of them."

"Why didn't he kill Howard himself?"

"The same reason he didn't try to kill you. If he does, his life is forfeit on my star system. There are some rules he dare not break, not as long as I'm still alive to report them."

"You're breaking them, and you're a cop."

"Not a very good one."

"Maybe Zye is not a very good bounty hunter."

"They do have a kind of sick code of honor, but I've never understood it. My government doesn't officially acknowledge their existence. Unofficially is another matter. Because humans killed their own, Zye would not face what you would call a criminal indictment. This whole dabbling in another world is a lot more complicated than I imagined."

"Could your blue light thing have protected Howard from the gun shots?"

"He'd have to be in physical possession of one like you were on the street. If I put the force field on maximum, it would probably have protected you and me from a mile wide asteroid dropping from the sky."

"Probably?"

"That's the best I can do. We're both dealing with physics and technology which I do not understand."

"I was afraid of that."

"What is a 'deep tunnel'?" Joe asked. "Howard's memory is of a tunnel far underground with an access somewhere in the countryside south of Kankakee."

"That's the same general area we've got that phone number from. The 'Deep Tunnel' project is around there. It's supposed to provide flood relief."

"Where is Kankakee?"

Mike gave directions as Joe started the car and drove to Interstate 80. Mike asked, "Isn't this kind of nuts?"

"What?"

"Driving around in the middle of the night without knowing exactly where we're going is a little goofy."

"It's got to happen. I've got to follow the clue now. Who knows what Zye will find or what Vov has done in the meantime? Vov could move his operation. Zye hooking up with humans is a bad sign. If you're tired, you should get some rest, but I've got to look now. It's likely he might have the power to cause major disruptions. He'd have better tools, and he would have more technical knowledge at his disposal. He would be far more ruthless and destructive than anything this planet has ever known."

Mike felt himself shiver.

"I want to find him," Joe said. "For you and your planet. It is imperative that we do."

"Before he destroys my world."

"Preferably."

FORTY-FOUR

They rushed through the middle of the night. Ten miles south of Kankakee, they stopped at an all-night gas station and picked up a detailed local map. They examined it. "Near as I can figure out from this," Mike said, "the location has got to be east and a little south of here..."

For several hours they drove through the darkened countryside. Mike kept the window down to help view the passing addresses on the mail boxes. The faster they drove, the more bugs squashed onto their windshield. The dying bugs and the whining tires and the rushing wind were the only sounds. The humidity was rising, and the September night remained unseasonably warm. The breeze through the open window helped dry the sweat from their bodies.

"Could Vov or Zye follow us?" Mike asked.

"They aren't behind us."

"You didn't detect Zye in the clinic."

"He wasn't there when we got there, that's for sure. Once we were in, I didn't think to check if either of them was behind us, because I desperately wanted any information Howard had. I was also concerned with his physical condition. I wish I could have done something about it. Sometimes I think they were right to demote me. I never seem to get anything right."

"Self pity is a universal characteristic?"

"I guess."

"You're doing the best you can, which is all any of us can expect. Like you said earlier, there's no training manual for this."

"No, there isn't."

After several moments of silence Mike said, "I hope Kyle is all right."

"I do, too."

Mike began to feel himself nodding. "I'm tired," he announced. "How are you going to be able to find the place down here?"

"His memory told me a county road. I got a picture of what was nearby. I'm trying to find that picture."

"In the dark?"

"If I have to. That's when he saw it. If we need to, we'll look in daylight as well."

After two hours they were back at the Interstate. Mike pulled off on the frontage road and checked the map. He said, "We're about ten miles north of Kankakee."

"I hate to give up," Joe said.

"The only thing left is that gas station, which I believe we may have passed at least once before." Mike pointed to what looked like an abandoned Stuckey's. He saw remnants of the oddly shaped blue roof. He remembered the little diners/gift shops from his youth as places his parents never let him buy anything.

"It's got a pay phone," Joe said.

"With the receiver hanging off. If it's been used in years, I would be stunned."

They pulled the car around to shine the headlights on both the phone and the front of the building. Mike saw crumpled pavement, broken glass, and felt a few random mosquitoes. On the front of the building, Mike could make out two painted-over numbers.

"That's two of the four numbers Skipper gave us," Joe said.

They walked over to the phone. The glow from the headlights wasn't the most efficient. They examined it as best they could.

Mike held the receiver to his ear. "Probably hasn't worked in ages," he said.

Joe took out his communicator. "I don't know what kind of radar or other protections Vov might have out." For several seconds Joe tapped at the front of his communicator. Mike heard the phone come to life with a dial tone. After ten seconds the noise stopped.

"It's the right number," Joe said. "Why would Vov be calling the middle of nowhere?"

"If your guy is that good technologically, maybe he's managed to connect into the phone lines. There could be a thousand reasons."

They returned to the car. Joe began driving down the country road away from the Interstate. Mike yawned again.

"You don't have to stay awake," Joe said.

"Sorry, I'm really bushed. It's been a lot of late nights recently."

"Yeah."

"Don't you get tired?"

"We're trained not to."

"Must be nice."

"Sometimes."

As they continued to drive slowly along, Mike felt his eyes nodding shut. He awoke to find himself alone in the car. It was parked on a deserted road next to an open field. It was still dark out. Starlight glittered around him. Mike heard footsteps approach. He crouched down.

"I think this is it," Joe said.

Mike sat up. "Where are we?"

"I have been down every dirt road I could find. We are almost due east of Kankakee near the border with Indiana."

Mike got out of the car and gazed at the countryside. "I don't see anything."

"We're in a shallow dip in the ground. The car headlights caught or caused a glint of light off metal in the distance. I explored."

They walked for a few minutes in the direction Joe indicated. At the top of a small rise, the alien pointed toward a clump of buildings and a tall mound of dirt a hundred yards away.

"The access road comes from the opposite direction. We could have taken the car to it, except I don't know where it comes out. I didn't want to waste time finding another road in the dark."

They strode over the uneven ground. As Mike's eyes adjusted to the light and as they neared their goal, he saw huge cranes, different shaped and sized buildings, and enormous earth-moving machines.

They crouched behind a large bulldozer that smelled of rust, oil, and metal. Joe looked carefully over everything. No lights of any kind shone. He pointed to the cluster of metal huts.

Mike eyed the large, silent, black shapes in the declivity before them. "Tell me again why this is not an insane thing to do," Mike said.

"You've stuck with me this far."

"The old it-seemed-like-a-good-idea-at-the-time defense. Not the most convincing argument you could have used."

"You want something magical and other worldly, find yourself another alien."

"Do you know one?"

"The only safe ones are several zillion light years away."

Mike eyed the entrance then gave a searching look in all directions. "There must be guards around here somewhere. The workers at this site can't just leave this open to casual strollers like ourselves who want to wander on down any old time."

The alien peered over the rim of the mammoth earth mover. "It looks pretty deserted to me, like somebody abandoned construction."

"The tunnel itself? I thought I heard they lost funding for a while. I'm not sure."

Joe checked his communicator. "There's no live alien down there."

"You mean there's a dead one."

"No, I don't know what my readings mean. Something is odd

down there, but there are no live, lurking enemies."

After a last careful glance around, the alien stood up, dashed across the mud and cinder ground, and entered the building. Mike gazed up at the stars. The wind was up and gusting brutally from the south. The humidity was as uncomfortable as a night in mid-July. Because of the harsh breeze, his sweat dried almost as quickly as it formed on his skin. A stray trickle of sweat rolled down his spine. He shivered in spite of the heat then hurried after the alien.

FORTY-FIVE

Inside the hut Joe had his communicator on top of a desk. From its faint glow, Mike saw more signs of disuse: mounds of dust on piles of equipment, used fast food containers strewn hither and yon with cobwebs lacing them together, crumpled newspapers gathered in a corner topped by several flashlight batteries with acid stains around them, a deflated condom and torn foil packet rested on the tattered cover of a pornographic magazine.

Joe was at a computer console.

"That can't be working," Mike said. "You were right. This place is abandoned."

"It's supposed to look that way," Joe said. "Watch."

Joe hooked two wires together and plugged them both together into the back of the computer. Immediately the screen sprang to life. Joe moved his fingers rapidly over the keys for several minutes.

"What are you doing?" Mike asked.

"Vov has used some Earth technology here, but it is mixed with a great deal from my planet. Howard saw the ship here. My communicator still can't locate it. It might be too far underground. Maybe he's been able to build a force field around it. I won't know until I check. It may have to be a visual sighting."

"What if it's gone?"

"It's the best lead I've got. I've still got to look. He's definitely been here. There's got to be a way down to where Howard saw the ship. Those elevators over there are broken. I tried them before I came back to get you." The alien's fingers were almost a blur as they tapped the keys.

"How do you know what to try?" Mike asked.

"I'm using codes I'm familiar with from my planet, and I'm

experimenting. Some of this is just trial and error."

Mike watched Joe work in the blue light from the screen. His concentration on his mission was complete. As close as Mike remembered them being last night, now he felt as if Joe was indeed from another planet or more like when he was a kid and the adults didn't want him bothering them. The being's eyes glowed in the electronic emanations from the computer screen. The intensity of Joe's concentration and the fixity of his gaze disturbed Mike. He hadn't felt this distant from the alien since they'd met.

Mike moved away from the desk with the computer. He found a swivel chair ten feet from the alien. He plopped into it, propped his feet on a table, and leaned his head against the wall. He yawned. He wished he'd had more sleep in the past week. He wished he'd had more time to stop and think about what had happened.

He found his mind wandering and refusing to focus. He wiped his hands against his eyes. The room was dark and slightly less humid than outdoors. The tap of the computer keys was monotonous and soothing. The alien worked relentlessly and without pause. Mike found himself nodding off.

He woke to find the alien standing over him. Joe kissed him lightly on the forehead.

"What?" Mike asked.

"I found the way to get in."

"How long was I asleep?"

"A little over an hour. You should stay up here. Better yet, get in the car and get away. It took me too long to break his code, and I may have set off an alarm. He could be on his way here."

"I'm going with you."

"Mike, please."

"I've stuck with this goofy escapade from the beginning."

"Mike... all right. We better hurry. Come on."

Using his communicator for a feeble guiding light, Joe led them out of the room. They walked through a series of passages, down flights of stairs, and across landings. After traversing a lengthy corridor lined with cement block, they came to a cavernous opening. The floor was as smooth as ice up to where it ended in an immense hole. The roof was at least two or three stories above them.

"This is where they took the heavy equipment down to do the digging." He pointed at a massive door fifty feet beyond them. "There might be another way out that way, but is at least several miles and could be blocked."

Joe looked at a crumpled piece of paper in his hand. Mike glanced over his shoulder and didn't recognize the writing.

"I feel like Indiana Jones in the Temple of the Future," Mike said.

Joe smiled at him. "I remember that hero from one memory I read. I could get into that kind of action-adventure scenario."

The alien led the way across the floor to the open space. Near the edge, the alien halted and studied the floor carefully. He stooped, squatted, and finally knelt on the floor a foot away from the precipice.

Mike walked to the edge of the elevator shaft and glanced down into darkness. "Is this working?" Mike asked.

"Got to be," Joe said. "It's how he got his ship down there."

The alien brushed dirt from a space about the size of a shoe box. Mike saw a flash of light. The alien ran his fingers over rocks that glowed slightly. Then the floor began to rumble. They listened to the elevator rise and then watched it slowly appear. Mike thought the device was large enough to put at least two, maybe three, eighteen-wheeled trucks side by side on it. There was no gate on the front. They simply strode forward. The alien found the control panel on the right side of the car.

He hesitated before pressing the down button.

"What?" Mike asked.

"He's tricky," the alien said.

"Down is down," Mike opined.

"Yeah, but my guess is he'd have safeguards at each point. After I got the code from the computer, I tried to fix it as if I'd never touched it. I'm not sure I succeeded. Then the control panel here performed functions I did not command it to. In attempting to override what was happening, I think I short-circuited the entire thing, or maybe it was programmed to self-destruct if it was tampered with. I know several times I found locks on the codes he'd put in that I couldn't unlock. I had to go around each one. If I'd actually opened one, I'm not sure what would have happened."

"The elevator has to work," Mike said. "He's got to be able to get up and down, or could there be another way?"

"Everything I've been able to find so far points to this being the only entrance. There's got to be a trick." Joe's fingers flew over the display on his communicator. He stood in the middle of the elevator and then began running the communicator up and down the wall.

"What are you doing?"

"Using it to scan for remnants of him having been here. You would call it DNA testing or maybe using a high powered microscope. This will detect the smallest fleck of skin he could have dropped, dried spit, whatever." Joe was silent for several minutes as he walked slowly around the car, the communicator pointing outward from the palm of his hand. Finally, he pointed to the wall just outside the elevator car on the opposite side from the obvious controls. Mike saw only blank space. The alien walked to where he pointed. He passed his communicator over the wall several times. There was a slight flash, and the elevator lurched downward. Joe leapt aboard.

FORTY-SIX

After the first lurch, the ride down was reasonably smooth. At the bottom of the shaft the way to the left was crammed with broken and twisted machinery and piles of debris. The way to the right was filled with mounds of dirt.

"Which way?" Mike asked. While Joe worked the front of his communicator, Mike strode over to the small hills of Earth. A wide doorway opened up on the right. He approached the opening and stopped.

"Joe," he called softly.

"What? I'm a little busy here."

"You need to come see this."

The alien joined Mike. He held up his light. They looked into a cave. On the right were rows of black metallic bookcases from the floor to the ceiling and as far back as the light permitted the eye to see. Each shelf contained a black plastic body bag. At times Mike saw a foot or hand sticking out. Closest to them on the floor on the right were ten bodies placed side by side. They were all naked males. They were all dead.

"What does this mean?" Mike whispered.

Joe was working his calculator quickly.

"Something is wrong here," Joe said.

Mike felt his stomach become queasy. He gulped quickly several times. Mike recognized one of the bodies. It was the man with the welts and whiplashes on his torso who had been in Sally's Leather Boutique and later at the bar.

Joe shook his calculator. "This can't be right."

"What?"

"This says that every one of these people is from my planet or is at least in part. That's what it says, but that is impossible."

"Why?"

"Our anatomies are different. The differences between your and my physiology aren't great, but they are significant enough to be measurable. My communicator says the anatomies are wrong for my planet, but I still get alien readings. It's as if they've all been infected with DNA from my planet somehow." He shrugged. "The genes, blood cells have molecules that are non-Terran."

"Is that possible?"

"I don't know." Joe walked up to each of the figures lying on the ground. He knelt next to each one, touched them, and examined his communicator.

Mike felt the chill of the cavern begin to seep into his bones.

Joe rejoined Mike at the cave entrance. "I can't explain it. These have got to be humans, and I presume he killed or caused the death of all these people. Maybe he was experimenting with them although I didn't find any implant evidence like we did with Howard."

Mike looked at the mounds of earth. "He was burying them. Did he bring all these down here himself? Who was helping him? Does he have people from your planet doing his bidding?"

"I am reasonably certain there are only the three people we know of from my planet here. I have little doubt he's formed some kind of criminal organization." They stood for a few more moments of silence. Joe said, "There is nothing you or I can do for them now. We have to get back to our main task."

The alien scanned with his communicator. "The force field which I presume surrounds his ship is in the other direction past the machines."

They began clambering over the cold metal. The earth-moving equipment seemed to have been jumbled about haphazardly. Parts of it seemed to have been welded or even fused together. The sides of the metal were slick. Handholds were often difficult because of the jagged edges on the twisted and broken ends. They climbed and descended carefully. After they'd gone for about a quarter of a mile, Mike asked, "Couldn't he have booby-trapped this stuff?"

Joe placed his right foot on the outer edge of the bucket at the end of a steam shovel on its side. His foot slipped. He caught himself on the solid metal. Mike gave him a hand up. They teetered on slabs of metal and faced each other.

"You should go back," Joe said.

"Since we've entered this complex, I've felt like the kid who's been in the way. Last night I chose to forget about the impossibilities of a relationship. Now last night seems like several forevers ago, and you are someone I don't know. You're different."

Joe placed his hand on Mike's arm. "I meant what I said last night, but right now I'm working. I'm sorry. This is what I was sent here for. This is my real job. I've got to succeed."

"I know. I realize how serious it is. I'm not trying to have a ridiculous lovers' quarrel."

"It will be different after this is done. I promise."

They resumed scrambling ahead. Mike estimated they'd gone another quarter mile when the piles of machinery abruptly came to an end. The floor became smooth. The alien held up his communicator. The feeble glow showed a ceiling about twenty feet above them. A smooth floor led into darkness. They walked slowly forward. A few minutes later Mike felt the alien's hand reach for his. They walked for some time, hand in hand. Mike liked the tingle and the closeness.

Abruptly Joe slowed. Ahead Mike dimly saw an obstruction. Again Joe held the communicator up, but this time the light from the small machine began to grow. Soon the cavern became almost as bright as day.

"If that gets that bright," Mike asked, "couldn't you have used that to light our way before?"

"That's it," Joe said. As they hurried forward more quickly, Joe added, "The light is growing because I'm able to draw on his ship's power with this."

"Through a force field?"

"You want a physics lecture, find another alien."

"When things are physically impossible, you get awful surly."

"Radio waves travel through the air. Can you?"

"No."

"They can get through a force field, but you can't. Communication still works though."

As Mike got a better view of the ship, he thought it looked more like a truncated space shuttle mixed with a little of the space capsules from the first Earth-orbiting missions back in the early sixties.

About ten feet from the ship, the alien abruptly stopped. Mike stood next to him and put out his hand. He yanked it back. He felt as if his flesh had been scorched, but there was no visible burn.

"What is it?" Mike asked.

"It's the force field. This shouldn't take long." Again Joe took the communicator and passed his fingers rapidly over the surface. The light from it dimmed.

"What is that thing, really?" Mike asked.

Joe said, "Pretend that the tricorders in the *Star Trek* world are real, then multiply their power ten thousand fold. That's not a good comparison, but it's the only one I can think of that makes sense."

"With it can you leap tall buildings in a single bound?"

"Why would I want to do that?"

Mike took out the device the alien had given him. He examined it carefully. He saw nothing he understood. Reluctantly and gingerly, Mike replaced it in his pocket.

Joe continued working for several minutes. For the first time, Mike saw sweat break out on the alien's skin. The amount of time lengthened. Mike heard the alien muttering under his breath in what he presumed was Joe's native language. Fifteen minutes passed with no difference in the alien's posture.

Finally Joe said, "Let me have your communicator."

Mike handed him his. "What's wrong?"

"I've gotten through most of the layers of protection, but there is more here than I can move. He's made a new shield partly with Earth materials less susceptible to the communicator, but I can still handle it."

Joe took both devices and held them side by side. Slowly he extended his hands, palm up, towards the barrier. Mike thought he heard a crackling sound. For an instant the air seemed to shatter. A loud boom echoed and reechoed. Mike covered his ears and shook his head. Flecks of dust drifted down from the ceiling. Joe began to hurry toward the ship. Mike followed.

At the nearest end, the alien stopped. "You okay?" Joe asked.

"I'm sure the ringing in my ears will stop this century."

Joe handed Mike the other-worldly tricorder. "Hang on to this. Whatever you do, don't let it go."

Joe ran the remaining communicator in his hand over the hull of the ship. Abruptly a panel slid aside.

"Good," the alien said. They entered.

Inside what Mike saw looked mostly like stainless steel: pristinely neat, very cold, very cramped, and very empty. They passed through this first chamber, little more than a hallway, into a second chamber the size of a small walk-in closet.

Once inside, the alien hurried to a console filled with soft lights, multi-colored schematics, and symbols Mike did not recognize. After several seconds of pressing buttons, Joe said, "Mike, you have got to leave. He could be here any second. If nothing else, the alarm on his ship was set. If he didn't know from what I did before we came down here, he will know now that I am here. As soon as I touched the force field, he was aware of me. It took me too long to penetrate his blocks up above, much less the stuff down here. No matter where he was in the Chicago area, he could have managed to get here by now."

Mike was exasperated. "I'm going to climb back over all that debris, figure out how to work the elevator, and then get out of the building myself? Does any of that make sense to you?"

The alien caught Mike's gaze and let it linger. "You're right. I'm sorry. What he's done here is dangerous. I didn't know he'd set it up to be this sophisticated. Although..." He gazed at the instrument panel.

Mike said, "At the moment I don't think I'd want to be anyplace else."

Joe nodded. "I can only get a few basic systems to work. Maybe he's building a new one. This model isn't a fighting ship. He could be trying to construct something more lethal than I want to think about."

"Can you stop him from here?"

"I thought I would be able to do a great deal once I found his ship. I'm not sure now. It's going to take a while for me to check all of this." Joe worked the console in silence for fifteen minutes. He could stand in one place and reach the entire surface of the control panel. To Mike it looked as if Joe was placing his hands on Braille-like bumps.

"What are you touching?" Mike asked.

"What look like small black dots to you are thousands of coded instruments." Joe shook his head. "It's worse than I thought. He's in communication with his ship the way I am with mine. That isn't supposed to be possible with this model. He must have altered it. I might be able to tell for sure if..."

"Can't you turn it off?"

"It's too late."

A third voice said, "I agree."

FORTY-SEVEN

Mike and Joe whirled around. Mike's heart banged as if he'd been main-lining caffeine. He remembered the face from the communicator. The man was taller than he thought from what he'd seen on Joe's screen. Up close the new alien looked very much like a United States senator is supposed to look: a shock of silver gray hair swept back, a dignified face with several deep grooves. Vov smiled pleasantly at him -- as if he were a friendly doctor about to give you pleasant news about your test results.

The newcomer spoke directly to Joe. Mike recognized the melodic humming punctuated by occasional deep bass notes that he remembered listening to when Zye and Joe spoke in Howard's apartment.

"Hey," Mike said. "If you guys are going to destroy the Earth or me, I think you should at least speak so I can understand."

Vov spoke to Joe in English, "Your Earth buddy doesn't understand. I'd hate to have him even more confused than he already is for the last few moments of his life." Vov turned to him. Mike distrusted the silky smile. "You poor fool. You think you're on the adventure of a lifetime, but you'll be a wretched corpse in a few moments. Do listen in. I enjoy an audience."

Vov turned back to Joe. "You should have put the force field back up after you got in. That would have given you some warning that I was here, but you didn't. Who are you? Are you a cop or a bounty hunter?"

"Detective Third Level Joe 36/444 operating on special leave."

"Aren't you the one who screwed up, and all those people died on Ruvum II?"

"Yes."

The older alien laughed and turned to Mike. "You do know you've been wandering around with a broken down rookie detective. Doesn't have the brains to make it on the regular force."

"I'm going to take you back," Joe said.

"No you're not. There is not the slightest possibility of that. You shouldn't have gotten in here, but my organization is far from perfect. I still have to handle too many details myself."

"We were at the clinic," Joe said. "We found Howard. Zye killed him."

Vov chortled. "Ask me how much I care. Howard was a little more persistent than most. He was about to tell all. I would have killed him at the bar, but you came a moment too soon." Vov turned to Mike, "He's told you I'm some kind of evil mad scientist, hasn't he?"

Mike forced himself not to nod yes.

"Perhaps," Vov went on, "I'm not the evil one here. I am capable of giving Earth technological secrets you won't discover for hundreds or thousands of years. Why is that a bad thing? He wants to keep knowledge from you. I want to give it to you. He's the one who is a danger to humanity."

"People are dying because of you," Mike said. "You come here and kill and control, and you call that progress?"

"As a wise earthling once wrote, if you want to make the world a better place, you need, as Kurt Vonnegut said in *The Sirens of Titan,* 'A genial willingness to shed other people's blood.' Did you notice my little experimental models nearby? Humans are not very resilient, but they are very gullible. I needed money, of course. To get money, I needed a gimmick. Through a happy chance about six months ago, I made a unique discovery. Turns out our blood cures people of AIDS."

"The cure at the clinic," Mike said.

"That's why I got those odd readings," Joe said. "I was picking up traces of your blood in their bodies."

Vov explained, "I was forced to do some testing to perfect it. There turned out to be an unfortunate side effect. In one or two months after a daily dose of drinking fluid with microscopic traces of my blood in it, the patient was cured of AIDS. Unfortunately, within a few months after that, he was also dead. In continuous doses over a long period of time, our blood is toxic to humans. Desperate people flocked to my clinic, people who were going to die anyway. They felt better for a month or so. Word spread. I started making a great deal of money. Building a criminal organization isn't cheap, and I had the indigent and those who didn't have health insurance come to me, never in sufficient numbers, but I could experiment on them."

"How could you make money off of those?" Mike asked.

"How do indigent heroin addicts get money?" Vov asked. "These people did the same. I found those who had no families or whose families would have nothing to do with them, and I experimented on them. The failures I kept here."

"You're a murderer," Mike said.

Vov ignored Mike and spoke to Joe. "Third level, incompetent whatever-you-are, neither of you will live to see the outside of this ship. I built a criminal organization that you have seriously interfered with. That clinic scam is out, and the fire in the factory-bar complex ruined what was going to be a new laboratory."

"Zye said he started it."

Vov laughed again. "No, it was I, or maybe we both started it. That night I could have killed you all. Zye was clever enough to evade me outside, but I thought the fire might trap you. Ah well, that complex was going to be the heart of a very legitimate empire with simple earthlings making the components to their own enslavement and ultimate destruction."

Neither alien moved or even looked in his direction, but Mike felt himself wrenched off his feet, picked up, and thrown. He slammed hard against the wall three feet behind him. All the bones in his body seemed to crumble to jelly. The back of Mike's head throbbed. He slumped to the floor. He tried shaking his head to clear it. The blue light appeared around him in fits and starts.

"Leave him alone," Joe said.

"You gave him a communicator. I thought only earthlings were that stupid. You'd be dead if you brought me back to our planet."

"Depends."

"Why would you give him a communicator?" Vov looked at Mike then Joe. "I see. You care for him. Humans have something they call, 'love.' How amusing. If you go back to our planet, the police scans of your mind would find that emotion eventually. You would be ostracized and shunned."

"Why?" Mike asked.

"Falling in love with a human is bad enough. Falling in love with another male? It's as sick on our planet as on yours."

"I'm not sick," Joe said. "I'm not trying to enslave a planet."

"Oh, please!" Vov said.

Again Mike's body began to move. He willed himself still, and this time he only slid a few inches.

"You're stronger than I thought," Vov said to Joe, "but you can't protect him and attack me at the same time. That force shield you gave him is rather puny."

"It kept you from killing him outright."

"It won't stop me for long."

Joe said, "It works both ways. You can't attack the two of us at the same time."

Vov laughed. "Sure I can."

Several things happened at once.

Mike tried pushing up with his hands on the floor. He managed half an inch and slumped back. His muscles weren't in the mood to respond to any commands his brain gave them.

For several minutes the two aliens faced each other unblinking. The blue light around Joe grew steadily brighter. Mike's own aura solidified as well.

The next changes in the cabin Mike noticed began subtly.

Although they were indoors, deep underground in an enclosed space, Mike began to feel a stirring of a breeze against his cheek. Slowly the air in the cabin began to whirl and increase in speed. Moments later an outline formed on the floor around both of the aliens' shoes and began to turn yellow, then orange, and finally red.

Seconds after that, circles of metal with a diameter of about three feet glowed bright red on the ceiling directly above and then around the feet of each alien. Mike felt the space under his butt begin to get warmer. Wisps of smoke started drifting from the reddish-tinted floor and ceiling. Mike heard a vague, rumbling, grinding noise.

Neither alien touched a communicator or any part of the physical space Mike could see. What Mike had suspected and feared from the start must be true. The alien did have hidden powers, mental powers. Joe had lied to Mike from the beginning. Mike was angry, but his fear rose faster. He was far underground with one and very possibly two beings who didn't care the slightest about whether he lived or died.

Mike's muscles began to come back under his own control. He rubbed his arms briefly. He hesitated for several seconds, gathered himself for a spring, and tried to leap toward the older man. His leap came out as little more than a feeble flailing at the air. He tried again. The air was thicker than stew that had been left on the stove a week.

The muffled rumbling grew louder. The wind buffeted his clothes and forced him back against the wall and to the floor. He again tried to rise to his feet but found he could barely stand, much less make headway against the gale.

Both aliens' eyes sparkled as their glares bored into each other. At the same instant, both glanced toward the instrument panel. Abruptly the wind died. Joe's hand hit the controls a second before the older man's. At that instant Mike felt as if he'd been released from the tightest shackles. He hurled himself at them. He bashed into the older man's side. The grinding noise rose to ear-shattering decibels. He felt himself flung through the air again. He tried moving, but his body felt encased in Lucite. Dazed, he could do nothing more than watch the titanic struggle play itself out in front of him.

Joe kept his hand desperately on the control panel. The older alien bashed at Joe's fingers with both of his fists. The entire control panel began to glow red.

Joe bellowed in agony but kept his hand on the controls. The grinding noise increased. Wisps of vapor began to ooze from the panel. Mike saw small licks of flame rise from the deepest red portions of the floor and ceiling. Smoke obscured his vision. He began to cough. Joe looked toward him then back at the older man who was still trying to pry Joe's hands off the controls. Suddenly Joe wrenched his fists from the computer switches and, cupping his hands, slammed both of them against the side of the older man's head.

Vov bellowed then staggered back. Joe flung himself forward. The older man dodged sideways, missing the full brunt of the attack, but he was thrown off balance. He stumbled and fell to the ground.

The force of his own lunge landed Joe hard against the wall of the spaceship. The older man picked himself up. He glanced around the smoldering cabin and nodded in Mike's direction. Mike felt himself losing consciousness.

He heard Joe scream, "No!"

FORTY-EIGHT

The next thing Mike remembered was smoke and the feeling of being carried, then being gently placed on a cold floor. When he became fully conscious, he realized he was just outside the bottom of the elevator shaft.

Joe sat on the floor near him. His eyes were closed. His clothes were burnt, scorched, and rent in numerous places. Mike could see one palm, burned through to the bone.

"You carried me from the ship or did you use your mental powers?" Mike found himself coughing and gasping when he tried to speak. When the alien spoke, he sounded at least as bad off as Mike.

"My mental powers are nearly exhausted. Yes, I carried you."

"Thank you."

The alien nodded.

"Where's Vov?"

"He got away."

"What happened?" Mike asked. His voice croaked. The smoke he'd inhaled inhibited his voice box.

"We might get out in time." Joe's voice croaked worse than Mike's.

"What does that mean?"

With frighteningly loud creaks and groans the elevator arrived at their level. The alien staggered to his feet.

"Can you walk?" Joe asked.

Mike tried to stand. The alien stumbled to his side, put his arms around him, and tried to help him rise. Each of them tottered and swayed, neither firm on his feet. They shuffled onto the cage floor.

"How'd he get out?" Mike asked.

"I don't know where he is or how he got out. After you passed out, we fought for another ten or fifteen minutes. I was beginning to overcome his defenses, not by much, and it was still touch and go. His ship has a self-destruct device. He managed to activate it while we fought. He chose to set his device and run. He was strong enough to make following nearly impossible, but I had to do something about his ship, and I was worried about you. I made sure you were all right. He knew I'd have to stop the explosion. I managed to damage him severely, but he isn't dead, not even close to it. He has managed to damage me severely as well."

They both lay on the elevator floor as it took them closer to the surface. At every lurch, Mike expected it to tumble to the bottom of the shaft and smash itself and them to pieces.

At the top the alien took faltering steps off the elevator, steadied himself with one hand against the wall, and turned around. Mike leaned his shoulder against the wall and breathed heavily. He felt like he'd run a marathon with people beating on him with baseball bats the entire time. He slumped to the floor.

Joe staggered several feet back toward the elevator car. He was about fifteen feet from Mike. The alien took out his communicator. His fingers moved slowly over the surface.

"I thought you stopped the explosion."

"I'm double checking. I had to be closer to the surface to draw on the power in my ship."

"You can do that from here?"

"Enough so that it will help. I must work."

Joe kept his full attention on the opening to the shaft. Abruptly, the elevator plunged downward. Horrific metallic screeching filled the air for several seconds. Then Mike heard a thunderous crash. In moments billows of dust and debris filled the space where they were. Both he and the alien choked. Mike took out his hanky and held it in front of his face. He concentrated on breathing.

When the smoke cleared, the tiny communicator still provided light. From its glow, Mike saw the alien's ashen face. The alien tapped on the front of his communicator for nearly a minute. There was a brief flash from below. Then the alien, supporting himself with both hands against the wall, began to move slowly and awkwardly toward the long hall down which they'd come earlier. When he arrived where Mike was hunched against the wall, he said, "Help me," and began to fall.

Exhausted as he was, Mike leaned an arm out and steadied Joe. "What's happened?" Mike asked.

"I've sealed the shaft. There's going to be a tremendous explosion any time now. If what I've done works and if we make it above ground, we'll probably live, and life on your planet will continue as it has."

"My mom says there's an old Polish saying, 'great Russian comedy, everybody die.' If it explodes, who gets killed?"

"I have shielded it. If I hadn't, everything within five to ten miles could have been obliterated. Vov knew I'd have to try and stop the explosion rather than chase after him. He's not supposed to have the ability to even challenge me. He came very close to besting me. That is supposed to be impossible."

"You keep saying that."

"Maybe I can turn it into a magic chant to save your world. I kept him from gaining control of the ship, but I couldn't stop him from setting the self-destruct mechanism."

"When you first told me about this, Vov was simply a criminal. I heard him say 'enslavement and destruction.' This guy sounds like he's Hitler compounded past infinity with the weapons to match. You should have told me."

"Maybe I should have. Can we discuss this after I save your planet?"

"Isn't that a little melodramatic?"

"Only if it doesn't work."

Together Mike and Joe staggered down the hall. Mike wasn't sure who was supporting whom. They escorted each other to the landing and then up the stairs. They walked fifty feet down the corridor to the last landing and halted.

The alien stood with his eyes shut and his communicator in his hand. Every few seconds his body trembled involuntarily. When he opened his eyes, he said, "Deep underground, I could move enough materials in the way, as well as create a force field around it. Outside, I have to make final preparations. Somehow, after that, I still have to catch him."

In the room they first entered, Joe tripped and fell to one knee.

"What's wrong with you?" Mike asked.

"We've got to keep moving. I don't know how good my force field is. I... we've got to keep moving."

They struggled forward. Mike didn't feel adequate to helping a being with incredible powers.

"You have the power to move things with your mind without your communicator," Mike said. "You lied to me."

Joe breathed deeply as they reached the final exit. "I know that." They shut the doors behind them.

They stood in the shallow valley among the ruined and rusted hulks. In the dawn light, these loomed eerily among clouds of wispy fog. The deserted machinery appeared even more ominous than it did in the dark of night. The air was clammy with humidity and warmth. Mike listened carefully for the sound of anyone nearby.

"Are deadly aliens waiting in the fog?"

"Vov and Zye are not nearby. If there are humans, I don't know. I need your communicator."

Mike handed it over. "Keep it," he said.

The alien sighed. Instead of tapping on the front of each he held them palms up.

"All that tapping on the communicator was fake?"

"Please let me work." Mike watched him. The alien's features barely changed for more than thirty seconds. Then he shut his eyes for another fifteen seconds. When he opened them again, he staggered then reached out for Mike. They swayed together several moments. The alien gulped in great bushels of air. Finally he whispered, "I've done all I can. For what little good it would do if I've failed, we should get as far away from here as possible."

They struggled to the lip of the declivity. Mike could see maybe fifty feet. The fields around them seemed completely deserted. Mike felt occasional puffs of wind press moisture against his skin. Their progress across the fields was agonizingly slow. The alien was forced to stop several times. Mike was glad for the respites.

During one of the longer pauses, he looked carefully at the alien who was clearly in pain. "You don't want humans to tend to your wounds?" Mike asked.

The alien glanced at his hands. "I've got to get back to my ship to repair myself. I am totally exhausted and severely damaged internally."

"I can take you to one of our hospitals. They can fix your wounds."

Joe gasped. "I wish it was only what you see." He held out his hands. "These are easily fixed even by your doctors here. They couldn't possible fix the internal problems. In your terms it's as if someone has taken a laser as hot as the surface of the sun and beamed it inside my head, trying to burn and destroy it synapse by synapse. Whatever else happens, do not take me to an earthling doctor. Hurry. We must get to my ship."

"How powerful are you?" Mike asked.

Joe hung his head and spoke to the ground. "I can reach into any human being's mind and destroy it in less than a second. I can control earth, wind, and fire, and command them to my bidding."

At that moment Mike felt the Earth under him sway. He heard a muffled rumble. Joe shut his eyes. He groaned softly. For a few seconds, his muscles stretched taut. Then his body went limp, and he slumped to the ground. Joe muttered, "Get me to my ship, please." He lapsed into unconsciousness.

Nothing Mike tried revived him. Lifting Joe to his shoulders, Mike used a fireman's carry to move him. He found the warm tingle was far less, his worry far greater. At the car Mike placed Joe carefully against the side of the vehicle. He unlocked the door and placed him gently on the seat. Mike got in on the driver's side and sat in silence. He barely knew what to do. Finally, he started the car and drove as fast as he dared toward Interstate 57. He barely kept his mind on the road. He had no idea how he was supposed to get Joe to his ship. Mike knew there was no way he was going to bore down under the lake to find an alien spacecraft.

Mike touched the alien's hand. It was warm. Joe's breathing was shallow and raspy. Mike worried that the alien might die. He found that despite his anger at being lied to, he was appalled at the possibility. He desperately wanted Joe to live. He could be furious with him later.

FORTY-NINE

An hour and a half later they crawled with the traffic past the immense McCormick Place complex then up Lake Shore Drive past Soldier Field then around the Loop. The cars next to them were barely visible in the fog that had thickened the farther north they'd driven. Northbound traffic began to ease as Mike rounded the Oak Street curve. He could still barely make out the tail-lights of the car ten feet in front of him. He passed only three cars on the Belmont Avenue off-ramp. He turned right and made the sharp U-turn to the harbor.

Mike parked the car at the far end of the lot. The last ticks of the engine faded into the enveloping fog. Joe groaned softly. He opened his eyes and glanced out at the fog then at Mike.

"Are you okay?" Mike asked.

Joe drew several deep breaths before murmuring, "The rest helped a little. I think I can walk. Where are we?"

"The lake shore."

Joe groped for the door handle and clicked it up. The door swung part-way open. As he eased himself out of the car, Joe stumbled and fell to his knees. Mike tried to hurry to help, but all of his muscles felt as if they'd been worked in a gym for a solid week. He had to lean one hand on the car to keep himself from falling as he staggered to Joe's side. He helped the alien stand and clutched him, so he wouldn't fall. They stared at the fog. The alien's face had serious burns and deep gouges down the sides of his arms.

Although they could hear the occasional rhythmic slap of shoes against pavement, they couldn't see any of the runners who usually inhabited the nearby stretch of pavement. Without waiting to see who might appear out of the fog, they stumbled to the Belmont Rocks. Several times Mike needed to keep Joe from falling. At the lake's edge, Joe reached into the hiding place for his traveling disk.

It was gone.

Joe carefully placed his hands onto one of the rocks. "One of them must have it," he whispered.

"Maybe the cops discovered the hiding place?"

"Only someone from my planet could have found it and dislodged it. We must find a boat. If one of them has the thing, they might be keeping watch." The alien tried to move quickly. He groaned and fell to the ground. Mike helped him up. "We've got to keep moving," Joe said.

"Where?"

"Get me to the side of the marina."

When they reached the concrete walkway, they paused. The mist swirled around them. Moisture seeped into Mike's eyes as he looked from the alien to the amazingly placid lake water.

"Now what?" Mike asked.

The alien said nothing. He stood with his eyes closed. Mike peered into the foggy half-light. He heard the gentle swishing and lapping of the water against the cement barrier.

"I'm not sure I'm going with you," Mike said.

"You've got to." The alien spoke earnestly. "I need your help." Joe gasped, clutched his head with one hand and his side with the other. "I do not have the strength to argue."

Mike supported the alien as he began to hobble around the harbor. As far as Mike could see in the fog, all the vessels were too far out for them to get to.

Joe pointed. "There."

Next to the boathouse, Mike spotted a small dinghy without an outboard motor. "That should do," Joe said. The boat slowly began to float in their direction.

"You're moving that with mental powers?"

Joe nodded. Once the boat arrived, Mike helped Joe in despite his own pain. Joe said, "You'll have to row. I'm too tired." Mike took the oars and rowed into the fog.

Two men appeared from behind a stand of bushes and shouted for them to halt. They began to draw guns. The alien barely glanced at them. Mike rowed furiously, but the boat moved far quicker than he rowed. Seconds later, they were swallowed by the fog. For a few minutes they heard shouts.

Joe braced himself against the edge of the boat. "I cannot do much more of this. I moved the boat as much as I could."

"Where am I going?" Mike asked.

"To a bigger boat."

Mike rowed for five minutes until a gray darkness appeared on the water. For a moment Mike thought it might be the alien's spaceship. Then he recognized the shape of a cigar boat. Mike's last boyfriend had tried to seduce him on one. This was the kind of boat that could probably hit ninety miles an hour and slurp up gas at the rate of one-and-a-half-miles-per-gallon with a one hundred fifty gallon tank.

The boat rocked and swayed in the slight swell as they tried to climb aboard. At the last second the alien tripped and fell to his hands and knees on the boat deck.

"I can't use my mental powers to move this boat. You'll have to start it and drive out. I can maybe push it a little bit, if you can get it started. Moving that small boat has almost completely exhausted me."

"Where are the keys?" Mike asked.

Joe took out his communicator. "I can jump start it with this." Moments later, the engine gave a cough and then roared to life. The alien slumped down on the deck, eyes closed, arms and legs still.

The cockpit for passengers and driver had two sections. The forward part had two seats with the controls in front of the one on the right. Mike noted the door down three steps between the passenger and driver's seat.

Mike vaguely recalled how to handle the relatively simple controls. The alien lay in the open area just behind the seats.

The engine roar sounded monstrous amid the gray and silent fog. In the distance he thought he heard another motor start up. Mike could barely see ten feet in any direction. He had to risk turning the lights on. Then he spun the wheel. As Mike inched the craft forward, he saw mostly their own lights reflecting off the fog. Occasionally a boat loomed nearby. There were fewer in September than in high summer, but the harbor was still crowded. He was forced to go slowly enough that he didn't run into anything.

He had no real idea where the harbor entrance was nor where to go after that. If the alien died, he was sunk. The smile at his unfortunate word choice was fleeting. Vov would find him and kill him in short order, and woe to the rest of humanity after that.

Mike looked back at Joe. The alien hadn't opened his eyes. His head lolled to the side. He looked worse than in the car. A shiver ran through Mike. He feared that the alien might be dead. He wasn't sure if the feeling came from fright for what might happen to himself or from fear that if the alien were dead, he'd miss a companion who'd taken him on an adventure no one from Earth could duplicate.

Mike remembered that there had been a dampening switch. He wasn't eager to find out which one it was by trial and error, but he felt he had little choice. He also wanted to try the controls to find the one that would activate the radar.

As they eased forward Mike felt the damp on his forehead, saw droplets beading on the surface of the deck. Mike angled around several small crafts. From the configuration of the boats, he tried making a reasonable guess as to where the exit was. As he neared where he thought it might be, he slowed the engine to the lowest it would go without stalling.

He thought he heard another boat. He saw no lights through the impenetrable fog. The bottom of the boat gently scraped against the bottom. A rock outcropping appeared to his right. He'd found the wall around the harbor. If he followed this long enough he'd come to the exit. A few moments later the rocks slid away. Cautiously Mike swung the boat right and ran it out onto the lake.

FIFTY

Mike drove what he thought was about twenty-five feet beyond the opening and put the engine on idle. He knew the alien's ship was deep under the lake. He had no idea how to get to the rendezvous point. There was just him, oceans of fog, and billions of gallons of opaque water.

Mike looked back at the alien. He might have moved. He couldn't have heard him moan.

He could barely make out the sound of another boat's motor. Definite this time. Theirs was not the only craft out on the lake. Mike shivered uneasily. His shirt clung to his skin.

He put his hand on the throttle. A mad dash in this fog would be insane. For all he knew, he'd turned the boat completely around. He could rush for ten feet and crash himself, the alien, and the boat into oblivion.

Mike thrust the throttle forward and began creeping toward what he hoped was further into the lake. The hum of the other motor increased.

Suddenly the lights of another cigar boat loomed out of the mist. It came at them on a perpendicular angle from the right and straight on toward the center of the boat.

"What the hell?" Mike asked. He had a brief flash that it was maybe a Coast Guard boat or the police or FBI, someone official not taking kindly to morning excursions. Maybe it was simply someone befuddled by the fog.

But as the boat neared, it did not swerve in the slightest in its course to impact in the center of their boat. Mike didn't wait for identification or explanations. He shoved the throttle forward. The engine gave a full-throated roar, and the boat leaped forward over the calm, black surface of the lake.

The lights of the other boat swerved to pursue them. Mike could see at least three people on the other boat. One he thought looked like Zye. One of the people on the boat stood on the passenger seat, swung a leg over the windshield, then pulled himself up, and stepped over. He lay down on top of the forward deck, brought a rifle to his shoulder, swung the barrel in their direction, and sighted through his scope.

"What's happening?" came a faint voice from the rear. Mike snapped his eyes from death on the right to the back of the boat. The alien was sitting up. Mike realized that Joe was taking a great effort to shout again. "What's going on?"

"We're being chased, and we're about to be shot at."

Abruptly a piece of the wood an inch under the windshield erupted into fragments.

"We are being shot at," Mike corrected.

The alien attempted to rise. Mike couldn't leave the controls to help him. Mike prayed that they were racing toward the open water.

The alien eased himself between the two seats. Mike leaned back with one hand to help him. Joe managed to rise far enough to glance at the other boat.

"It's Zye," he shouted, "and some unfriendly buddies."

Another shot blasted into the radar scope followed in quick succession by two more that tore into seat cushions. So much for trying to get the radar to work. Mike couldn't duck. He had to keep control of the wheel and watch where they were going. He glanced at the other boat. The shooter seemed to be having a hard time getting another shot off, or perhaps with the pitching of both boats, even on these calm waters, he couldn't aim accurately. Maybe he'd fired all kinds of rounds, and all the others had missed. The ones that hit so close might have been simply random luck.

"Can you help?" Mike asked.

The alien shook his head. "I'm too exhausted." Mike could barely hear him over the wild cacophony of noise.

"Try," Mike yelled.

"I am trying. Be thankful it's Zye and not Vov. Just keep us moving forward." The minutes stretched slowly as boat followed boat. Mike had no idea how far they'd gone into the lake.

Mike peered forward. "There's a light in front of us."

"What?"

Mike couldn't tell if it was the buoy of a water filtration marker or another boat. It might be a small light at the end of a pier, although Mike thought they were too far out for this to be true. He had no idea if within seconds he would be smashed into oblivion on a shoal of rocks or guided helpfully through the thick fog.

They'd begun to pull ahead of the other boat. For the longest time, it had been twenty or thirty feet to their right and about ten feet back. Now it was maybe forty to fifty feet to the side and twenty feet behind. The lights of the enemy were beginning to shimmer and grow dim in the enveloping fog.

Mike looked ahead. The light he'd seen was growing brighter. Now he could see it was on the prow of a boat and heading straight for them.

Another alien?

Joe was grasping his side and leaning against the bulwark. He stared intently forward.

"It's the cops," he said.

"Should we stop for them?"

"Vov could be with them," Joe said. "How fast can this thing can go?"

"My boyfriend claimed his could outrun almost anything on the lake. He used to brag about it. I don't want to run from the cops."

"You want to explain what's been going on?"

Mike shook his head. Mike aimed their boat to the left. He saw the police boat begin to turn. It was closing on them fast.

For the first time Mike heard the loud blast of a foghorn. He peered intently into the darkness but couldn't see where it came from.

The boat that had been ahead of them was close enough that Mike could see a uniformed man reach for a microphone. What came next sounded like the voice of god at the last trumpet.

"Come about and prepare to be boarded."

Mike ignored him. So did their pursuers. Mike passed the prow of the police vessel with five yards to spare. The alien boat wasn't so lucky. Their choice was to smash into the police boat or slow down and turn. Mike didn't see what happened as he was forced to hold onto the wheel and gaze forward in an attempt to see what was ahead. At one point he managed to glance back. He'd heard no crash so assumed there hadn't been a collision. After a few seconds, he could barely see the outline of their pursuers. He thought he heard gun shots.

The alien gave a gasp of pure horror. Mike turned back forward. He flinched involuntarily. Directly in their path a black monster towered eight or nine stories above them.

"Hang on," Mike screamed. He wrenched the wheel far to the right. The boat heeled over. He thought they might capsize. The cigar boat leaped and shuddered through the wake of the behemoth. The huge freighter made no sound that could be heard over the throb of their engines. Its silent, fog-enshrouded passing made it all the more frightening. They had no indication that any human agency controlled the mammoth hulk in front of them.

Mike cut their speed as they danced over waves kicked up by the ship. Abruptly a huge hole appeared in their windshield and webs of crinkling spread out in the plastic.

The original boat pursuing them ran a parallel course maybe thirty feet to their right. Mike could see the guy with the rifle wedging himself to the edge of the cockpit and windshield to get himself some balance.

Mike couldn't hear the shots, but he could see small flashes of red and occasional spouts lift out of the water. Perhaps twenty feet beyond the second boat, farther to the right, Mike saw the faint glow of more lights. He thought perhaps they might be the police boat.

Another fusillade of bullets raked the rail, shredded the passenger seat completely, and thumped into the instrument panel.

Brass, fabric, and plastic flew around their heads. Mike scrunched as low as he dared to the floor, but his head was still exposed. He had to see above the windshield or risk a crash.

They were bouncing in the wake of the freighter. Their enemies couldn't turn toward them and make a lot of headway because all of them were still in the wake of the ship. The pitching and swaying of the boats prevented accurate shots no matter how close. Of course, a hail of bullets no matter how randomly fired could eventually hit something vital, especially himself, Mike thought.

Mike also guessed that along with trying to shoot them, at the moment, Zye would be quite happy with simply sinking them. He wondered how far out they'd gone and how cold the water was. He had no idea what speed they'd reached or for exactly how long they'd headed straight out on the lake: at least a mile or two and probably much more. Mike was a good swimmer, but he was exhausted from his ordeal earlier. Also he'd have to drag the alien with him. He didn't relish a swim with deadly enemies trying to take pot shots at him while he stroked for shore or worse some alien trying to fry his mind into nothingness.

The mass of the freighter passed, and they quickly edged through the last of the wake. Mike swung the boat out toward open water and pushed the throttle to the utmost. They raced forward.

The deadly fog, the lights of the boat, the slumped-over alien, the shattered portions of the cockpit and windshield -- Mike took them all in, pulled in a deep breath and took an even tighter grip on the wheel. He hunched himself deeper into his leather jacket. Small sprays of water occasionally landed in the boat. Joe sat on the top step. He held his head in his hands. For five minutes

Mike thought he heard the other boats. Slowly their sound faded. After another ten minutes of flat-out speed the boat abruptly raced into clear air. A glorious sun-drenched morning sparkled on the water. When next he dared glance back, he saw a wall of fog. He saw no lights emerge from the looming gray. He strained to listen, but he heard no other engines. At least their pursuers couldn't be close.

After ten more minutes at top speed, Mike cut the engines. Nothing frightening disturbed the glory of the vast expanse of bright blue. Behind him the menacing fog placidly swirled and eddied. He didn't know when something untoward would leap out of the dank gray.

Mike tried to get his bearings, but he had no real notion of where they were. He kept the boat headed away from the fog. He presumed from the position of the sun that they were moving east out onto the lake. Certainly he saw no shoreline nearby. For the moment the going was clear and unhindered. Mike took stock of his surroundings.

Shattered pieces of boat lay strewn about the cabin. Mike thought he saw a few puffs of smoke come from the engine on the left. Nothing he could do about that now.

Keeping one hand on the wheel, he knelt next to Joe. "Are you okay? Can I help?"

The alien opened his eyes and stared at the glorious firmament above. "I have to rest. I have to get to the ship."

"Which way do I go?"

The alien pulled out his communicator. "We're about ten miles away from where we need to be."

"Which way?" Mike asked.

Joe pointed.

Mike felt water in his shoes. He looked down. An inch of water was in the cockpit. He couldn't tell if he was simply noticing it now because of the sloshing of the boat in a gentle swell, or maybe at least one of the gun shots had penetrated the hull and they were sinking.

Mike muttered, "I want to be beamed up."

FIFTY-ONE

The rising sun gave Mike a sense of time and place. "What I need is a good physicist," Mike muttered.

"What?" Joe asked.

"An old joke that I like. According to an old friend of mine, all problems we face can be reduced to problems of time and space, and to solve problems in that realm one need only call your local physicist."

"Guess you had to be there," Joe said.

Following the alien's directions, they sped quickly toward the northeast.

He felt the water in the cockpit rise to his ankles. His look down confirmed the dampness.

"We may sink before long."

The alien looked back toward the barely visible fog bank. "I think we've lost them. If we hurry, we'll make it. Once we're inside my ship, no one can find us."

The boat began slowing perceptibly.

"Are you doing that?" Mike asked.

"No."

"Now what's wrong?" Mike rose to his feet and looked behind. Gasoline trailed from the engine on the left. A thin stream of smoke drifted in the boat's wake.

"They must have hit at least one of the engines," Mike said. "Can you fix this thing or move it with your powers?"

The alien shut his eyes for a few moments. "I certainly can't fix it. I doubt if I can move it. Keep driving for as long as you can."

"If they find that trail of fuel, they'll be able to follow us."

"I know."

At the lower speed the noise was much less. Mike propped some of the debris around the wheel to hold it steady and searched in the compartments on the side of the cockpit. He found several life jackets. He put one on and helped the alien into one. He also found several oars.

"I can't imagine these being much good," he muttered to the sunlight.

Abruptly the alien sat up. "We're close," he said. "Help me stand."

"Are you better?" Mike asked.

"A little. This close to my ship I can draw limited amounts of energy from it." They stood together. The alien leaned heavily against Mike. Joe took his communicator out of his pocket. He tapped the front for a few seconds.

"Turn off the boat," Joe said.

Mike complied.

The ensuing silence was pleasing.

Joe said, "Now appearing, one alien spaceship."

Mike didn't know what he expected. His vision of any ship was shaped by a variety of science fiction movies from the fifties, plus *Star Trek,* and *Close Encounters of the Third Kind.* His glimpse the other day had been of a stainless-steel surface. He presumed he'd have more time to watch. The water to the left of the boat about fifty feet from them began to foam. Slowly, sunlight began to gleam off sloping metal.

Joe pointed the communicator at the rising metal, pressed once or twice at the face, and the upward movement stopped, and the ship pulled up right next to them. Another few taps and a door slid open. They exited their boat carefully. When they were at the opening to the ship, Joe looked back. He raised the communicator, pointed it at the cigar boat, which in the next second completely disappeared.

"What the hell?"

"I couldn't afford to leave any trace of where we are."

"There wasn't any explosion."

"I rearranged all of its molecules. Don't worry, it didn't suffer. If you could help me, please."

Mike put his arm around the alien's waist and helped him inside. Immediately after they cleared the opening, the panel slid shut. This ship, like Vov's, seemed to be mostly stainless steel, pristinely neat. The room they were in was much larger than the entry way in Vov's ship.

"Home to Tara," Mike said. He helped the alien further down the hallway. Mike asked, "Are we still on the surface?"

"No. It's already descending. I set the controls automatically."

The side of the alien's face still pulsed where it had been scorched with second- and third-degree burns. The ragged gouges down the side of his arm and on his hands oozed small amounts of colorless liquid.

The next room was about as big as Mike's bedroom in his apartment. After they entered, the door slid shut. Where the opening had been, there was only solid wall. Chairs and a bed which seemed to be made out of the same stainless steel as everything else were seamlessly attached to the floor and wall. Mike couldn't tell what the source of light was in any of the rooms. Everything gleamed brightly.

"I need to be at that console." Joe pointed at a desk-shelf area.

Mike helped him to the console and then stood next to the alien as Joe began touching Braille-like knobs, the same as those he'd seen on Vov's ship. To Mike it looked as if this console had three times as many controls as Vov's did. Pale pink light began to bathe the alien who leaned heavily against the shelf. "Mike, you can't stand near me."

Mike stepped back to the middle of the room.

Joe's voice seemed to come from a great distance. "Whatever happens, do not touch me. Do not move to help me. Promise me this."

"I promise."

Mike watched Joe shut his eyes. The light around him turned to a bright pulsing yellow. The alien's arms rose to stick straight out from his shoulders. He spread his legs wide. As the light changed to blue, the alien's clothes disappeared. Mike watched the body he'd explored not that many hours before rise off the floor several inches then begin to rotate in the light. Mike felt completely helpless. He also knew he was in a presence far more powerful than any he had ever known. The heat in the cabin increased.

Mike stumbled back and felt one of the chairs behind him. He sat in it, expecting it to be cold and metallic. Instead whatever material it was made of instantly conformed to his body, as if it were a metallic marshmallow waiting to do his bidding. Whenever his body moved, the chair's contours adjusted themselves to his new position, each time making him as comfortable as he could have wished.

He looked over at Joe. The alien's skin was bright pink. The light around him was now bright red. Mike watched in awe. He saw the burned skin on the side of the alien's face begin to transform. At first he wasn't sure what was happening. For several moments he feared that the alien would be revealed to be a shape shifter and that in actuality the thing was a multi-limbed gorgon. This fantasy soon passed as he realized that almost pore by pore the skin was being repaired and turned back to match the pink of the rest of the body.

The process was slow. The alien's body continued to slowly twirl. Mike wished he had the nerve to leave the room and explore the ship, but he hardly dared move. He didn't know what he might accidentally set off with some random touch.

Mike wondered about Vov and Zye and what they would be able to do about their plans. He wasn't sure if Joe really did either. So many times Joe had said the other alien wasn't capable of something, and then Vov had gone and done what was supposedly beyond his power. Mike feared that once again the evil alien might suddenly appear in the doorway.

But nothing happened, except that the glow continued unabated. Mike felt his exhaustion creep up on him. Tired as he continued to be, he hesitated about falling asleep.

An hour passed before the burns on the alien's face were completely healed. As this was finished, the light changed to a soft violet, and the gouges on the alien's arms slowly began to disappear. All that happened occurred in silence. For a while Mike thought about the fact that they were hundreds of feet under water and underneath the bottom of the lake.

He stuck his knuckles under his eyelids in an attempt to keep them open. His lack of sleep and his own physical exhaustion combined to cause his eyelids to droop involuntarily. As he began to drift off, he wondered if the alien weren't in some way causing him to fall asleep. Suddenly the alien gave a horrific scream. Mike leaped to his feet. The light around Joe was now dark purple. The alien's eyes were still closed, and he made no further sound.

The cry brought Mike fully awake. He remembered Joe's admonishment not to touch him. He prowled the space in the cabin for a half an hour. He touched the walls but felt only cool steel. He sat on the bed for a moment. It began gently undulating. He jumped back up.

After another half hour the alien, looked completely whole on the outside. The pillar of light surrounding him was nearly black. Mike couldn't see where the light source originated from. It was as if a column of color simply appeared and existed on its own.

He sat back on the chair. He felt its comfort and his tiredness. He had no idea how long this would go on. He settled back and let his mind drift over the fantastic experiences he'd had. Again, he found himself falling asleep.

FIFTY-TWO

When Mike awoke, he felt a crick in his neck. He stretched. The alien no longer glowed and rotated. Joe was lying on the bed with his eyes closed. Mike sat on the edge of the bed and examined the still naked body: strong, slender, and still breathing. Mike took out his cell phone, checked the time, and noted that over ten hours had passed since he'd last awakened. He felt fresh and in much less pain. He only heard the soft breathing of the alien. He didn't remember any lack of sound as profound as this in his life. In repose and naked, Mike thought Joe was as sexy as at any moment in the past few days. Still he did not touch him.

The alien awoke and smiled at Mike. His hands roved over his healed skin. He pressed his side. Joe said, "I feel better."

"You wouldn't be able to give me a dose of that?" Mike asked.

"I wish I could. How do you feel?"

"I've rested," Mike replied. "I think I'm okay. Are you cured?"

"Patched is more like it. I'm not a hundred percent, but I am much better than I was. Thank you for helping me to get here."

"Now what?"

"We use what we've found out to destroy Vov."

Joe stood up, stretched mightily, and then walked to the console. He ran his fingers briefly over the strange little knobs. Seconds later a panel opened to reveal a pair of bright white briefs and socks, faded blue jeans, gym shoes, and a sweatshirt. The alien spoke as he dressed.

"I have to find Vov and stop him. I've also got to figure out what Zye is up to. He must be around someplace. I can work better from the master controls in the next room. Let's go."

"No," Mike stated.

Joe stopped. "What do you mean?"

"Which part of 'no' is culturally alien to you? Don't think I'm not grateful to you for saving my life. I am, but we need to get some things settled before anything else happens. I think we're perfectly safe here, so we've got at least a little time. You lied to me."

"You've just seen me practically raised from the dead, and you're worried about being lied to?"

"I don't care if you're the son of god. You lied to me from the start. You said you love me."

"I did. I do. I didn't know I was going to fall in love. We don't do that on my planet."

"You're not going to stay. You'll leave. You told him you were going to take him back. You never planned to stay."

"Mike, what did you think was going to happen?"

"I don't know."

"What do you want to happen?"

"I don't know."

"For now, you are stuck with me. Vov will find you. He can rip minds apart. That would be worse than killing you. He might let you live a life worse than being completely physically paralyzed. He won't care who he hurts to find and destroy you."

"Why does he want to kill me? You're the threat to him. I'm not."

"He is not omnipotent. If you go to the police, they might not believe your story completely. They may not know precisely what destroyed that tunnel, but they'll know something enormous did. The most brilliant Earth scientists working for centuries could not reconstruct a centimeter of what came from my planet. If you know that Vov is a killer, he has to figure that the authorities will gain that knowledge soon enough. With all the civil authorities actively against him, it would make his work infinitely more difficult."

"If you're going to destroy this planet because of politics or crimes on your planet," Mike said, "why not just get it over with? You're saying we have no say in the future of our entire planet, that all the lives of the billions of people on this rock are nothing compared to your intergalactic machinations. Well, screw it. I'm tired of it. Just blow us all to hell and be done with it. Even if I could get out of this ship, report you to every police force on the planet, and we had years to prepare for you -- you could still wreck the place with a blink of your eyes."

"You done?"

"Until you let me out of here."

"I don't want to kill people. I want to save people. I don't want you to die. Against all directives, training, orders, decrees, programming, inserts, and implants, I care for you very deeply. I want to stay with you. I'd like to make my life with you."

Mike found himself pacing around the chair he'd slept in. He stopped himself behind it and gripped the top of the back with his hands. He was torn. He wanted what he was being told to be the truth. He'd overcome a lot of his own fears to declare his interest. He let go of the chair and said, "I wish I could believe you."

"What can I do to make you believe?"

Mike pointed toward the control panel. "Can you cure Darryl with your technology?"

"Unfortunately no. This is set to my anatomy. It would kill him. We've tried it on other planets, and it doesn't work. I'm sorry."

Mike looked around the magnificent ship which contained powers far beyond his ability to comprehend. Finally his gaze returned to the alien's eyes. "I don't know what you could say," Mike said. "Maybe there isn't anything." He sighed. "As the only representative of the human race here, I feel required to ask on our behalf, will we survive the three of you? Will you leave us alone? Will we ever have our planet back?"

"I cannot leave you alone with a crazed killer on the loose."

"Let Zye have him. That way your work is done. Then you can leave."

Mike fell silent. He stopped at the console, looked at Joe, looked down at the incomprehensible buttons. He knew his objections were made from fear of losing the alien, of the unknown, of his own helplessness in the face of such sheer power and might, of being out of his depth with no one to whom he could appeal for help or even talk with. "I'm sorry," Mike said. "I have no skills to deal with you and what you represent. I thought I did. I don't. I'm just a guy."

"You have the skills. You're kind, thoughtful, smart. You try and puzzle things out based on the best available information. That's the most anybody can do."

"I wish you hadn't lied."

"I wish I hadn't also. I shall not lie to you again. There is no need at this point."

"What do you mean?"

"I need to finish my mission. For the time I have left here, I would like you to be a part of that. You may not be able to share your adventure with others, but I am inviting you to be part of saving your planet."

Mike shook his head. "This is too overwhelming. I'm sorry now that I have any feelings for you." Mike continued to gaze into the alien's eyes until Joe turned away. "You didn't tell me about your powers," Mike said.

Joe spoke softly. "No, I didn't."

"What else haven't you told me?"

"Probably several million things. Where would you like me to start?"

"I'm not sure."

"I would like to start my explanation over from the beginning."

"What good is that supposed to do? Is that supposed to make up for every lie? And how am I supposed to believe them?"

"I wish I knew."

"How much of our minds can you control?"

"On my planet we can greet each other telepathically. With a lot of practice, I could probably snap a human's mind, and over time I could control people. I don't want to."

"Why not?"

"I have more than implants controlling me. You would call them morals, although they are stronger than that. Going beyond all my training to have sex with you was a tougher choice than I have ever had to make. I'm glad I did. I would do it again. I don't want to rule or control you. You know, Mike, if I wanted to use my powers to alter your mind, I'd have stopped you asking questions days ago. I didn't."

"If you told me the truth about being an alien, what was the big secret about revealing your powers?"

"I am not a good cop. I wanted help, and I wanted to connect, and I wanted to be liked. I thought revealing all those powers might scare you."

"I was scared anyway."

"Wouldn't you have been more frightened if I'd told you about my powers?"

"We'll never know, because you didn't give me the chance. In so many movies, people are frightened of the alien. I know that's all fiction, but in real life, you give people choices. You took away my choice. In my mind secrets and relationships don't mix."

"I told you as much of the truth I thought you could handle."

"You told me as much of the truth as *you* could handle. Don't put this all on me, the poor weak earthling."

"Compared to me you are."

"That does not make me feel better."

Joe held out a hand as if pleading to be understood and accepted. "First you say you want reality and truth, and when I give you some, you don't like it."

Mike didn't respond to the hand held out to him. He was still too angry and confused.

"Against all logic and in peril to my mission, I chose to save you. Doing that does not make me a good cop. I have never experienced the attraction I feel to you. I wish I knew what to say to get you to believe me, to convince you that I care for you. I'm sorry, very sorry that your feelings are hurt. Can't you try and put yourself in my place for a while? What choices did I really have?"

Mike felt the reasonableness of the arguments. His emotions were still in turmoil. He wanted to believe the alien.

The alien touched Mike's arm and spoke softly. "If we were both honest, we'd admit we've known each other an awfully short time to be lovers."

"Yeah, but I was getting used to the idea."

"So was I. Can we at least agree to work this out when my job is done?"

Mike saw the sensibleness of the request. He nodded agreement. He paused and pulled in a deep breath. He asked, "What happens now?"

FIFTY-THREE

They moved into the control room. Innumerable little black knobs covered a console that circled the entire room. The only thing Mike could think of as comparable was the sound and lighting controls at a major rock concert, although this dwarfed that completely.

"If he gets this ship, Earth could be destroyed," Joe said. "He cannot be allowed to have that much power. I'm afraid if he gets Zye's ship, his power might be unstoppable."

"How could Vov be as powerful as you?"

"Mentally, he was my superior. I expected that. He's got years of experience. He's had at least a year to work untrammeled on Earth. It is a long time for someone as bright as he is to do some great damage."

Joe sat down at the controls and ran his hands over sets of knobs. "I wish I knew where he was now. I'm worried."

Mike asked, "Where are we going?"

"I've programmed the ship to rise to the surface far from where they chased us. Want to cruise around in the ship for a few minutes? Might be a lot of fun."

"Like in space?"

Joe nodded.

"We've got time for a trip?"

"My body is getting used to its cure. For injuries much less severe than mine, we're supposed to wait twenty-four to forty-eight hours before resuming activity. We don't have that much time, but I want to take at least several hours. Where would you like to go?"

"Can we go to your planet?"

"That would take more time than we have. Something a little closer."

"The rings of Saturn?"

Joe ran his hands over the controls for a few seconds.

Mike did not feel the ship move. A few seconds later part of the wall slipped aside revealing a blur of rapidly moving lights.

"What is it?"

"We're passing through your solar system. That's what it looks like when the ship moves."

"Is this full speed?"

"It isn't intergalactic speed, just ordinary runabout-the-solar-system speed."

"How long will we take to get to Saturn?"

"Couple minutes."

"Oh." Mike watched the blur of lights. "How do I know this isn't simply a video?" he asked.

"I like the way you doubt everything," Joe said. "Nobody on my planet asks questions the way you do. What you are looking at is not a screen. It is an electronic portal to the universe. You are looking at the real thing."

The rapidly passing lights began to slow. The stars began to shine distinctly. He gave a small gasp as he got his first glimpse of Saturn's rings. He was astounded at the incredible beauty. Looking up he saw the gray swath that was the Milky Way. For a few moments the vastness and majesty of the universe comforted him. "That's one of the most beautiful sights I ever hope to see."

"It's not that rare throughout the galaxy."

"Incredible."

They made a circuit of Saturn. "We should be getting back," Joe said.

"Yeah."

The portal blurred again.

"Are you going to land in the lake again?" Mike asked.

"I'm going to land at the north end of the lake and travel

under water. I can jam Zye's radar, but amazingly enough, Earth radar is so primitive that my instruments are not good at jamming it. Once again your police will know something left the lake a few hours ago and then something reappeared."

"They won't be able to follow underwater?"

"Not readily. No submarine could keep up with me. Currently, there aren't any of those in the lake anyway. First, I want to find Zye and his ship."

Several minutes later Joe said, "We're as close to shore as we can get. We need to move quickly. When this thing is on the surface, it is at its most vulnerable." From a compartment Joe took another of the disc-shaped flotation devices.

When the outer portal opened, Joe flung the disc onto the lake surface. Above Mike could see a canopy of stars. To the east however, there was a faint glow of dawn. The air was warm and humid. The water was near a dead calm. There wasn't a hint of fog.

"How long were we in your ship?" Mike asked.

"It's been almost twenty hours. I can do miracle cures, but they aren't easy or quick."

They stepped onto the flotation device. The ship quickly disappeared under the surface. They began to move almost simultaneously.

"Where are we?" Mike asked.

"Just at the north end of the city. We're a little over two miles out. We'll be on shore before anyone can react to us being here."

"It's clear weather. Someone could see us."

"We've got a few minutes before full sun up. I'll stop at a breakwater and summon a boat."

"Hurry."

"The boat is already on its way to meet us."

"You're using your full powers."

"Yes."

As the shoreline came into view, Mike also saw a small motorboat drifting toward them. When it got close enough, they climbed in.

They pulled into the lagoon just north of the Noyes Center on the Northwestern University campus on the lake front in Evanston. Several early joggers waved at them. They left the boat and let it float away. Joe put the transportation disc on the surface of the water. He tapped his communicator, there was a flurry of sand, and it disappeared.

"I buried it under the surface. If anyone ever finds it besides me, it will disintegrate."

As they stood on the shoreline Mike said, "Thanks for saving me."

Joe smiled, "You're welcome." Joe took the second communicator out of his pocket and held it out to Mike. "Here."

"You keep it."

"I'd feel better if you had it." Mike reached out and took it.

From the Noyes Center, Mike called his mother. She sounded wide awake. "Michael, the police were here looking for you. Where were you yesterday?"

Mike wondered how he was supposed to answer her. His mother broke into his silence. "What is going on, Michael?"

"Nothing."

"It can't be nothing. The police don't investigate nothing."

"I can have my lawyer call you, Mom, but I have not broken any laws. What did the police say?"

"They just wanted to know where you were. You know I'm not a worrier, but something weird is going on."

"I'll explain as soon as I can."

"Now would be better."

"Later is all I can give you, Mom, sorry."

His mother was silent several moments. "You've always been

sensible, Michael. I've always been able to trust you, unlike your sister, and to be honest, your brother as well."

"Is Jack's dad in prison?"

"For now, but your lawyer called. He's afraid they're going to offer him bail. I don't know if he'll be able to pay it. We need to keep him away from Jack."

Mike called Meganvilia.

"Thank god, it's you," Meganvilia said. "While it is always lovely to hear your voice, my dear, I was effusively grateful this time for a very specific reason. I heard it on the news after those two went clattering out to play butch with the tools. The Luxor is on fire. I was afraid you were inside."

"No, I was busy elsewhere."

Mike felt his stiff muscles and his fatigue. For all the sleep he'd gotten in the alien's ship, it certainly didn't feel like enough. "What happened?"

"I don't know. I heard it on a traffic report. They've got streets closed around the place."

"Is Jack all right?"

"He's outside helping my lover fix his truck. How can you fix a truck at this hour of the morning? Noon is the most sensible hour I can think of to rise. I was forced to disturb my slumber to fetch them toast and juice. The boy is no trouble."

"Can you keep Jack a little longer?"

"I've got work tonight, but Ray can watch him. They like each other."

"Thanks. I owe you big time."

"I know."

He called his lawyer and told him the police had been to visit his parents. David said, "Why don't you stop by my place? I'll make some calls while waiting for you to get here."

Mike gave Joe the information from the phone calls.

"We can go to David's, but then I'd like to try and stop at the Luxor," Joe said. "We may not find anything, but like all good cops throughout the universe, I don't believe in coincidences."

"What if they're waiting for us?"

"We'll be careful. I've got to find them. I can't stop or hide."

"Why not?" Mike asked. "Why is this so immediately important? Can't you just lie low and plan more carefully?"

"Every day that clinic is open more humans die. His plans for destroying, taking over, or simply ruining everything good on this planet could be set in motion even as we speak. If I stop, there is no guarantee he will. I have to keep going." Again they took a bus to get where they needed to go.

In David's condo just north of Lincoln Park overlooking Lake Shore Drive, they had breakfast. David claimed he was going to no trouble as he prepared artichoke hearts, thin slices of salmon, and poached eggs all covered with fresh Hollandaise sauce. Mike thought they were the worst Eggs Benedict he'd ever tasted. The alien gobbled them down.

David wore a white silk robe over white silk pajamas. When the sun hit his body and outfit just right, Mike could see he had on white boxer shorts and a white t-shirt underneath. Mike wouldn't have been surprised if they were of white silk as well. David made very little comment about the alien, other than greeting him and admiring his excellent appetite.

"I made inquiries," David said. "I have been unable to find out anything. If there is an investigation or if they think you have committed a crime, I don't know about it."

"I was on the roof of Balls, Whips, and Chains the night of the fire. We had to be rescued."

"Did you know that no one who was in the bar was arrested? The fire and riot prevented that. They arrested several people at the riot itself. Fortunately, most people had the sense to run like hell when massive amounts of police showed up. Still I've been on the phone a great deal. One of my clients got caught in a sweep. He claims he was just out walking his dog. I've got to get him out today."

"Did you hear the Luxor was burning?" Mike asked.

"The Luxor was a death trap waiting to happen."

"We were staying there," Mike said.

David looked from one to the other of them. He spoke very quietly. "Mike, what is going on? Why were you staying at the Luxor?"

"I can't tell you, yet."

Silence from David accompanied by a fierce stare.

Joe said, "Could you come with us to the Luxor? We may run into the police, and we'll want you there."

David nodded. "So that I can give you protection from something about which I know nothing?"

"Pretty much," Mike admitted.

"I think I don't want to know, is what I think," David said.

Mike and Joe took separate showers. David lent them clean underwear and socks. It was the first pair of silk boxer shorts Mike had ever worn. They took another bus to Belmont harbor and retrieved Darryl's car from the parking lot. Mike took the parking ticket off the windshield and vowed to pay it as soon as possible.

At the Luxor several fire trucks remained. The building was completely gutted. Wisps of smoke still curled up from several locations. One hose continued to throw water on these spots. Gawkers stood behind police barricades. Mike found a parking space north on Halsted, and the three of them walked back.

FIFTY-FOUR

Joe, Mike, and David stood on the fringe of a group on the other side of Halsted watching the activity.

"Why are we here?" David asked.

Joe turned to a man with a salt and pepper beard and asked, "Anybody hurt?"

"I saw them carry out one person. Don't know how serious it was. They didn't have his face covered so I guess he wasn't dead."

Agents Henry and Hynes walked up to them.

"Heard you were staying here," Henry said.

David pushed himself forward.

"I don't like lawyers," Henry said.

"Why are you here?" David asked. "A simple fire isn't the FBI's bailiwick."

"Why haven't you been in your apartment?" Henry asked Mike.

"Have you been conducting a surveillance of my clients?" David asked.

"Just curious," Henry asked. "Were you at Balls, Whips, and Chains?"

"Taking a bar survey?" David asked.

"Can't they answer?"

"As their lawyer, I'd advise them not to, until I know more about what is going on."

"At which point you will order them not to say a word?"

"More than likely."

The FBI agents glared at the three of them and then drifted away.

Joe asked, "Isn't that the bartender from Oscar and Alfred's?"

Mike looked. "Yeah. What's he doing here?"

"Gawking like everybody else?" David suggested. "Look, I can't play nursemaid to you two for the rest of my life. I'll have to begin charging you double time. I'm going to contact my friend in the police department again. If any police officials approach you, just keep repeating the word, 'lawyer.' Eventually, even the slowest of them will catch on. I'll want a full explanation of this whole affair, Mike. Right now, I have to get to work."

They thanked him for his help. David left.

"The bartender doesn't seem to be paying much attention to the fire," Mike said. "He seems to be hanging around almost too casually. Maybe he set the fire."

"Let's make sure he doesn't see us, and then we can follow him. I have no other leads. You can't believe how many times police follow clues that go nowhere."

For an hour they played shadow tag with the bartender. Finally, they saw him go up to one of the uniformed cops and talk for a few minutes. After that he began to walk away.

They followed.

The bartender walked up Halsted Street as far as Lincoln. He stood at the bus kiosk. A bus pulled up. "We better get the car," Joe said.

The bus pulled away, but the bartender was still on the pavement.

"What the hell?" Mike asked.

Joe and Mike were north of the corner at the other side of the little park, keeping several visual barriers between them. Mike hurried back, got the car, and came around the block. He parked half in and half out of the bus zone north of Fullerton. For another half hour, they watched the bartender. He did the approach-the-bus-but-not-get-on trick three more times.

"Who's he waiting for?" Mike asked.

"Zye. His memory is clear on that point. He's also anxious that he has not arrived."

"Does he know where the ship is?"

"I checked while we were waiting at the fire. No, but he's seen Zye in the past few hours. He's got some suspicions about him, but the bounty hunter is paying him a great deal of money. He doesn't know that Zye is an alien. He thinks the bounty hunter is some kind of kinky trick, but your bartender will do just about anything for money."

"You mean they had sex?"

"No, it's money for non-sexual services rendered."

"Is the bartender gay or straight?" Mike asked.

"He's had sex with both but mostly women."

"I like inside information," Mike said. "I could make Hugo look like a piker."

"Anything to keep you ahead of the game."

Mike saw him first crossing Fullerton Avenue. "It's the fake cop in his fake-cop outfit."

The fake cop walked up to the bartender. They talked briefly. The cop pulled out a pair of handcuffs.

"He's arresting him?" Joe asked.

"How?" Mike asked.

"How isn't the problem, but he's doing it."

"He's not going to walk him to the station? I wonder if the bartender is going to notice that it is odd that he's not calling for any kind of back-up."

Mike started the car as the cop and bartender walked away. He turned left and followed them east as they strode down Fullerton a half block to Burling. They turned north. The cop stopped three cars from the corner and placed the bartender into the back seat of a nondescript car.

"Ugly enough to be an unmarked car," Mike said.

"He's facing south," Joe said. "We need to turn around."

Mike backed into the entrance to Children's Hospital. This

way they were prepared for whichever way the fake cop turned out of the intersection.

The cop pulled out and signaled for a left turn going east on Fullerton.

"Let's go," Joe said.

They followed three cars behind. They almost lost them at the eternally congested corner of Clark and Fullerton. Mike managed to slip through just before the light turned red. The fake cop pulled onto Lake Shore Drive and headed south.

"Why don't we take your ship?"

"By the time we got to it, we'd have long since lost him."

"Can you defeat Vov without your ship?"

"The communicator is very powerful. I would rather have my ship, but I cannot hover around hundreds of miles of cornfields for hours on end. I'd be noticed by some very unfriendly people. I couldn't be shot down, but I'd be inconvenienced, and I don't want to announce my presence to this planet. If he is underground, as his ship was, we'd have to get out and walk eventually."

"Couldn't your ship displace dirt like it does the sand at the bottom of the lake?"

"It takes too long. On the surface it would leave obvious traces that something huge had passed through. If it was night time, I might be able to take a chance. We'll simply have to follow."

"Could you read the fake cop's mind?"

"No. Vov has altered it significantly."

"Is it an implant?"

"I don't think so, although it is certainly some kind of mind control."

An hour and a half later, they passed the deserted gas station with the useless pay phone they'd been at before. They drove several miles past where they'd found Vov's ship. On Interstate 57 they could stay nearly a mile behind and keep large trucks between them. They only had to close the distance when they neared exits. Once they were on the country roads, they had to fall even further behind. Mike was worried they'd miss him, and finally after the fake cop had been out of sight over the horizon for a minute, he was sure they had lost him. They drove slowly to the top of a slight rise.

A half mile farther on, they arrived at a deserted factory complex: no trees, lots of debris, no cover between the road and the factory. The fake cop's car was parked by itself next to a gray brick wall. None of the factory's windows were broken. It looked like someone had tried to remove the grime from the outside of the wall. No other cars were in the lot.

"We've got to follow," Joe said.

They parked the car as far off the road and as deep in a culvert as they could. The air was damp and humid, the wind rising from the south. There was nothing to do but take a chance at hurrying across the empty open space. They walked past the other car and arrived at the door. They eased it open.

FIFTY-FIVE

This factory was filled with materials from front to back. Neither the cop nor the bartender were in sight.

"No dust," Mike muttered.

The alien had his communicator out. "They've both been here," he murmured

"Are they here now?"

"One of them is, with Zye." Joe pointed. "The bounty hunter is that way. Something is wrong with him, very wrong."

Their footfalls were silent as, while watching for the cop and bartender, they made their way in the direction the alien said the bounty hunter was. They passed work stations filled with computers. Others had beakers, test tubes, and microscopes. Other places had lathes, machine tools, tool and die works. A lot of the machinery gleamed in the soft light of the factory. The humidity from outside reached in here. Mike found his T-shirt and jeans almost uncomfortable.

At the top of a set of stairs, the alien pointed down.

Mike whispered, "I'm pretty much burnt out on this underground-cavern routine."

"We've got to. The cop and the bartender are down here as well."

The stair railing was cool to Mike's touch. Ten feet past the bottom of the stairs was a doorway with light streaming out of it. The corridor proceeded about another twenty feet beyond with six closed doors branching off it.

Mike heard the bartender say, "This isn't a police station. You're not a cop. I'm leaving."

There was an unpleasant sound as of a hard object hitting human flesh. The bartender whimpered. "What is this? I've done nothing. Are you even a cop?"

Mike and Joe eased to the doorway.

They saw the fake cop gently tapping a truncheon into his hand.

As best he could with his hands tied behind his back, the bartender cringed away from him. The left side of his mirrored sun glasses was broken, letting them see one eye clearly. Numerous bruises and welts shone on the bartender's face. The eye was puffy and nearly closed.

The fake cop moved backwards away from his victim, turned and saw Mike and Joe, and moved toward them. The cop said, "You must wait here. You will be dealt with in turn."

Joe walked swiftly forward and grabbed the truncheon from the surprised man. Seconds later the human fell to the ground unconscious. Joe hadn't touched him.

"You can do that?" Mike whispered.

"I can't kill him. I can render him temporarily inactive."

"What are you doing here?" the bartender asked.

"You were following us," Joe said. "We saw what happened. Where is your boss?"

The bartender addressed Mike, "What's going on?"

"You need to tell us that," Mike replied.

The bartender shrugged. Joe used the bartender's belt to secure his still manacled hands to the back of the chair.

"Hey, you can't do that," he protested.

"Sure I can," Joe said. "It was easy." He secured the fake cop then turned to Mike. "We need to find Zye."

They walked back out into the corridor. A quick glance at his communicator, and Joe pointed to the third door down on the left.

They listened carefully at the door and then Joe began the painstaking process of slowly opening it. No humans were present. Mike thought it resembled a hospital room. Numerous apparatus surrounded a bed. The lights blinked with letters and symbols that did not make sense to Mike.

"Is that your language?" Mike asked.

"Yes. He's built a sort of hospital room mixed with torture chamber." As they approached the bed, they saw it was Zye lying unconscious. "It must have been Vov who did this to him. I would never want to be hooked up to one of these."

"They make you tell the truth?" Mike asked.

"We have the truth with our implants. These are made to give pain. They are completely outlawed in my star system. They exist secretly on some of the outer rogue planets and those less civilized."

Joe touched Zye's body. "He's dying."

"Is there anything you can do?"

"No. I could return him to my ship, but his mind is almost completely destroyed. I doubt if he would survive the trip. Worse, Vov has this set up so that if Zye is disconnected, he dies instantly. If you could keep watch at the door for a few moments, I've got to try and read what's left in there."

"He's unconscious."

"This is what I am trained and implanted for."

Mike moved to the door and watched the empty corridor. He had no idea what he would do if suddenly a horde of Vov's minions invaded or even if a couple of legitimate cops showed up and asked what the hell he was doing. In less than five minutes Joe joined him.

He put his hand on Mike's shoulder and hung his head. "It's worse than I thought. Vov has Zye's ship. The complex we found with Vov's ship was a small part of a vast underground network. We only destroyed a small part of it. We've got to go back there."

They freed both the cop and the bartender and let them go.

Mike asked, "You're just going to let them go? Aren't they dangerous?"

"Not anymore."

"Oh." Mike paused. "Your mind is that powerful?"

"With my implants, yeah, I can change them that fast."

They quickly returned to the empty factory, and then once outdoors they strode into a howling wind. Directly overhead the sky was clear, and the sun beat down. To the south and west, vast anvil-topped thunderheads rose thousands of feet into the sky.

"We've got to hurry. Vov with a more powerful ship is terribly dangerous."

"Going to storm," Mike said.

"We've got to find him. There has to be another entrance somewhere to that complex."

"We can't get back in the way we did last time?"

"That way is buried forever."

"Where is Zye's ship?"

"I don't know. The bounty hunter used it to try and defeat Vov. Zye lost."

Using his communicator, Joe tried to locate Zye's ship. "Nothing. How can there be nothing? The ship or a portal large enough for it has to be somewhere near here."

They took the car and drove as best they could in circles on the back roads trying to take every road as close as they could to the entrance they had found.

"I get some kind of odd reading in that direction," Joe said, pointing. They tried to find a road that lead to it but couldn't. "We'll have to walk."

They left the car and began trudging forward. The fields were mostly harvested. They walked between rows of corn stubble. The clods of earth were dry, and their feet kicked up small puffs of dust, quickly dispersed by the rising gale. After a mile and a half, they crossed a dirt road with a small ditch running along the north side and climbed over a wooden fence.

Mike turned and looked at the approaching storm behind them. Lightning flashed almost continuously, thunder rumbled ominously. The sky was nearly black. After he saw one flash that seemed to split the sky, he counted ten before the sound of thunder arrived. Ten miles away, he thought automatically. "We better think about getting to cover," Mike said. "We're going to get soaked."

"I think we're close. We've got to find him. With the combination of his power and Zye's ship, he could begin destroying huge parts of this planet very quickly."

Mike gaped back on the storm-filled horizon. Thunder crashed and lightning crackled. The sky was turning greenish black. "I don't like this," Mike said.

"I've got him," Joe spoke loud enough to be heard over the storm. He gaped at the front of his communicator.

"Where?"

"And he's got me," Joe said. "Zye's ship has a flash return that tracks someone that is tracking him. He'll be coming for us."

Rain began pelting down. They were soaked instantly. Unbidden into Mike's mind came the line from the old Bob Dylan song, apt here, "The wind howled like a hammer." "We're going to be dead from the storm first," Mike said.

"You have your communicator?"

"Yes." Mike took it out. He watched the saturated alien. "Can this thing protect me from a direct lightning strike?"

"It should."

"I don't want to chance it. We're the tallest things standing in this field. Even an invasion by an alien army is going to have to wait. We gotta get into that ditch we crossed, and we better hurry. Run!"

The wind was behind them as they raced for any kind of safety from the storm. What Vov could do from this distance with that ship, Mike wasn't sure, but the more immediate danger was from the storm. Half a mile further on, Mike thought he saw the wooden fence off to their left. He grabbed the alien's arm. "There," he said.

They switched directions and dashed away. The black dirt of central Illinois squished and mushed under their feet, making them mix their running with slips and slides. Mike stumbled at one point and would have fallen, but the alien lifted him up. They slogged through the instantly sodden earth. Halfway to the ditch lightning struck a lone tree in the distance. The rain quickly doused the fire. They ran on.

Moments later they dove into a ditch. The wind there was somewhat less as they flattened themselves to the ground as best they could. Every bit of the surface of the planet they came in contact with was wet, and in the ditch water ran an inch deep. They lay with their heads close to each other and their feet pointing in the opposite direction.

"This is better?" Joe asked.

Mike raised his head to examine their limited protection. They were maybe five inches below the level of the land. Joe propped himself on his elbows and had his head bent over his communicator. Mike had never been caught in such a storm, never had the elements so totally overwhelmed him with their indifference and might.

He looked toward the heart of the storm then said, "Tornado's coming."

FIFTY-SIX

Lightning flashed. Thunder roared. Rain poured down. Mike gaped at the horizon. He tapped Joe on the shoulder and pointed.

"Nothing in or beyond the Earth is going to protect us from that," Mike said.

"I've seen them in people's minds," Joe said. "Hell of a wind."

Mike asked, "Can you stop the storm?"

"If I had my ship, I could lessen the intensity. To alter this storm would require far more than I am capable of."

The wind howled around them. Rain continued to pelt down. The fat drops stung Mike's back through his light shirt. His jeans were plastered to his butt and the back of his thighs and calves. His chest, legs, and crotch lay in the deepening run off. Mike glanced at Joe who looked almost like he was enjoying himself. Their faces were inches from each other.

"We don't get storms like this on my planet," Joe said, "Nothing half so much fun as this." The alien laughed, turned on his back, and opened his mouth to the rain.

"You should try and cover up," Mike said.

Water beaded over the alien's face. Earth and sky, alien and human were totally sodden. The alien leaned closer, put his hand behind Mike's head, and pulled them together. They kissed amid some of the most powerful forces on the planet.

"I'm sorry I lied to you," Joe said. "I'm sorry I made you angry. I love you. If we had such a thing as marriage on my planet, I would propose to you. You have taught me much. I love you, Mike Carlson."

Mike's emotions whirled and spun. His feelings of loss in the middle of impending doom were too much.

"Hell of time for making love," he said.

Joe moved his head to kiss him again and stopped. He gazed

over Mike's shoulder. Joe drew in his breath. He said, "I do believe this is it."

"What 'it'?" Mike turned.

A pin point of glowing light formed in the west and began advancing over the prairie toward them. It neither swerved nor altered course despite the encircling cataclysm. Slowly the bright white light began to grow.

Around them the wind howled, and above them the dark clouds rolled black and terrifying. Mike guessed the rotating menace skipping along the ground was about three quarters of a mile to the south of their position.

The pin point of light rapidly grew. The stubbles of corn in the field were turned into opalescent gold by the fantastic glow. Everything became stark and clear.

"What is it?" Mike asked.

"Him. With power unimaginable. That has to be Zye's ship with the power at full force. He wants me and my ship, and he intends to have them."

"What can we do?"

"I'll need your communicator."

Mike dug into the jeans that were plastered to his skin. He handed it to the alien.

Joe said, "Always remember, I love you."

"What are you going to do?"

Joe did not respond. He lurched upward. Halfway to his feet the wind pushed him down. For an instant he leaned a hand on Mike's shoulder then drew himself up to his full height and stepped to the lip of the ditch.

"You'll be killed!" Mike yelled. "Get down!"

"I was sent here to stop him. I must."

Mike cupped his hands around his eyes and lifted his head slightly. He saw that the approaching light had one central, intense focus but also had occasional flashes like a strobe around this core. What had begun as a pinpoint of brightness had risen to the size of the entire front end of a tanker truck. As it rapidly approached, it expanded exponentially.

Joe yelled, "Don't look up. Don't try to follow me. Stay down."

Mike tried to rise, but the wind forced him to his knees. The swirling debris stung him. He lay down and lifted himself up on his elbows. The elements still made this difficult, but he was not going to obey the alien and not look.

The tornado was less than half a mile away. Lightning flashed almost continuously around them. The unworldly light was almost upon them. It was now as big as a house and beginning to rotate. Joe planted his feet wide apart and raised his arms to the sky. Mike saw light flash in Joe's hands. The alien held a communicator in each one. Joe spread his arms as far up and apart as he could and marched toward the light.

Then lightning flashed, and to Mike it looked as if Joe was calling down bolts of energy from the heavens. Great gouts of energy seemed to radiate to the alien's fists and then bounce toward the approaching light. Unrelenting lightning streamed down from the heavens, struck the alien's fists, and then blasted toward the still expanding light. As the stream of energy radiating from him increased, Joe slowly approached the fiery white brilliance.

"No!" Mike screamed.

He tried to rise, but the storm was upon him. The noise was incredible. He felt as if the roaring was in his head, as if he were ready to implode. He managed to raise his head slightly in the direction the alien had gone.

He saw a swirling light, as if lightning were shooting up from the ground of its own volition with its own swirling, tornadic force. It pulsed around Joe. The approaching, great white light was dimmer and had begun to waver. Joe's light continued to grow and brighten until Mike could see him no more.

There was a titanic explosion.

Fifty-seven

Mike didn't remember how long he lay there. He thought it must have only been seconds. Mike peered over the edge of the ditch. Of the light and the alien, there was nothing to be seen. The remnants of the tornado roared away to his left. He saw the stem of the twister rip into a barn and smash it to smithereens. A few spatters of rain fell around him. A clearing line of clouds with soft blue sky beyond them was closing in on him.

He stood and walked over the denuded earth to where he thought he had last seen Joe. The ground was scoured clear while mud squished under his feet. His muscles felt weak. Escaping the storm was an emotional relief. The destruction of the man he loved was agonizing.

He inspected the area where he thought the alien had disappeared. Carefully he trod the ground. His feet slopped in the mud, but he barely noticed the clinging muck. The sky slowly brightened to an incredibly clear blue. The land and sky had been washed beautifully clean. There was no trace of either alien or spacecraft. The departing storm to the north and east was a black backdrop to a part of his life torn away.

He saw a piece of metal glint in the sunlight and stooped to pick it up. The device was burnt and twisted, but Mike recognized it as one of the alien's communicators. He searched diligently for any other trace but could find no other remnant of the alien, the other ship, or that his world had been disturbed in any way from beyond the solar system. Whether the tornado had swept away all remnants of the struggle or the explosion itself had obliterated everything, he wasn't sure.

He walked slowly back to where he remembered leaving the car. The Chevrolet was on its roof half way in the middle of a cow pasture. Mike plodded down the country road. He walked half an hour before he came to the highway. He saw the lights of emergency vehicles in the distance and strode toward them.

Talking to police and the towing company and waiting in the police station were mostly a blur. Injured people and damage control were the main concern of emergency personnel. He wasn't about to tell what really happened, and his injuries were slight cuts and easily treated.

He called his brother to come get him. On the way to Chicago, his brother gave a long monologue on the dangers of being out in a storm and the unusualness of a late September tornado. He intermixed this with a running commentary on the current football season and the Bears' chances of making the playoffs. Mike barely nodded or grunted at appropriate places as they sped back to town.

His brother did ask at one point, "What the hell were you doing out here, anyway?"

"Driving."

"Gonna cool off tonight. Be less humid."

"Yeah."

They arrived at the city after midnight. Back at his apartment, Mike took a long shower. Drying off felt wonderful after spending so long in damp clothing. He thought for a while he might want to toss out the clothes, then he thought he might save them. He put the ruined communicator on the table next to his bed. He stared at it briefly. He closed his eyes and had no idea how he managed to fall asleep. When he finally succumbed, he slept deeply.

FIFTY-EIGHT

When Mike awoke, he had no sense of the time. He glanced at the clock next to his bed. Four o'clock. But the sun was shining dimly through his bedroom window. He'd slept through to late the next afternoon.

He felt dazed. He pulled on briefs, black jeans, white athletic socks, a flannel shirt, and running shoes. In the kitchen he drank a glass of orange juice. He poured himself some more and took the glass into the living room. He let himself sink into his easy chair. He remained unmoving. Through his front window, he watched the sunlight dim on the houses across the street. He saw the street lights go on and darkness descend. He heard footsteps pass his door. His neighbors coming home after a normal day's work.

Darkness gathered around him. Mike didn't turn on any lights.

The phone rang. He let his machine answer. It was Agent Henry from the FBI asking him to call.

Mike didn't recall when he'd put his empty glass down, or when he'd moved to the couch and stretched out to sleep. When he woke again, there was dim light, daylight, shining into his windows. There was a very soft tapping on his door.

"Mike?"

He recognized Mrs. Benson's whisper.

He stumbled to the door and opened it. She looked worried. "Are you all right?" she asked.

"Yes, Mrs. Benson."

"You look a fright."

Mike touched his tousled hair and unshaven chin.

"I heard you come in yesterday, and you haven't moved outside your apartment since then. I've been worried."

"I'm okay."

"I brought you some fresh, homemade bread in case you haven't had a chance to buy groceries. I know you haven't been home much lately. I brought you some fresh-squeezed juice as well."

She handed him a basket redolent of home and safety along with a glass jar, cool to the touch and filled with bright orange liquid.

He thanked her.

She shook her head. "You eat something and get some rest. Do you want me to call anyone for you?"

"No, Mrs. Benson. Thank you."

"If you need to talk, I'm here."

"Thanks, maybe later."

She patted his cheek softly. "You take care of yourself."

Mike took the food to the kitchen table. He pulled off a hunk of the still warm bread. It was delicious. He sat at the table, ate the whole loaf, and drank all the juice.

He showered and dressed again. He called his lawyer to tell him about the call from the FBI. As he talked, his call waiting beeped in. He asked David to wait and answered. It was Darryl.

"Where the hell have you been?" his friend whispered.

"Joe is..." Mike couldn't say the words.

"Can you come to the hospital? Please."

Mike had nothing else to do. Darryl sounded weak, and his saying, "please," was a sure tip off that things were not well. "Are you all right?" Mike asked.

"No."

"I'll be there."

Mike switched back to David who suggested they set up a meeting for noon, after Mike had been to the hospital.

The phone rang. Mike ignored it until his nephew's voice spoke on the answering machine. "I want to find out what's happening.

I called my mom. She's really mad at you, but Grandma is making her calm down. My dad still might get out on bail."

Mike picked up the phone. "You'll be safe at Meganvilia's."

"He won't try anything now, will he?"

"I won't let anything happen to you."

"Is Joe there? Can I talk to him?"

Mike felt tears well up in his eyes. He had no idea what to tell the boy or what he would tell the friends who had met Joe.

Mike said, "He's not here right now. I'll tell him you asked after him."

FIFTY-NINE

Mike sat on the side of Darryl's bed. His friend's body had become considerably thinner even in the past few days.

Darryl whispered, "I've wondered what my last conversation would be like, my last words. When you and I first made love, I thought about whether we'd know each other when we were thirty or seventy-five, if we'd love each other forever." Darryl patted the bed covers. "I want to say some famous last words to you, but I don't know any. And don't tell me to keep quiet to keep up my strength. A little extra strength is not going to cure what ails me. Let me ramble."

Mike held the dying man's hand tightly.

Darryl breathed deeply for several minutes with his eyes closed. Finally they opened a slit. He said, "You have my instructions?"

"Yes. Big funeral ceremony. Loud wailing opera music. Lots of tears. Snub your family."

"I wrote it all down. You've got my will."

"Darryl, I love you."

"No, you don't. You love Joe."

"I..."

"Don't lie to a dying man. I was able to tell the first time I met him. He loves you, too."

"He's dead."

Darryl's eyes opened completely.

"Why didn't you tell me?"

"You're dying."

"At a time like this I can afford not to be selfish. What happened?"

"It's a long story."

"I'm not going anywhere. If I die listening to your voice, I won't mind. I've always liked that basso profundo you speak in. That alternating between a high-pitched squeak and that low rumble is what attracted me to you when we were teenagers." He smiled briefly. "Tell me what happened."

Mike told the story from the beginning, the entire truth. Darryl listened mostly with his eyes closed. He opened them fully when Mike talked about Joe being an alien and the proofs he'd given. At that point Mike asked, "You think I'm crazy, don't you."

"Honey, you want to fall in love with a visitor from another planet, it's your business. I'm in no position to disapprove. If I wasn't good enough for you, probably no one on Earth would be. Is there a point to your lying to me at a time like this?" Darryl answered his own question. "I doubt it. No one I know has a better grip on reality than you do. I'm only sorry I can't go to his ship with you or share your lives or wish you good-bye as you whisk off into the universe." Darryl paused and breathed deeply for several moments then resumed. "You probably still better do safe sex. You don't want to catch an interstellar disease. Did you and he have sex?"

Mike nodded.

"Good for you. Maybe you'll have an interstellar love child. I hate to miss it. Continue the story."

When Mike finished, Darryl was quieter for longer than Mike had ever known him to be. The warm hand continued to clutch his. He watched the slow rise and fall of the emaciated chest.

After a few minutes Darryl asked, "Are you sure he's dead?"

"There was absolutely no trace of him, the other alien, or the ship. The blast must have obliterated everything. What the explosion didn't get, the tornado must have. I doubt if he was strong enough or had time enough to save us both."

Darryl smiled. With great effort he put his left hand on top of where his and Mike's right hands already held each other. He patted his friend. "You've had the most unique and marvelous experience anyone on Earth has ever had."

"I've been afraid to tell anyone."

"And you're stuck with me, and I'm dying. Course, that is a bit safer. You don't have to worry about me thinking you're a raving loony and trying to have you put away."

"There's that. Do you think I'm a raving loony?"

"I believe you, but I'm fairly demented as it is."

"I loved him."

"I know."

"He'll never come back, just like you're never coming back. I don't know how much of this I can handle."

"You're strong and beautiful and brave and the person I've met who is most worthy of being loved. I should have never stopped loving you. Don't worry, someday, sometime, you will meet your true love."

"This better not be a song cue."

"Don't despair, Mike. If love ever comes to you, say, 'yes.' It'll happen to you again."

"I'm not sure I want it to. It's too hard if this is all it's going to be like in the end."

"But love is always like this in the end."

Darryl gasped briefly and choked.

Mike helped him sip water through the straw in the plastic container beside the bed. Darryl lay back with his eyes closed and breathed evenly.

Mike leaned over and brushed back Darryl's hair from his forehead. He caressed the ravaged face. For a moment he thought his friend might have fallen asleep. Then he realized the quiet was filled with lack of movement. The sheet covering Darryl's chest no longer rose and fell. Mike leaned down and hugged his friend.

When he sat back up, he hung his head. At the moment tears did not come. He'd wept his tears for Darryl after he'd first learned of the diagnosis. Now he held his dead friend's hand and let his mind remember as much as he could of his experiences with Darryl.

He didn't know how long it was before the nurse came in and found him there.

Mike didn't remember walking out of the hospital. He found himself out by the Belmont Rocks watching the full moon rise over Lake Michigan. He thought it was heart-breakingly beautiful. The air was cool and crisp, waiting for autumn and winter not far behind. His reverie ended when a young male couple rose from the rocks below him, where he had not observed them. They giggled and left, adjusting pants and jackets as they sauntered away.

Mike walked along the lake front all the way to the renovated Soldier Field. The stadium was totally deserted. He walked out to the planetarium. As he turned to go back, the lights of the city spread out before him in all their glory. The view of Chicago from the small slip of land was among the most spectacular. He walked through Grant Park and into the Loop. From there he turned north and wandered the streets for most of the night, deserted, empty, haunted streets with memories of Darryl and Joe scraping away at his consciousness.

As the first gray light of dawn spread over the city, he found himself in front of his apartment house. He was glad there was no light on in Mrs. Benson's apartment. He wanted solitude, not solicitude.

Climbing the stairs to his place was like climbing a mountain without equipment. Inside the apartment, he dropped his clothes one by one as he trekked to his bedroom. He tumbled into bed and surprised himself by falling instantly into a deep sleep.

Sixty

His phone rang at nine in the morning.

"You missed our appointment," David said.

"Darryl is dead," Mike informed him.

"I'm sorry. What can I do to help?"

"I honestly don't know."

"Let's meet this afternoon around four. I'll bring the FBI, and we can put this whole thing to rest."

Mike didn't bother to ask about why the FBI wanted to see him some more. He didn't really care.

When Mike awoke next he heard knocking on his front door. He threw on jeans and padded to the living room. He heard Mrs. Benson calling his name and continuing to knock. When he opened the door, he saw she had a new basket of goodies. They sat at Mike's kitchen table. He inspected the basket and saw it included more fresh bread, homemade soup, and a bottle of brandy. Mrs. Benson got him a bowl and poured him some soup. Mike ate.

"I heard about Darryl," Mrs. Benson said. "I'm sorry."

"Thank you."

"I know you want to be alone."

"Yes."

"I know this is hard to listen to, but life will go on. Things will get better. I've seen a lot of death in my time as have you with friends dying of AIDS. Life can be terrible, but it can be beautiful too."

"I know. I'll be all right."

Mrs. Benson left a few minutes later.

Mike finished the food. He took a shower long enough to run the whole apartment house out of hot water. He dressed slowly. When done, he called Meganvilia and checked on Jack. All was fine. He checked with his mother and his lawyer. Through legal machinations David had finally managed to convince the state's attorney to keep Jack's father from getting bail. So Lennon Kazakel was out of the picture entirely. Rosemary, his incompetent sister, was recovering.

SIXTY-ONE

That afternoon David, the FBI, and a lieutenant from the Chicago police showed up at Mike's apartment. They tried asking about his movements for the past week. David fielded, thwarted, or deflected most of the questions. The lawyer demanded to know what crime it was they were investigating. Neither the FBI nor the representatives of the police gave him specific answers.

David said, "This isn't some kind of *Law and Order* episode where the poor ignorant schnook gets tricked by the cops into confessing to some kind of guilt. What the hell is going on?"

"Can your client at least tell us about the man he was with when we talked to him the other night? We discovered he was staying with him at the Luxor Hotel."

Mike said, "He was a guy I wish I could see again."

"Where is he?"

"I wish I knew."

"Is he a criminal?" David asked.

"No," Agent Henry confessed. "We just wanted to talk to him."

"He is my client as well," David announced. "If there has been no crime, you'll have to back off."

The Chicago police lieutenant said, "As far as I can see, there has been no crime committed at any point here." He jerked a thumb at the FBI agents. "I think these people have seen one too many episodes of *The X-Files*."

"What the hell does that mean?" David asked.

The Chicago cop stood up. "It means no crime has been committed. As far as the Chicago police are concerned, your client, and anybody he knows, are free and clear of us."

David turned to the FBI agents. "And you?"

They grumbled, mumbled, and admitted little, but before they left, David got them to once again agree to leave his client alone.

After he closed the door behind the visitors, David returned and sat next to Mike on the couch.

David said, "That was my friend from the police department. It took me quite a bit to get him to be here today. He can really be a help."

Mike leaned back, shut his eyes, and listened to himself breathe.

David asked, "Mike, what the hell has happened?"

Mike sighed. After a few moments he murmured, "Do you really want to know?"

David stared at his friend. "The truth, as I've said before, is a highly overrated commodity, but you sound weird."

Mike opened his eyes. "I never want to feel this exhausted again. Every muscle in my body hurts. Every cell in my brain aches. My nerves feel like they've shut down for the duration."

"Can I get you something? Do you want me to stay with you? I think maybe I should."

"No, thanks. I appreciate your offer. Right now I need peace and quiet."

"Do you want to go away for a vacation? I know this sedate little spa about fifty miles north of San Francisco. I could help pay for your vacation."

"I'm not hurting financially. I invested my tips for the past four years in all the smart things you told me to. I'll want to go back to work, but right now I need to take care of Darryl's last requests and his will. I've still got a few days of vacation I can take."

"I can do the funeral arrangements."

"I want to. It'll be good for me to remember him."

"You're sure?"

"Yes."

"I still don't think I should leave. I'd be happy to stay."

Mike wanted to sit and remember Darryl and the alien. He missed Darryl as one does a longtime friend. The hurt was salved a little by shared memories. Joe he missed and was surprised at how much the ache hurt. He knew he'd fallen in love with Joe, and that surprised him a little. He'd give a great deal to see Joe's intelligent smile.

Mike said, "Really, no, David. I'd like to sit quietly for a while. I'm going to be all right."

David stood up. "I'll call to check on you every day."

"There's no need, but okay. I really appreciate all of your concern. You've been a big help lately. Thanks."

After David left, Mike stared at the poster above the couch. It was of an attractive man wearing only his briefs. He was turned halfway to the camera. The shadows in the room had lengthened considerably before he began making calls about the services for Darryl. At his friend's request, he had arranged for him to be buried in St. Basil's Cemetery in Centerboro where they'd grown up.

SIXTY-TWO

Mike found it quicker and easier than he had thought to make the formal arrangements for the funeral. Mike's parents gave him as much comfort as they could. They invited him to stay at their house for the duration. Mike gently refused.

The funeral itself was more heavily attended than Mike had expected. A constant stream of people came for the wake. Darryl may have been a pain in the ass, but he had affected many people's lives.

The weather was pleasantly warm for late September. Many of the people were in short sleeves. At the gravesite Mike read what Darryl had referred to as his farewell address. It was a much calmer and more mature document than Mike expected. Mostly Darryl had exhorted those who knew him not to grieve.

Mike's mother stayed next to him after everyone else had gone. She kept her arm hooked in his as the unstoppable tears streaked Mike's face. When the crying eased, she handed him a tissue. They stood together as the morning sun rose to noon.

"I have to go," she whispered.

He nodded.

"Jack's safe," she murmured.

"I heard. Is Rosemary ever going to forgive me?"

"Your sister will have to learn to cope with you being able to do the right thing. I'll handle her."

"Thanks."

"I'll call you," she said.

"Okay."

"I love you," she said and kissed his cheek.

After everyone was gone, Mike moved under the shade of the giant oak that commanded this low rise of the cemetery. The dappled sunlight and the soft breeze soothed him.

"Good bye, Darryl," he murmured. The wind rustled the tree leaves.

"Hello, Mike."

Mike whirled around. Ten feet away, the alien was leaning against the trunk of the oak.

"Joe?"

"Yeah."

"How?"

The alien walked toward him. When they stood two feet apart he said, "I survived. It's taken a while to heal myself. I didn't have the strength to come sooner. I shouldn't be away from my ship yet. I'm still a little woozy."

Mike reached out to him and held him by the arm.

"You're not a ghost," Mike said.

"Nor am I a hallucination. The laws of physics work."

"You said that before."

"I'm not going back to my planet."

"You're staying here?"

"With you, if I may."

"Yes."

"What did you report back to your planet?"

"That I'd been unsuccessful here and was moving on to the next sector. I've set a probe in a far off direction that will transmit news of my failures at regular intervals. They thought I was an incompetent and a fool. This will prove them right. They can think my ship and I are merrily wandering into even farther reaches of deep space."

"You didn't report Vov and Zye dead?"

"Then they'd expect me to show up."

"How did you find me?"

"The Internet had the newspaper report of where the funeral and internment were going to be. I took a bus."

Mike smiled. He reached out and pulled Joe close. They held each other tightly. Mike felt the strong arms enfold him, hands grasping him tightly, the now familiar tingle.

"Will they let you stay? Will someone come for you?"

"I'm not important enough."

"To me you are."

Mark Zubro is the author of twenty-three mystery novels and five short stories. His book *A Simple Suburban Murder* won the Lambda Literary Award for Best Gay Men's mystery. He also wrote a thriller, *Foolproof*, with two other mystery writers, Jeanne Dams and Barb D'Amato. He taught eighth graders English and reading for thirty-four years. He was president of the teachers' union in his district from 1985 until 2006. He retired from teaching in 2006 and now spends his time reading, writing, napping, and eating chocolate. His newest book *Another Dead Republican*, is his thirteenth in the Tom and Scott series. One of the keys in Zubro's mysteries is you do not want to be a person who is racist, sexist, homophobic, or a school administrator. If you are any of those, it is likely you are the corpse, or, at the least, it can be fairly well guaranteed that bad things will happen to you by the end. And if in Zubro's books you happen to be a Republican and/or against workers' rights, it would be far better if you did not make a habit of broadcasting this. If you did, you're quite likely to be a suspect, or worse.

TRADEMARKS ACKNOWLEDGMENT

The author acknowledges the trademark status and trademark owners of the following wordmarks mentioned in this work of fiction:

Chevrolet & Chevy – General Motors

CNN – Cable News Network

Detroit Tigers – Detroit Tigers

Dockers – Levi Strauss & Co.

Field and Stream – Bonnier Corp.

iPod – Apple Inc.

Kmart – Sears Brands LLC

Law and Order – NBCUniversal Media, LLC

Lexus – Toyota Motor Corporation

Lucite – Lucite International Inc.

Mylar - DuPont Teijin Films

Nancy Drew – Simon & Schuster, Inc.

Star Trek – Paramount Pictures

Stuckey's – Stuckey's Corporation

Sun-Times – Sun-Times Media, LLC

Superman – DC Comics, a Warner Bros Entertainment company

The X-Files – 20th Century Fox Television

Tower Records – Caiman Holdings, Inc.

Transformers – Hasbro